Between Two Worlds: The Heart Between the Tides

TRINA BORDEAUX

Florida

First Edition: July 2025

This book is a work of fiction. Names, characters, places, and incidents either are products of the author's imagination or are used fictitiously. Any resemblance to actual events, locales, or persons, living or dead, is entirely coincidental.

Library of Congress Control Number: 2025915300

ISBN: 979-8-9991594-1-0

TABLE OF CONTENTS

THE HEART BETWEEN THE TIDES

1 Troubled Waters

The sea is supposed to sing. Today, it only groans.

Mara Ondine carves through the dull gray water, copper hair trailing in a ragged banner behind her. Every kick of her tail stirs up clouds of silt and loose flecks of plastic. Sunlight above shivers in streaks, fighting through an oil-slick shimmer that sits heavy on the surface, casting everything below in anemic twilight. The reef—her reef, her home—rises in a graveyard hush. Where once it pulsed with color and gossiping fish, now only dead fingers of coral remain, reaching for the current, empty.

A shredded net drapes a rock like a rotted shroud. From its folds, a parrotfish twitches, half its body flayed raw where the plastic line sawed into scale and skin. Its gills flutter in frantic time, eyes rolling with the old mammal terror of drowning in one's own element. Mara's jaw goes hard. The muscle tics, and she has to bite down on the rush of bile in her throat.

She hates the way her body reacts here—tenses, coils, grows sharp at the edges. She hates the way her mind picks out the human trash with the same hyper-focus as a predator: bottle cap, plastic straw, the skeleton of a six-pack ring. She hates, most of all, the way her people's song is smothered by silence, as if the ocean itself is holding its breath.

Mara loops around the jagged coral head, careful not to brush the scars on her tail against the abrasive rubble. She remembers each line—every angry, pink-edged mark—a story of narrow escapes and stubborn returns. Today, the pain is background noise.

A meter ahead, a knot of fish clusters near a darker mass. They hover in panic, pressed together by some primal pact of prey, but none dare get too close. The shape resolves into a chunk of commercial net, tangled with beer cans and plastic ribbon, anchored by a starfish crushed flat beneath. Three clownfish flicker in and out of the mesh, their movements skittish and staccato, the bright orange of their bodies a sick joke against the sunken palette of decay.

Mara closes on the net, the water around her thickening with rot and fear. Her fingers curl into fists, nails biting into the soft webbing of her hands. Her eyes slit, scanning for an angle, a seam, a moment of weakness in the tangle.

The nearest clownfish jerks toward her, then away, fins shuddering so fast they blur. She pulses a silent apology in its direction. It will not help, but it's all she can give.

She presses her palm to the net. The synthetic fibers bite back, scraping the curve of her thumb. Instinct begs her to rip and tear, to use brute force, but that only tightens the snare. Mara knows this routine; humans design their traps with malice, and she's learned the lesson in blood and old scars. Her rage is useless here. Precision is the only weapon that matters.

She centers herself. Draws the Current-Calling up from the pit of her chest. At first, it's a flicker—cold, briny static humming along the lines of her ribs. Then it grows. Her gills flare open as she gulps a mouthful of water, muscles tightening in her shoulders, her spine arching with the pressure. The ocean answers her, reluctantly, like a stubborn child. Mara sets her teeth and pushes harder.

The current obeys. It's a living thing: a surge that buckles the net and rattles the entire reef. For a moment, the world blurs at the edges. Mara's vision white-outs, then snaps back. Silt swirls in angry vortices, twisting between her fingers and through the net, carrying the loose strands with it. The mesh billows, then jerks free from its anchor.

A clownfish tumbles backward, rolling ass-over-fin in the current. The parrotfish thrashes, more frantic than before. Mara ignores the ache spreading through her tail and the burning in her arms. She's not done.

She threads a hand into the net, using the last spasm of magic to hold the current steady. The synthetic line cinches tight around her wrist. She doesn't flinch. Her other hand slides in, finds the weak spot she's mapped in her head, and pulls.

The line gives. A slit opens in the mesh, just wide enough for a desperate fish to slip through. The clownfish are first, one, then two, then three, gone in a heartbeat. The parrotfish lags, confused, trailing blood, then blasts free in a streak of blue and orange. Mara twists her hand out, leaving a thin crescent of skin behind on the razor-sharp edge.

She lets the current go. It collapses all at once, like the snap-back after a deep breath held too long. The net floats, limp, half-shredded, and useless. Her hands shake. Her gills stutter, greedy for oxygen. She drifts for a moment, adrenaline slowly leaking from her muscles, and watches the newly freed fish disappear into the void beyond the reef.

Mara looks down. Her tail shivers with the aftershock, scales flashing dull green and silver. The effort leaves her hollow, as if someone scooped the meat from her bones and left her skin to float. She scans the perimeter: more nets, more trash, more casualties than she can count. Some fish will make it, most won't.

The tide always keeps its own ledger.

A shape floats past her face, barely recognizable—a battered piece of candy wrapper, its colors long since bled away by the salt and sun. She thinks of the word "candy," and the taste is both sweet and bitter.

She can fix a net. She can't fix the ocean.

She forces her fins to move, clawing her way to a ledge of coral that still holds a little life. There, she slumps, letting her tail drape over the edge and her arms rest limp at her sides. The water around her is thick with the churn of her magic, the silt and debris settling slowly.

Far above, the sunlight fights to break through the chemical haze, but fails.

Mara blinks, her eyes grainy with exhaustion, and stares into the endless debris field. It spreads in every direction, far past the reach of any single mermaid. Far past the reach of hope, if she's honest.

Still, she can't bring herself to stop. Not yet.

She doesn't notice the cut until the blood beads up, darkening in the cold and diffusing into the current. It's nothing—a surface thing, easily forgotten—but the sting wakes her from the stupor of magic fatigue. Mara flexes her hand, feels the skin pull taut along her knuckles, and grins at the pain. It is honest. It is real.

Her tail droops along the coral shelf, every flicker of its muscles sending a warning tremor through the rest of her body. Even her scales feel bruised. She lies back, the pressure of the water a heavy blanket pressing her into the stone, and lets her head tip toward the surface.

Above, the water blisters with oil, a thin slick that shimmers in malignant rainbows whenever a stray shaft of sun dares pierce through the clouds. Mara tries to recall what this patch looked like as a child. She remembers colors—so many they made her dizzy—rising like a living wall from the sand. Schools of fish packed tight enough to block her view, a rumor of dolphins echoing from the edge of the drop-off. Now, even the dolphins are gone.

The clicks and pops that used to fill the water—shrimp, crab, the secret language of reef dwellers—are gone too—instead, a sticky, suffocating silence. Mara listens harder, hoping for even a hint of the old music, but hears only the distant groan of a human ship engine far overhead, and the brittle, hollow snap of dead coral fracturing.

She peels herself from the ledge and drifts down. The closer she gets to the sand, the stranger the world becomes. Plastic beads fill the cracks between rocks—straws just up from the bottom like a new species of plant. A discarded fishing lure flashes briefly in the gloom before something—probably a crab, maybe a rat—drags it deeper.

She pushes forward, feeling smaller with every meter. There are too many wounds here. She'd need an army to heal even a fraction.

Her mind drifts to old stories: ancestors weaving tides to build new reefs overnight, moving whole armies of fish with a single song. She wonders if they ever felt as hopeless as she does now, or if the legend is just another kind of lie.

Something shifts above her, blotting out what little light there is. Instinct pulls Mara flush against the coral, flattening her body and pressing her gills tight to her neck. The scent in the water sharpens—old sweat, salt, a note of iron—and she tastes the tang of warning.

The shadow floats closer, resolves into the unmistakable silhouette of a mermaid in full acceleration, slicing through the water with the efficiency of a torpedo. Mara tenses, unsure if she should run or fight, then lets herself relax as she reads the signature movements: the careful, calculated arc of approach, the perfectly controlled tail flicks, the deliberate avoidance of obstacles. She knows that stroke. She's seen it a thousand times.

Relief and dread tangle in her stomach.

Lyla Pearl emerges from the gloom, a streak of platinum hair first, her face following a second later. Even in the ruin, Lyla's features are impossibly sharp. Her silver eyes scan the debris with the cool detachment of a surgeon, missing nothing. Mara is pretty sure her sister could spot a seahorse at a kilometer, and still be annoyed by the way it swam.

She floats upright, posture rigid, and doesn't bother with pleasantries. "You're bleeding," Lyla says, her tone flat as basalt.

"Not much," Mara replies, tucking the wounded hand behind her back.

Lyla's gaze shifts down, taking in the torn skin, the trembling tail, the webbing at the edges of Mara's fins where the effort of magic still leaves its aftertaste. "You're also exhausted. You shouldn't have come alone." The sentence carries the weight of a hundred arguments, none of them new.

Mara shrugs, which, in water, is a slow, heavy gesture. "Someone has to start. The others want to wait for the current to fix things."

A flicker of irritation passes over Lyla's face, gone before it lands. She surveys the wreckage—oil, plastic, the dying silence. "The current is sick," she says finally. "You can feel it. If you can feel it, so can they."

Mara lets the words hover between them. She knows what Lyla means: the elders, the council, the whole crumbling hierarchy that will talk the reef to death while arguing about whose fault it is. She's heard the debates, the blame, the paralyzing fear. She's tired of it all.

She floats a little higher, meeting Lyla's gaze. "We can't just hide. Not anymore."

Lyla's response is pure muscle—her shoulders tensing, arms crossing in front of her chest, tail sweeping behind her in an involuntary gesture of defense. "You know what happens when you draw attention. We've talked about this."

"They already see us," Mara spits. "Or do you think the nets just fall here on their own?"

A standoff, then. Neither was willing to break the gaze. For a second, Mara wonders if Lyla will turn and swim away, leave her to the emptiness. Instead, her sister's expression softens, just a fraction.

"Come home," Lyla says, but her voice is different this time. "Please."

Mara's chest aches. She wants to say yes, but the word sticks in her throat.

She sweeps her hand in a slow arc, indicating the ruined landscape. "It won't fix itself."

"No," Lyla agrees, and her voice is so quiet Mara almost misses it. "But neither will you, if you keep going like this."

They float there, surrounded by the shrapnel of two worlds colliding. Mara tries to find something left that's worth saving, but all she sees is brokenness.

Still, she doesn't leave. She can't.

She waits for Lyla to speak again, for the argument to reignite, but instead her sister just hovers, watching, as if expecting Mara to figure it out on her own.

Maybe that's what family is. Not protection, not even love, but the patience to watch someone else's heart break and stay close anyway.

Mara closes her eyes, lets herself rest on the current, and feels her sister's presence settle beside her like the ghost of an old melody.

It's almost enough.

The silence thickens until it hurts.

Mara tries to fill it with movement—flicking her tail, tracing lines in the water, tapping her claws against the brittle shell of a dead mollusk. None of it helps. Lyla hovers a few body lengths away, not so far that Mara can relax, but just distant enough to signal there will be no easy reconciliation.

The sisters are trapped in the standoff, each waiting for the other to speak first. Lyla wins, as always.

"You risk everything with these excursions," she says, voice low and cold. "The humans have already taken so much. Would you offer yourself to them as well?"

The words strike harder than intended, and Mara's body reacts before her mind does. She pushes off from the coral, slicing a sharp arc that brings her nose to nose with her sister. "What else am I supposed to do?" she snaps. "Watch from a cave while they strip the ocean to its bones?"

Lyla doesn't flinch. Her eyes narrow, and her jaw sets into that infuriating line of finality. "You know the cost. If you get caught—"

"They'll kill me? Or worse?" Mara snorts. "Let them try. I'd rather die fighting than rot in a sanctuary."

Her hands move when she talks—always have—punctuating every sentence with a jab or a sweep. Right now, both fists are tight, the knuckles white beneath the scales. Lyla watches the display, unimpressed.

"It's not just about you," Lyla says. "It's never just about you."

Mara almost laughs. "Funny, coming from the chosen one."

A flush creeps into Lyla's cheeks, silver eyes flashing. "That is not how it works, and you know it. We all have a place. We all have a duty." She gestures at the devastation beyond them, the horizonless stretch of poison and death. "If you die, that duty dies with you."

Mara rounds on her, voice rising. "And if we do nothing, the ocean dies with us." She spins in place, arms flung wide. "Look around, Lyla. Look at what waiting has done!"

The motion sends a ripple through the water, stirring the debris, the plastic snow that now coats the reef. A soda can bounces along the bottom, skittering between their tails. Lyla's gaze follows it, her face a mask of distaste.

"You're being reckless," Lyla says. "There's a reason the old ways exist."

"Old ways?" Mara laughs, but it's ugly, a bitter bark. "The old ways are dead, sister. They died with the last clean tide."

Lyla's tail lashes, a whip-crack of irritation. "The old ways kept us alive."

"So did hiding," Mara fires back. "And look where that got us."

The tension breaks into a physical confrontation—brief, instinctual, but real. Lyla surges forward, and Mara braces, shoulders hunched, expecting a blow. Instead, Lyla catches her by the arm, grips iron-strong, and yanks her in close.

"You think you're the only one who cares?" Lyla's voice shakes. "You think I want this?" Her other hand trembles, as if she's barely holding herself together. "I remember what it was like, too."

They're close enough to see the microscars on each other's faces. Close enough to remember the nights spent chasing squid through forests of kelp, the secret games, and shared songs. Mara wants to look away, but can't.

She softens, just a little. "Then help me."

Lyla's grip tightens, then loosens. She releases Mara and takes a long, measured breath. "Help you do what? Throw yourself at the humans' mercy? That's not a strategy, Mara. That's a death wish."

"There must be humans who would help if they knew," Mara says. She can't keep the plea out of her voice. "Not all of them are monsters."

Lyla's answer is immediate and absolute. "Humans help only

themselves. That is the one truth our people have always known."

Mara feels the last of her hope slip away, replaced by something colder. "Maybe that's why our people are dying."

They separate, both breathing hard. The argument is over—at least for now—but nothing is resolved. The reef is still dead, the water still poisoned, the sisters still alone against it all.

Mara floats upward, away from the ruins, needing distance. Lyla lets her go, arms crossed, watching.

Above, the oil-slick surface warps the light, refracting Mara's silhouette into something unrecognizable. She wonders if Lyla sees it, and what her sister thinks of the distorted shadow that remains.

She's halfway to the surface before she hears Lyla's voice again, faint and echoing in the current.

"I just don't want to lose you," Lyla says.

Mara almost turns back. Almost. But there's nothing left to say.

She slips into the thinning water, toward the surface, toward whatever comes next.

Below, Lyla watches until Mara is gone.

2 Surface Tension

The surface splits with a sound like bones breaking.

Mara explodes from the water, copper hair slicked against her skull, eyes burning from the slap of salt and sunlight. For a heartbeat, she hovers in the arch between worlds, suspended, the ocean streaming from her arms and tail in curtains. Then gravity wins. She crashes back, a deliberate, practiced breach—not for joy, not for the sport of it, but for air, for information, for rage.

The brine above is worse than below. Chemical tang cuts through her mouth, the usual tang of salt soiled by something sharper, metallic, and slick. She coughs, gills fluttering hard against her neck, and immediately tastes fuel. Gasoline. Diesel, maybe. It's thick enough to film her tongue.

She floats at the edge of the breakwater, tucked in the shadow of a decayed buoy. The surface here is chaos: human voices, engines, gulls wheeling overhead, a stadium of sound that flattens the water's natural rhythm—Mara's headaches from the volume alone.

She scans the coast. The town sprawls along the sand in drunken tiers—cement blocks and neon signs leering down at the waterline, tinny music and the smell of frying meat rolling down to meet her. On the beach, children shriek and run; parents corral them with shouts, towels, and umbrellas that stab the sky like regimental flags. Further along, a carnival ride whines, a Ferris wheel turning slowly as the moon in the midday haze.

Beneath the bright, Mara sees the rot. She tastes it in the foam, feels it in the way her scales itch and crawl. Oil floats in languid sheets over the bay, refracting the sun in poisonous rainbows. On her arm, droplets gather, each slick spot a badge of shame. She wipes her scales with the back of her hand, but the colors just smear, and her hand comes away smelling like old paint thinner.

A fishing vessel grinds along the outer harbor, nets trailing, gulls in complete riot at its wake. Even from here, Mara sees the stains along the hull, the blackish smears where something toxic bleeds from the engine. A boom swings out, dumping refuse—shredded netting, severed fish-heads, a slurry of plastic fragments—directly into the water. The current will drag it all straight into the bay, to the reef's shallow grave.

Mara's jaw locks. Her tail flares, sending a pulse of pain up through her hip. She forces herself to go still, to watch.

She closes her eyes and opens her senses. The trick is not to reach, but to allow. Let the Tide-Sensing rise in her, let the ocean speak through the scars. At first, it's pressure—an ambient static that hums along her bones. Then, as she tunes deeper, the shapes come.

The pollution is alive, in a way. It drifts in ribbons, each chemical and plastic strand glowing with the dark light of contamination. The bay is a soup of them: one tendril is pesticide, sweet and heavy, curling from the mouth of a storm drain; another, sharper, is a spill of antifreeze leaking from the dry docks upriver. Microplastics dust the shallows, fine as silt, inhaled by every fish dumb enough to filter-feed.

She gags, gagging harder as she tracks the flow. It all collects in the lee of the harbor wall, exactly where the baby fry, hatchlings, larvae would gather to hide from predators. Human trash disguised as a sanctuary.

Her body tenses with indignation. Magic, here, is agony.

She opens her eyes. Above her, a gull dives for a half-eaten sandwich floating on a foam cooler. It pecks at the bread, chokes, then flips the crust into the wind, which carries it right back into the water.

On the beach, nobody notices. A group of teenagers vaults off a jetty, plunging into the toxic surf with wild, unselfconscious glee. The water here's so turbid that it's nearly opaque, but they surface with teeth bared and eyes stinging, high on the recklessness of not knowing or not caring. Mara feels both envy and pity.

She watches a small boy wade in, clutching a bright orange bucket. He scoops at the water, holding up a prize—a writhing, shell-shocked crab. The boy's mother laughs and takes a picture. Mara can see, even from here, the flecks of black oil caught in the crab's legs. She wonders if they'll notice when the creature dies by sundown.

The vessel in the bay swings around, lining up for another pass. Mara shades her eyes and sees the pilot: a broad-shouldered man, pale skin sunburnt to raw red, lips pursed around a cigarette as he pilots one-handed. He isn't even pretending to avoid the slick; he cuts straight through, wake foaming with bits of Styrofoam and kelp.

Mara's gills tighten, refusing to open. Her whole-body rebels against the idea of breathing here, but she forces herself to gulp the surface water. The taste burns a path down her throat, settling like acid in her chest.

She tucks her legs under, careful to keep her tail submerged. The lower half still twitches with the aftermath of the earlier spell work, the ache radiating from where the net had gnawed into her flesh. She glances down, half expecting to see blood, but the wound is already starting to seal—Merfolk heals fast, necessity bred by a world that offers little mercy.

Not fast enough. The pain is a warning: you are not invincible.

Mara listens. The ocean's voice is everywhere and nowhere here—drowned by the static of human machinery, the endless loop of their music and noise. But beneath that, she hears the actual sound. It is not a song anymore. It is a scream, stretched thin by hunger and poison.

She lets the anger fill her because anger is better than despair. She surveys the shoreline again, her eyes scanning for threat, for weakness, for anything to justify the risk of surfacing at all. The answer comes in the form of two men, standing knee-deep in the surf, pulling a seine net toward the sand.

The net is heavy with catch. As they haul it in, the contents tumble onto the shore—a writhing mass of silver fish, glinting in the sun, peppered with bright plastic fragments and the occasional jellyfish blob. The men laugh, separating the live fish into buckets, stomping the rest into the sand. Mara wants to shout, to storm the shore and show them the consequence of their harvest.

Instead, she sinks lower, letting the buoy mask her presence, and watches.

Her eyes are drawn to the outflow pipe at the far end of the harbor. A slick the size of a small boat spreads from its mouth, the edges ringed with dead algae and the pulped remains of smaller creatures. Every few seconds, a bubble erupts from the depths—methane, or something worse. Each bubble bursts at the surface with a tiny pop, the smell reaching Mara even here.

She wonders if anyone on shore can sense it. Suppose any human nose is sharp enough to tell clean water from contaminated water. She doubts it. Perhaps they all live in denial, or maybe they've forgotten what the world is supposed to be.

Mara thinks of her home, her sister, and the dead reef. She thinks of the generations who once commanded the tides, now reduced to scavengers and ghosts. She thinks of the children on the sand, their careless inheritance. Something hardens in her chest.

Her body is shaking—not from cold, but from the tight coil of restraint. It would be so easy to call a current, to twist the water into a force they could not ignore. To take the nets and the boats and grind them against the rocks until nothing remained.

But she is not a monster. She is here to watch, to learn, to decide.

A girl, maybe twelve, sprints along the water's edge, her feet sending up plumes of wet sand. She runs past the fishermen, past the beached net, and stops to stare at the same outflow pipe Mara is watching. The girl's face contorts in disgust; she pinches her nose, then darts back to her parents, arms waving as she points at the slick.

Nobody looks. They shake their heads, dismiss her, and bury their faces in their screens.

Mara finds herself smiling—barely, but it's real.

She files the moment away, then ducks under a low swell, letting the cold water close over her. She scans the bay one more time, mapping every anchor, every net, every weakness. The pollution glows in her mind, a web of sick light, but she traces the connections, memorizes the pathways, commits it all to memory.

Next time, she'll do more than watch.

The tide shifts, just enough to hint at change. Mara flicks her tail and slides under, vanishing in the shadow of the buoy, already planning her next move.

The trick is not being seen.

Mara hugs the shadow line, darting between the hulls of moored skiffs and the tangle of dock pilings. There's plenty of cover—old tires, barnacle-scabbed fenders, floating mats of weed and trash. Humans might rule the land, but under the planks, the ocean still belongs to her.

She slips through the marina's backwater, muscles bunching and releasing in quiet rhythm. Now and then, a paddleboard glides past overhead, bright-painted fiberglass slicing the surface. Mara holds her breath, waiting for the shadows to pass, then glides onward, trailing a wake no bigger than a minnow's. Her tail is a blade, movement pure efficiency.

She listens as she goes. Human voices roll over the water, echoing strangely and fragmentarily: laughter, arguments, music blasting from waterproof speakers. At the end of the boardwalk, someone's grilling meat; the smell makes her gag, but also her stomach growls in betrayal.

She doesn't stop until she hits the open bay. Here, the town's noise is a little fainter, though the shoreline pulses with energy—people everywhere, as if the whole species is compelled to flock to the water and then spend the day ignoring it. Mara scans the beach and picks her target: a rocky outcrop jutting from the breakwater, shielded on three sides, perfect for spying.

She times her run between the sets, catches a lull in the surf, and launches herself forward. A wave rears up, threatening to expose her, but she ducks beneath, letting the cold churn blast her toward the rocks.

As she surfaces, she nearly collides with a trio of human children. They're splashing in the shallows; faces painted with the kind of wild joy Mara hasn't seen in her own world for years. The kids shriek as a stray wave knocks them off balance; one girl emerges sputtering, her tangled hair plastered over her eyes. Mara freezes, hiding just beneath the foam, heart hammering against her ribs. The girl blinks, stares straight at Mara's position, then giggles and flings a handful of water at her brother. For a second, Mara wonders if the girl saw her, then dismisses it. Humans see only what they want.

She lets the children's noise fade behind her, then slithers along the rock face, muscles burning as she fights the current. There are barnacles here, sharp as broken glass, and old loops of fishing line ghosting the cracks. Mara is careful to keep her wounded fin clear, but even so, she scrapes a fresh line across her hip. The pain is sharp, but it reminds her she's alive.

The view from the rocks is perfect. She props her elbows up, chin in her hands, and watches the show.

The beach is chaos, but not the kind she knows. Here, humans spread themselves in layers: the front line—closest to the tide—is dominated by children and teenagers, running obstacle courses of sandcastles and plastic buckets. Parents hover just behind, herding the smaller ones, half-watching, half-dreaming. Further back, an army of umbrellas and towels, every color jarring against the dun sand, every family group staking a claim to territory.

Vendors prowl the periphery, pushing carts of ice and sugary water. One man shouts over the din, offering neon bracelets and inflatable toys. Another pace with a tray of sun-bleached starfish, shells glued with rhinestones. Mara cringes at the sight, but even more at the humans who buy them—she can't decide if they are naive or just cruel.

At the far end of the strand, fishermen work the tide pool. Not for food, she thinks, but for the sport of it: their buckets overflow, fish squirming in the heat, every so often a winner held up for a photo before being tossed back. None of the fish will survive, not in this water. Mara can even taste the chemicals and microplastics from here.

She surveys the entire tableau, a mix of disgust and fascination. What a strange, reckless species. So clever with their tools, so careless with their world. She wonders if they even know the extent of the damage they cause, or if ignorance is part of their mythos.

She's still musing when she spots the man.

He stands apart from the rest, posted near the jetty with a cluster of other humans. There's something different about him, something that draws the eye. Maybe it's his stance—shoulders squared; feet planted like he's facing down a storm. Perhaps it's the way he moves: not with the lazy shamble of the sunbathers, but with the kinetic edge of someone always about to act.

His hair is a dark mess, tangled by wind and salt, the ends bleached almost to copper. His skin is tanned and scarred, with lean muscle visible under weathered field clothes: boots, cargo pants, and a faded jacket stained with old brine and a green hue. Mara can see from here that his hands are cut and calloused, and when he gestures, it's with knife-precision.

He's talking to the fishermen and not talking—arguing. The words don't reach Mara, but the shape of the conversation is obvious: the fishermen are stone-faced, arms crossed, every inch the portrait of stubborn old blood. The stranger's voice rises and falls, hands slicing the air, sometimes jabbing a finger at a laminated sheet he keeps rolled under his arm. Whatever he's saying, it isn't landing.

She narrows her eyes, tunes her ears. The wind shifts, and a snippet of his speech floats out over the water: "—pulling juvenile stock that hasn't had a chance to reproduce! It's unsustainable—" The fishermen laugh, one of them making a rude gesture, Mara doesn't quite understand. The stranger presses on, not cowed in the least.

She watches as he unfurls the sheet—a series of charts and photographs, each one marked with glaring red lines. He points, the other hand fisted at his side, and talks faster. The fishermen roll their eyes, but they can't look away from the evidence. Mara catches flashes of dead coral, massed fish kills, satellite images of the coast gone pale and empty.

She feels a chill run through her. The data matches what she has seen and what she has lived. The stranger is proper, even if the humans refuse to hear it.

One fisherman turns away, spitting on the sand. Another shrugs and takes a long drink from a can, clearly finished with the debate. But the stranger doesn't let up. He moves closer, lowering his voice, and gestures toward the water, as if he can sense the disaster lurking below.

Mara's curiosity spikes. She inches forward, bracing her tail against the rock, and studies his face: strong jaw, lines cut deep by sun and wind, eyes a stormy blue-gray that flickers with every shift of emotion. There's a scar above his right eyebrow, a thin arc like a lightning bolt.

She wonders who he is. What drives him to fight when no one wants to listen? She wonders, too, if he's like her—an exile, or just the last believer in a lost cause.

As the argument dissolves, the fishermen scatter, laughing and shaking their heads in disbelief. The stranger stands alone for a moment, hands at his sides, staring at the empty net as if it holds the answer to a riddle. He sighs, shoulders sagging, then bends to pick up a piece of trash from the sand. He crumples it in his fist, eyes sweeping the horizon before he drops it into a battered canvas bag.

Mara watches him work his way down the shore, pausing every few meters to collect debris. He moves with the focus of a predator, never missing a piece, sometimes kneeling to pluck microplastics from tide pools with tweezers. The task is endless, but he doesn't slow down.

She finds herself rooting for him.

The sun begins to dip, shadows growing long on the sand. Families pack up, the noise fading to a tired murmur. Vendors retreat, the air thick with the scent of hot pavement and seaweed. Only a few fishermen remain, cleaning their gear, and the stranger, still scouring the beach.

Mara's fingers grip the rock, nails digging into the barnacles. Her gills strain in the shallow water, breath coming ragged with anticipation.

This human is not like the others. She knows it, feels it in her bones.

He is dangerous, and he is exactly what she needs.

She waits until he moves out of sight, then slides back into the current, her mind already racing with plans. If she's going to change anything, she'll have to start with him.

The tide is rising. It's time to act.

The bay trembles with voices.

Mara floats just beyond the buoy line, using its rusted chain as cover. The orange float above bobs in the chop, concealing her as she scans the shore. The afternoon hums with tension, every sound sharpened by anticipation: the thud of volleyballs, the bark of a lifeguard's megaphone, the wet slap of fish guts on a vendor's table.

But today, it's not the noise that draws her. It's the fight.

Finn Gallagher is back—holding his ground at the jetty, locked in a heated argument with two weathered old-timers from the dock. Mara hears the first sharp volley as she drifts closer, flattening herself like a stingray against the shadowed shallows.

The men's voices tear across the air like pelican beaks. The fisherman's laughter carries, mean and cracked, while Finn's stands taut and trembling—his jaw set, his hands barely steady. From her vantage, Mara watches his fingers twitch each time the scarecrow-shaped fisherman spits near his boots.

She tucks herself tighter behind the buoy's chain and listens.

"...you haven't logged a legal catch in months," Finn says, voice raw as if scraped across coral. "It's not quotas. Your nets are coming up empty."

The scarecrow grins wide, teeth like broken shells. "Heard this doom talk since before your mama was wet behind the ears. Sea takes; sea gives back. We wait."

"You'll wait yourselves into extinction." Finn jabs a gloved finger toward a trawler swaying in the shallows. "That's a gill net violation. Everyone sees it. Everyone knows it. You're killing everything for a hundred kilometers and calling it tradition."

The second fisherman—hulking, diesel-slick, walrus-shaped—crosses his arms and spits. "Why don't you go back to counting sea slugs, college boy?"

"I'm trying to save your job," Finn snaps, clipboard clutched in white-knuckled fists. "At this rate, there won't be anything left to catch in five years."

He pulls a folder from his pack, unfurling a flurry of data like prayer flags. Pages catch the wind—color photos, maps, charts. Mara's sharp eyes skim the contents: bleached reefs, trawler scars, a graph stained red like a wound.

"That reef was alive last spring," Finn says, pointing to one image. "Now it's bone-white rubble. No shiners, no crabs, no life. It's dead. You killed it."

"Wasn't us," the scarecrow shrugs. "Foreigners. Red tide. Cold winter." The walrus snickers, picking his teeth with a plastic straw.

Mara's stomach twists.

Finn stares up at the sky like he's begging the clouds for patience. Then, jaw clenched, he gathers the loose papers—only for the fishermen to stomp them into the mud.

The scarecrow spits again, this time nailing Finn's boot. "Good luck with your grant money," he sneers, then ambles off, bucket slapping against his leg. The walrus follows, laughing without shame.

Finn doesn't move. Not at first. He stands there, fists shaking, lips white. Then slowly—like someone releasing a long-held breath—he loosens. He kneels and starts gathering trash from the high-tide line. Cigarette butts. Bottle caps. Shreds of old net.

Mara stares, stunned. He's not looking around for credit. He's not performing. He's just... cleaning.

The water around her reeks of diesel; it clings to her skin like guilt. But she doesn't pull back. She watches as Finn plucks a plastic straw from the sand with the care of a surgeon.

He mutters under his breath. Mara catches the words.

"Point zero one seven kilograms. Just here. Multiply by... a million, minimum. Per meter."

Then louder, to no one: "Two-point-five kilometers of shoreline. Daily tide. Seventeen metric tons a year, easy."

He starts collecting again.

Mara smiles—unexpected, involuntary. The expression tugs at muscles she hasn't used in months.

She follows him with her eyes as he works his way down the coast. He bleeds from a rusted nail but doesn't flinch. He untangles the monofilament line and carefully loops it, stuffing it into his pocket. Every so often, he glances at the water—searching for something—a sign. Maybe hope.

Finally, he slumps onto a concrete bollard, peels an orange with his teeth, and eats half of it in silence. The rest goes into the trash bag, along with everything else discarded by his kind.

Mara considers surfacing.

She won't. Not yet.

But she doesn't retreat either. Instead, she follows him. Just a shadow behind a shadow. Just beneath the shimmer of the surface.

Finn stops at an inlet fouled by runoff. He kneels in the sludge, still muttering, still working. His hands tremble now—not from rage, but fatigue.

Mara drifts closer, near enough to see the calluses on his knuckles, the rust-stained lines on his palms. He moves with care. As if the ocean matters.

When he finishes, he lingers at the end of the jetty. The sunset ignites the water in flames of orange and red—the oil slick gleams like gold.

Mara surfaces a meter behind the rocks, barely disturbing the water.

She watches him. The set of his jaw. The posture of someone who is worn down but not broken. The quiet conversation between man and sea.

And then she knows.

Not tonight.

But soon.

She'll show herself. She wants to see what he'll do. If he'll run, or fight. Or—maybe—listen.

Her heart pounds like a drumbeat in the deep.

Mara dives, cutting through the dark. She follows his shape to shore, her hair a copper banner in the current.

She won't hide anymore.

Not from the humans.

Not from her choices.

Not from herself.

3 First Contact

The shadow under the jetty is thin but enough. Mara curls herself into the crevice, her spine pressed against the barnacle-scarred concrete, her jade and silver scales catching stray shards of light. The air at the surface is raw—burns her gills, dries the membranes in her mouth. She risks a single breath, gills flaring in shallow pulses, each one a stab. Her tail, still pink at the tip from the morning's net, throbs in rhythm with her heart.

She hates being this close to shore. Hates the noise—engines, gulls, music that never matches the beat of the surf. Hates the way the human stink sours every lungful, as if the world is dying from the top down.

Worse than the pain is the visibility. She is a ghost against the stone, but if the sun hits at the wrong angle, she'll flash like a lure. There's safety in the blue, but today she needs the shallows.

She rechecks the beach. The town is in weekend mode—half-naked bodies stacked three deep on sun-bleached towels, every square of sand claimed by a different tribe. Children batter the tide, their shrieks carrying past the breakwater. Further up, the fishermen cluster at the jetty's tip, beer in one hand, line in the other, all eyes on the water.

They don't see her, not yet.

Mara shifts her weight and peers through the cracks. A familiar figure paces the water's edge, alone. She recognizes the man by his walk: all momentum, like he's late for his own funeral. The scientist. She watches him sweep the beach with practiced fury, laminated charts clutched under one arm, boots kicking up arcs of dead kelp. She'd seen him on other days, constantly arguing with locals, always cleaning up after their carelessness. He moves with the edge of someone who knows the odds and spits on them anyway.

She wishes she could hate him, but mostly she envies his stubbornness.

The gill pain spikes. Mara tucks her head and draws a lungful through her nose. Salt, oil, old gasoline—her body screams for relief, for home. But there's no retreat. She closes her eyes and summons the Sea-Speaking.

It's not a power so much as a surrender. She lets the old melody uncoil in her chest; the ghost of a song her mother taught her before the coral died. The note vibrates in the hollow of her bones, at first too soft for even the fish to notice. She pushes, risking the backlash, and sends it out—a pulse, a question, a plea.

The water listens.

At first, nothing. The harbor is too dirty, the signal muddied by millions of microplastics and the hum of distant motors. She pushes again. The ache in her tail sharpens, nerves lighting up as if the old wound is freshly sliced. She ignores it.

Somewhere past the buoys, the call lands.

A ripple. Then two. The first dorsal fin breaks the surface fifty meters offshore—quick and tight, gone again in a blink. Mara holds the note, working it into a higher register. She can't see them yet, but she knows the shape of their thoughts: curiosity, irritation, hunger.

Dolphins. A whole pod, likely three generations riding the current together. The juveniles are reckless, chasing a battered mullet through the slick; the elders are wary, circling the edges, testing the edges of the sound.

They never come this close to shore—not anymore. But Mara sweetens the melody, layers it with promise and urgency—the dolphin's bite.

Two leaps, crisscrossing each other in a practiced display, their wet bodies flaring silver in the rotten sunlight. The beach crowd erupts: first a gasp, then the insect hum of cameras and phones. Children scream with new purpose, mothers point, and the fishermen abandon their lines. Every eye is fixed on the spectacle.

Mara eases back, hiding deeper in the shadow. The dolphins do their job: a dozen breaches in rapid succession, tails slapping the water, showboating for the primate audience. One of the elders' spins, flicks a fish into the air, and the crowd loses its mind.

Perfect. No one is looking at the rocks.

Mara slides from her crevice, careful to keep her silhouette low. Her tail protests, but she powers through. The adrenaline clears the pain for a few seconds, long enough to reach the lee side of the jetty, where the scientist stands, oblivious to everything except the page in his hand.

She lets herself rest, halfway in the shadow, and watches him.

He's not like the others. The skin at his throat is raw from sunburn, but he doesn't wear the standard human armor: no sunglasses, no hat, just the open stare of someone who's given up on secrets. The charts in his hand are spattered with mud, edges warped from water, but he clings to them like gospel.

He paces, double-backs, muttering numbers and names. Every so often, he checks the dolphin show, shakes his head, and scribbles something down. His focus is surgical. Mara finds herself drawn in, almost laughing at the intensity.

She knows this type: the lone crusader. The world is ending, but they think they can tape it back together with enough data. She respects it, even as she pities him.

She waits until the dolphins are at the peak of their riot—a synchronized leap, three bodies twisting midair—then risks moving closer. She needs to see his face, needs to be sure before she risks everything.

The water at her hips is only a meter deep now. Her scales catch the light, and for a moment, she fears she's exposed. But the beach is blind with dolphin-fever. All safe.

She remembers Lyla's words, the threat beneath the concern: "If you get caught, it's not just your death." Mara shoves the memory down. She's past caring. If the old ways are dead, then let them die. The world needs something new.

She inches closer to the scientist, her copper hair floating out behind her, darkening as the ends soak up the oily water. She is sure he'll see her, call out, ruin everything. But he doesn't. Instead, he kneels, eyes locked on a patch of dead seaweed, and begins collecting specimens into a baggie.

This is her chance.

Her heart slams against her ribs. The gill pain is a howl now, almost drowning her thoughts. She risks a breath through her mouth, lips just below the surface. Every instinct says run. Instead, she braces her hands on the sand and prepares to breach.

The last dolphin leap fades, the crowd's cheers dying down. The spell is almost broken.

Mara goes.

She bursts from the water, silent and sudden, her upper body gleaming in the low sun. For an instant, she's exposed—scales, hair, sharp black nails, the whole horror show of Merfolk myth. But the scientist doesn't see a monster.

He sees a miracle.

His eyes widen, jaw slack, every chart and theory evaporating in the wash of adrenaline. The bag of seaweed drops from his hand, forgotten. Mara stares him down, the two locked in a wordless standoff.

She does not speak. Not yet.

He blinks, shakes his head, and starts to backpedal, boots sliding on the wet sand. Mara watches, measuring his fear, waiting for him to shout, run, or call the others.

He does none of these things.

Instead, he whispers, "No way," voice barely a breath, like he's afraid to scare her off.

Mara risks a smile. The pain in her tail is gone now, replaced by a wild, intoxicating clarity. She holds her ground, muscles coiled and ready.

The scientist takes a step forward. "Are you—" He stops, swallows, and starts again. "Are you hurt?" His gaze flicks to her tail, the raw edge barely hidden below the surface.

Mara blinks, unprepared for the question. She almost laughs.

Instead, she nods once.

The scientist fumbles for words. “I—I saw you,” he says, “last week. I thought—” He gestures helplessly at the water. “I thought I was losing my mind.”

Mara remembers the old stories: humans as monsters, hunters, thieves. This one looks nothing like a threat. He looks like he’s about to pass out.

She dips her head, just enough to show she understands. “Not losing,” she says, voice rough from disuse. “Finding.”

He staggers at the sound, but doesn’t run.

They stare at each other, suspended in the moment.

Behind them, the dolphins begin to slip away, their job done.

Mara feels the world tilt, a new current taking hold. She’s not sure where it leads, but for the first time in years, it doesn’t feel like drowning.

She smiles again, and this time, it’s real.

Finn’s reaction is everything Mara expects—and nothing she could have prepared for.

First: a full-body jolt, like he’s been struck by lightning. Then the classic human freeze, eyes locked, breath held, every cell trying to decide between fight and flight. His hands—those strong, capable hands—clench tighter around the rolled charts before muscle memory forgets them entirely. The bundle slips, lands in the tide with a wet smack, papers fanning out like a wounded bird.

He doesn't notice. He's staring at her—really staring, like he's trying to memorize the pattern of her scales, the texture of her hair, the line of her jaw.

She waits, letting the silence stretch. Humans need time to recalibrate when their reality breaks.

He blinks twice and says, "You're—" but the rest of the sentence drowns in the slap of a wave.

Mara cocks her head, curious. "I am."

He backs up, tripping over a slick rock, but keeps his eyes on her. "It's impossible," he mutters, voice already dropping into the monotone of denial. "There's no way. Must be—costume, some kind of—" He's talking to himself now, words tumbling out, desperate to stitch the world back together.

She interrupts. "Your ocean is dying, scientist-man. My people die with it." The sentence comes out almost as a song, the vowels stretched and strange, tinged with the accent of the deep. Mara doesn't know if he hears the plea beneath the declaration.

Finn stops moving. The color drains from his face, then floods back in a blotchy, uneven wash. "You can talk," he whispers, as if this is the most incredible part.

Mara laughs, a brittle sound. "You can't hear much," she replies, and flicks her gills in emphasis. "Even now, you miss what screams."

His gaze drops to the gills, and Mara can feel him cataloguing her anatomy: the slit along her neck, the ridged scar above her right rib, the shimmering layer of jade and silver just beneath her skin. His eyes widen further.

"I saw you," he says, voice steadier. "Not just now. Before. You were in the kelp beds, near the outlet." His hand gestures vaguely toward the ruined reef, fingers trembling.

"Cleaning," Mara says. "Fixing what you break."

He ignores the jab. "How is this possible?" The question isn't for her; it's for the universe. But Mara answers anyway.

"We have always been here. Hiding. Fading." She lets her tail rise a fraction above the water, enough for the glimmer to catch his eye. "You stopped looking. Made us ghosts."

Finn nods, half-entranced. "Nobody would believe me. Hell, I don't believe you." His voice cracks, but the awe never leaves his face. "Are you… Are you alone?"

The words cut sharper than he could know. Mara grits her teeth. "Almost."

They stand there, the tide licking at their ankles, the dolphins still making a circus of the outer bay. Mara feels the urgency mount: the show won't last much longer, and once the humans lose interest, the risk increases tenfold.

She has to make him understand.

Mara edges forward, water sheeting off her scales. "Listen," she says. The word is both a command and an invitation.

Finn obeys, still in that analytical trance.

Mara focuses, channeling the Current-Calling into the bones of her arms. The magic is heavier near the surface, but she's practiced enough to twist it. She holds her palms out, fingers splayed, and lets the energy build.

The water beside her arm trembles. First a ripple, then a cyclone: a spiral no bigger than a child's toy, but spinning with impossible speed, pulling debris and air into its center. She shapes it, tightens the gyre until it hums like a tuning fork, then snaps her fingers. The vortex collapses in a perfect circle, sending a shockwave across the shallows.

Finn stares, mouth open. "That's—" He gropes for the language, falls back on science. "That's not hydrodynamic. There's no turbulence-no source—how the hell did you—" He trails off, rubs at his eyes, and tries again. "It's like micro-laminar flow, but with… intent."

Mara frowns, not quite parsing the jargon, but gets the gist. She points at the dissipating spiral. "Proof," she says. "Not costume."

Finn laughs—high, nervous, but genuine. "Yeah. No costume does that."

Behind him, the dolphins breach again, one arcing over the other in a move so precise it could have been choreographed. The crowd on the beach goes wild, a sea of phones lifted overhead.

Finn doesn't care. He's fixated on Mara, on the impossible. "Why me?" he asks, voice almost pleading. "Why show me?"

She thinks of Lyla, the anger, and the heartbreak. She thinks of the silent reef, the suffocating water. "You listen," Mara says. "Others don't. Others hunt."

He absorbs this, weighing the risk and the hope. "So, what do you want?" he asks.

Mara doesn't hesitate. "Help." The word is stark, stripped of pride. "You can't fix all. But maybe you can slow the end."

Finn's face hardens, the scientist giving way to the fighter. "I've been trying," he says, a pulse of defiance in his voice. "Nobody listens."

Mara nods. "I know."

They stand in the shallow, neither moving, both stunned by the new order of things. The dolphins begin to drift away, their contract with Mara fulfilled. The show is ending.

Mara risks a last step, close enough to read Finn's eyes. She sees the fear, but also the hope.

"Will you help?" she asks, and it's as much a challenge as a plea.

Finn doesn't flinch. "Yes. Whatever it takes."

The water between them is electric.

Mara smiles, and this time, Finn mirrors it.

The dolphins vanish beneath the chop, taking the last of the old world with them.

They retreat a few paces from the open water, Finn crouched at the edge, Mara half-lurking behind a drift of kelp. The beach is already returning to its default state—families dragging children up the dunes, fishermen re-rigging lines, the crowd's dolphin high fading into ordinary boredom. Nobody looks twice at the strange tableau of man and myth in the tidal zone.

Mara risks another breath, gills flaring raw. She's been out of the blue too long, but she won't show weakness.

Finn regains a fraction of composure, his scientist's brain snapping back into gear. "How—" he hesitates, then clears his throat. "How long have you been watching us?"

"Longer than you've been watching anything," Mara replies. She gestures at the foamed-over patch of water near the storm drain, the rainbow slicks, the scum. "You poison without seeing. It's always been this way, but faster now."

Finn's gaze follows her point. "We try to stop it," he says, sounding even less convinced than she feels. "Some of us, anyway."

"Not enough," Mara says, softer. She motions to a battered can rolling in the backwash, then to the broken fragments of coral at her feet, bone-white and brittle as old teeth. "The reefs scream, but you don't hear."

Finn absorbs this. "I do," he says. "I've been trying to tell people. I have—" He stops, remembering the ruined charts. "Well, I had data. Trends. Satellite images, species counts. Nobody cares until it's already dead."

Mara smiles bitterly. "Humans love tragedy when it's past tense."

He almost laughs, but the sound dies. "How many of you are there?"

She doesn't answer right away. The real number is a secret even among her kind. "Fewer every season," she finally says. "We hide. We die. Soon, there will be nothing left to discover."

Finn swallows. The word extinction hangs between them.

"I've spent my life looking for something like this," he admits, "but I always thought if I found it, it would be some fossil, a piece of DNA, not—" He gestures at her, helpless.

"Not a warning," Mara says. "Not a plea."

They fall silent, but it's not empty. Mara reads the shifting tides of Finn's mind—already calculating risk, reward, what-ifs. She's seen this before: the instant a human decides to make a cause his own.

"I can help," Finn says, almost to himself. "I could get you in front of people who might actually do something. Researchers, conservation groups—hell, the press, if you want." His face lights up with the possibility, but then he sees Mara's expression.

Her gills stutter. "No press," she says sharply. "No more stories. Stories bring hunters."

Finn hesitates. "But how else—"

She cuts him off. "You want proof. But proof is a trap. The first scientist brings the second, the second brings cameras, then money, then nets, then—" She gestures at herself, the ruined tail, the long scars. "That is how it always ends."

He looks away, stung by the truth of it.

Mara softens, just enough. "If you want to help, start smaller. Fix this." She points at the slick, at the dead patch of reef. "No one will listen to a myth. But maybe they will listen to you."

Finn's hands tremble, but he sets his jaw. "I've been trying. Alone, I get ignored. But if I had…" He stops, the idea forming in real time. "If I had something from you. Not you—just evidence. Guidance."

Mara considers. It is a risk, but risk is all that's left.

"I can give you warnings," she says. "Where the water turns bad. When the currents shift or the nets deteriorate. But you must swear not to bring others. Not yet."

Finn nods, fierce and fast. "You have my word."

She studies him, weighing the promise. Merfolk are not known for faith in humans, but Finn's eyes hold a kind of desperate honesty she hasn't seen in years. Maybe never.

The tide begins to rise again, a cold surge lapping at Finn's boots. Mara knows she needs to leave, to heal, to carry the news back to the deep. But she lingers.

"One more thing," Finn says, voice suddenly shy. "Your name. I can't just keep thinking of you as—"

Mara grins, baring sharp teeth. "Mara," she says. "Mara Ondine."

He repeats it, as if tasting a new element. "I'm Finn. Finn Gallagher."

She's heard the name, in the water, whispered by fish and sea rats who scavenge the town's edge. A friend to the blue, if such a thing exists.

"Until next tide, Finn Gallagher," Mara says.

He nods, and for a moment, they are equals.

Mara slips back, scales catching one last flash of light. She disappears beneath the water without a ripple, the world closing behind her like she was never there at all.

On the shore, Finn stands alone, watching the place where myth just became mission.

The dolphins are gone, the crowd has vanished, and the ocean returns to its long, patient dying.

But now, a new current is running underneath, swift and invisible.

Change.

4 Guardians of the Deep

Mara's tail is a ragged banner behind her, every beat sending up a pulse of red into the black-green water. The wound sears, but she doesn't slow. She has to get home before the pain betrays her—before it calls in predators, or worse, the city guards.

The world below the dead reef is a second ocean. The surface sunlight sours into a dull gray the further she goes, then blinks out entirely. Only the city remains: a maze of phosphorescent coral spires, pulsing with slow light, all ringed by kelp fronds so neon-bright they leave afterimages when she blinks. Each tower is carved from living reef, each window a bubble of air kept by patient magic. The city sprawls along the old continental shelf, not built for beauty anymore but for survival—a fortress in the gloom.

Mara angles downward, following the cold current toward the outer gate. She passes a flock of juveniles practicing tail-flips through hoops made of discarded human netting. Their laughter echoes, pure and sharp, but she knows what comes next. As soon as they see her—see the blood, the limp in her stroke—the laughter collapses into silence.

"Hey, Ondine!" one calls, but the voice trails off as it notices the damage. Mara ignores them, eyes locked on the city gates.

She barely makes it to the perimeter before Lyla intercepts. No warning. Just a flash of white-blonde hair, then the bruising grip of fingers on Mara's forearm.

"Not here," Lyla snaps and hauls her into a side passage.

It's all muscle. Lyla's hands clamp down, steering Mara up a spiral corridor flanked by barnacle-tough walls. The only light is from small, bioluminescent worms stitched in careful patterns overhead. There's no time to protest, and anyway, Mara wouldn't. She knows the drill.

They emerge into a hollowed chamber; walls lined with the fossil shells of ancestors. The place smells of brine and old anger.

Lyla slams the door behind them, then whips around. Her face is blank, but the tail flick gives it away—Lyla is furious. "You're leaking blood halfway across the shelf," she hisses, voice tuned to a frequency only family can hear.

Mara forces a shrug, even though it spikes agony up her spine. "There are worse things in the water."

"Not for us." Lyla's eyes are quicksilver, shot with micro-currents of distrust. "What happened, Mara?"

She tries to play it off, but Lyla's not having it. "Don't lie."

Mara sighs, lets herself fold onto a ledge. The wound is ugly—a gash with fibers of net still caught in the edge. She plucks one free, flicks it to the floor.

"Surface nets," Mara says. "Got caught. Fought out."

Lyla doesn't move, but the tension in her arms ramps up. "You're supposed to avoid the surface. If the elders catch you up there—"

"They're not watching," Mara spits. "Not really. They talk."

The accusation hangs, and Mara instantly regrets it, but Lyla doesn't rise to the bait. Instead, she kneels, tilting Mara's tail to inspect the wound. Her hands are gentle now, even as she rages.

"Idiot," Lyla mutters. "They'll know."

"Let them know," Mara says. "I'm not ashamed."

"You should be."

There's a pause, thick as oil. Lyla goes to the wall, pulls a strip of kelp from a hook, and wraps it around the gash, her movements precise. When she finishes, she sits across from Mara, arms folded tight.

"Tell me," Lyla says.

Mara doesn't want to. But she owes her sister the truth.

"I surfaced near the old breakwater. Watched the humans." She hesitates, then, "One saw me."

Lyla's gills flare open, sharp and involuntary. "You let yourself be seen?"

"Not on purpose," Mara lies. But the truth is, she needed it. Needed someone to see the pain, the proof that the ocean is dying. "He's different. Not like the others."

Lyla laughs, a bitter, whalebone-cracking sound. "They're all the same. They pretend to care, but they take. You know the stories."

"I know the stories," Mara shoots back. "That's all they are now. Stories. While we wait down here and rot."

Lyla's hands are close to fists. "Our people are alive because of those stories, because we hide. Because we do not trust the surface." She jabs a finger at Mara. "You risk more than yourself every time you breach. You risk all of us."

Mara stares at the shell wall. Generations of their kind, etched into the spiral. She feels small. "If we keep hiding, we'll die anyway."

The silence is absolute.

Lyla paces the small chamber, her fins bristling with agitation. "Do you know why the old songs forbid contact?" she asks, not waiting for an answer. "Because the last time we trusted a surface-dweller, it ended in slaughter."

"I read the histories—" Mara begins, but Lyla cuts her off.

"You don't know. You haven't lived it." She grabs a loose shard of coral from the floor and slams it into the wall, sending a dust cloud through the water. "They came with nets, with poison. They promised peace, and then they hunted us for meat. For trophies. For stories to tell their children. It was a purge, Mara. Our numbers—" her voice breaks, the music gone flat— "never recovered."

Mara's tail curls in, unconsciously protective. But she can't give up. "This one isn't like that," she insists, even as she feels the words thin out. "He wants to help."

Lyla snorts, pure contempt. "They all do, until they get what they want. Then they forget."

"He's a scientist," Mara tries. "He's spent his life fighting for the ocean."

Lyla turns, fixing her with that ancient, judgmental stare. "And what happens when he tells his tribe? When the news spreads, and the cameras come? Do you really think they'll just let us live?"

Mara can't answer. She wants to believe, but the memory of the hungry faces on the beach—the nets, the knives, the indifference—crowds her mind.

Lyla's voice drops, low and lethal. "The surface-dwellers hunt what they fear, and they fear what they cannot control."

The sentence resonates; a chord struck deep in the bone. For a moment, neither speaks.

Mara feels the urge to fold, to let Lyla's anger wash her away. But she forces herself upright, chin up, even as her tail droops.

"We can't win by hiding," Mara says. "Not anymore."

"Then we lose faster," Lyla says.

Mara's gills flutter. "What if we could fix it? What if—just once—we trusted the right human?"

Lyla closes her eyes and rubs the bridge of her nose like she's fighting a migraine. "There is no right human," she says, but the edge is gone from her voice. "Only survivors, and the ones who feed on them."

Mara lets it hang. She senses Lyla softening, just a hair.

"I don't want to watch us go extinct in the dark," Mara whispers. "I'd rather try, even if it kills me."

Lyla's face is unreadable. The currents between them swirl with old loyalty, new fear. "You always did like impossible odds," she says, but this time, there's a trace of pride.

She stands, gestures for Mara to follow. "Come. I'll clean the wound properly. Then you tell me everything about this scientist."

Mara obeys, and as she passes Lyla, she catches the faintest shimmer of a smile. It's gone in a blink, but it's there.

They swim through the pale corridors, Mara limping, Lyla holding her upright. Neither speaks, but the air between them is less jagged. Hope may be contagious, after all.

In the distance, the city lights pulse, defiant against the dying world.

The training pools lie at the city's edge, just past the shell barracks and the old arena. Once, they hosted competitions—show trials of power, where young Merfolk would sculpt the currents, race the tide, court the favor of watching elders. Now, the pools serve as a classroom and a refuge, a place for those willing to fight the slow poison seeping in from above.

Lyla ushers Mara past the outer guards with a curt nod, her grip never loosening from Mara's elbow. The guards don't question, but their eyes linger, tracking every movement. Inside, the water is colder, the walls lined with grids of hollowed coral, each cell holding a flicker of phosphorescence or a captive crustacean. The floor slopes gently to a bottomless blue pit in the center.

Lyla releases Mara at the edge. "Sit," she orders, and Mara obeys, muscles humming with fatigue.

Lyla circles the pool once, scanning for eavesdroppers. Satisfied, she drops to a crouch across from her sister. For a moment, she watches, lips pressed thin, as if weighing the risk of even speaking.

"You know what will happen if the council finds out," Lyla says.

"They already know," Mara replies. "They just don't want to admit it."

Lyla shakes her head, but the fight is out of her. "Then we have to make you better. Fast." She gestures at the pool. "Show me what you can do."

Mara draws a breath, bracing herself for the pain. She stretches her hands over the water, fingers splayed. The old way, the way her mother taught: feel the rhythm, follow the pull, then push. The first attempt is clumsy. The water shudders, then goes still.

"Again," Lyla says. "Don't force it. Let it come through."

Mara closes her eyes. There it is: the pulse, faint but steady. She latches onto it, and this time, when she moves her hand, the current follows—a thin thread, curling through the pool like a ribbon of smoke.

Lyla grunts approval. "Good. Now split it."

Mara flicks her wrist, and the ribbon divides into two, then four, each one writhing in a different pattern. It's exhausting, holding the shapes in her mind, but she manages a brief lattice before it unravels. The effort leaves her dizzy.

"Again," Lyla says, but there's less bite to it now.

Mara tries again and again. Each time, the current grows finer, more precise. On the tenth attempt, she manages to braid two flows together—a double helix of motion, holding for three full breaths before collapsing.

Lyla actually smiles. “Better.”

They work in silence for a while, Lyla only speaking to correct Mara’s hand or posture, sometimes just flicking her own fingers in demonstration. When Mara’s arms shake too hard to continue, Lyla calls a halt.

She gestures to the side wall, where a battered mesh bag hangs. Inside, a half-dozen shellfish clack against each other, alive and wary.

“Now Sea-Speaking,” Lyla says. “Use the song, not the current.”

Mara hesitates. She’s never been good at this part—the empathy, the tuning of oneself to something not entirely human. But she tries. She centers herself, lets her mind drift past pain, past the noise of the city, to the quiet place where only the song exists.

The first note is a whisper. The shellfish go still, antennae quivering. Mara builds the sound, weaving memory and feeling into the shape of her need. “Come,” she sings, not with her voice, but with the part of her that remembers the old reef, the one before the silence.

For a moment, nothing. Then, a single shell creaks open, a tentative response.

Mara pours everything into it, calling to the others. Two more shells open, then the rest. They emerge, all six, paddling toward Mara’s hands at the edge of the pool.

Lyla’s smile is genuine now. “You, see? You have the touch.”

Mara doesn’t answer, holding the song as long as she can. But then a shadow flickers over the pool, and the shellfish scatter, diving for the bottom. The song is gone. Mara feels the connection snap, like a broken string.

Lyla stands, scanning the ceiling. "Polluted current," she mutters, face hardening. "It's worse every day."

Mara knows what she means. The magic works, but only in fits and starts—never as easy as the old stories made it sound.

"Try again," Lyla says, but Mara can't. She's wrung out, her head pounding.

Lyla notices, and her tone softens. "We have to get you stronger. If you're going to play at being a surface spy, you can't leave traces. The current must flow beneath, never above."

"Like you," Mara says, and it's almost an accusation.

Lyla doesn't rise to the bait. Instead, she sits beside Mara, their tails almost touching.

"I used to be like you," Lyla says, voice low. "I thought I could change everything if I were just loud enough." She gestures to the training pool. "Now I teach kids to swim in circles, because that's all we have left."

"Not all," Mara says. "We have the surface. We have—"

"The humans," Lyla finishes. "Don't be naive."

"Is it naive to hope?"

Lyla snorts. "It's dangerous."

They watch the shellfish for a while, both thinking of the world outside—of nets, and oil, and cities built on the bones of the sea.

"Will you help me?" Mara asks, unsure of the answer she wants.

Lyla doesn't hesitate. "Of course. But you have to promise—if it goes bad, if you're caught—"

"I'll protect us," Mara says. "I swear."

Lyla nods, as if sealing a pact. "Then we begin tomorrow. At dawn."

She stands, shakes out her hair, and stalks to the exit. "Rest. You'll need it."

Mara waits until her sister is gone, then slides into the water and sinks to the bottom of the pool. She stares up at the slow-moving lights in the ceiling, letting the cold numb her wounds.

For the first time since breaching the surface, Mara feels something close to hope.

She drifts and dreams of currents braided tighter than any net.

The path to the Elder Council cuts through the city's oldest bone.

Mara and Lyla swim in silence, passing through tunnels worn smooth by centuries of tail and tide. Each archway is ribbed with ancient shell, stained by the fingerprints of the generations that fled here after the surf gates sealed. Every few meters, a guard in polished scale armor eyes their passage, but Lyla's reputation clears the way—no one stops a Pearl unless they want a new orifice chewed.

The final approach narrows, light dimming, until it opens on a chamber so vast that Mara's vision bends around it. The dome rises from a base of black coral, each bench a tier above the last, spiraling up to the apex. The benches are packed: elders in their formal sashes, apprentice scribes, old soldiers with tails like battered pennants. The crowd hisses and mutters as Mara and Lyla glide into the open.

At the center, seven thrones—alive, not carved, the coral pulsing faintly as if breathing. The Elders are arrayed by age, their bodies armored in the thickest plates, every segment etched with runes. Pearls the size of fists stud their brows and shoulders, each one a badge of victory or loss. Mara recognizes the faces from a hundred nightmares, and from every history lesson: Elder Nerissa, silver-scaled and severe; Elder Caspian, blue-black with eyes like deep current; Elder Mira, spotted and half-blind but still rumored to out-swim a shark.

Lyla bows first, and Mara follows, tail tucked low.

Elder Nerissa's voice cuts across the dome, soft but pitched to travel. "You come before the Council, Mara Ondine. Stand, and account for yourself."

Mara straightens, suppressing a wince. Her tail is wrapped in fresh kelp, but the wound throbs.

Nerissa's gaze is clinical, dissecting her. Reports reach us of reckless surfacing. Unmasked use of magic near the human settlements. Are these reports correct?"

Mara tries to keep her voice level. "They are."

Murmurs ripple through the benches, a few outright jeers from the rowdy old guard. Lyla glares them down.

Nerissa nods, satisfied. "And for what purpose do you risk our extinction?"

Mara looks to Lyla, then squares herself. "To find help. The reefs are dying. Our magic weakens every year. We can't fix it from down here—not alone."

Elder Caspian leans forward. "Help from whom?"

"From a human," Mara says, and the word detonates in the chamber.

Gasps, some hissing, a few outright curses in the old tongue. One scribe faints, or pretends to.

Nerissa lets the uproar simmer, then gestures for silence. "We have tried this before, child. Humans hunt; they betray. They poison for profit. You believe one will save us?"

"I don't know," Mara says, honest and raw. "But it's better than drowning slowly in the dark."

A dry chuckle from Caspian. "Some would call that optimism. Others, suicide."

Elder Mira stirs, her voice a low rumble. "Who is this human?"

"Finn Gallagher," Mara says. "He's a scientist. He's spent his life—"

"Collecting corpses for study?" Nerissa interrupts. "Or pinning us in jars?"

"No," Mara says, louder now. "He listens. He fights for the water. He's different."

Nerissa glances to the side, where a smaller councilor, gilled and nearly translucent, whispers in her ear.

Elder Caspian's eyes never leave Mara. "Demonstrate," he

says.

Mara blinks. "What?"

"Your Tide-Sensing," Caspian says. "Prove that the water above is as poisoned as you say."

Mara hesitates, but Lyla gives her a tiny nod. She steps forward, eyes the open well in the center of the chamber.

She draws the current up, like she practiced—find the heartbeat, feel the filth. At first, she's terrified it won't work, that she'll fail in front of all of them, but as she focuses, the world sharpens. The water here is old, but the pollution seeps down even this far. She tastes the tang of antifreeze, the metallic echo of pesticide. The microplastics catch on her tongue.

She holds her palms out, channeling the sensory overload into a visible pulse. Tiny motes of plankton, dormant until now, burst to life in a blue-green flash, illuminating the water in a spiraling pattern that climbs the walls of the dome. For a split second, the chamber glows with a terrible beauty.

But then, as the plankton swirl, dark threads snake through the light—heavy bands of toxin, ropy clouds of silt and rot. The display is unmistakable: the poison runs deeper than any of them wanted to believe.

The chamber goes dead quiet.

Caspian stands. "That is enough."

Mara lets the spell drop, her hands shaking.

Nerissa looks away, as if the truth has a taste she can't stand. "And what is your plan, Ondine? You and your human?"

Mara's mind whirls. "We study the flows. We warn you where

the poison is worst. We try to stop the damage before it reaches us. Maybe, if we learn enough, we can fix it. Or buy time for the young to grow."

Nerissa scoffs, but Caspian seems intrigued.

A voice from the benches: "And if the human betrays us?" It's the old guard again, their tails beating in angry rhythm.

Mara straightens, ignoring the pain. "Then I take the blame. Alone. No one else suffers for my risk."

Lyla's hand finds Mara's, squeezing once. Solidarity.

Elder Mira peers at her, one eye milky. "You love this human?" she asks, out of nowhere.

Mara blushes, scales going iridescent at her cheeks. "No," she says, but then, "Maybe. I don't know. Does it matter?"

Mira grins, sharklike. "Sometimes, it's the only thing that does."

The Council withdraws, conferring in a knot of scales and whispers. The dome seethes with speculation; the crowd fractures into camps: some argue for isolation, some for war, and a few hold out hope for an alliance. Mara listens, but tunes it out.

Her fate is decided in less time than she expects.

Nerissa rises, voice ringing. "The Council will allow your experiment, Mara Ondine. You will act as liaison with the surface-dweller, but under strict conditions: any betrayal, any threat to the city, and the gates seal again—this time forever."

Mara bows, tail dragging the floor.

Caspian steps forward, breaking protocol. He gestures for Mara to join him at the center of the well.

"Come," he says, and Mara follows.

He speaks quietly, for her alone. "There are techniques lost to most of your age. Old Tideweaving, for defense, for escape. I will show you one. If things go bad, you use it—no hesitation. Understand?"

Mara nods.

Caspian's eyes, old as anything, soften a hair. "I hope your faith is not misplaced," he says, "but the world above is crueler than you think."

He presses a hand to her brow, and for a second, Mara feels her mind expand—like a river breaking its banks. She glimpses secrets, currents hidden beneath the city, the silent calculus of predator and prey. She sees, for a heartbeat, a future where all of this is ash and silence, unless someone changes the tide.

Then it's over, and she's just Mara again, dizzy but alive.

The Council adjourns. Nerissa leaves without looking back. Mira winks, then vanishes into the crowd. The benches are clear, the guards relax. The rest of the city will take days to learn what happened here, but Mara knows the rumors will be wild.

She turns to Lyla. "Well?"

Lyla's face is unreadable. Then she laughs, soft and strange. "Congratulations. You just made yourself the most dangerous thing in the city."

Mara grins, teeth bared. "Not in the city."

They swim up, toward the thinning light. Outside, the city's glow is almost lost to the darkness, but above, a thread of current calls—faint but insistent.

Mara follows, knowing the whole world is watching now.

But for the first time, it feels like the current is hers to shape.

5 Secrets of the Sea

Dawn in the cove is not a sunrise but a slow defeat of the dark. The sky above is a rumor of gold, all the warmth stopped cold at the horizon, bleeding into the water in thin, sickly lines. The rocks here are sharp, black, and barnacle-clawed, and the tide, even at its gentlest, is a battering ram. Mara drags herself out of the surf, hands digging into cold sand, copper hair plastered to her neck and cheeks by salt and sweat. Her tail—still a little ragged from the last council summons, the tip a swollen echo of old injury—catches on a barnacle and she hisses, the sound so inhuman it startles even the gulls overhead.

She is already late.

Finn waits on the shore, boots leaving moon-cratered impressions in the morning-damp sand. He's pulled his hood low and wears sunglasses, despite the clouds. His jacket is zipped, one hand in the pocket, but his other hand hovers by his side like it's ready to catch a falling star. He keeps glancing over his shoulder, nerves visible in every micro-movement. Beside him stands another human, this one perfectly still. She is smaller than Finn, but only in the way that a coiled eel is smaller than the current: you know the force is in there, waiting. Her black hair is tied back in a line so precise it could slice kelp. She clutches a clipboard, and the look she gives the water is the look Mara has seen in a shark just before it bites.

Mara slows, lets the last ripple carry her to the shallows. She stays half-submerged, tail hidden by the churn, and pulls herself upright, exposing only her head and shoulders. The water beads along her arms in silvery droplets, catching what little light there is and refracting it along the line of her collarbone. Her gills flutter, then close. She takes the moment to scan the cove. It's empty, except for the three of them and a single plastic bag caught in the rocks, flapping like a stranded jellyfish.

Finn is the first to move. He lifts a hand, an awkward wave. "Morning," he calls, voice pitching up at the end.

The other human—Ava, she remembers from Finn's briefing—does not wave. She lifts the clipboard and starts writing.

Mara pushes herself further up, the water receding to reveal the latticework of her scales. The old stories say the first thing humans notice is the tail, but in her experience, it's always the eyes. Ava Chen's eyes are obsidian behind her glasses, but the way they widen as Mara approaches is unmistakable. The scientist in her is already chewing the data.

Finn clears his throat, the sound clipped and businesslike. "Mara, this is Dr. Ava Chen. She runs the coastal hydrodynamics lab at Scripps." He glances at Mara, then back at Ava. "Ava, this is—well, I guess the word is 'liaison.'"

Ava Chen doesn't smile. "I prefer empiricist," she says. "Are you going to demonstrate, or do I need to take water samples first?"

Mara tries to parse the sarcasm, but it is too thin, almost flavorless. She nods, a motion that feels both too formal and too eager. "Ready when you are." The words sound thick in her throat. She has practiced the human tongue, but the vowels are always a little off, vowels stretching like kelp in the tide. She hopes they won't notice.

Ava steps to the water's edge, her boots sinking a centimeter in the wet sand. "I need measurable data," she says, voice neutral, but the pen in her hand clicks with every other word. "No more handwaving." She points at a line of small, boxy devices arranged along the shoreline; each connected to a coil of cable that snakes back to a battered tablet. Wave sensors. Three-axis current meters. Temp and salinity logs. If what Finn claims is true, we need scientific documentation."

Mara studies the setup, eyebrows knit. The boxes look like toys, but the way Ava handles them suggests they are more dangerous than they appear. Finn kneels beside one and taps the screen, scrolling through columns of numbers. "We're live," he says. "It'll auto-log everything for the next hour."

The conversation is so tight, so stripped of excess, that Mara wonders if they are nervous, or just always this efficient.

She slides fully into the water and finds a flat stone just deep enough for her tail to rest. The wound at the tip throbs, a low pulse in time with her heart. She raises her hands above the surface, her fingers webbed and trembling slightly from the cold. She focuses, finds the pulse of the current beneath, the deep muscle memory of her people. She draws the first trickle of energy up her arms, and the water between her fingers starts to vibrate—not enough to see, but enough to feel.

Finn watches, kneeling at the ready, his own fingers curled around a waterproof camera. Ava Chen sets her pen down, eyes tracking every twitch.

Mara breathes. Then she lets the Current-Calling go.

The effect is slow at first—a ripple, nothing more, spreading outward from her palms in perfect circles. The human eye would barely register it, but the sensors start to chirp, the lights on their panels shifting from green to yellow, then to red. Ava's eyes flick to the readout, then back to Mara. The ripple grows, each wave chasing the last, building amplitude without losing its symmetry. Mara narrows her focus, amplifying the pull, and the water between her hands begins to glow, faint but discernible —a soft jade halo that pulses with every beat.

Finn's jaw drops. He forgets the camera; eyes locked on the light. Even Ava steps forward, feet almost touching the water.

Mara keeps the pattern going for three full breaths. She lets it expand, the circles widening until the whole cove is trembling, the sand beneath Finn and Ava's boots shivering in resonance. Mara's gills open and close, the pressure in her lungs building. Her arms want to drop, but she holds the pose, eyes fixed on Ava's face.

The pen in Ava's hand has stopped clicking. She doesn't move, barely breathes.

When Mara finally lets go, the water calms instantly, the only sign of disturbance a few concentric ripples racing for the shore. The jade light gutters, then vanishes. Mara slumps, catching herself on the rock, chest heaving with the effort.

Finn is the first to speak, his voice half-whispered. "Jesus."

Ava says nothing. She turns to her tablet and begins scrolling through data, lips pressed so tight they're white. For a minute, the only sound is the slap of the outgoing waves and the rapid-fire tap of Ava's finger on the touchscreen.

Mara tries to read their faces. Finn is half-exhilarated, half-terrified, like he's just seen a god and realized it bleeds. Ava is unreadable, the scientist mask drawn so tight it seems to cut off all emotion. But Mara can smell the adrenaline on her, the spike of hormones that says not fear, but awe.

Ava finally looks up. "Rerun it," she says, voice smaller than before. "Increase the frequency if you can."

Mara nods, gathers her strength, and readies herself for round two.

Mara steadies herself and shakes out her arms. The cold has crept into her bones, but adrenaline and pride keep her from shivering. Finn is on one knee at the sensor bank, phone ready, his face split in a smile that looks more like a threat than joy. Ava Chen positions herself dead-center on the shore, as if daring Mara to impress her twice.

The first demonstration had been simple: the pure circle, the easiest shape, the way a child might draw magic in sand. This time, Mara closes her eyes and digs deep, searching for the twist in the current that will let her bend the rules.

She feels the rough grit of the wound at her tail tip, the ragged edges catching on every microshift in water pressure. She lets the pain anchor her, focusing her mind into a hard, sharp point.

She lifts her hands again, this time stretching her arms wide, palms up like an offering.

The water responds instantly. Where before there was a ripple, now there is a spiral—a tight, hungry cyclone no wider than Mara's chest, but deep as a whirlpool. It starts at her left hand and whips around to her right, gathering speed until it throws a spray out three meters. The spiral draws in the cove's surface scum, shredding it to mist, and even the sand at the bottom stirs in a rising column. The entire shoreline vibrates with the effort.

The spiral holds for a count of ten, then Mara flicks her wrist, and the cyclone collapses. The air is heavy with mist and salt, and for a moment, everything is quiet.

Ava's face breaks, the first crack in the scientist's glass. "Again," she says, voice hoarse. "This time, see if you can do a vertical oscillation. We're not getting enough amplitude on the Y-axis."

Mara's lips twitch. "Vertical, then." The words feel strange, as if speaking them makes them true.

She draws the current in, then slams her hands together, palms cupped. The water between them jumps—a shockwave that surges up and out, climbing the invisible ladder of pressure until it breaks the surface in a standing wave. The column rises, higher than a human head, almost three feet above the baseline. The wave holds, wobbling but never collapsing. It's a thing Mara has never tried before, not even in secret.

Ava's jaw drops. The pen slips from her fingers, rolling down the sand and into the water. She doesn't notice.

Finn makes a whooping sound, loud enough that it nearly breaks Mara's concentration.

Ava recovers, breathless, eyes darting between the standing wave and the readout. "That's impossible," she whispers, then louder: "Finn, you seeing this? The sensors are pegged."

Finn only nods, snapping shots with the waterproof camera, the grin on his face feral.

Mara lets the wave fall, timing the release so it slams into the shore in a perfect, directed crash, no spillover. She is careful to keep the energy contained; there's no point in showing them how much damage she could really do.

Ava is still staring at the water, the boxy sensors half-submerged and blinking frantically. "Nothing natural could produce that. Nothing. It would take a hurricane-grade pressure differential to make the water behave that way." She wipes her hand down her face, leaving a smear of seawater on her cheek. "Show me the third sequence."

Mara hesitates. She remembers the rehearsal with Finn, the theory he'd drawn in the sand with a stick: two currents, opposite direction, perfectly synchronized. The move is a signature, the kind of magic that gets you noticed by your own people, and she has never attempted it in front of anyone, let alone a human.

She glances at Finn. He catches her look, nods encouragement. "You got it," he mouths.

Mara takes a long, steadying breath, gills fluttering open and shut, and lets her mind go flat and blank. She calls up the energy, more than before, more than is safe, and channels it straight down her arms. The water in her hand hums, then splits—literally divides, left spinning counterclockwise, right clockwise, each a mirror of the other. The two whorls start at her fingertips and twist outward, growing in speed and size until they form matched gyres, opposite but perfectly balanced. The air above the water vibrates with the frequency; Mara can feel it in her teeth.

Ava stumbles back a step, nearly falling into the sand. "That's not… that's not possible." She squints at the sensor display, then at Mara, then at the water. "You're splitting the vector. That can't be done, not at this scale. Not with—" She stops, at a total loss.

Mara holds it as long as she can. Ten seconds, twenty. The exertion is immense—her arms shake, sweat prickles her forehead, and the old wound at her tail tip throbs with a fresh, insistent ache. She is close to the edge, close to losing control, but she clings to the motion, makes it her own.

Then, as Finn had asked, she forces the two whorls to meet. The collision is silent, but the water between them flattens, a split second of mirror-stillness, before the combined pressure explodes upward in a spray so fine that it rains back down on all three of them.

Mara collapses to her elbows, face inches above the water—her vision swims. For a second, she thinks she might blackout, but she holds on, blinking away the salt.

Ava is speechless. She moves closer, boots in the wet, and bends down so she's eye-level with Mara. "How are you doing that?" The words are almost reverent, a prayer in the church of science.

Mara blinks, lets the air clear. "Practice," she says, voice thin.

Ava stands up and paces, muttering numbers. "The energy readings are off the charts. I don't even know how to model this. You're creating a pressure gradient, but there's no temperature delta, no wind effect, nothing." She turns to Finn. "Do you realize what this means? If we can quantify the input—"

Finn interrupts, voice low. "It means she can move the ocean, if she wants."

Ava laughs, not mocking but incredulous. "No one can move the ocean." She turns to Mara. "Can you do it again?"

Mara is still catching her breath, but she nods, though shorter this time. "Not today," she says, and the admission burns, but she is empty.

Ava is smart enough to see it. She kneels, hand hovering inches from Mara's shoulder, as if afraid to touch. "You're tired."

Mara manages a smile, though it feels like lifting a stone with her teeth. "Little bit."

Ava stands and brushes sand off her knees. The skepticism is gone, replaced by something wild and hungry—a need to understand, to see the world with new rules. "You're incredible," she says, and there is no sarcasm this time.

Finn moves closer and offers Mara his hand. She takes it and lets him help her to an upright position. The touch is warm, electric.

Ava is already at the sensor bank, hands moving in a blur over the controls, pulling up the raw data. "I need to analyze this," she says, "but I can tell you right now, nothing on the planet does what you just did. No animal, no weather system, nothing."

Mara sits on the flat stone; tail curled around her. She glances at the horizon and sees a shape—a fishing boat, white hull slicing through the water, headed for the mouth of the cove. She tenses, instinct ready to drop below and vanish.

Finn sees it, too. "We need to move," he says, voice tight. "If they see you, we blow everything."

Ava snaps the tablet shut, grabs her clipboard, and the three of them retreat up the rock line, Mara using her arms to haul herself out of the surf, Finn and Ava moving in step. They duck behind a driftwood log, hidden from the open water.

The fishing boat passes, oblivious, its wake a minor aftershock compared to what Mara just unleashed.

When it's gone, Finn laughs, breathless. "We did it. We actually did it."

Ava is silent, staring at the data on her screen. After a moment, she turns to Mara and says, "Tomorrow, same time?"

Mara hesitates, then nods.

Ava smiles. Not wide, not warm, but real. “Good. We have work to do.”

They linger in the cold for a minute, Mara’s skin prickling with the leftover energy. She feels light, dizzy, unmoored. She watches Finn and Ava argue over the numbers, then realizes she’s smiling, too.

It is not a happy smile. It is the smile of someone who knows exactly how dangerous she’s just become.

The cove is different at midday. The light is higher, less forgiving, and every shadow is sharper, every sound closer to a threat. Mara has retreated to the stone shelf at the cove’s edge, the water just deep enough to keep her tail free. Her arms and gills ache with the aftershock of magic, and the old wound is a constant throb, but the exhaustion is almost pleasant—a proof of work, the ache that follows not a beating but a victory.

Finn Gallagher kneels beside her, his jacket gone now, sleeves rolled past the elbow. He’s spread out a fan of charts, some already wet and curling at the corners. A set of laminated printouts and sensor logs is weighted down with pebbles. He taps a line on one of the sheets, glancing at Mara for a sign she’s following.

“Here,” he says, “see this? This is you.”

Mara squints at the chart. It means less than nothing. The lines wiggle and cross, some in blue, some in red, and beside them a forest of numbers, dense as kelp. “Looks like a fish spine,” she says, tone half-tease.

Finn grins. "Yeah, a little. But watch: this section—" he traces it with a blunt finger, rough skin catching on the printout "—is baseline. Nothing. Normal coastal turbulence." He shifts down the page. "But this spike? That's your current calling. It's—" he hesitates, searching for the right word— "not normal. Not even close."

She watches the line. "It listens," she says, almost to herself. "Water doesn't move like that unless you ask."

Finn looks up, and for a second, there's something gentle in his eyes. "You talk to the ocean."

Mara snorts. "Ocean never talks back."

He slides a new printout under her hand, this one a series of images, each with a time-stamp. They're photographs, snapped in rapid sequence during the test. One shows the standing wave, crisp as a blade, the next the spiral, a blur of white spray. In each, Mara's silhouette is at the center, arms outstretched, face set in lines of pure focus.

"These," Finn says, "are going to change everything. If you're willing."

Mara traces one of the images, her webbed fingers smudging the ink. "Change for who?"

He hesitates, then says, "For everyone, maybe."

Mara tilts her head, and the old bitterness returns. "Or just for you."

Finn flinches. "Not just me," he says, quick and raw. "This is about the ocean. About saving it."

She studies his face. The words are valid, but there's another truth below, a desperation that has nothing to do with science. She lets it go for now.

Ava Chen appears at the top of the rock line, her lab coat replaced by a sun shirt and hiking pants, but the clipboard is still glued to her hand. Her face is flushed, not from the sun but from speed—she's been running calculations, even on the way back to the cove.

She plops down cross-legged on the rock, barely glancing at Mara. "You know you broke the sensors, right?"

Finn gives her a look. "You said they could handle a full typhoon."

Ava flips a page, jabs it with her pen. "This wasn't a typhoon. This was… I don't even know." She looks at Mara, finally, and the skepticism from before is gone, replaced by pure, ravenous curiosity. "Can you do other things? Not just move water, but—" She flips back through her notes, eyes darting. "Can you sense chemical composition? Pollution? Temperature gradients?"

Mara blinks. "Of course." It's like asking if a human can taste salt. "But it hurts sometimes. When the water is wrong."

Ava's lips part, the beginning of a question, but Finn jumps in. "We talked about this. Remember? Tide-Sensing?"

Ava looks to Finn, then to Mara, as if the world has split and both are equally real. "Show me," she says, then, softer, "please."

Mara sighs, flicks her tail to the side, and closes her eyes. The magic is slower this time, the current thin and laced with exhaustion, but she can still find the pulse. She reaches with her mind, lets the water seep in through every pore, every slit in her gills, until she can taste the cove's memory on her tongue.

"There's runoff," she says, eyes still closed. "From the last storm. It's old, but not gone. Tastes like metal. Iron, copper, something from the hills." She opens her eyes, meets Ava's. "But not too much. The water is healthy, but stressed. Like a fish in a net that's too small."

Ava is silent, scribbling, then looks to Finn for confirmation.

"She's right," Finn says, and his pride is naked. "There was a mudslide up the river last week. The runoff matched exactly what she described. And she did it without a sensor or a sample."

Ava's skepticism is gone. Now there's only hunger. "What about temperature? Can you sense gradients, like a thermocline?"

Mara shrugs. "Warm water floats. Cold water sinks. Even a human can feel that."

Ava bites her lip, then says, "But can you find it blind?"

Mara nods, then focuses. She lets the current wash her, finds the thin line in the water where the cold and warm fight for space. She points, eyes still closed. "There. Three arm-lengths down, it changes. Cold below, warm above."

Finn slips a sensor into the water, glances at the readout, then nods. "Exactly right."

Ava stares, and for the first time, she looks at Mara not as a threat or an oddity, but as a peer. "We could use that," she says. "For monitoring. For conservation." Her brain is already running a hundred simulations, and Mara can see it in her eyes.

They conduct more experiments—chemical traces, pH shifts, and even the way the ocean's sound changes with variations in density and pollution. Mara is a fast study, and Finn is patient, guiding her through the logic of the machines. She learns the names: spectrophotometer, D.O. probe, fluorometer. Each has a weakness, a blind spot, but Mara fills the gaps with intuition.

Finn leans over her shoulder, showing her the way the numbers stack, how a change in current can ripple for kilometers down the coast. Their faces are inches apart, voices low, and every time their hands brush, a shock runs up Mara's arm. She wonders if Finn feels it, too.

Ava is relentless, never satisfied, always pushing for the next test. But there's a respect now, a recognition that Mara's senses are not just a curiosity, but a tool.

The afternoon wears on. The cove is quieter, the human world on the beach now a distant murmur. Finn and Mara sit side by side, hunched over a spread of wet charts, their heads almost touching. Ava stands nearby, arms crossed, watching the horizon for threats.

Mara points at a data point on the graph. "This one is wrong," she says. "It doesn't match the others."

Finn studies it, then grins. "You're right. Sensor glitch. That's incredible—you caught it by eye."

Mara laughs, and the sound is not bitter this time.

Ava sets her clipboard down and crouches beside them. "What you can do… It's beyond anything I've seen." She meets Mara's gaze, and there is no fear, only respect. "You don't have to help us. But if you choose to, we can make things better. Maybe slow the end."

Mara considers. "You believe me now?"

Ava smiles, small and hard-won. "I'd be an idiot not to."

They share a look—one that says, we are in this together now, whether we like it or not.

A shadow moves on the far side of the cove. Mara tenses, but it's just a pair of gulls, squabbling over a chunk of crab. The world is safe, for the moment.

Finn gathers the papers, tucking them into a waterproof bag. "Same time tomorrow?" he asks, and it's clear he means more than just the experiment.

Mara nods. "Tomorrow. Bring more sensors."

Ava snorts, then says, "We'll need more batteries, too." She glances at Mara, then at Finn. "I'll run the analysis tonight. But I'm not telling anyone. Not yet."

Finn nods, serious. "It's not safe. Not for her. Not for us, either."

Mara is already backing into the water, the cold a balm against the heat in her face. She glances once at Finn, catches his eye, and there's a flicker of something between them—hope, maybe, or just the relief of not being alone.

She slides under, tail slicing the surface in a final, perfect arc. The water closes behind her, the cove sealing off the secret of what just happened.

Above, the humans gather their things, voices low and urgent. Mara hears them, even down here, their words muffled but clear: "Unbelievable," "Game-changer," "Careful, don't leave a trace."

She smiles in the dark. The tide is turning, and this time, she is the current.

6 Tides of Doubt

The town's docks at midnight are a different animal than the cheery cliché in a postcard—raw, reeking, alive with the slow, cancerous rot of diesel and salt. Even at this hour, men are still working: sullen shapes in waders and headlamps, stripping scales and loading ice chests under yellow sodium bulbs. Some have nowhere else to go. It's these that Finn Gallagher finds himself among now, breath fogging in the cold, arms braced against the dock rail as if he can physically hold back the ocean.

The fishermen circle him in a loose perimeter, each man a diagram of the same life: corded forearms, bellies gone soft around the edges, sun-stained faces with permanent goggle tans and eyes that squint at all the world's bullshit. But tonight, there's no boredom in the stares. Just a thick, fetid wariness that floats over the dock, heavier than the sea mist.

Nobody speaks at first. Finn recognizes three of the men from the wharf. The fourth—the one with a homemade tattoo of a squid wrapping his neck—he doesn't know, but the guy's hands are full of old breaks and new nervousness.

Squid Tattoo breaks the silence. "You've been out on the water late, doc," he says. "Heard you running that skiff up and down the cove last two nights. Way past fishing hours."

Finn shrugs. "Tide's better after dark."

A snort from the short one, the one who always smells like rotten clams. "Tide's better for what? Ain't no blues running, unless you know some secret nobody else does."

They close in, one step at a time, like wolves not quite sure if the deer is worth the trouble.

Finn tries to keep his voice casual. "Collecting samples," he says. "Coral, krill, salinity checks. You know, science."

"You've always been an odd one, Gallagher." It's the big guy, Don, who once threw Finn into a bait tank for talking about ecosystem collapse at the wrong bar. "But now you're just weird."

Finn tries to move, but the circle tightens. "Look, if this is about that pier incident—"

"It's about what's in the water," Squid Tattoo snaps. "We see things out there. Weird things. Stuff that doesn't belong."

Finn holds his ground. "Like what?"

There's a shuffle as they all look at each other, none willing to go first.

The clam-scented guy cracks. "Saw something last night. Something with a face. Staring up through the breakwater. Gave me the goddamn chills, man."

The others nod, more eager now.

"Had a tail," Don says. "Not a fish tail. A real one. Long as my arm."

"Copper-red hair," Squid Tattoo says. "Like a flare in the

water. Could see it even after dark. And those eyes—fuck, I never saw anything like it."

Finn feels his skin go tight. His heart rate ticks up, but he keeps his face blank. "Probably a seal," he says. "Light does weird things in the water."

Clam Guy shakes his head. Seals don't have scales. And they don't scream like that."

A shiver down Finn's spine. "Scream?"

He nods, voice hushed. "High-pitched, made the boat engine skip a beat. Set off every gull in the bay."

Finn is about to deflect again when Don gets in his face, whiskey breath and all. "Why are you out there, Gallagher? You hunting it? Or are you working with it?"

The air shifts. It's not a joke anymore.

Finn knows the script: small towns, old men, new fears. But this time, he's not sure who's hunting whom.

He looks Don in the eyes. "I'm trying to fix the water, not add to the ghost stories."

Don pokes him in the chest, hard enough to hurt. "Maybe you should stay off the water just until things calm down. Friendly advice."

Finn doesn't back up. "I appreciate it," he says, voice as flat as the dock.

They stand there, breathing in each other's anger, until finally the circle breaks and the men drift off, muttering.

Finn waits until they're gone, then sags against the rail. His hands are shaking, but not from fear.

In the dark beyond the floodlights, a shape peels itself off the shadow of the nearest warehouse. If the fishermen are wolves, this one is a shark—sleek, predatory, all dead eyes and momentum.

Captain Marcus Blackwell watches the exchange with a smile that means nothing good.

He's taller than Finn, but moves with the slow, deliberate confidence of someone who's never lost a fight. His jacket is military surplus, but expensive; the boots are new, the watch on his wrist glints in the sodium glow. His hair is silver at the temples and cropped to regulation length. The only sign of old age is the way he favors his left leg, just a fraction of a limp.

Blackwell carries a harpoon gun, not as a tool, but as an extension of his body. He rests it over his shoulder, finger tapping the trigger guard.

He stands beside Finn, staring at the water.

"Rough crowd," he says.

Finn snorts. "They're not subtle."

Blackwell grins. "Neither are you. Heard you riled up the old man council with your presentation last week."

Finn doesn't answer.

Blackwell lets the silence build. "People talk, Gallagher. They say you're chasing something out there. Something big."

Finn looks away. "Just research."

"Sure." Blackwell scans the bay, head cocked. "You know, I've seen things, too. Out past the buoy line. Used to think it was the cold, or maybe the whiskey. Now, I'm not so sure."

Finn tenses. "You see a lot, Captain?"

"Enough." Blackwell's voice drops, almost in an intimate tone. "Tell me, if you had the chance to catch it—bring back proof—would you?"

Finn hesitates, thinking of Mara, her eyes, the way the world feels different when she's near.

Blackwell leans in, his breath warm against Finn's ear. "Because I would. And I will. One way or another."

He pats Finn on the back, then drifts away into the dark, the harpoon gun gleaming.

Finn watches him go, a cold pit forming in his gut.

He looks down at the water, at the black mirror, and wonders if Mara is watching, too.

Above him, the gulls circle, hungry for anything new.

And in the shadows, Blackwell is already planning his next move.

In the seminar room, the air is thick with the scent of burnt coffee, dust, and the unspoken hunger of colleagues waiting to see someone fail. Finn stands at the front, hands white-knuckling the clicker, sweat ghosting the collar of his shirt. The projector hums behind him, painting the wall with his last six months of work—thermal maps, satellite overlays, spectral graphs that look like bad heartbeats. The title slide is a dare: "Anomalous

Hydrodynamics and the Case for an Unknown Predator."

He knows, even before he starts, that it's going to end in blood.

The department is all here, packed into the back rows: the professors with their plastic smiles, the grad students with their wide eyes, even the tenured fossils who show up only for free food and the chance to tear someone apart. A few faces are friendly, most are not.

Finn clears his throat. "As you can see from the readings—" he gestures to a slide, the laser pointer shaking more than he'd like—"there's a persistent disturbance in the tidal patterns along the shelf. Too regular for a ship. Too erratic for a whale. I've matched the timing to the reported local incidents."

A murmur ripples through the crowd.

He pushes ahead, voice getting stronger. "Traditional models can't explain it. I've tried simulations for rogue current, mass fish movement, and even illicit dumping. Nothing fits. The pattern is—"

A hand goes up. Dr. Metzger, who hasn't had a new idea since the Clinton era. "Are you proposing a Loch Ness monster, Gallagher?"

Laughter. Not friendly.

Finn bares his teeth. "I'm proposing that there's something we don't understand in the water. The data support it. I have sample runs, video, even tissue traces from the last net entanglement."

Another voice: "Maybe it's just a new kind of shark. The fishermen said they saw teeth, right?"

More laughter. Finn's pulse rises, but he doesn't back down.

"Nothing with teeth like that moves this way," he says. "And—" he clicks to the next slide, a freeze frame of the night-vision GoPro from the last survey run. In the center of the image is a streak of iridescent green and a flash of copper, blurred but unmistakably out of place. "The fishermen saw a tail. They said it looked like a woman's. I'm not saying—"

He doesn't get to finish. The back row explodes; someone makes a dramatic mermaid-swimming gesture, and the room goes into a feeding frenzy.

Finn tries to push through the noise. "There's more. If you look at the chemistry—"

But Dr. Hargrove, the department chair, cuts in from the front row. "I think that's enough fantasy for today, Dr. Gallagher. Let's save time for real research presentations."

The laughter drops instantly, replaced by the brittle silence of authority.

Hargrove stands. He's an ex-Navy man who never let the uniform go—every gesture is an order, every smile a warning. He doesn't even look at Finn as he gathers his briefcase.

"Some of us have grants to write," Hargrove says, and the room empties on cue.

Finn is left at the podium, slides flickering on the wall, heartbeat in his throat.

He wants to throw something, break the window, and shout at the retreating backs. Instead, he waits until the last of the students filters out, then kills the projector, packs his laptop, and walks the longest possible route to his office, just to burn off the adrenaline.

Hargrove is waiting at the door, already installed behind Finn's

own desk, hands folded.
"Sit," he says.

Finn stays standing.

Hargrove looks up, eyes hard as cold steel. "You know why I'm here?"

Finn says nothing.

Hargrove sighs, as if this is all beneath him. "You were a good hire, Gallagher. Young, aggressive, right resume. But this—" he gestures at the pile of printouts Finn left on his desk, now crumpled and marked with red pen—"is not science. It's tabloid shit. And it's making us look bad."

"It's the data," Finn says. "I'm following it where it leads."

Hargrove's smile is as thin as a knife edge. "Do you know how many emails I get a week from donors and board members asking if you're really chasing mermaids? Do you know how many reporters want to run a story on our 'resident cryptid nut'?"

Finn grinds his teeth. "I'm onto something. You said you wanted innovation. This is it."

"I want funding," Hargrove says. "I want stability. I want not to have to answer questions about why my junior faculty is quoting old sailors and running around the bay at three in the morning."

Finn leans forward, hands on the desk. "If you would just look at the numbers—"

Hargrove slides a folder across the desk. "This is your warning, Gallagher. One more word about mermaids, and this becomes official. Grant support? Gone. Lab space? Gone. Maybe even your job."

Finn opens the folder. Inside is a formal notice of disciplinary action, already signed.

Hargrove stands and straightens his jacket. "You're too smart to throw it all away on a fairy tale. Stick to the grant. Write the paper on the jellyfish bloom. Let this go."

He pauses at the door, face softening for a second. "You're a good scientist, Finn. Don't be an idiot."

Then he's gone, leaving Finn alone in the office, fluorescent lights buzzing above.

Finn sits, stares at the notice, then at the wall behind the desk. There's a framed diploma with his name in gold.

He wants to smash it.

Instead, he grabs the stack of printouts, the video freeze-frames, and the tide charts. He stuffs them in his bag, slings it over his shoulder, and leaves.

The door slams so hard it rattles the diploma off its hook.

Down the hall, the laughter has already started up again.

Night in the tide pool is blacker than black—ocean above, rock on all sides, the world shrunk to a glass coffin. Mara floats just below the surface, her copper hair fanned out in a spiral, blooming red where the moon cuts through. She hovers, not swimming, not breathing, just holding herself in place and letting the current do what it wants with her.

She's been here since dusk. There's no time in the pool, only the slow retreat of the tide, the world growing smaller with every minute.

Her hands are raw, fingertips tracing the knife-edged edge of dead coral. Each ridge is a memory: the first net she ever cut, the first blood she ever drew. The old pain helps. It's the new kind she can't handle.

Above her, the sky flickers with a distant storm. Lightning for a moment, then gone. She lets herself drift closer to the rock wall, feeling the cold bite through scale and skin, the water too shallow now for any real escape.

She's tried to forget what happened on the beach, the shouting, the way the fishermen looked at her. But the faces stick, printed on the backs of her eyelids. The man with the cigarette, the one with the tattoo, all of them staring like they'd seen a ghost and wanted to make sure it stayed that way. And Finn, her only anchor to this world, was caught between loyalty and terror.

She saw him from the water—saw how he didn't run when they circled, how he tried to play human while being nothing of the sort. It made her want to laugh and cry at the same time.

She shudders, gills fluttering, breath coming too fast.

The memory of the other man—Blackwell, Finn called him—haunts her most. He was on the dock, just out of the light, watching everything. He didn't laugh or shout, just smiled, small and precise, like a shark sighting blood in the blue.

Her whole-body recoils at the memory. She pushes herself down, sinking to the bottom of the pool. The sand here is littered with fragments of shells, bits of plastic, and other debris that the tide brings and leaves behind. She blends in, folds herself tight, pretends for a moment she's already part of the wreckage.

A school of glass minnows drifts past. For a second, she thinks they'll comfort her, but they sense the wrongness and scatter, silver streaks flashing away from her shadow.

She watches them go, heart stuttering.

She reaches out, touching a piece of coral that has been bleached so many times it's pure white. Once, her city looked like that—alive, singing with current and color. Now, it's just memory, fading every day.

She lets the ache roll through her; a wave she has no energy to fight. The surface is closed to her, the deep is poison, and in between there is only this: a pool, a box, a cage.

Mara presses her forehead against the wall, lets her scales go dull, and her hair go limp. For a moment, she thinks about slipping under and never coming back up. It would be easy, just a small surrender, a letting go.

The thought is a comfort and a terror.

She holds it tight, then lets it drift, like so much detritus.

Above, the storm comes closer—the air hums with electricity. Mara floats up, just enough to break the surface, and lets the rain strike her face.

She wonders if Finn feels the storm, too.

She wonders if it even matters.

Finn is halfway through a cold microwave burrito and a half-dozen tabs of spreadsheet hell when the world explodes.

The front door slams against the wall hard enough to send a cheap print of the Monterey Bay Aquarium tumbling to the floor. Mara stumbles inside, hair a sodden flame, water streaming down her arms and pooling in a tight, angry circle at her bare feet. She's wearing a stolen rain jacket over what looks like gym shorts, but even with legs, she moves like a force of nature—ungainly and predatory at once.

Finn yelps, almost bites his own tongue off. "Christ, you scared me—"

She shuts the door with a slam. "They know."

He's up and moving, shoving aside the pile of reports on the battered kitchen table. "Who knows? Slow down—are you hurt?"

Mara ignores the question and paces the tiny room like a caged shark. "The men at the docks. They watched you. Watched us. They're talking."

Finn's brain scrambles for the script—comfort, reassurance, procedure. "Nobody would believe them," he says. "You're just a rumor. People see what they want."

"Not this one." Mara's eyes are wild, pupils dilated, gills along her neck fluttering in panic. "He was watching. Different than the others. He hunts."

Finn's heart rate spikes. He thinks of Blackwell's smile, the threat in every word. "Blackwell?"

She nods, hair flinging droplets everywhere. "He follows. He asks questions. He smells like death."

Finn tries to soothe, but Mara grabs his arm, nails biting deep. "Listen. They will come. They always do."

He flinches, then pulls her hand off, not roughly, just enough to break the grip. "You can't be here," he hisses, shoving her towards the windowless bathroom. "If anyone sees—"

"They already have!" She leans against the kitchen counter, breath coming in short bursts, water running down her calves, soaking the bathmat. "It's done. My people—they were right about you."

The accusation cuts deeper than he expects. "That's not fair. I've put everything on the line for this. For you."

She sneers. "For data. For your name on the grant. Isn't that what matters to you?"

He feels the heat rise in his face. "If you'd seen what they did to me today, you wouldn't say that. They laughed me out of my own department. The only reason I'm not unemployed is that I—" he hesitates, then lies—"that I shut up about you."

She snorts, no humor in it. "So, you hide, same as us. Maybe we are not so different."

He wants to rage, but instead, he slumps into the only chair in the room. "If you want to give up, just say it."

She stands over him, water dripping on his leg. "You still don't understand. If I am caught, I die. If I am seen, my people die. You—" She gestures at the chaos of his desk, at the spiral-bound notebooks and empty Red Bulls. "You get a new job. You forget."

He meets her eyes. "That's not true."

She flinches, then, and for the first time, he sees the crack in her armor—the edge of an absolute, deep terror.

Finn stands, puts a hand on her shoulder, gently this time.

"We can fix this," he says. "We just need time. I have friends. We can lay low, work the data, build up proof that won't get anyone hurt."

She shrugs off his hand, but more softly now. "Data is useless. They only believe what they see. And once they see, they will never let go."

He sighs, rakes a hand through his hair. "Then we don't let them see."

She laughs—bitter, exhausted, wet. "You forget what you are up against."

"No," he says. "I just believe we can win."

For a second, she looks at him like she believes it, too. Then her gaze drops, and she hugs her arms around herself, legs trembling with the effort of standing.

Finn realizes she's never done this before—been on land, walked, balanced on two feet. He grabs a towel from the laundry pile and drapes it around her shoulders. She buries her face in it, and he pretends not to see the way her jaw clenches, the way she refuses to cry.

He opens the fridge, scans for anything resembling food, and finds a single yogurt cup. He offers it to her, wordless.

She takes it, sniffs, makes a face, but eats it anyway.

"Why do you do this?" she says, not looking up.

He shrugs. "Because you're real. Because I want to help."

She shakes her head. "No. Why do you care?"

Finn leans against the counter, watching the rain streak the window. "Because if we don't change something, everything ends."

She lets the words hang. The storm outside grows louder, thunder rolling in from the bay.

Finally, she looks at him. "Trust is for fools."

He manages a smile. "Then let's be fools together."

They stand in silence, storm and all.

Neither moves, but something shifts in the air—less fear, more a grim understanding.

For now, it's enough.

The first warning is the shatter—high, sharp, and final.

Finn and Mara both duck instinctively as the window above the sink blows inward, glass skittering across the tile like hailstones. Something metallic and round clatters onto the linoleum, bounces twice, and then begins to spit out thick, white smoke that smells of burning sugar and copper.

"Move!" Finn grabs Mara's wrist and yanks her away from the spreading fog. She's faster than he expects—already halfway to the back door before he's got his feet under him. The kitchen fills with smoke in seconds, acrid and blinding.

He fumbles for the door handle. Mara pressed against his back, her breath hot on his neck.

He gets the door open just as the first man crashes through

the hallway—black fatigues, full-face respirator, gun up and ready. Finn slams the door into the man's shoulder, sending him sprawling. The gun discharges with a hiss, and a silver dart embeds itself in the ceiling.

"Target acquired," the man barks, voice muffled by the mask.

A second man appears behind him, aiming a matching weapon at Mara.

She doesn't freeze—she ducks low, slides past Finn's knee, and takes the legs out from under the shooter. The man goes down hard, weapon clattering out of reach.

Finn doesn't think, acts—he grabs the gun and swings it at the first intruder's head. The plastic butt connects with a dull thunk, and the man's helmeted head snaps back.

Mara scrambles to her feet, but there's nowhere to run. The kitchen is boxed in, smoke rising fast, the only exit back through the kill box of the hallway.

And then, as if conjured by their fear, Blackwell steps into the frame.

He's unmasked, face perfectly calm, pistol raised. "Well, well," he says, eyes locked on Mara. "The rumors didn't do you justice."

Mara bares her teeth, a snarl that doesn't sound remotely human.

Finn puts himself between her and Blackwell, but the captain only laughs.

"Step aside, Gallagher. This is business."

"Go to hell," Finn says, aiming the tranq gun with shaky hands.

Blackwell doesn't even blink. "You wouldn't shoot me. You're not built for it." He cocks his own gun, a real one, and points it directly at Finn's chest.

Mara makes a sudden move, and Blackwell swings the pistol at her. "Easy," he says, voice steady, almost bored. "I'd prefer the specimen undamaged, but I'll settle for dead if necessary."

The words are cold, practiced, and absolute.

Behind him, the two men in black regroup, training their weapons on Finn and Mara both.

Finn calculates quickly: two darts, one bullet, no cover, one way out.

He lunges.

It's not a plan, just raw impulse—he barrels into Blackwell, driving the tranq gun up under the captain's jaw. He squeezes the trigger, feels the soft recoil as the dart punctures skin.

Blackwell staggers, but doesn't go down. Instead, he brings the pistol up and jams it into Finn's ribs.

Finn freezes. For a second, time is syrup.

"You're outclassed, son," Blackwell whispers. "Let go."

Finn's arms shake, but he doesn't drop the gun.

From behind, Mara moves—she leaps, a blur, all muscle and velocity. She hits the nearest intruder in the back, sending him face-first into the countertop. The second one fires, but the dart goes wide, thudding into the fridge.

Blackwell squeezes the trigger.

Pain, hot and immediate, blooms in Finn's side. He gasps, staggers back, dropping the tranq gun.

Mara shrieks, a sound so alien and sharp it cuts through the smoke. She grabs Finn, pulls him out of Blackwell's grasp, and hurls herself through the open back door.

They tumble onto the deck, Finn's blood leaving a hot streak on the wood. Mara drags him to the stairs, down toward the dunes.

The smoke and pain blur everything, but Finn hears Blackwell's voice behind them, cold and precise: "Bring them back. Alive if possible."

They stagger into the rain, down the narrow path toward the beach: Finn's head swims, his vision tunneling.

Mara half-carries, half-drags him to the tide line, where the world is nothing but storm and surf. She drops him in the wet sand; hands pressed to his wound.

He tries to speak, but she shakes her head. "Not yet."

The water is up to their ankles, then knees, then waists. Blackwell's men follow, flashlights and weapons slicing the night.

Mara looks at Finn. Her eyes are all desperation and fury. "Hold your breath."

Before he can protest, she pulls him under.

The shock is instant, electric, but then she's beside him, arms around his chest, legs kicking strong and steady. They cut through the surf, away from the shore, the sounds of pursuit fading behind them.

Finn is bleeding, the cold stinging every nerve, but Mara's grip is relentless.

He blacks out before he ever sees the open ocean.

He comes back to himself, coughing up salt and blood.

The world is dark, roaring, full of water. Mara is there, pulling him up by the collar, her face inches from his. Her hair floats around them in a nimbus, fire red even in the moonlit green of the shallows. Finn chokes, coughs again, and claws at the sand until he feels land beneath him.

On the beach above, lights slash the rain—flashlights, headlights, shouts echoing down the dunes. Blackwell's men are coming. Some of them are already at the waterline, guns ready, voices barking commands.

Mara checks Finn's side, finds the bullet wound, and presses her hand tightly over it. The pain is distant, a shockwave, but Finn is too busy watching her face. Her eyes are no longer afraid. They're something else entirely—ancient, endless, mad with purpose.

"Mara—" he croaks, but she shakes her head.

"Breathe," she says, and stands, drawing him up with her.

They stagger up the sand, Mara half-carrying, half-dragging him. The men close in, fanned out, black shapes against the white chaos of the surf.

One of them fires, a dart this time—tranq or poison, Finn doesn't know—but Mara flings her arm, and the dart veers away, slapping harmlessly into the sand.

Finn's head spins. "What are you—?"

But Mara's not listening. She faces the men, plants her feet in the wet, and screams.

It's not human. It's not even an animal. The sound is pure force, a frequency that shakes the air, the sand, the bones inside Finn's head. He clamps his hands over his ears, but the scream gets through, vibrating his teeth.

The men drop to their knees, weapons falling. Blackwell himself is at the front, lips curled in a snarl, eyes wild.

Then Mara falls silent, lips parted, breath ragged.

The ocean answers.

Finn hears it before he sees it—a rumble in the undertow, a hiss of wind, then a wall of water rising from the deep. The wave builds in the dark, gathers mass, and looms taller than the men on the shore. Blackwell sees it, too, and for the first time, his mask slips.

He screams at his men to run.

The wave hits.

It crashes over the sand with the sound of a thousand engines. It lifts the men, the guns, the trucks, and hurls them back toward the dunes. Blackwell stands his ground until the last second, then dives, disappears into the foam.

Finn and Mara are already running up the beach, away from the wreckage. Finn can barely keep upright, vision tunneling, world reduced to Mara's grip on his arm.

They reach the lot where Finn's battered truck sits. Mara wrenches open the passenger door and shoves Finn inside. He slumps against the seat, barely conscious, watching through the windshield as water pours off the roof of the world.

Mara climbs in beside him. Her skin is gray, her eyes sunken, every muscle twitching with aftershock.

"Can you drive?" she asks, voice barely above a whisper.

He nods, fumbles for the keys in his jeans, and starts the engine. The truck lurches into gear, tires spinning on mud and grit.

They careen down the access road, headlights cutting through the storm. Behind them, the wave recedes, leaving Blackwell's men scattered and soaked, their vehicles stranded in the sand.

Blackwell himself stands in the wash, dripping, fists clenched, eyes fixed on the retreating truck. He looks more alive now than he did in the kitchen—hungry, pissed, hunting.

Finn watches him in the rearview until the taillights fade.

He drives blind, one hand pressed to his side, the other gripping the wheel so tight it aches. Mara sits beside him, head back, eyes closed, face calm for the first time since he met her.

They reach the edge of town, then the highway. Finn floors it, no plan, just movement.

"Where to?" he asks.

Mara doesn't answer for a long time.

Then, quietly: "Anywhere. Just not here."

He nods, pushes the truck faster, and watches the mile

markers flick past. Rain drums on the roof; the world is still chaos, but for the first time, Finn feels hope. Fragile, stupid, real.

He glances at Mara, her fingers tangled in the frayed towel, her body humming with silent power.

He thinks of all the things he still doesn't know—about her, about the ocean, about himself.

But for now, the only thing that matters is the road, the storm, and the fact that they are both still alive.

He drives.

Behind them, the tide begins to rise again.

7 Allies from the Abyss

Mara slips into the city at low tide, riding the fractured current beneath the limestone cliffs. She keeps to the shadow of the overhang, fingers dragging along the pitted stone. Above, the surface is a bruised mirror, more threat than refuge. Below, the world glows with its own fever—sick but beautiful, pulsing with the last traces of wildness.

The main gate is a theater, all show: rows of sentry trout in military stripes, scales polished to blue-black sheen, jaws fixed in perpetual snarl. Mara has no interest in playing villain for them tonight. She veers left, down a crevice half-filled with moss and grit, through a bone-thin tunnel lined with barbed polyps that sting her wrists as she passes. The pain is a comfort—a reminder that she is not home, not ever, but at least she is not dead.

She follows the old contraband route, the one used by exiles and the barely tolerated, past the carcass of a scavenger crab and into the outer reef. Here, the water temperature shifts, and the chemistry changes. Mara's gills flare, tasting the surge: more brine than blood, but she can still pick out the faintest trace of diesel from the inlet above. The pollution is everywhere, but she's adapted.

She passes beneath a drift of jelly, their bells lit with stolen color, and darts around a curtain of silt. The city proper blooms beyond—a spiral of phosphorescent coral, rising in lazy whorls from the shelf floor to the dome above. It looks fragile, like a cloud made solid, but every inch is reinforced by centuries of magic, tradition, and paranoia.

Mara ghosts past the first tier. No one challenges her. The city is tired, slumped inward, with most of its denizens curled into private caves or huddled in the feeding grounds, trading gossip and scraps. The further she moves from the city center, the less alive everything seems. The outlying towers are near-deserted, their windows pulsing with faint blue light, but there are no voices, no movement.

The training grotto is on the edge of the blue zone, tucked into a dead-end alley where the old coral meets the new. Mara hesitates just before the entrance, flattening herself against the wall and letting her senses sweep the cave. Inside: five Merfolk, all young, barely past molt. Their heartbeats are loud, their nerves a thunderclap. Mara recognizes one—Coral, her first friend, her last mistake before everything turned sour. The others are strangers, but all are marked by the city's slow starvation: lean bodies, thin arms, eyes that can't quite decide if they're hungry or just angry.

Mara steps into the mouth of the grotto, and all five heads snap up. The oldest, Coral, has her hair coiled in a practical knot and her scales buffed to a dull gray, the color of surrender. She bares her teeth in something not quite a smile.

"You're late," Coral says.

Mara shrugs. "Had to take the scenic route."

The others edge back as Mara slides in, settling herself on a ledge that overlooks the training pool. The water here is shallow, almost still, the surface tension strong enough to hold dust.

Mara's reflection is a warning: hair wild, eyes dark, tail still raw from the last council session. She looks exactly like what she is—a risk.

Coral gestures for the others to gather in. They arrange themselves in a semicircle, carefully keeping Mara at the center.

Mara addresses them all, voice pitched low. "You know why you're here?"

A thin boy—barely adolescent, with a jagged notch in one fin—mutters, "To learn to die, apparently." His tone is bitter, but it's a brittle defense.

Mara smirks. "Not today."

Coral cuts in, firm: "The city is dying. The elders will never admit it, but everyone knows." She looks at Mara, and for a second, the old loyalty flashes behind her eyes. "We want to hear your plan. All of it."

Mara doesn't waste breath. She unfolds the proposal she's been carrying in her head since the first time she met Finn: a plan to use the surface, to trade information, to weaponize the things the city has always feared. She tells them about the pollution, the poachers, the humans' own power, and their hunger for control. She talks about Finn—not by name, but by function, as if he's a tool that could save them, if only they dare to wield it.

The others are silent. Only the ripple of their tails betrays anything. Mara watches their faces as she speaks, gauging the progress of doubt, fear, and hope. She is practiced at this—the calculus of revolution, the slow accretion of belief.

When she finishes, Coral is the first to move. She leans in so close that her nose almost touches Mara's.

"The elders will kill you if they catch you," Coral says.

Mara matches her gaze. "Only if you let them."

Coral grins, this time for real, and grabs Mara's forearm in a warrior's clasp. "Suits me. When do we start?"

One of the other trainees, a girl with a white streak in her hair and a nervous tic in her left hand, asks, "What about the city? They'll never follow."

Mara considers. "They don't need to. Not at first." She glances at the others. "It starts with us. With proof. We show them that a new way is possible. The rest will come after."

There's a brief, electric pause.

Then, from the mouth of the grotto, another voice cuts through: "Or you'll just get everyone killed faster."

All heads whip toward the entrance. Lyla stands in the shadows, arms folded, jaw set hard. Her platinum hair is slicked back in rows of tight braids, every strand barbed with tiny shell shards. She appears to have been waiting for hours.

Coral's hand drops from Mara's arm, and the whole group shrinks back instinctively. Lyla's reputation is legendary.

Mara doesn't flinch. "Come to help, or just to watch me fail?" she asks.

Lyla stalks forward, each step measured and deliberate. "You're risking everything on human promises. You're trusting the enemy."

Mara's tail flicks, splattering the surface. "And you're risking everything on doing nothing."

The two sisters face off in the blue-lit gloom, silence expanding between them like a wound.

Coral shifts, uncomfortable, then says, "Someone has to try. The old ways are killing us. If we don't adapt—"

"If we don't adapt, we die," Lyla finishes, her voice flat. She doesn't look at Coral; her focus is locked on Mara. "But you want to change everything, right now. That's not adaptation, that's suicide."

Mara shrugs, forcing nonchalance she does not feel. "If we're already dead, might as well do something interesting on the way out."

The room is on a knife-edge. Mara senses the others looking to Lyla, waiting for a decree, a sign.

Lyla closes her eyes, just for a heartbeat, then lets out a breath. "Fine. But if we're going to do this, you'll need more than talk." She opens her eyes. "You'll need training."

Mara blinks, uncertain.

Lyla steps into the circle, addresses the trainees in a tone that brooks no argument. "You'll learn the old magics, the ones we don't teach anymore. You'll learn to move the currents without being seen. You'll learn to fight dirty."

The trainees look at each other, suddenly a little more alive, a little less afraid.

Lyla glances at Mara, and for the first time since the city fell, Mara sees something like hope in her sister's face.

"Tomorrow," Lyla says. "We start at dawn."

Mara nods. She can't help the smile that cracks her lips.

In the center of the grotto, the water is still, but underneath, the current is already shifting.

The training arena is a dent in the shelf; a perfect circle scored into the seabed by some ancient violence. Around the rim, twelve stone pillars tilt inward, each one carved with spiral motifs that catch the light and throw it back in dizzying shards. At dawn, the place looks abandoned. By midmorning, it hums with purpose.

Lyla is already at the center, waiting. The water is obvious today, a small gift from the night's upwelling, but the stench of rot lingers beneath—a reminder of everything they fight against.

The five trainees, led by Coral, hang back at the edge. Each looks smaller in daylight, less sure, their rebellion already folding in on itself. Mara waits with them, flexing her hands, trying to shake the cold out of her bones.

Lyla raises one hand. The gesture is minimal, almost lazy, but a green current spools instantly around her wrist, dense as rope. It tightens, then releases, sending a pulse through the water that hums in Mara's skull.

"First lesson," Lyla says, voice crisp. "No one cares about your pride. Not in here."

The trainees shuffle forward, reluctant. Coral masks her nerves with a wry smile; the boy with the notched fin flexes, trying to look tough. The white-streaked girl clings to the back, eyes darting between Mara and Lyla.

Lyla turns to the group. "Current-Calling is not just a strength," she says, "it's precision. You move the sea, or the sea moves you." She circles the arena, slow predator's grace. "Pollution weakens us. Adapting is the only option."

She points at Coral. "You. Show me."

Coral hesitates, then sweeps her hands in a practiced arc. A thin ribbon of water peels from the arena floor, spinning up like a dancer's veil. It holds for two seconds, then shreds into pieces, dissipating into a cloud of silt.

Lyla snorts. "Try again."

Coral does. It's better, but still weak. The next trainee—Notch, the boy—overcompensates, and the current he conjures rams straight into a pillar, scattering fragments of barnacle.

"Worse," Lyla says, unimpressed.

The third tries, then the fourth. Each result is more mess than magic, the energy barely holding before it breaks.

Lyla beckons to Mara. "Your turn."

Mara forces her hands to be steady. She channels the current up from the floor, feeling it twist through her fingers, gathering just under the surface. For a moment, it sings—a clean, sharp line. She pushes, tries to shape it into a circle, but halfway through the maneuver, pain lances up her arm: her concentration slips, and the current collapses. Water snaps back, exposing the pale scar where the net sliced deep.

Lyla's eyes catch it. "You're favoring your left," she says. "Is it pain, or fear?"

Mara wants to snap back, but Coral's eyes are on her, hopeful. She shrugs. "Both."

Lyla doesn't smile. "Then fix it. Or you'll die before you make a difference."

She sweeps the group together with a cutting gesture. "Again. All of you. Together this time. Channel into the pillar, not each other."

The trainees hesitate, not sure how to coordinate. Mara remembers the old games—seaweave and tag, where it was less about force and more about anticipation, matching tempo. She glances at Coral, who nods once. On instinct, Mara lets Coral take the lead, and they synchronize their movements.

The others follow, awkward at first. The currents tangle, eddies pulling in all directions. For a second, it looks like it will fail again, but Coral plants herself and calls out, "Feel the pulse—don't fight it."

They listen. Mara slows her breathing, lets the tide carry her arms. The following current builds smoother, each trainee feeding into the spiral rather than tearing it apart. The energy thickens, brighter, denser. Lyla nods, barely perceptible, but it's there.

"Now," Lyla says, "combine."

Mara and Coral focus, funneling the spiral around the nearest pillar. It wraps clean, climbing up the groove in the stone and holding, a liquid helix glowing with faint blue. For a moment, even the dead coral at the pillar's base trembles as the ancient architecture awakens.

The trainees look at each other, shock and pride bleeding together. Even Notch grins, teeth flashing.

Lyla's approval is as minimal as her disdain: a single, sharp nod.

"You're not useless," she says. "But you're not ready either. Tomorrow, we do it again."

Coral whoops, a sound Mara hasn't heard since they were kids.

Mara massages her arm, wincing, but the pain is different now:

less wound, more promise. For the first time, she can almost see a way forward.

Above the arena, the current shifts slowly and steadily. The city is still dying, but today, the water obeys them.

After the third drill, Lyla dismisses the group with a flick of her wrist and a terse, "Outside. Sea-Speaking this time." Mara takes the cue, leading the trainees out of the arena and through the city's outer wall.

The passage is narrow, chiseled ages ago when the reef was alive, and the city needed less defense. Now, it's all caution and compromise. The wall itself is limestone, streaked with old growth and new scars from collapse. On the far side, the open ocean yawns—darker, deeper, full of risks. But there's more life here, too, for anyone brave enough to look.

They emerge onto a ledge overlooking the slope of the old reef. Schools of damselfish twist in the eddies, picking at whatever food the last tide left. In the distance, a pod of manta rays hovers near the surface, their wings catching the morning light and flicking it down into the gloom. Mara sees them and feels a jolt of longing—a memory from childhood, when the world was still wild.

"Watch," Mara says, and lifts her hands. She spreads her fingers wide, channeling the ocean's pulse into the tips of her fingers. The jade glow is faint in daylight, but it travels. The nearest manta flinches, then tilts its great head and glides closer, curiosity blooming in its alien eyes.

The trainees follow her lead, each reaching out in their own style. Notch is reckless, flaring energy too fast; the white-streaked girl is tentative, barely disturbing the water. Coral, by contrast, is all patience—her arms move with the slow surety of the tide, never forcing, only inviting.

Within minutes, the manta pod closes in on them. Six enormous rays sweep around the group, their bodies moving as if on invisible rails. The air is electric, every trainee hyper-aware of the power just overhead.

Lyla appears beside Mara, arms folded, watching. "Don't let them box you in," she says. "They're gentle until they aren't."

Mara nods, but keeps her focus. She opens her mind to the Sea-Speaking, not as a command, but as a request: "Help us. Watch for us." The thought radiates outward, braided with images of the city, the trainees, and the dangers beyond.

One manta circles lower, wings nearly touching Mara's hair. She feels its interest, its wariness, and a hungry edge that's all instinct. Still, it does not attack. Instead, it settles above the ledge, blocking the sun for a heartbeat.

The next trainee tries, but fumbles the frequency. Instead of a manta, an octopus uncoils from a nearby crevice, eyes bulging with irritation. It launches a jet of ink at the group, clouding the water, then squeezes itself into a hairline crack in the limestone.

Notch laughs, shaking off the embarrassment. "Guess I need more practice."

Coral doesn't laugh. She kneels on the ledge, lowers her face until she's eye-to-eye with the fish. She hums, soft and low, letting the song ripple through her hands. A small reef shark drifts in, drawn by the sound. It noses at Coral's palm, cautious but curious, then curls around her tail in a lazy spiral.

Mara crouches beside her, voice low. "They can be our eyes

beyond the city," she says. "First warning, if anything comes."

Coral nods, never looking away from the shark. "Or protection. If we feed them right, they might even fight for us."

Lyla hovers behind, silent until now. "They'll fight for food," she says. "But never for love."

Mara turns. "They don't have to love us. Just warn us."

Lyla considers, then inclines her head. "And perhaps, when the time comes, die for us."

The group looks at her, surprised. Lyla is not one for optimism—or for making plans that risk anything but herself.

Mara catches Lyla's eye, and for once, finds no anger there.

The manta pod disperses, sweeping away in a slow, deliberate spiral. But one remains, gliding above the group like a sentinel.

Mara feels the connection, the understanding. The city is dying, but the wild is still out here, waiting to be called.

She shares a look with Coral, then with Lyla, and knows the message is clear: They are not alone.

The air in the boathouse lab is a cocktail of bleach, cheap coffee, and salt-wet neoprene. Finn Gallagher paces the far side of the folding table, his boots squeaking on the warped linoleum, while Dr. Ava Chen loads the last of the video files onto her battered laptop. Around them, the new resistance—three environmental activists and two biologists from the university, one of whom still has a DUI ankle bracelet blinking beneath her jeans—try to look like this is just another night, not the start of a slow-motion mutiny.

Finn checks his watch. He wants to vomit, or run, or both, but instead he taps a cracked glass beaker with a pencil until everyone shuts up.

"I'll keep this short," he says, voice hollow. "What we're about to show you is, um, not normal. It's not even technically illegal unless we get caught. But it will change how you think about the bay. About everything."

Ava Chen glances at him over the rims of her glasses, a look that says: Don't oversell. Finn ignores her.

He plugs the HDMI into a battered projector. The screen is a wrinkled bedsheet, duct-taped to the drywall. The first slide is all numbers—hydrocarbon counts, dissolved oxygen, the kind of stats that get grants but never riots. The biologists nod, eyes flitting from the screen to their battered notepads. The activists yawn.

"Now," Finn says, voice tight, "watch this."

Ava cues the video. It's night-vision footage from the previous week: the breakwater, the darting shadows, and—at the four-minute mark—a glimmering, unmistakable shape arcing through the water. The face is pixelated, the body a blur, but the outline is unmistakable. The crowd goes silent.

Finn pauses. "This is not a seal."

One of the activists, a red-haired woman with calloused knuckles, squints at the screen. "Photoshop?"

Ava pipes up, deadpan. "This is from the city's own marine cam. I pulled the raw data. Timestamp is real."

The next slide is a chemical readout. Then sonar, then more video. Each new frame brings the same shape, the same impossible flash of color—sometimes red, sometimes a pale shimmer, always just at the edge of believability.

Finn's pulse hammers. He skips to the last slide: a short, silent loop of Mara Ondine calling up a microcurrent, lifting the tide just enough to snuff a net full of poachers' gear. The force, the precision—no marine mammal can do that. No human, either.

Someone drops a pen.

Finn clicks off the projector. The only sound is the whir of the minifridge.

Ava steps in, crisp and professional. "What you just saw does not leave this room. We've already secured offsite backups, and these—" She pulls a Ziploc bag from the table, filled with labeled thumb drives, each encased in waterproof resin—"are for when things go sideways. Each drive has a coded identifier. If you get picked up, burn your copy. If you need to contact us, please use a secure drop-off location. No email. No calls. Nothing digital after tonight."

The ankle-bracelet biologist raises a hand, voice trembling. "Is it… dangerous? Is it violent?"

Finn shakes his head. "No. Not unless you threaten it. Or us." He lets that sink in. "Right now, it just wants to survive. Same as us."

The red-haired activist grins, teeth white and sharp. "We could use this. For the protest."

Ava nods. "That's the plan. But you need to be smart. If anyone on the other side gets this data, it's not just you in danger. It's everything in the water."

There's a pause, then the room ignites with whispers and

strategy. The activists pull out their battered phones, but Finn glares, and they tuck them away. The biologists review the files again, faces flickering with awe and fear.

Ava steps back, crossing her arms, gaze fixed on Finn. "You did well," she says, voice low.

Finn almost laughs. "We're just getting started."

They watch as the new plan takes shape and gains momentum. The memory sticks vanish into pockets, the team breaks into subgroups, rehearsing their stories and their lies. In less than an hour, the seeds are planted. Tomorrow, the protests will start. The world will notice, and maybe—if they're lucky—Someone will finally listen.

Finn closes his laptop, hands shaking. He looks at Ava, who nods once, grim and proud.

Outside, the bay is dark and quiet. But Finn knows: nothing will ever be the same.

At sunset, the cove is a wound in the coast—raw rock, gnarled driftwood, the tide clawing at the shore as if it could eat the land itself. Mara surfaces first, copper hair slicked against her scalp, eyes darting for threats. The water is glass, tinted pink and gold by the dying sun, but underneath: shadows, waiting.

She floats just offshore, motionless. Around her, the new pack—Coral, Notch, the white-streaked girl, the others—rise in a careful spread, forming a perimeter. They've drilled for this: never surface alone, always cover your escape. Lyla lingers deeper, eyes on the mouth of the bay.

On the rocks, Finn stands with his hands shoved deep in his pockets, posture hunched against the wind. Next to him, Dr. Ava Chen checks her watch, then scans the horizon for signs of the boat they're expecting. The activists and biologists from the meeting cluster near a battered row of skiffs, muttering and glancing at the water with a mix of reverence and raw terror.

One of the biologists' points. "There—did you see that? In the kelp."

Finn tries not to smile. "Just stay still. They'll come to us."

Mara's heart drums so loudly she feels it in her teeth. The last time she risked the surface, it nearly killed her. But this is the plan, and Lyla was right: sometimes, the best way to hide is to be so obvious no one believes what they see.

Coral is the first to breach, hands up, palms open—a universal sign of peace, or at least nonviolence. The activists flinch back, but the red-haired leader steps forward, lips parted in awe.

Coral speaks first, voice tremoring just enough to betray her fear. "We help you, you help us," she says. Not perfect English, but it lands.

The biologist stares, jaw slack, then reaches out. Coral clasps her forearm, grip strong, and the others exhale as if a spell has just broken.

Finn moves to the waterline and waves Mara in. "You made it."

Mara shrugs. "Not dead yet."

They keep it business. There's no room for sentiment. Finn lays out the plan in crisp, clipped phrases: "We monitor the coast. You track the poachers, the worst polluters. We hit them together—data, protests, and, uh, less conventional means if needed."

Ava adds, "We use the waterproof comms for all contact—no digital. No phones. We keep it off the grid."

She hands out the comm devices—compact, hydrophobic, patched together from old dive computers and smuggled military tech. Each one fits in a closed fist and has a single emergency button. Mara tests hers, feels the pulse of the signal in her palm.

Lyla surfaces then, silent as a ghost. She takes one look at the humans, then at Mara, and nods. It's all the approval Mara needs.

The sun drops below the horizon, and the world shifts to indigo. Above, the activists and scientists load their skiffs with battered cameras, protest banners, and buckets of chalk for tagging piers and breakwaters. Below, Mara leads her team through last-minute drills, including current calling, evasive maneuvers, and synchronized breaches.

At full dark, the first target approaches: an illegal drift net, lit by a green lamp and trailed by two outboard skiffs. Mara's team splits, Coral and Notch circling wide, the others angling for the net's anchor line.

On shore, Finn gives the signal. The activists paddle out, silent as seals, cameras pointed at the operation. The netters see the boats and curse as they try to pull their gear. But Mara and her team are already at work, weaving the currents under the net, twisting it into a perfect spiral that jams the winch and yanks the outboard into a dead spin.

The netters panic, tossing knives and screaming at the sea. But the protest boats stay just out of reach, their cameras capturing every second.

On the comm, Finn's voice is low and fast: "You got it. Go, go, go."

Mara's group dives, leaving only a burst of bubbles.

The next morning, the video is everywhere—on social feeds, news sites, and even the city council's inbox. The netters claim sabotage, but the authorities laugh. Who would believe in sabotage by a mermaid?

Mara and Finn watch the coverage from the boathouse, crowded around a busted tablet. Ava reads the news aloud, but Mara barely hears. She's watching the waterline, waiting for the next crisis to arise.

Finn touches her shoulder. "You did it."

Mara shakes her head. "Not yet."

He grins. "That's the spirit."

Outside, the tide is already turning. This time, it's on their side.

8 Siren's Song

The cove is a skeleton at low tide: bones of driftwood, ribs of black basalt, the hollowed mouth of a cave that only empties at the solstice. Mara slips in before dawn, hugging the shelf, and tastes the copper of spent diesel on the first breath. The rock is cold, but she has grown to like it. Its edges are honest.

Finn is waiting, same as always, perched on a boulder with his bag of human instruments. He's early. He always is. The morning fog blurs his outline, makes him look softer than the last time she saw him, but the tension in his shoulders is real. When he spots her, he lifts a hand, unsure whether to wave or salute. It ends up somewhere in between.

She's already laughing as she pulls herself up the rock face, tail braced against a tide pool slick with green. Finn offers his hand. Mara pretends not to see it, hauls herself up with two fists and a grunt, and lands beside him, scales scraping the stone. Only then does she glance at his outstretched hand.

"You look tired, Finn Gallagher," she says, brushing the sand from her elbows.

He drops his hand, embarrassed. "Pulled a double shift at the sensor bank. Chen wanted the raw telemetry by eight." He tugs at the collar of his shirt, which is stained with sea salt and coffee. "You, uh, look—healthy."

She snorts. "You mean wet."

"I mean, not… injured." He's staring at her tail, which is healing faster than it should.

"Thanks to your friend's sticky bandages." Mara flicks her tail in demonstration, sending a spray of droplets onto his leg. He winces, but she's learned he doesn't actually mind.

The next minute is comfortable silence. Finn unzips the bag, lays out his tools in a neat row: a waterproof tablet, a tangle of leads, glass vials, and two mystery canisters with hazard symbols. Mara leans in, eyes the array.

"You always bring more," she observes. "Does Chen not trust her own readings?"

"She says you're an anomalous data point." He hesitates, then adds, "In the best way."

Mara likes the sound of that. She likes the way Finn won't meet her gaze, how he's more comfortable with wires and code than with anything living. She likes that he never asks the questions she doesn't want to answer.

He holds out a slender probe. "Ready?"

Mara nods, slips off the rock into the pool. She stretches out, letting her gills flutter. The instrument touches her side, just above the rib. It's cold, but his fingers are careful.

Finn glances at the readout. "Oxygen saturation is… wow." He bends closer, double-checks. "That's not possible."

She grins, teeth sharp. "That's the point, isn't it?"

He flushes, then shoves the probe into the sand and fumbles for the next instrument. Mara props herself up on her elbows and watches him work.

"What does the sticker mean?" she asks, pointing to the yellow triangle on the canister.

Finn blinks. "Oh, that's just—" He frowns, reconsiders. "You remember last week, when you did the standing wave?"

Mara nods. "You made me do it three times. Said it was for 'statistical significance.'"

He bites back a smile. "Yeah. Anyway, Chen thinks we should try to capture the microbubble effect. See if the gas is… special."

Mara arches a brow. "Your words, or hers?"

He ducks his head, but she can see the answer on his face.

"I can do it," Mara says. She slips both arms forward and positions her hands over the deepest spot in the pool. She calls up the current—not much, just enough to make the surface shudder and pop. The water sings under her touch, and the microbubbles rise in perfect spirals, catching the morning light. The canister snicks open, and Finn collects the first pulse, then the second. His hands are steady. His eyes, when he dares to look at her, are not.

"Good?" Mara asks, dropping the current.

Finn checks the canister. "Better than good." He wipes a bead of condensation off his brow, then glances at her again, softer this time.

She holds his gaze a second longer than before. There is something new in the silence. Not tension—never that—but a question neither wants to voice. Mara thinks of Lyla, the warning in her voice: "Surface-dwellers hunt what they fear." But Finn is not a hunter. If anything, he's the hunted, always a step ahead of his own guilt.

He packs away the canister, then holds out the waterproof tablet. "Chen wants you to try the diagnostic test."

Mara groans. "The one with the shapes?"

Finn grins. "She programmed it with fish."

She groans louder. "Cruel."

He sets the tablet on a flat rock. Mara taps the first icon. A virtual sardine flits across the screen, chased by a pixelated shark. She's supposed to track both at once and react when the pattern changes. Mara is bored in seconds, but she makes a show of trying, swiping her fingers in erratic zigzags.

"Your world is so binary," she says after a few rounds. "Either you win, or you die."

He shrugs. "Sometimes you win and die. That's most of grad school."

She laughs, the sound rolling out over the pool. The sardine survives another round, and Mara leans back, victorious.

"You're getting good at this," Finn says.

Mara flexes her webbed fingers. "I learn fast."

He looks at her, really looks, and Mara can feel the heat under her scales. She wonders if Finn feels it too, or if he's just cold from the wind.

A gull cries overhead, loud enough to break the mood.

Finn clears his throat. "You want to see something cool?"

Mara feigns indifference, but she likes this game. "Impress me."

He digs into his bag and pulls out a tiny drone—no larger than a crab, all legs and sensors. "They're using these for marine mapping now. It can get into places divers can't. And it's waterproof, so if you want to—" he hesitates, then "—race it?"

She grins, all teeth. "You think I'd lose?"

He flips the drone on and sets it skittering across the tide pool. Mara gives it a one-second head start, then launches herself after it. The chase is a blur of spray and laughter—hers is wild, his is tight and nervous, but it's laughter all the same. The drone dodges, but Mara is faster; she grabs it between two fingers, gentle but triumphant, and pops back up to the surface.

Finn claps, delighted. "I've never seen anyone catch one bare-handed."

She tosses the drone back to him. "Not fair. It can't sense the currents."

He sits down beside her, closer now. The drone clatters across his knees, but he ignores it. He's looking at her again, and Mara realizes she's waiting for him to say something important.

But instead, he asks, "What does it feel like when you use the magic?"

She considers. "Like listening to a song, you almost remember, but can't quite name. It's loud, but not with sound. More like a feeling."

He nods, as he understands. "Sometimes I think that's what science is. Chasing a pattern you can't see, hoping it makes sense if you listen hard enough."

She studies him, the shadows under his eyes, the way his hands tremble when they're not holding something. "Do you ever rest, Finn Gallagher?"

He shrugs. "There's not much time left, is there?"

She doesn't answer. Instead, she places a hand on his wrist. Human custom, she thinks, but it feels right. His pulse is frantic under her palm, but he doesn't pull away.

"Maybe tonight, you rest," Mara says.

He swallows. "Tonight's the full moon. Best readings for bioluminescence."

She arches a brow. "Is that what you want to study?"

He meets her gaze, and this time he doesn't look away. "There's something I want to show you. Out past the old jetty. If you're free."

She doesn't laugh, not this time. "I'm always free at night."

He grins, sheepish, but the fear is gone from his face.

Mara stands, water cascading off her scales, and gives him a mock salute. "Then I'll see you under the moon, Finn Gallagher."

He stands too, shoulders a little straighter. "I'll bring snacks."

She shakes her head, already sliding into the water. "Just bring yourself," she says, then vanishes into the blue.

For the rest of the day, she thinks only of the way his hand felt in hers and what he might show her when the world is dark.

Mara waits just beyond the breakwater, poised on the edge of the dark. She listens to her pulse in the cold and to the distant drone of the town, the shouts and gull cries, the brittle music of the marina bars. All of it is background noise compared to the white-hot silence inside her.

She watches the moon, a thin-boned coin stamped with scars, and feels a wild urge to break the surface before Finn is even in position. But she waits. There is something sacred in the timing.

When the hour is right, she breaches slowly, careful not to slap the water's surface. The cove is alive in moonlight—each ripple a silvered brushstroke, the rock pools shining like the eyes of nocturnal things. Out near the mouth, Finn waits in a borrowed rowboat, his outline cut against the sky. He sits hunched, arms crossed, but the way he stares at the water says he's already seen her.

Mara circles once, then twice, burning off nerves, then slips to the side of the boat. "You're early," she says, chin just above the surface.

Finn startles, nearly dropping the oar overboard. "Jesus, you swim quietly."

She laughs, which feels like popping a bubble. "I thought you were a marine biologist. Don't you know how to spot the apex predators?"

He grins. "Not when they look like you."

He's brought a blanket, a thermos, and a battered tackle box. The blanket is folded and unused on the bow. Mara wonders if he means to invite her up, or if it's for himself, a barrier against the chill. The thermos is propped at his feet.

He offers her a cup. "It's just tea. Chen says caffeine slows reflexes, so—"

She cuts him off by grabbing the cup and downing it in one swallow. It's sweet, with a sting of something alcoholic. Mara arches a brow. "Tea?"

Finn flushes. "I spiked it. For courage."

She bobs in place, letting her tail drift below the hull. "What did you want to show me?"

He sets the oar aside, fixes her with a look that's pure Finn—earnest, a little too intense. "Look up," he says.

She does, but the sky is just sky—cloudless, bright, dotted with stars.

"Not that," he says, and gestures at the water.

The surface is perfect, unbroken. Mara opens her gills and listens. It's not until she lets her eyes unfocus that she sees it: a hundred microcurrents, each twisted by hand or moon, each mapped by the wind. She narrows her focus, and beneath the silver is a second glow—a blue so sharp it hurts.

She's stunned for a second, then realizes: bioluminescence—a whole patch of water, blooming with it.

She stares up at Finn, who is now rocking side to side, watching her reaction with shy pride. "I seeded the cove," he says. "Last week. I wanted to see if it would work. Looks like it did."

She wants to tease him, but the wonder of it is too much. "It's beautiful," she says.

He beams. "Not as good as your magic, but—"

She cuts him off. "Not magic. Just practice."

He tilts his head. "So, show me."

Mara takes the challenge. She sinks below the hull and lets her hands skim the mud. It takes more effort this time—she's never tried to bend the wild glow before—but she calls the current anyway, and the water obeys. The blue pulses, then flares, a double helix of light climbing up the sides of the boat.

Finn shouts, delighted, and Mara feels a flush that's not just the effort.

She surfaces, hair plastered to her neck, and grins. "Human technology is clever. But nature wins."

He nods, breathless. "You win, Mara Ondine."

They're silent for a minute. The only sound is the lapping of the hull and the click of Finn's teeth as he fidgets.

She floats closer to the boat until her face is even with his. "You look like you want to ask something," she says.

He hesitates, then: "How old were you, the first time you used the—" he can't say 'magic,' so he says, "—the gift?"

She thinks. "I was five seasons old. My mother showed me how to read the tides. Said it was our duty, but also our joy." She shrugs. "It didn't feel special until I saw what it could do. For others."

He listens so intently that it's almost a magic in itself.

"Why do you do this?" she asks. "The ocean doesn't belong to you. You could leave, go anywhere."

He watches his hands for a while, then says, "When I was a kid, my mom ran a charter boat out of Morro Bay. She'd take tourists whale watching, fishing, whatever paid. One winter, we hit a pod of orcas—huge, way too close. I was supposed to be scared, but it was—" he grins, remembering. "I thought they were saying hi. I tried to jump in."

Mara laughs, picturing tiny Finn flinging himself at a killer whale.

He shrugs. "It stuck with me. The idea that we share the ocean with things we can't even understand. Maybe never will." He looks up, not at her but at the moon. "When I met you, I realized I'd been looking for the impossible my whole life. And I found it."

She's quiet, taken aback. "You found a headache, Finn."

He shakes his head, then looks her dead in the eye. "I found you."

There it is again, the silence, but this time it's charged. She lets herself drift until her arms rest against the hull.

He holds out a hand, tentative. "Can I—"

She takes it, pulling herself halfway onto the boat. The scales on her arms catch the blue light, refracting it onto the wood. He traces one with his thumb, awestruck.

She waits, breathless, for him to make the next move.

He does. It's awkward, his first attempt missing her cheek and landing on the corner of her jaw. But she leans into it, catches his hand, and draws him closer.

Their lips meet, and it's nothing like Mara expected. It's softer, slower, the heat building from nothing to everything in a second.

She tastes the sea on him, and something else—fear, hope, the tangled mess of a human heart.

He breaks first, gasping. "Sorry," he says, but she laughs and yanks him back.

The next kiss is hungrier, all teeth and tongue and shared breath. Finn's hands, uncertain at first, find their place on her face, then her neck, then tangled in her hair. Mara loses herself in it, the pulse of the ocean forgotten, her body electric with need.

The boat rocks hard. Finn almost topples, but Mara steadies him, her tail curled around the prow for leverage.

When they break apart, both are breathing hard.

"I've never—" Finn says, then stops, embarrassed.

Mara grins. "You're not terrible at it."

He laughs, and the sound is music.

They sit together, Mara draped over the side of the boat, Finn kneeling before her, arms resting on her shoulders.

The water glows beneath them, a world apart from everything else.

"Do you ever wish you were human?" Finn asks, not cruel, just curious.

She shakes her head. "I wish humans would listen better. But I don't want to be one."

He nods. "Good. I like you the way you are."

She kisses him again, quickly, then releases him.

The moon is high now, the cove silent but for their breaths.

They remain like that for a long time, neither moving nor speaking. Just alive in the dark, together.

The jellyfish pulse beneath, and above, the sky is endless.

The blue hush between them is broken by a shiver that runs from Mara's gills to her spine. She stiffens, senses scraping raw.

Finn blinks, confusion clouding his face. "What's wrong?"

She lifts her head, eyes unfocused. There's a vibration in the water now—a hum, low and wide, like distant thunder smothered by flesh. She filters it out, piece by piece, until only the pattern remains.

"Something's coming," she says, voice gone flat. "Not a storm. Not normal."

Finn tries to process; his hands still tangled in her hair. "A boat?"

She shakes him off, slides overboard in one practiced motion. She hangs there, just below the hull, letting the current speak through her. It's worse than she thought. Dozens of pressure wakes, each moving in parallel, then splitting and reforming like a net with thinking edges.

She breaches, face close to Finn's. "It's a fleet. Maybe ten, maybe more. All in line."

He scrambles for his phone, thumb flicking through weather,

then to ship trackers. "I don't see anything—" but the words die as Mara's expression goes from concern to horror.

She closes her eyes, tuning in. Each engine, each hull, has its own taste. One of them—there it is, the largest—drags a signature current, a twist of oil and rust and something else. It's familiar. It's infamous.

Blackwell.

She flashes to the stories: how he hunted her kind in the cold seas, how he'd circle for days, not with nets but with blades. They said he could smell Merfolk on the wind, and that his ship was painted black to match the blood on his hull.

She opens her eyes and speaks in a rush. "The captain from the docks—the one who found you. He's here. Leading them."

Finn goes pale. "Blackwell?"

She nods. "They're closing the gap. Six knots, maybe seven. Fast."

He looks at his phone again, hands shaking. "Still nothing on AIS. They're running dark."

Mara sees the realization dawn on him: this is not a drill, not a test run. It's a hunt.

She grabs his wrist. "I have to warn the city."

He nods, but doesn't let go. "Wait. If he's hunting you, he'll be scanning for any anomaly. If you make a move—"

"They'll see," she finishes. She wants to curse, but the language doesn't fit.

She thinks fast. "He's targeting the shallows. Where the young train."

Finn's face twists. "That's the nursery. There'll be dozens—"

"Hundreds," Mara says, voice gone sharp.

Finn's hands find her shoulders, holding her at the edge of the boat. "Let me help. I can warn Chen. We have activists in every port. If we jam the signals—"

Mara shakes her head. "Blackwell's not like the others. He doesn't need comms. He watches the water."

He releases her, but his face is set. "Then we fight with what we have."

She feels the urge to run, to get ahead of the fleet, but Finn's presence is an anchor. "If I don't come back—"

He doesn't let her finish. "Don't," Finn says, voice trembling. "You're coming back."

She wants to believe it. But the current in her chest is pure dread.

Mara slips from the boat, shivering once at the cold water. She centers herself, eyes half-closed, and lets the new sense spool out from her. This is the skill Lyla drilled into her, the talent the old city honed for generations: become the water, read its wounds, track every pulse of disruption until you know the shape of every enemy long before you ever see them.

It's worse than before. The fleet is fanning out, forming a perfect crescent along the outer reef. The big ship—Blackwell's—sits at the center. Mara feels its engines churning, heavier than anything else in the bay. She tastes the chemical tang of its wake, the microfractures it leaves in the current, the premonition of nets opening wide and slow. She's seen this tactic in memory—stories from the elders, and from her own nightmares.

Finn calls to her from above, his phone's glow casting him in a lunar-pale light. "You're right. There's nothing on the public logs, but my tracker app's spiking noise on the trawl bands. Like someone's jamming everything."

The water muffles Mara's voice, but he hears her anyway. "That's how he hunts. Silence first, then the kill."

Finn's face goes hard; all the fear burned away by something colder. "How long do we have?"

Mara scans the current again, heart sinking. "Two hours, maybe less. They're fast. They'll hit the city before sunrise."

He clutches the edge of the boat, knuckles white. "What do we do?"

It's the first time he's ever said 'we.' She almost laughs, but there's no room for that now. "You go to Chen. Tell her to call off the protest and evacuate everyone. If the netters catch the activists on the water—"

He cuts her off. "They'll just shoot." He knows. He hates knowing.

Mara floats beside the hull, letting herself hover. The memory of Blackwell is sharp now, a knife against her gills. She flashes back to her childhood, the story every Merfolk knew but none dared tell in full:

A fleet comes at night, silent as death. The first sign is always the taste of metal in the water, then the shadow of the hull overhead, then the weight of nets, heavier than gravity. Her mother's fin caught in mesh, the panic-smell of blood, the way the water filled with bubbles that weren't air but agony. The sound of a blade cutting through bone, clean as a song.

Blackwell always kept a trophy. Sometimes a tail, sometimes a jaw. Sometimes a live one, starved and strung for the press. He'd been myth once, then a rumor, then a man, then worse.

"Finn," she says, "when you see the boats, don't try to reason. Just run."

He shakes his head. "What about you?"

She's honest because there's no point in lying now. I go to the city. Try to get the young out, get the Council to run. Maybe they'll listen."

"They'll listen," Finn says, and he means it, though she knows how hard it is to move a city built on secrets.

He looks down at her, and Mara sees the raw hope in his face. "Promise you'll make it back. I won't leave if you don't."

She wants to. But hope is not a currency she trades in.

"I'll try," she says, and the words sting like salt.

He's leaning over the side now, desperate. "Mara—" He wants to say more, but the words tangle and choke.

So, she does what she can. She reaches up, takes his hand in hers, and squeezes hard, letting him feel the strength in her bones, the promise of what she's about to do.

"Tell Chen not to call the Coast Guard. Blackwell has half of them paid. Use the university network. The activists. They'll listen to you."

He nods, already scrolling his phone, setting plans in motion.

Mara gives him one last look, the waterline splitting her face: half world, half air.

"Don't die," he says, voice breaking.

She grins, all teeth. "That's your job."

And then she's gone, a streak of silver and green cutting through the black, headed for the reef city with every muscle burning.

Finn scrambles to the shore, boots slipping on slime and stone. He calls Chen before he's even dry. "It's happening," he says, voice raw. "They're coming for the Merfolk. We have less than two hours. Lockdown the bay, get everyone out."

Ava Chen doesn't waste words. "Coordinates?" she asks, and Finn feeds her everything: the trawl band spikes, the gaps in satellite feeds, the triangulated path of Blackwell's lead ship. "Copy," Chen says. "We'll go dark and scramble the rest. You?"

Finn glances at the horizon, the impossible dark. "I'm going to the marina. If I can stall them—"

Chen interrupts. "Don't be stupid, Gallagher. You're not James Bond."

"Neither is Blackwell," Finn spits, "but he's going to kill every one of them if I don't do something."

Chen goes silent, then: "Don't get caught. We need you."

He hangs up, fingers shaking.

On the water, the black hulls are already visible—a dozen, maybe more, all running silent. Finn counts them, bile rising in his throat. He sprints to the battered pickup parked near the cove, throws it into gear, and peels out, tires screaming.

The marina is a mess: security gates locked, alarms blaring, every light in the dock house on. He sees the first of Blackwell's men before he even stops the truck—two silhouettes, dressed like workers but moving with military precision, ducking behind a crate of crab traps. Finn kills the headlights, slides out, and keeps low.

He knows the plan: Blackwell always lands first, secures the dock, then sweeps the cove in a tightening spiral, each wave of crew more ruthless than the last. The boats have custom matte-black paint, numbers filed off, no flag or logo in sight. This is not fishing; it's war.

Finn texts Chen the update, then heads to the old research shed. He fumbles with the lock, gets inside, and checks the cabinets for anything he can use. Emergency flares, a gas mask, and a flare gun with three cartridges. It'll have to do.

He scans the water for Mara, but she's gone—nothing left but a ripple. He closes his eyes, wills her to be safe.

In the city below, Mara is already at the gates, shouting warnings with every ounce of breath. She finds Coral and Lyla in the training grotto, barely awake, but they sense the panic before she even speaks.

"They're coming," Mara gasps. "All of them. The Black hull. We have to run."

Coral blanches, but Lyla is all business. "Evac routes?"

"North tunnel. The old mine. It's collapsed in spots, but it's the only way past the shelf."

Lyla nods, grabs the youngest first. "Move!"

The alarm spreads fast, wordless, primal, every Merfolk catching the pulse of fear in the water. The city empties like a vein cut open: mothers clutching fry, old soldiers herding packs of young, the few guards left marshaling a hopeless defense.

Mara's tail is shredded from the last fight, but she ignores the pain. She helps the slowest, the wounded, the ones too proud or too scared to run. The city is breaking apart, but if they're lucky, some will make it.

She gets a flash, then, of Blackwell's hull grinding overhead, and every old scar in her body sings in warning.

Up above, Finn hears the first engines rev. He sees two of Blackwell's men—faces familiar from old mugshots and news reports—moving down the pier with AR-15s and night vision. He crouches behind the research shed, watches them set up motion sensors along the dock.

He knows what happens next: the thermal sweep, then the flash-bangs, then the net. It's the same every time.

He waits until they're past, then sprints for the fuel depot. The tanks are old, marked for demolition, but they're full enough. He pulls the flare gun from his pocket and wedges it into a crack in the main valve. A single spark will turn the pier into a firestorm.

Finn ducks back to the shed, breath coming in gasps. He checks his phone. A single message from Chen: "Backup coming, ETA 20."

He knows it'll be too late.

Back in the tunnels, Mara and the survivors push through the mine shaft, the light gone but for the faintest glow from the algae on the walls. The air is thick with silt and terror.

Coral is the first to panic. "We're lost," she whispers, voice thin. "They'll catch us."

Lyla slaps her hard, and the sound echoes. "Keep moving," she says. "We die if we stop."

Mara pushes ahead, feeling for the thinnest hint of current. She finds it, a trickle of cold, pure water. It means escape.

She gestures. "This way. Hurry."

They claw through the rock, tails and hands bloodied. Behind, Mara can feel the city dying, the current going thick with loss. She won't let herself look back.

Above, Finn sees the first black hull tie up at the pier. Aboard, the silhouette of Captain Marcus Blackwell, standing straight and still in a coat of midnight, his face unreadable from this distance.

Finn sights down the dock, takes aim with the flare gun, and waits for Blackwell to step onto the planks.

When he does, Finn fires.

The flare punches through the dark, arcs to the fuel tank. There's a second of nothing, then the world erupts in white fire.

The dock is a warzone—screams, explosions, burning rain falling everywhere. Blackwell's men scatter, diving for cover, but the smoke is everywhere, blanketing the water.

Finn runs. He dashes past the chaos, down to the beach, hoping the distraction buys Mara the time she needs. He sees a shape moving at the water's edge—Mara, battered, covered in ash and kelp, dragging two children behind her.

He runs to her, arms open, and she nearly collapses into him.

"You did it," he says, breathless.

She shakes her head. "We did it. But they'll be back. Always back."

Finn looks over his shoulder. The fire is spreading, but the black hulls are already regrouping, drawing guns, sweeping the shore.

He glances at Mara. "We have to go."

She nods. "There's a cave. Northwest of here. It'll hold, for now."

He grabs her hand, the kids clutching her tail. Together, they slip into the surf, vanishing beneath the waves.

On the surface, Blackwell stands at the edge of the burning dock, face smeared with soot and blood, eyes scanning the water for any sign of them. He grins, slow and sure, like a man who's never lost a hunt.

The sun rises, red as a warning.

Far below, Mara and Finn hold tight, the younglings pressed between them, the current guiding them through the dark.

It's not a victory. Not yet.

But it's survival, and for now, that's enough.

They swim, the cold bite of the new day slicing through everything. Finn never lets go of her hand.

And for the first time, Mara thinks they might make it.

9 Depths of Deception

At midnight, the cove is a locked room, and Finn and Ava are breaking in. The moonless dark is their camouflage, the roaring surf their white noise. Above them, on the bluff, floodlights sweep the perimeter—arcs of sterile daylight that make every shadow ten times sharper. The only way through is under.

They crawl the last fifty yards on their bellies, wet to the chest, the fine gravel grinding through the knees of Finn's jeans. Ava moves like she's done this before, which, Finn realizes, she probably has. Her night-vision goggles glow ghost green; she stops every few meters to scan the fences, then gestures for Finn to follow.

He tries not to breathe too loudly. The ocean air tastes of rot, and the closer they get to the warehouse, the more it smells like chemicals—bleach, formalin, something sharp and metallic. It's worse than the usual stench of dead kelp.

The fence is a joke: single coil of razor wire, sensor units' duct-taped to the posts, nothing Finn and his wire cutter can't handle. He kneels, slicing slowly, counting to ten before each snip. Ava covers him, pistol drawn and low. The gate gives with a soft metallic whine. They're in.

For a second, Finn's heart is a hummingbird in his chest. He waits for an alarm, a shout, the blue-and-red strobe of the private security, but nothing. The only sound is the distant thunder of surf and the nearer yelping of dogs, which Finn fervently hopes are leashed.

Ava elbows him, hard. "Move."

They skirt the edge of the compound, hunched below the window line. At the north wall, Finn finds a service hatch with a biometric pad. He plugs in the reader from his kit, fingers trembling so bad he nearly drops it. The hack runs its cycle—thirty seconds, thirty years. The light blinks green, and Ava's in first, then he.

Inside: darkness, but with a heartbeat. The room is climate-controlled, cold as a tomb. Rows of tanks line the walls—each one a miniature ocean, neon-lit, humming. Some are full of rare fish, pulsing with color and confusion. Others are empty but for hunks of coral or bundles of tubing.

Finn slides down the aisle, eyes wide. Every few feet, he stops, snaps a picture with the infrared camera. He catalogs what he sees: tropical lionfish, Pacific eels, a glass tank with nothing but a cluster of live sea urchins. Then, farther down, a series of bell jars—each holding something not quite right.

Ava goes straight for the back wall, where a rolling ladder leads up to a mezzanine crammed with boxes. Finn hears the faint click of her boots, then the clatter as she starts rifling through the shelves.

He focuses on the jars. The first holds a piece of what looks like pale, scaled skin, five centimeters across, the edges cauterized. The label reads: "Specimen 4C. Collected from a drift net." Next to it, a fragment of bone, not fish but not mammal either, just the tip of a delicate fin or maybe a finger. The third jar stops him cold. Inside: a fan of scales, iridescent blue and green, not unlike the ones he's seen on Mara when the sunlight hits just right. These are torn, with ragged edges.

He takes a shaky breath, wipes his hands on his jeans, and snaps the picture.

There's a whir and a blue flicker from the loft. Ava's silhouette is framed in monitor light, her hands moving fast over the keys.

"What did you find?" he whispers, climbing the ladder two rungs at a time.

She doesn't look up. "Shipping manifests. Fish is a front—this place is a relay for something else. Look."

He leans over her shoulder. On the screen, a grid of names and destinations: shipments to Oceanic Industries, Global Fishing Consortium, a dozen other shell companies. Each line is timestamped, with coordinates and cargo descriptions. Several are flagged "urgent—specimen transfer." Finn's pulse kicks up another notch as he recognizes the pattern of the locations—each one a known hotspot for rare marine life, and a few that line up almost perfectly with Mara's migration stories.

He scans the files, then jabs at a line item. "That's the same cove where they dumped the waste barrels last winter. And that one—" he points "—that's the estuary where the netted pod was found dead last month."

Ava's mouth is set in a grim line. "This is more than poaching. They're running something big. Biotech, maybe, or weapons."

"Or something nobody's named yet," Finn says—his voice cracks.

Ava yanks a thumb drive from her vest and jams it into the

port. The screen flickers as she dumps the entire hard drive—the upload bar crawls. Down below, something crashes—a heavy thunk, then footsteps.

Finn and Ava freeze. A voice, guttural, half-laugh: "You do the rounds, or is it my turn?"

A second voice, bored: "Rock-paper-scissors for it?"

The two security guards lumber in, flashlights sweeping the tanks. Finn slides flat to the floor of the mezzanine, trying not to shake. Below, the guards are silhouetted by the aquarium glow—both big, both armed. One carries a baton, the other a shotgun slung loose.

Ava moves as silently as a cat. She signals Finn: wait, then vanish. She finishes the file dump, snaps the laptop closed, and creeps to the edge of the loft, pistol ready but finger off the trigger.

Below, the guards stop in front of the tank with the iridescent scales. The taller one whistles. "Boss says we get more of these; he gets a bonus."

"Hope he shares," says the other. "Heard he's got a line on something really valuable, out past the reef."

The first guy laughs. "If it's so valuable, why do they keep sending us to babysit these damn fish?"

Ava and Finn catch each other's eye. He can see her brain working a thousand meters per second, calculating risk and exit routes.

He creeps back to the computer station, scanning the other files. His stomach twists as he sees his own name and Ava's flagged on a security report: "High risk, likely to investigate," accompanied by photos and a bullet-point list of their movements over the last month.

He starts copying, hands moving on autopilot. He feels, for the first time, what Mara must have felt—hunted, dissected, counted down to extinction.

Ava's hand lands on his shoulder, steady. "We need to go," she mouths.

He nods, pocketing the drive.

They slide down the ladder as the guards move toward the far end of the tanks. In the brief confusion, Finn and Ava slip through a side door, out onto a maintenance catwalk over the cove. The metal grates shudder under their weight, but they move fast.

At the end of the catwalk, Finn pauses. From here, he can see the boats: three black RIBs, each bristling with antennae and spotlights, tied up along the private dock. On the deck, men in camo are loading crates stamped with the same logos as the manifests. Finn feels his blood run cold as he sees the emblem on their jackets—Oceanic Industries, the company that, two years ago, swore up and down at a congressional hearing that they had no interest in marine genetic harvesting.

Ava points down the line. "Boat house. We can use the launch to get clear, if we move now."

Finn hesitates. There's a glass panel overlooking the tanks, and on the other side, something moves—something familiar. It's Blackwell, hunched over a work table, talking with a third guard. On the desk: a series of vials, a tray of surgical instruments, and, at the center, a set of scales so bright they almost hum. They're just like Mara's—Finn's vision tunnels.

He fumbles the camera, clicks a dozen shots, and tries to steady his hands.

Ava grabs his arm, harder this time. "Finn. We have to move. Now."

He nods, barely, and lets her drag him down the walk, across the open dock. The wind is up, the clouds blowing in from the west. They stick to the shadows, ducking behind skiffs and crates.

At the last crate, Finn trips. It's his own fault—he's looking over his shoulder at the lab, not at his feet. The impact sends a stack of empty plastic tanks tumbling, clattering loudly like cymbals.

The security guy with the baton is on them in seconds, light and weapon raised. Ava doesn't run. She faces him down, gun at her side, badge flashing from the inside of her coat.

"EPA," she says, voice like a cold slap. "You violate six federal codes. Stand down."

The guy blinks, but only for a second. "Lady, I don't know what you think you're—"

He never finishes. Ava is on him, knee to the groin, then an arm bar. The guard hits the dock hard, winded and groping for his radio. Finn stands frozen, useless, until Ava shoves him toward the boathouse.

Inside, the air is even colder. The boat is prepped, and the engine is idling. Finn fumbles the ignition, nearly drops the keys, but then the RIB starts with a cough and a roar.

Ava jumps in next to him, breathless but grinning. "You drive?"

"I navigate. I don't—" but she's already untying the lines, pushing them out into the dark.

Behind, the alarm finally triggers. The whole compound lights up—search beams, shouting, the angry yelp of the unleashed dogs. Finn pushes the throttle, and the boat knifes through the black water, leaving a wake of phosphorescence behind.

They clear the cove in under a minute, but neither speaks until the dock, and the shouts are a mile behind. Only then does Ava let out a shaky laugh.

"You see the look on his face?" she says, half-crazed.

Finn shakes his head, can't find his voice. He checks his jacket, confirms the drive is still there, still safe.

He can't stop thinking about the scales, the way they shone in the blue light.

He can't stop thinking about Mara, and whether, when this is over, there'll be enough left to save.

Beneath the skin of the sea, Mara slips through the trench, every muscle taut. The water here is close to freezing, and the silt along the canyon walls whispers of ancient things, but Mara focuses on the pull of the current ahead, ignoring the ache in her tail. Lyla follows at her right, never more than a half-body length away, her eyes always on the darkness behind them. Coral brings up the rear, small and sharp, quick to dart to cover at the faintest tremor.

They move in silence, but for the pulse of the water and the electric thrum of nerves. Mara's gills flare as she tastes the surface: exhaust, diesel, the faint ammonia of human fear. It's worse than she hoped. The poison is everywhere now.

A thousand meters from the cove, Mara halts, fanning her tail for stability. She gestures—flat palm, then two fingers to her own eyes. Lyla nods, alert. Mara draws in the cold, then raises her hands and calls the current, being careful and subtle so it bends the water rather than shattering it. She shapes a small vortex, no wider than her outstretched arms, and pushes it upward, through the trench ceiling and toward the surface. As it rises, it coils around the thin thermocline, capturing stray bubbles and particles, and climbs up to where sound can carry.

The vortex is more than a listening device: it is a periscope for the senses. Mara shudders as her mind latches onto it. The hum of boat engines. Human voices, muffled but clear enough. The clatter of equipment on metal. She drifts, suspended in the trench, and filters the signal.

Above, the night is alive with movement. Blackwell's men are on the dock, hauling crates, shouting orders, laughing too loudly. Mara's jaw tightens as she recognizes the cadence: these are not the casual poachers or weekend fishermen who haunt the inlets. These are professionals, drilled and cold.

She focuses, drawing the vortex tighter. The next sound is a voice, smooth and heavy, slicing through the white noise.

"Tomorrow at dawn," it says. "Three teams. Northern coves first, then south."

Another voice, higher, jittery: "You think it's real? What did they find in the nets last week?"

A dry chuckle. "The boss says it's better than real. Says it's the jackpot."

Lyla drifts close, brushing Mara's shoulder. "What do they want?"

"Everything," Mara says, voice thin.

Coral pushes ahead, closer to the surface, then points with a flick of her fin. "They're loading sonar," she whispers. "Big set. Maybe industrial."

Mara follows her gaze. Through the shimmer of water and oil, she can see the hull of a launch, black and slick as whale hide. Four men stand on the deck, three with rifles, one in a jumpsuit, working a panel of electronics. The device is ugly, bristling with wires and dish antennae.

"Sonar, and a signal jammer," Coral says, almost impressed. "They're planning for anything."

Mara's stomach knots. She senses the danger—not just to her, but to all of them. The humans know, or suspect, too much.

She closes her eyes, lets her mind sink into the water, and calls the deeper magic. Tide-Sensing isn't like the other tricks—it costs more. It pulls at her bones, makes her heart beat slow, but if she can tune it right, she'll see the whole picture.

At first, nothing but the constant static of poisoned water. Then, under that, a vibration. It's not natural—too regular, too sharp at the edges. It's the signature of the sonar, but worse, she realizes: it's amplified by the pollution, bouncing through the silt like a death knell.

She opens her eyes. "We can't get close," she tells Lyla. "The water's too fouled. Our magic won't work for more than a minute."

Lyla's mouth twists. "So, we get in, get out. Fast."

Coral is already moving, her tail cutting a sharp angle through the trench. "They're testing the dish. We have to see what it does."

Mara glances at the surface again, then signals the others. She leads the way, rolling tight to the rock wall, using every shadow. At the mouth of the cove, she slows, holding her breath as a patrol boat idles overhead. Its propeller chops the silence, the sound a physical force. Mara waits until it's past, then pushes through.

They rise, one at a time, until their heads are barely a foot from the surface. The water here is slick with oil, and its taste makes Mara's teeth ache.

She focuses upward, and her world becomes a telescope.

On the dock, Blackwell himself stands at the center of the chaos. He's taller than the others, lean and mean, his head bare, face lit blue by the glow of a tablet. Mara's gaze lands on the screen: a map of the coast, each cove marked with a red dot. Next to him, two men haul a crate the size of a small coffin, marked with the same logo as the poachers' boat: Oceanic Industries.

Blackwell turns, and his voice cuts through again. "This is a sweep and clear. No mistakes. We want them alive."

A man in a red jacket shuffles nervously. "You ever seen one, boss?"

Blackwell grins, a mouthful of shark teeth. "I've seen enough to know they're out there. And that they bleed."

A ripple of nervous laughter. Mara feels Lyla tense at her side.

Coral edges upward, trying to get a better angle. Her hand brushes a floating bit of plastic—one of the dozens of wrappers and bags that litter the shallows. The plastic shifts, and the sound is microscopic, but instantly, a flashlight beam knifes through the dark, cutting right across Coral's head.

"Did you see that?" a guard yells.

Mara slams her tail, pushing all three of them deeper, out of sight. For a second, her heart is in her throat, waiting for the crack of a rifle or the thunder of a net cannon. But nothing comes. The guards curse, then laugh, and then return to their work.

They drift at the bottom, letting the cold calm their nerves.

Coral is pale, but grinning. "Close."

Mara wants to scream, but Lyla shakes her head. "We have to warn the city," she says. "If they sweep the coves, we're trapped."

Mara nods, then looks up one last time. Blackwell is there, still staring at the water, eyes hard as stone.

She memorizes the map, the pattern of the dots. "They start at dawn," she whispers. "We have maybe six hours."

"Less, if they get smart," Lyla says.

They kick off, moving down the trench, Coral taking the lead this time. Mara hangs back for a second, glancing at the surface. Above, the men are already moving on to the next task. The water vibrates with anticipation, and Mara knows: this is it. The war has started, and she's on the front line.

She swims hard into the cold.

They almost make it to the woods.

It starts with Finn, head down, barreling through the moonless dark behind Dr. Ava Chen. The two of them are all adrenaline and clumsy speed, boot soles biting the wet planks of the marina dock. At first, it seems straightforward: the guards are still clustered at the main gate, alarms shrilling in two-second bursts. Finn keeps his eyes on Ava's back, refusing to look left or right, certain that if he does, his nerves will short out and freeze him.

At the end of the dock, they break left, aiming for the tree line where they can come back to the old logging road. They're halfway there when Finn catches his foot on a coil of hose, pitches forward, and slams into a stack of plastic crates. The sound is thunder. One crate explodes open, its contents—a dozen rare clownfish, each the size of Finn's thumb—splatter across the deck in a rain of saltwater and glass.

The nearest guard whips around, flashlight beam searing the dark. "Who's there?"

Finn scrambles to his feet, soaking wet and off-balance, one hand clutching the thumb drive in his pocket. He tries to run, but his legs are stuck in a state of panic. Ava is already moving, a blur in the corner of his eye, but Finn can't help himself: he tries to gather the spilled fish, hands slick and clumsy. One wriggles free and bounces into the water.

The guard is close now, boots pounding the dock, gun up.

Ava doesn't hesitate. She grabs the nearest tank, hoists it over her head, and hurls it down the dock. It bursts at the guard's feet, sending a tidal wave of saltwater and parrotfish into the air. The guard yelps, blinded, slips, and goes down hard.

"Come on!" Ava hisses, hauling Finn by the collar.

They run, splashing through a low tide pool, feet slipping on seaweed and slime. Behind them, more shouts—another guard, maybe two. The spotlights whip across the dock, but Finn and Ava are in the reeds now, hidden by cattails and the ruined hull of an old tugboat.

Ava yanks him behind the wreck, and they crouch, panting. Finn's lungs are razors. He feels the urge to puke, but swallows it down.

Ava leans in, voice low and fierce. "Get a grip, Gallagher."

He nods, hating himself. "Sorry."

She checks her pistol, eyes narrowed. "You get the drive?"

Finn pats his jacket. "Yeah."

Ava's shoulders sag, just a little. She's all steel, but even steel bends. "Good. Next, we—" She stops, cocks her head.

There's a new sound: a rush, like a firehose aimed straight up, and then a wet slap as something big breaks the surface of the cove. Finn cranes his neck. For a second, he thinks it's a dolphin, but the shape is all wrong—too long, too smooth, the color not gray but a shifting palette of blue and green.

Then he realizes.

"Mara," he whispers, heart slamming.

She's at the end of the dock, just below the waterline, using the shadow of the pilings as cover. Finn catches the flash of her hair, copper against the black water. For a heartbeat, they stare.

Ava sees it, too. "Is that—?"

Finn nods, eyes burning. "Yeah."

On the dock above, guards are still chasing ghosts, but one is close enough that Finn can hear his boots. Mara's head bobs up, just enough to make eye contact. Finn risks standing, waving an arm slowly and wide, hoping she understands. Then he points at the boats, at the guard, at the cove—trying to spell out, in the dumbest possible human semaphore: massive hunt. Danger. Run.

Mara's eyes go wide. She glances to her left, then back at him. She nods once, sharply—and then she's gone, a ripple in the surface all that's left.

Finn ducks behind the wreck as a flashlight passes overhead.

Ava checks her watch, then the tree line. "Five minutes to the service road. Can you make it?"

He grits his teeth, nods.

They sprint, hunched low, keeping to the reeds and rocks. The mud sucks at their shoes, but it's covering, and by the time the guards recover enough to organize, Finn and Ava are at the tree line, hidden by darkness and the noise of the surf.

They don't stop moving. They scramble up the incline, through brambles and slick grass, then into the maze of stunted pines. Finn stumbles, more than once, but each time Ava catches him, drags him upright, keeps them moving.

Behind them, the dock is a confusion of shouting, the spotlights sweeping wildly and uselessly.

They hit the service road, duck into a culvert, and collapse, out of breath and trembling. Finn holds the thumb drive in his hand, squeezing it so hard it bites into his palm.

Ava's voice is a rasp. "Did you really see her?"

He nods, grinning like an idiot.

Ava shakes her head, then laughs, sharp and wild. "Let's hope she got the message."

Finn closes his eyes, already picturing Mara's face as she dives. He prays she'll be faster than the humans.

Below, Mara is already in motion.

The moment she sees Finn's signal, she knows what it means. The hunt is bigger than they guessed, and the time is shorter.

She flicks her tail, signaling to Lyla and Coral, and they cut left, deeper into the trench, aiming for the currents that run parallel to the shoreline. The water here is so cold it burns, but Mara is too busy thinking to notice. She replays Finn's gestures in her mind: the boats, the guards, the sweep of his arm along the cove.

"They're moving now," Mara says. "We have to beat them home."

Lyla's eyes are hard. "We'll make it."

Coral is ahead, guiding them through the silt cloud that rises with every stroke. The world is blurred and rushed; the only clear thing is the need to get to the city before the sweep starts.

At the halfway mark, the water tastes of blood and copper. Mara risks a glance up—already, the sound of boat engines is overhead, a low drone that shivers through the bones. She doubles her speed, ignoring the agony in her muscles.

The current fights her, but she's stronger, and in minutes they're at the outlying reef. Mara signals a halt, and all three tuck into a hollowed coral head, catching their breath.

"We have to warn everyone," Coral says.

Mara nods, but her mind is still on Finn and the terror in his eyes. "We will," she says. "But we'll need a plan."

Lyla's mouth is grim. "The elders won't listen."

"Then we make them," Mara says, voice like glass.

They slip through the city's shield wall, and the race is on.

At the top of the bluff, above the chaos, Blackwell stands with his second-in-command. He studies the map, tracing the dots with a battered finger.

The guard asks, "Where do we start?"

Blackwell grins, all teeth and cold light. He circles a spot on the southern cove, right where the trench meets the shelf.

"Here," he says. "We start at dawn."

He folds the map, tucks it into his jacket, and walks back to the dock.

The moon slips behind a cloud, and the world goes dark again.

But beneath the surface, the current is already shifting.

10 Riptide of Conflict

At twilight, the ocean is a field of knives. The lead activist boat slams over each crest with a hollow bang, the bow slapping foam so hard it leaves bruises. Finn stands at the prow, both hands white-knuckled on the safety line, binoculars up, horizon smudged by squalls. His stomach is a fistful of glass. The smell is diesel and cold salt, every breath searing his lungs.

"Contact," he says, voice clipped, radio pressed to his ear. "Visual on Blackwell's flagship. Bearing zero-seven-zero. Two miles and closing."

Behind, three other skiffs fan out in an imperfect wedge. Every boat is patched together from borrowed money, welded steel, and the kind of reckless hope only true believers keep alive. Each one carries a skeleton crew: a grad student with a night-vision scope, a retired fisherwoman with arms like a rope haul, an IT guy who quit his job the week before and hasn't stopped shaking since. Ava Chen is at the tiller, lips tight, eyes already bloodshot from the wind. She catches Finn's look, then thumbs her own radio.

"Copy. We've got movement on the deck. Looks like they're prepping nets."

Finn swings the binoculars left, past the horizon line, and finds the sleek black hull of Blackwell's main ship. It's ugly and beautiful, a fifty-footer disguised as a pleasure yacht, but Finn knows every inch of it. He has mapped the transponder logs, watched them from shore, and plotted their locations on charts. The name stenciled on the bow is a lie, but the men in red oilskins dragging gear across the deck are real.

"They're deploying nets," Finn says. "Get ready to document. All cameras live in thirty."

Ava nods, already signaling to the other boats. In the orange wash of dying light, every gesture is a semaphore.

Finn's heart pounds. He tries not to think of Mara—tries, but fails. He can't help picturing her in the water below, every muscle braced for the coming violence.

Below the hulls, Mara moves through a storm of shadow and refraction. The world here is thick with noise: the churn of twin engines, the metallic pulse of sonar, the endless hum of hungry water. She leads her strike group in a slow spiral, keeping low to the sediment, bodies nearly invisible against the gloom. To her left, Coral tracks perfectly, eyes up, every scale camouflaged to the silt. To her right, Notch flexes his hands, itching for the fight.

Mara surfaces just enough to taste the prop wash, then signals the others with a flick of her tail. She waits for a heartbeat—one, two, three—then calls up the current. It's like pulling on a wire wrapped through her ribs; the magic fights her, raw and uncut, but she's grown used to the pain. She pulls harder. The water beneath the poacher ship begins to twist.

She pushes the current up and left, then inverts it, creating a torqued eddy that climbs the keel and into the mouth of the net. The shift is so small, so delicate, that no human would notice. But Mara sees it: the net folds inward, then catches itself, the line going slack, the mesh tangling around its own dead weight.

She hears the men on deck cursing, the slap of boots as they scramble to fix the failure.

Notch grins, all teeth. "Again?"

"Again," Mara says. Her gills flare as she channels more force, muscles straining against the undertow.

Coral adds her power, and the water blooms with a faint, bioluminescent halo—visible only if you know to look for it. The second net snaps up, then hangs limp, the floats bobbing uselessly in the wake.

Mara lets go, gasping, the pressure in her chest so sharp she nearly blacks out.

Above, the deck explodes with shouting.

Blackwell stands at the starboard rail, hands behind his back, watching the water with a predator's patience. His first mate, a thickset man with a busted nose and the eyes of a cornered animal, hovers at his shoulder.

"They're here," Blackwell says, not even hiding the satisfaction. "Tell the men to ready the harpoons. Special gear, too."

The mate blinks. "You think it's—?"

"I know it is," Blackwell snaps. "We only lose gear like that when something's fighting back. And these aren't amateurs."

On his signal, the crew splits: two to the fore-and-aft harpoon guns, two more to the cages in the hold. Blackwell watches them work, then turns his gaze to the activist skiffs closing in from the north.

He smiles. The smile is old and practiced, all hunger and inevitability.

"Let them come," he murmurs.

Finn feels the first wave of victory when the net tangles. He sees it through the binoculars: the line jerks, then whips out of control, men on deck swearing and scrambling to reel it in—Ava whoops, a thin, desperate sound.

"Nice job, Mara," Finn whispers. Then, louder, to the radio: "First net compromised. Repeat, first net down. All teams, record everything—switch to backup if you have to."

The grad student in the boat behind holds up a camera, steady even as the skiff bucks in the chop. "We're getting it all," she says, eyes never leaving the viewfinder.

The second activist boat peels off, circling wide to get a profile shot of the black hull. The poachers ignore it, too busy with their own chaos. Finn sees the subsequent net rise, then snap back, the floats shivering like a live wire.

"They're losing it," Ava says, voice cracking over the engine noise. "You seeing the deck?"

Finn nods. He sees more: two of Blackwell's men moving to

the rail, hefting what look like small rocket-propelled harpoons.

"Shit. We've got harpoons on deck. All boats, maintain distance—repeat, stay outside effective range."

The grad student looks up, mouth a perfect O. "They're really going to shoot at us?"

"They'll shoot at anything," Finn says, teeth clenched. He keeps the binoculars glued to his face, refusing to miss a second.

He watches the harpoon men brace at the rail, aiming. The angle is off, but Finn knows the range is real.

"They're lining up," he says, radio trembling in his hand.

"Just get the footage," Ava says, knuckles white on the throttle.

Mara feels the shift in the water—a hard, fast pulse as the humans above ramp up their machinery. She recognizes the vibration of the net winch, the sharper bite of a winch cable under tension. She also feels the hum of something else, something colder. She risks a glance up: the black hull looms overhead, shadow slicing the twilight. She sees the harpoon gun's shadow, then the shape of a man leaning over the rail.

"Time to go," Mara says. "Pull back, slow. Keep the currents spinning—let them think they've got us."

Notch is already gone, kicking back toward deeper water. Coral lingers, as always, watching the net with a scientist's hunger.

Mara focuses. She lets the current go limp, then snaps it back with a hard jerk. The net twists on itself, binding in a double coil. She pushes until her vision blurs, then lets the spell collapse.

She surfaces, just her eyes above the water, and sees the harpoon splash ten meters to her left. The thing is brutal, a meter-long steel shaft, trailing a line of wire.

She ducks under again, heart galloping.

The next harpoon lands even closer.

Coral is waiting for her, wide-eyed, as Mara breaks the surface again.

"Did we win?" Coral whispers.

"We made them mad," Mara says. "That's enough for now."

On deck, Blackwell watches the patterns in the water. He sees the eddies, the way the foam breaks and resets in perfect intervals. He's seen this before—in the North Sea, in the straits where the old men talked of sea-witches. He knows what it means.

"They're toying with us," Blackwell says, voice like stone. "But they'll slip. They always do."

He signals the mate. "Deploy the cages. If they're close enough to tangle the nets, they're close enough to catch."

The mate yells down to the hold, and two more men scramble up, manhandling a pair of steel cages the size of bathtubs. The cages are baited—live mackerel, writhing and bleeding from the gills.

"Drop 'em!" the mate barks.

The cages plunge into the sea, lines spooling out behind. Blackwell tracks the splash, then the wake, watching for any sign of disturbance.

He waits. He's patient. He's always been patient.

Finn sees the cages go in, and for a second, he panics. "They're baiting them," he says, voice hoarse. "They're using live bait. Mara, if you're down there—"

He swears, wishing he had a way to reach her.

But Ava's got his back. "Keep filming. That's what we're here for."

He obeys, but every muscle is ready to spring.

The grad student gets it all: the bait cages, the harpoons, the faces of the men as they hurl weapons into the deep. She narrates in a breathless monotone: "Illegal netting… live mammal traps… multiple violations…" Her voice is flat, but her hands don't shake.

Finn focuses on the flagship, watching the hull for any sign of Mara or the other Merfolk.

The next wave of cages drops. The first hits the water, bobs, then jerks violently to one side.

"Holy shit," Finn says. "Something's got it."

He doesn't know if it's Mara or one of the others, but the bait cage lurches again, nearly wrenched out of the crewman's grip.

On deck, Blackwell shouts for a winch. The steel cable goes taut, then starts to unspool, the motor whining in protest.

Then, suddenly, the cage line goes slack, and the steel mesh disappears under the hull.

Finn holds his breath.

Ava's lips peel back in a wild smile. "They stole it," she says.

Finn nearly laughs, then raises the binoculars again. He scans the water, searching for the telltale flash of Mara's scales.

He sees it—just a shimmer, blue-green and gone in a heartbeat.

"They're okay," Finn whispers.

Mara drags the cage down with Coral and Notch flanking her. The thing is heavy, but together they can muscle it into the trench, out of reach of the poachers above. The bait fish is still thrashing, but Mara ignores it. She's more interested in the harpoon that splintered the sand ten feet behind her.

Notch is giddy. "You see how mad they got?"

Coral laughs, but Mara is too tired for jokes. She feels every pulse of pain in her arms, her tail. Her gills are raw, her vision swimming.

She signals the others to back off, then lingers at the edge of the shadow, watching the hull above.

"They'll try again," Mara says. "He won't stop until he gets what he wants."

Coral nods, all humor gone. "He never does."

They slip away, leaving the bait cage wedged in a rock crevice.

Mara looks back once and sees the black hull looming above like a storm.

On deck, Blackwell slams a fist on the rail. "They're learning," he says, not even bothering to hide the anger.

The mate is white-faced. "What now?"

Blackwell turns, eyes glittering. "Now we set the trap."

He signals two men to the stern, where a crate waits, chained to the deck. Inside: a net shot designed for whales, illegal in every country. Blackwell doesn't care.

He checks the lines himself, then signals to deploy.

Finn watches as the new weapon is brought on deck. It's huge, ugly, and bristling with hooks. The grad student gasps.

"They're really doing it," she says, voice shaking now.

"Keep filming," Finn says. "Every second. This is how we bring them down."

He wipes sweat from his brow, even as the air grows cold.

In the distance, lightning cracks, illuminating the entire bay.

For a second, Finn swears he sees shapes in the water, darting around the hulls—too fast, too elegant to be anything but Mara's people.

"We're going to win," Finn says, almost to himself.

Ava glances at him, eyebrows up.

He grins, though his hands won't stop shaking.

Below, Mara feels the charge in the water. A storm is coming, and not just the human kind.

She locks eyes with Coral, then with Notch. They're tired, but not broken.

"Ready?" Mara asks.

They nod; determination set in every line.

"Then let's give them hell," Mara says.

They vanish into the dark, ready for round two.

On deck, Blackwell's eyes never leave the sea. He knows they're out there, just beyond reach.

But tonight, he thinks, maybe they'll make a mistake.

He waits, and the storm rolls in.

The first harpoon misses Finn's boat by three feet, spearing the sea with a banshee shriek. It punches through the surface and vanishes, leaving a line in its wake. The next land is closer, showering the crew with cold spray. The grad student drops her camera, scrambles to the floor, then pops up with both hands raised in a victorious V. "You seeing this?" she shouts to no one in particular, face split by an adrenaline high.

Finn's heart hammers, but he refuses to duck. He plants his feet on the deck, braces against the pitching, and shouts into the radio: "All boats hold position! Keep recording! Do not engage!" His voice barely clears the wind.

Ava Chen grins, wild-eyed, steering them closer to Blackwell's flagship. "You want a better angle, Gallagher? Because I can put you in the captain's lap."

"Just get us the shot," Finn says, hating how much he means it.

He trains the binoculars on the poacher ship. Blackwell's men are running the deck like rats, loading the whale-net cannon. At the stern, the net launcher pivots, grinding in the wind, its ugly mouth pointed right at the activist flotilla.

Finn's palms go slick. He glances over the side, half hoping, half dreading that Mara is somewhere out there—then the sky cracks open with lightning, a white-hot rip so bright it blinds him.

For one second, the world is a snapshot: three skiffs, battered but unbroken, bearing down on the biggest predator in the ocean.

Below the surge, Mara's world is thunder and vertigo. The storm has shifted from threat to promise—the pressure in the water is dizzying, every sense stretched to its limit. Notch and Coral keep pace, but Mara knows they're close to the red. Every spell hurts more; every current they twist is harder to tame.

But they have to. Above, the humans are shooting to kill.

Mara signals: arms crossed, then open wide—maximum force. The others nod. They begin to circle, fast and tight, feeding power into the gyre. Mara closes her eyes, lets the magic spool through her bones. She imagines the current as a living thing: angry, hungry, hers to command.

She draws it up, higher, then lets it snap. The eddy slams into the hull of Blackwell's ship, rocking it hard enough to stagger two men overboard. The water pulses with blue-white light, visible even in the chaos.

Notch whoops, voice carrying through the bubbles. Coral's lips twist in pain, but she keeps the current alive.

Mara risks a glance upward. The poacher ship lists to starboard, the deck a riot of panicked men. She sees the whale-net launcher swing, then backfire as the current jams the mechanism. A metal shudder echoes through the water.

Mara feels it: the net is jammed. The trap is broken.

She grins, blood in her mouth, and signals the others: again.

On deck, Blackwell is apoplectic. He smashes a fist into the railing, then yells over the wind: "They're sabotaging us! The tide's all wrong—she's out there! Find her!"

The mate is pale, one hand clutching a wrench, the other locked white-knuckled on the rail. "The net's jammed, boss. The launcher's—"

"I don't care," Blackwell barks. "Ready the fallback." He pivots to the foredeck, where the real monster is waiting: a box marked with hazard tape and fitted with a remote detonator.

The mate hesitates, staring at the box as it might bite. "You're sure?"

Another pulse of lightning already lights Blackwell's face. "I said, do it!"

On the lead skiff, Finn feels the change in the wind before he sees it. The air goes electric, all hair and teeth, every wave suddenly taller and sharper. The other skiffs struggle to keep formation—one nearly capsizes, righted only by a panicked leap from the retired fisherwoman.

Ava Chen leans into the tiller, whooping with every impact. "Storm's kicking up!" she shouts.

Finn looks behind. The grad student is soaked but grinning, clutching the camera to her chest like a newborn. "We've got them!" she hollers, high and clear.

The poacher ship is less than a hundred yards away now. On the deck, Blackwell and his men are fighting the elements and each other. Finn sees, in a flash, the mate hauling the hazard-marked box to the rail.

"What is that?" Finn says, voice flat with dread.

Ava Chen's eyes go wide. "Looks like… fuck. Depth charge? Something homebrew."

Finn's stomach drops. "Everyone back off!" he screams into the radio. "Fall back now!"

The grad student freezes, then throws herself to the deck as the box sails from Blackwell's ship, trailing a white line behind it. It splashes down, floats for a second, then is swallowed by the next wave.

Below, Mara sees the box's shadow too late.

"Down!" she screams, but Notch and Coral are already diving, muscles screaming as they kick for the bottom.

The charge detonates. The world splits, the shockwave rolling through the water like a hand of God. Mara is thrown sideways, tumbling in a whirl of pain and pressure. She feels the magic flicker, almost break.

She claws her way to the surface, lungs burning. When she breaches, the sky is insane—a swirl of purple and black, lightning strobing the clouds.

The poacher ship lists heavily, engine howling as it tries to right itself.

Mara scans the water. Notch surfaces ten meters away, dazed but alive. Coral is nowhere.

"Coral?" Mara calls, voice hoarse.

Nothing.

Mara ducks under, forcing her body to move, even as every muscle wants to curl in on itself. She finds Coral curled at the base of a kelp anchor, blood streaming from her gills. Mara grabs her, hauls her up, then signals Notch to help.

They surface together, gasping, salt and blood stinging every wound.

On the deck of the lead skiff, Finn is a mess of guilt and terror. The grad student is shrieking in triumph, pointing to the listing poacher ship, but Finn can't look away from the bloody foam near the hull.

He scans for Mara, desperate. Then, in the trough of a wave, he sees her—red hair plastered to her skull, arms locked around a limp body.

Finn grabs the radio. "Mara! Are you okay? Mara?"

Static. Then, faintly, a voice: "We're here. Coral is hurt."
Finn turns to Ava. "We have to help them."

Ava's face is all nerves now. "How?"

Finn looks at the poacher ship, at the chaos on deck, and at his own tiny crew.

"We run cover," he says. "Get their attention. Give Mara a chance."

Ava nods, slams the throttle open.

The skiff roars toward the flagship, bouncing like a toy in the growing swell.

Blackwell sees the activist boat coming and grins. "Idiots," he mutters, then signals to the last harpoon crew.

The men aim, steadying themselves against the pitch. Blackwell gives the order: "Fire!"

The harpoon thunks out, slow but deadly, the line arcing toward the skiff.

Ava Jukes left, misses the tip by inches.

Finn stands, arms wide, daring them to shoot again.

Blackwell laughs, but his crew is already losing nerve. The ship's engine is choking, the net is useless, and the storm is only getting worse.

"Get the anchors up!" Blackwell shouts. "We're getting out of here!"

The mate scrambles to obey, but the anchor chain is jammed. It's caught on something below.

Finn grins, watching the panic. He raises the camera and films every second.

Below, Mara fights to keep Coral afloat—Notch circles, scanning the hull for a way through. The current is insane now—Mara feels it like a fever, the magic gone feral. She wonders if it's the storm or if something in her has snapped.

She treads water, cradling Coral, watching as the poacher ship tries to break free. The anchor chain is wedged into the trench, and the more the engine strains, the deeper the hull digs itself in.

Notch surfaces, yelling: "They're stuck!"

Mara smiles, then waves at the distant skiff.

On the lead skiff, Finn sees Mara's gesture and understands: the poacher ship isn't going anywhere.

He grabs the radio and shouts to the other boats. "They're stuck! Get closer! Document everything!"

The grad student cheers, camera rolling.

In the storm, the activist fleet closes in. They circle the crippled flagship, lights blazing, voices raised in triumph.
Ava Chen whoops, steering them within spitting distance of Blackwell's bow.

Finn stands, arms high, grinning at the man who tried to kill them.

"Smile for the camera, asshole!" the grad student shouts.

Blackwell's face is pure murder, but there's nothing he can do.

Mara floats in the chaos, Coral limp in her arms, Notch at her side. The storm is a living thing now—each wave taller, each wind sharper. Mara feels the current pulse, then ripples out to the horizon.

It's over, for now.

She hugs Coral tighter, then kicks back toward open water.

Above, the human boats wheel and cheer, lights cutting through the darkness.

Mara watches, and, for the first time, believes they might actually win.

On deck, Finn can barely hear the voices over the wind. He's soaked, shaking, half-mad with relief.

Ava Chen slaps him on the back, then yells in his ear. "We did it, Gallagher. We really did it."

Finn wants to laugh, but all he can think of is Mara, somewhere in the wild water, alive.

He looks up at the sky—at the impossible, electric blue of the storm.

He grins.

"Yeah," Finn says. "We did."

On Blackwell's deck, the mate clings to the rail, eyes wide with terror. The ship is dead in the water, battered and helpless.

Blackwell rages, but even he knows when he's lost.

He stares at the sea, daring it to finish him.

The sea stares back, alive and unbroken.

Below, Mara and the others slip away, unseen.

The storm covers their Retreat, and, for once, the current is on their side.

They come in perfect formation: six Merfolk, bodies silvered and hard, faces set in lines of absolute focus. At their head, Lyla's hair streams like a banner of war, every braid crisp in the flow. The team arranges itself in a wedge beneath the boiling surface, a formation honed in a hundred battles that Mara has only ever heard of. She feels their power before she sees it—the water goes thin and electric, every current a live wire.

Notch sees them first. "Uh, that's—" he starts, but Mara is already scanning the squad, searching for the leader's face.

Lyla doesn't look at her. She's busy, hands rising in a martial rhythm, each gesture mirrored perfectly by her squad. The water around them pulses, then starts to spiral. It's more than Current-Calling—it's Ocean's Breath, the real kind, the kind that bends tides for miles and smashes ships to powder.

Mara's heart crumples. She flashes a warning, desperate: "Activists above. Human allies. Do not engage."

But Lyla's eyes are locked on the poacher ship, expression unreadable in the blue gloom.

The ritual begins. Each Mer turns in time, arms slicing the water, tails carving concentric rings—the current builds. At first, it's just a tightening—the hulls above begin to yaw, ropes strain, the wind shifts against the wave. Then the magic deepens. The tide becomes a wall.

Mara tries to signal again, but Lyla is lost in the spell, hands woven tight with her squad's—the pressure ramps, a physical crush, like the trench is trying to collapse her chest. Mara looks at Coral—still dazed but awake, eyes wide—and at Notch, who is holding on to the kelp anchor for dear life.

Above, the poacher ship is dead in the water, the engine screaming as it tries to break free. The activist boats spin in the churn, bows bucking with every surge.

Mara realizes what's coming a split second before it hits.

On the skiff, Finn feels the world tip. The sea lifts them, then drops them, then lifts again, every time higher. The horizon is gone, replaced by a wall of black cloud and rain.

Ava Chen yells, "That's not weather! That's—" but the words vanish in the wind.

Finn sees it first: a wave, tall as a building, forming at the edge of the trench. It glows at the base, a faint blue line, then rises, higher, until it blocks out the last of the sky.

He grabs the radio, screams, "Retreat! All boats, go! Go now!"

But the engine sputters, choking on foam. The skiff pivots, caught in the riptide, spinning them sideways to the wall of water.

He sees Blackwell's ship, the men abandoning station, diving for the hatches or the open sea. The wave bears down, slow at first, then impossibly fast.

Finn locks eyes with the grad student, her face a white mask.

"Brace!" he shouts, then flings himself to the deck.

Below, the ritual is at its peak. Lyla and her squad pour every bit of power into the spiral, arms blurring, tails rigid as spears. Mara feels the magic clawing at her own bones, as if it's trying to drag her in. She knows she should run—should grab Coral, Notch, and bolt for the deep.

But Finn's boat is in the path.

Mara makes a choice. She lets go of Coral, who sinks, safe, into a kelp hollow. She hauls Notch after her, but then, at the last second, kicks free and shoots for the surface, arms open wide.

She rides the wave up, then banks right, reaching for Finn's skiff.

She calls up every scrap of current she has left, every shred of magic, and slams it sideways, building a bubble around the boat. It's suicide, but she does it anyway.

The wave hits.

It's a good hammer. Water crushes the poacher ship, flipping it like a toy. Blackwell vanishes, swallowed by spray. The activist skiffs are tossed, two of them rolling end over end, a third speared by the broken mast of the flagship.

Finn's skiff is right in the kill zone. Mara slams her arms together, focusing the bubble and holding it as tightly as she can.

For a second, the boat rides inside a hollow of calm, the world white and silent outside.

She sees Finn, eyes wide, staring at her through the membrane.

He sees her, too—hair wild, blood trailing from her cheek, mouth open in a scream.

The bubble holds.

Then, in the next heartbeat, the force is too much. The membrane shatters. The wave picks up the skiff and hurls it into the air.

Mara loses sight of Finn as the water closes over her head. She is spinning, out of control, her tail numb, her gills filled with shock and sand.

She lands hard in a pocket of foam, her body pinwheeling until she smacks into something solid.

She blinks, tries to orient. Above her, the sky is a roiling bruise, but there's a gap—a hole in the center where the wave broke. In that hole, Finn's boat is upright, battered, but somehow afloat.

Finn is there, clinging to the rail, eyes wild.

He sees her, and for a second, Mara thinks he's going to jump in after her.

She shakes her head, mouthing, "Stay," and lets herself sink.

On deck, Finn is barely alive. The boat is a wreck, with half its gear missing, and Ava Chen is slumped but still breathing. The grad student is curled in a ball, hands over her head.

He looks for the other boats—one is gone, the other upside down, men clinging to the hull.

Finn looks for the poacher ship. It's nowhere. Blackwell's flagship is gone, or sunk, or smashed to driftwood.

He laughs, a wild, giddy sound.

"Did you see that?" he yells to Ava, who groans.

"Yeah," she says, voice wrecked. "That was not… normal."

He looks over the side, searching for Mara.

She's there, barely, a flash of copper in the foam.

Their eyes meet.

He mouths, "You did it," but he's not sure she can see.

She blinks, then vanishes.

Below, Lyla and her squad drift, spent. The ritual has cost them—two are barely conscious, one is bleeding from the nose, Lyla herself pale and trembling.

Mara floats down to them, body broken but spirit alive.

Lyla meets her gaze, and for the first time, Mara sees fear in her sister's eyes.

"They survived," Mara says, voice shredded.

Lyla nods, then looks away.

"Was it worth it?" Mara asks.

Lyla doesn't answer.

They drift in silence, the current a lullaby.

On the battered skiff, Finn holds on, watching the sea for any sign of another attack. But the water is quiet now. The sky begins to clear. In the distance, emergency lights strobe from shore, and Finn knows the world is coming to see what happened.

He closes his eyes, thinking of Mara, of the impossible wall of water, of the bubble that held just long enough.

He wonders if she's alive.

He hopes.

In the deep, Mara lets herself sink, arms limp, tail barely moving. She feels the pain in every cell, but she also feels something new.

Hope.

She laughs, then coughs, and then finds Coral and Notch; together, they swim home.

Above, the sea is quiet.

Below, the world is changed.

The last thing Mara remembers is Finn's face, lit by storm, alive with the joy of survival.

She thinks she could get used to that.

11 Echoes of the Past

At the crest of the squall, the world is whiteout and frenzy. Mara rides the seam between two swells, salt in her throat, blood in her teeth, the taste of it a goad. Above, the night crackles with fake stars—flares, searchlights, the cold geometry of radar beams. The activist boats are boxed in, every channel mapped and mined by Blackwell's fleet, but Mara's eyes are only for the water: how it pitches, how it fights, how it could be bent.

A net hisses past, so close Mara feels the filaments rake her shoulder. She ducks, spins, and kicks hard for the shadow under Finn's battered skiff. Already the water is chummed with engine oil and brine, and the surface flashes with the lost things of humans—oars, a shattered phone, a child's lifejacket sliced to ribbons.

Mara sees Finn at the prow, mouth open, yelling at someone out of view. Even here, in this hell, she can read the panic in his limbs: he's seen the net, and he knows what happens next.

"Now!" she screams, though he cannot hear her. The command is to herself.

She channels the current, wrapping both hands around the cold. The magic is thin, fractious, like pulling on spider silk strung across a canyon, but she yanks anyway, and the current obliges. Water bends, upends the net, flips it back at the poacher boat with a snap so sharp it stings her jaw. The hull rocks, nearly capsizes, and the men above scramble for their lines.

But the price is immediate: Mara's arms lock with pain, a barbed wire down each nerve. She wants to stop, wants to breathe, but there's no time—more nets, more engines, the war above and below reaching a fever.

Her gills flutter, desperate. Something is wrong with the water here. Each taste is flat, muffled, as if the world is wrapped in wet cloth. Mara blinks, tries to refocus, but her vision tunnels. Her pulse in her head, a drumbeat that will not quit.

She shakes it off, claws for the surface, just as the next wave lifts the skiff above her. For one impossible second, she's face-to-face with Finn. His mouth forms her name. He reaches out—not to save her, but to warn: something behind, something worse.

Mara twists. The harpoon is a black, rubbery, blunt-tipped device, meant for capture, not killing. It grazes her flank, wraps twice, and yanks her back into the undertow. She fights, but the cord bites deep, slicing her scales, filling the water with ribbons of red.

She thrashes, calls the current, but it's like shouting in a dead room—no echo, no power. The magic is gone.

No, not gone. Shifted.

She feels it then: a vibration, low and perfect, running through her skull and spine. It is not hers. It is not even now.

She sees, all at once, a different ocean.

A vision, but not the fever kind, not the way dreams used to come to Mara in the nursery. This is colder, sharper, older.

She's on the edge of a cove that does not exist, rimmed in basalt and barnacle, a place to clean, too symmetrical. Above the water, fog churns, but there is a clearing—a perfect circle.

In that circle: shapes. At first, silhouettes, but then the vision clarifies—twelve figures, six Merfolk and six humans, arranged in alternating sequence around a stone altar. Mara recognizes none of them, but knows, with the certainty of magic, that she is seeing the beginning of something.

They do not speak aloud. Their words are pulse, rhythm, the high click of coral, the slow beat of a human heart. Hands reach, not to clasp, but to hold the same thing: a shell, dark with age, spiraled three times around, marked with a symbol that Mara's mind struggles to keep. It is not a Merfolk sign, not exactly. She tries to focus, and the vision closes on the etching: a spiral, intersected by three lines, each at a different angle. She's seen it before, in the city's oldest cave, but never understood what it meant.

Now she does. It is a map. Or a recipe.

The humans in the vision raise their hands, palms bloodied. The Merfolk respond, slashing their own arms open, letting the current take the blood. The two flows meet in the water, mingle, and vanish.

A voice—female, but not Mara's, not anyone she knows—rises above the wind: "A pact, and a cost. Both, or nothing."

The others echo, a fugue of words in languages Mara almost understands.

Then, the vision shifts.

Hands touch the altar—a light, blue, and alive arc from stone to flesh. The humans flinch, but do not pull away. The Merfolk do not flinch at all. The glow intensifies, climbs the arms of the twelve, spills out into the circle, and into the cove. The fog above splits, and Mara sees, for a heartbeat, the shape of the magic itself: a helix, woven from two kinds of power, each incomplete without the other.

This is how it began, she realizes. Not from one, but from two. Not isolation, but cooperation.

The twelve collapse, drained, but the magic remains, seeping into the water, carried outward by the tide.

The vision fractures, time skipping forward.

The cove again, now empty but for the stones. New hands etch new spirals, this time in coral, this time in the city Mara calls home. The lines are not perfect, not even close, but the memory endures. The pact is passed on, not in words, but in ritual, in blood.

It is not a gift. It is a debt.

Mara surfaces, gasping, the world of now snapping back like a broken bone set wrong. Her lungs burn, her gills flutter uselessly. The net is still around her, the poacher boat overhead, but all else is different.

She's adrift, caught in the dead zone behind the skiff. Oil film above, net below, and the world pinched between.

For a second, Mara doesn't know which way is up. The vision claws at her, more real than anything she's ever felt.

A hand, slick and desperate, grabs her arm. Not a human

hand—a Merfolk. Coral.

"You went still as death," Coral hisses, hauling Mara into the shadow of the hull.

Mara tries to speak, but only foam comes out. Coral slaps her hard across the face.

"Wake up, wake up, wake up!" Coral's voice is a mix of panic and brightness, raw and unfiltered.

Mara coughs, spits blood and water, then shudders to herself. "I saw… I saw—" She can't finish.

Coral's eyes are wild. "They're closing in. We have to go. Now."

Above, the poacher's floodlight knifes the water, a cone of blue-white that incinerates every shadow. Mara sees, to her left, Notch tangled in the edge of the net, clawing at the surface, silent.

Coral launches herself upward, grabs Notch, rips the net, and shoves him toward Mara. "Take him. I'll distract."

Before Mara can protest, Coral is gone, a flash of silver, a tail breaking the surface in a perfect arc. She breaches right under the light, thrashes, then dives again, drawing the searchers off.

Mara can barely move. Notch is heavier than he should be, or maybe she is just that weak. She calls up the current—no, she tries. But the magic is

The thinnest it's ever been, like trying to draw from a spring that's been poisoned.

The skiff above bucks, shedding splinters and voices. Mara feels the new net drop, senses its path without even looking—the way it closes like a hungry mouth, eager for anything living. Her head throbs with the afterimage of the spiral, the taste of stone and blood, the pact running like mercury through her veins. She can't focus. Not on the current, not on her body, not even on Coral's frantic grip.

Notch is deadweight, scales splayed, eyes glazed. The net cinches around him, pinning his arms to his sides. Mara grabs his jaw, forces it shut to keep the ocean from filling him. Coral is yelling at her—soundless, just fury and urgency—but Mara can't pull the words from the water.

She reaches for the current again, trying to bend the water around the net to loosen its grip. The magic comes, but it's fractured—half memory, half now. She feels her hands moving, but also the hands of the vision, a thousand years ago, carving the spiral into wet clay.

In the vision, the current flows like fire, wild and uncut. Here, it's sludge.

The net yanks Notch upward, toward the poacher's hull. He writhes, still alive, tail lashing in panic. Mara kicks after, ignoring the riptide in her head, and bites down on the net's frayed edge. The taste is oil and human sweat and ancient wrongness, but she tears anyway, teeth grinding through nylon.

The pain is immediate. The net is laced with something—salt? Metal? It bites her gums, sends a pulse of heat through her brain. For a moment, she is twelve, in the nursery, learning how to strip a fish from its bones. For a moment, she is the old woman in the vision, cutting her palm open for the ritual, watching her blood dissolve in the tide.

Coral grabs the net too, and together they shred it, muscle and rage against the inevitability of nylon. Notch falls, limp, and Mara wraps him with one arm, holding his head above the water.

The poacher above yells, "Got one!" and the boat lurches, pulling the net up so fast it slices a groove into Mara's tail. She lets go, lets Notch go, and is almost sucked up with the net herself. Coral hauls her sideways, just in time, into the shadow under the hull.

Mara's brain is static. For a second, she thinks she sees the vision again: the circle of twelve, but now their faces are masks—Finn, Coral, Lyla, even Blackwell, the poacher, all locked in the same spiral. She shakes it off. The only real thing is Coral, shoving her forward, deeper into the black.

"Swim!" Coral screams. "We have to get clear!"

But Mara can't. Her limbs are stone; her head packed with voices. The vision is everywhere now—overlaying the fight, the pain, the desperate need to breathe. She gasps for water, but her gills don't work right; every gulp is thinner, drier, edged with the sharp ache of memory.

The world shrinks to Coral's hand, gripping her wrist, and the tunnel ahead, lined with the debris of battle: scales, net fragments, the snapped blade of a harpoon.

Coral drags her, not caring about the blood trail, not caring about anything but escape. Behind the water, the scene is alive with searchlights and the metallic snarl of propellers. Above, shouts in a human voice: "Lost the net! They're running!"

Mara wants to answer, to say she can't run, that she is split in two and cannot be put back together. But her mouth is full of water, and her tongue is thick with the taste of the altar, the pact, the spiral carved into her bones.

They burst from the hull's shadow and into the wild, open water. The storm is worse now, every wave a living wall. The activist boats are scattered, some upright, some overturned, all moving away from the center of the trap.

Mara sees Finn's skiff, the blue hull battered but afloat. He's still at the prow, bleeding from the head, eyes wild. He's shouting into the wind, but the words are for her, she knows. Even here, even now.

Coral tugs Mara downward, into the safety of the trench. They spiral lower, away from the reach of nets, away from the echo of the harpoons. Mara lets herself be pulled. She's got nothing left.

At the bottom, Coral finally lets go. She circles, panting, then grabs Mara by the chin.

"What happened?" Coral demands. "You were gone. Like you left your body. I thought you were dead!"

Mara blinks slowly, unsure if she's even real. "It was… old. A memory, not mine. Humans and Merfolk, together. A pact. The beginning."

Coral shakes her head, furious. "Who cares? We almost died!"

Mara wants to explain, wants to say that everything just changed, that the magic isn't just theirs, never was. But the words won't come.

Notch floats nearby, coughing, alive but barely. Coral moves to him, checks his eyes, his gills, his wrists. "Can you swim?" she asks, softer now.

Notch nods, but his body doesn't move. Coral sighs, tucks his arm over her shoulder, and kicks for the side tunnel, toward home.

Mara lingers, staring upward. The water above is chaos, the war still raging, but here in the dark, it's quiet. She lets the current carry her, neither fighting nor thinking. Her head is a spiral, her future a debt.

She looks at her hands. They are shaking, but not from fear.

From knowing.

Above, the battle goes on, but Mara's world has changed. Every pulse, every rush of current, is a reminder: the magic is not a birthright. It's a bargain. And it's been broken, over and over, for centuries.

She wonders what Finn would say if she told him. If he would still see her as impossible, or just as another animal, desperate to survive.

The thought stings. So, she doesn't dwell.

She follows Coral and Notch into the blue dark, away from the blood and oil.

But the vision stays, coiled in her chest, whispering: a pact, and a cost. Both, or nothing.

The current is thin; the magic is even thinner. But for now, it will have to be enough.

She swims.

Finn wedges himself into the last dry corner of the skiff's tiny cabin. Outside, the world is murder: steel hooks, spotlights, the juddering slap of waves against fiberglass. Inside, the air is a mix of boiled sweat and battery acid, every surface dripping. Radio chatter is a monotone scream, half the words bled out by static.

He checks the hatch. Still secure, though the last harpoon nearly sheared it clean off. The impact left a spiderweb of cracks in the forward port, each one allowing saltwater to dribble into the footwell. Finn's boots squelch with every shift, but he can't care—not with the timer running out, not with what's on the screen in front of him.

The tablet flickers between two feeds. Left: live deck cam, the view from the rail. Ava Chen is out there, hunched behind the console, teeth bared, knuckles white. Every ten seconds, the hull shudders, and Finn watches, helpless, as the poacher's circle for another run. Right: the archive, a half-terabyte of old scans and digitized logs, a project he started back when this was just activism and not open war. He scrolls, fingers slipping, eyes jumping from frame to frame.

It's not just a distraction. It's desperation.

Last night, before the storm, Mara handed him a shard of bone. "Memory stick," she joked, but her eyes were all business. "My people kept their history in song. This is as close as we get." He'd run it through every test he had, but the patterns made no sense—lines and curves, circles within circles, nothing even a cryptologist could love. But now, with the city on the line, he has to make it mean something.

The next volley of hooks hits. The boat lists, then rights itself, water sloshing over Finn's shins. He braces the tablet against his knee, ignoring the spray.

He drags two fingers down the archive, skipping to the folder flagged "Myth/Precontact." It's a mess: 18th-century ship logs, missionary fever-dreams, a few crumpled field notes from an archeologist who died chasing a hoax. He scans, discards, scans again.

One log catches his eye: 1723, coastal Oregon, Braque Judith Ann, Captain J. Herrera. Finn has read it a dozen times, but now he sees what he missed.

"...Third night, the water took on a queer light. Many of the men saw it and grew afraid. I took watch with the first mate, and at 3 bells, I heard the sound—high, shrill, yet with a sweetness. Soon after, the sea grew calm, and we passed the shoals without further loss. The crew called it the mercy of the 'ocean's children,' and I did not gainsay them."

Finn expands the margin, looks for the symbol that Captain Herrera sketched. There it is: spiral, three lines, a crude version but unmistakable. His pulse stutters. He calls up the photo Mara gave him last week—a shot of the spiral etched into the shell of a deepwater crab, the edges filed by someone with hands, not claws.

It's the same: different eras, different hands, same message.

He scrolls back to the log, breath quickening.

"...The local tribes speak of a 'pact' made in the old days, when the sea was wild, and ships were few. The pact was simple: we honor them, and they protect us from the rages of the water. To break this promise is to risk doom, not by storm, but by the cold cunning of those who swim below. Their mark is the spiral, with three points. One for us, one for them, one for the tide itself."

Finn fumbles for the following file—scans of ruins from a cliffside cave, the one Mara mapped for him. The spiral is there, too, only now it's ringed by glyphs Finn can't read. He tries to remember: when Mara first showed him the pattern, she called it "the wound that never healed." Said it was the oldest thing her people remembered.

The pattern is everywhere. All up and down the coast, anywhere humans and Merfolk ever crossed paths.

The implication slams through Finn, hot and mean: Mara's people didn't just hide. They made peace. They allied. And now, after centuries, it's coming undone.

His eyes flick to the deck cam. The activist boats are scattered, some limping, others lost. The poachers have split into three teams, driving their prey into tighter and tighter rings. Finn sees one of the skiffs—a blue one, maybe Lyla's—take a hit to the engine, then disappear behind a wall of spray.

He has to warn Mara. Not just about the trap, but about the old story, the one no one dared remember.

The radio crackles. Ava's voice: "Finn, you alive in there?"

He thumbs the mic. "Yeah. Please patch me into broadcast. Full power."

She laughs, high and reckless. "You want to call for help? In this mess?"

"No help," Finn says. "Just someone who'll listen."

Ava makes it happen. In seconds, every boat, every waterproof comm on the bay, gets its signal. Finn doesn't waste time.

"This is Finn Gallagher. I need Mara Ondine. Mara, if you're out there, listen to me. I've got something you need to see. There was a pact. Your people and ours. It was real. It's still real. The spiral—" He stops, hating the tremor in his voice. "It's a contract. If we break it, everyone loses."

He waits. No reply. Not even static.

Another harpoon hits, closer this time. The tablet jolts, almost lost to the bilge. Finn scrabbles for it, hands shaking, and pulls up the image. He holds it up to the cabin camera, hoping the signal gets through the jamming. "You showed me the spiral. I found it in the human records. They match. I think the magic—your magic—depends on both sides keeping the promise. That's why it's failing. That's why they want to catch you."

He lets the words hang, the silence as thick as blood.

Ava comes back on, voice brittle. "You done with your radio love letter? Because we've got a hull breach."

"Almost done," Finn says.

He shoves the tablet into a waterproof case and buckles it to his vest. He checks the window—outside, the enemy boats are almost on top of them, three black points on the angry blue.

He clutches the radio one last time. "Mara, please. If you can hear me, don't fight alone. I think there's another way."

Ava yells, "Brace!"

The next impact flips the skiff. The cabin goes dark, then cold. Finn's head hits the ceiling, then the water hits his face. He holds the radio in one hand, the tablet in the other, and kicks for the surface.

When he breaches, the world is on fire—flares, burning fuel, the sound of humans and the ocean at war. He sees the shore, impossibly far.

He tucks the tablet close to his heart and swims.

The surface is a minefield—boats, nets, broken hulls, stains of oil blooming in rainbow slicks. Mara breaks through, not to breathe, but to see. She expects the white-hot chaos of battle, the men screaming, the rotors and ropes, but not the sight of Finn, clinging to the gunwale of an overturned skiff, his face cut and bleeding and alive with purpose.

He sees her, too. For a split second, the war around them fades.

Mara cups her hands and calls, voice breaking through the wind: "There was a pact!"

Finn laughs, raw and helpless, then waves the waterproof case above his head. "I know! They called it the Covenant of Tides!"

Mara blinks. For a second, it's as if she's still in the vision, trapped in that blue-lit cave, Finn's voice echoing through the stone. But then a harpoon strikes the water between them, sending up a geyser of spray. She dives, reflexes, and memory in perfect sync.

Below, everything is slower. The pain in her arms, the ache in her gills, even the panic, is muted by the current. She replays Finn's words—Covenant of Tides, the spiral with three points, one for us, one for them, one for the tide itself.

She surfaces again, closer to his boat, dodging the sweep of a net. "If it's real," she shouts, "then it can be fixed. It can be shared."

Finn nods, clutching the case, already paddling one-armed for the next intact skiff. "But if they find out—" He jerks his chin at the nearest poacher vessel, Blackwell himself at the helm, surveying the carnage.

Mara's jaw tightens. "We keep it safe. We keep it secret. Until it's strong enough for everyone."

Another volley of harpoons, closer this time. Finn ducks, then stands again, teeth bared. "What do we do?"

Mara bares her own. "We finish what they started."

She flicks her tail, sending a shockwave through the water. She feels the magic, not as a song but as a conversation—her pulse, Finn's, the spiral, the tide. The old pact still resonates beneath the surface, fragile yet real.

She turns to Finn, points at the poacher ship. "Draw them in," she says. "Make them chase you. I'll break the trap."

Finn grins, eyes shining. "I thought you'd never ask."

He scrambles up the nearest hull, signals to Ava (still alive, by some miracle) and the grad student (filming, of course), and together they aim the battered skiff right at the flagship.

Blackwell sees them, roars a command. Three boats peel off and converge on Finn and the activists. Mara tastes the adrenaline spike in the water, the ripple of engines, the smell of fear. It is exquisite.

She dives deep and gathers the current to her. This time, it comes easier—like the spiral, once broken, is now mending itself, feeding on the blood and sweat of the present.

She rides the surge, up and up, then breaks the surface in the heart of the trap. She is visible, exposed, daring every hunter to see her.

Blackwell does. He leans over the rail, shotgun raised. "You're not getting away," he spits, the words almost lost in the storm.

Mara doesn't bother to answer. She slams her arms together, calls the current with every ounce of power left. The water bucks, then rises—an impossible wall, not a wave but a fist.

The poacher ships are too close, too hungry. They can't turn it in on time.

The wave collapses, slamming all three into the hull of the flagship. Men are thrown, nets tangle in the propellers, a harpoon gun snaps free and sails into the air, spinning like a child's toy.

Finn's skiff rides the crest, barely dodging the carnage, then slams into the side of the disabled vessel. Ava is up first, grabbing the rail and swinging herself aboard. Finn is right behind, one hand clutching the case, the other the spiral tattooed on his wrist.

Mara sees him, even though the chaos, and knows: the pact is working.

She dives again, circles the flagship, and finds Coral and Notch at the stern, hiding in the wake. Both are battered, but alive.

"Did you see?" Coral gasps, eyes huge. "You did that?"

Mara wants to deny it, wants to say it was all of them, but the truth is sweeter: "We all did."

She hears Notch laugh, delirious. "Let's do it again."

Mara nods, already gathering the current. Above, the deck is a riot—activists and poachers locked in desperate grappling, Finn and Ava fighting for the wheelhouse, Blackwell bellowing threats and firing into the sky.

But the tide has turned. The magic is back, wild and sharp, laced through every drop of water.

Mara feels Finn's heartbeat, even at this distance. She senses his resolve, the way the old pact is not just history, but hope.

She remembers the vision: the twelve, the circle, the spiral etched in flesh and stone. She wonders how many centuries it took to forget and how many seconds it took to remember.

She surfaces one last time, locks eyes with Finn across the broken deck.

He smiles, and this time, it's not just a matter of survival. It's a possibility.

Mara grins back, then vanishes, already planning the next move.

On the flagship, Finn wedges himself in the corner of the shattered cabin, radio at his mouth.

He doesn't need to call Mara this time. She's already listening.

"We have the proof," he says, voice raw and shaking. "It's all here."

Ava punches his arm, beaming. "Let's finish this."

Finn tucks the case under his arm and steps out onto the ruined deck.

Below, the ocean pulses, the spiral reborn, ready to write a new chapter in its history.

12 Captain's Log

The magic is wrong.

Mara tries to pull a current, but it whips back on itself, fracturing in her hands like splintered glass. Notch is dead weight against her, his tail trailing, limp. Above, the poacher's light splits the water into acid columns. The searchers have stopped even pretending to hunt fish; every harpoon, every net, every guttural curse is meant for her.

She's never felt the sea like this: thick, unwilling. Every ripple is a labor, each movement spools out at half-speed, then snaps back double-hard. Her gills can't keep up, lungs burning with the sour taste of diesel and something more bitter—fear.

Another net plunges down, stinking of blood and brine, and Mara ducks, pulling Notch under. She tries again, reaches for the thread of power, and this time—

Everything stops.

Her body goes cold, then rigid, as if every cell is being flash-frozen from the inside. The pain is clean, perfect, not even pain but absence, an instant where she exists only as a shadow behind her own eyes. Her gills flare, fluttering so fast they blur; her pupils dilate and flatten to nothing. The world silvers out. Every sound is gone, replaced by a deep, slow hum—the kind that lives in the marrow of old stones, or the blackest part of the trench.

Her hands clutch Notch, but she can't feel him.

A pulse starts in her jaw, moves through her skull, then down her spine to the tip of her tail. Each vertebra shudders in sequence, then goes slack. She's aware of the battle, distantly, as if watching it through a wall of clouded glass. The skiff above. Blackwell's voice, a blade of command. A body plunging into the sea and never resurfacing.

But then even that is gone, burned away by the white light behind her eyes.

She's somewhere else.

It's not a dream—dreams are colored by hunger, by wanting. This is raw and precise; a memory recorded in the bones of the ocean.

She is on a shore that should not exist. The stone is black, razor-sharp, spined with rows of glassy shells. The tide is low, every hollow brimming with life she has never seen—anemones the color of bruised fruit, barnacles like fused teeth, crabs so translucent they're made of water.

A wind pushes in off the sea, carrying the smell of something alive and wild, not the rot of the modern shallows but the shock of new blood.

And there are shapes on the strand.

At first, Mara thinks they are just driftwood, washed up and tangled in the weeds. But then the vision snaps into focus: twelve figures, standing in a loose ring at the edge of the surf. Six are Merfolk, tall and strange, skin so dark it shimmers blue, hair woven in heavy ropes down their backs. They stand upright, uncoiled, each with hands folded at the breast.

The other six are human.

No, not quite. Not like Finn, not like any above-dweller Mara has ever seen. These humans are lean, bones like cables, eyes black as obsidian. They wear only scraps of kelp; their arms are scored with lines that glow faintly under the moonlight.

The two tribes face each other in silence.

Between them, set on a stone plinth, is the shell.

It is enormous, wider than Mara's torso, carved in three spirals, each marked by a set of notches. The surface is stained with colors Mara cannot name—red and gold and something that hums violet at the edge of vision. It pulses, faintly, like a living heart.

A human steps forward. She is old, older than the stones, her hair a mat of salt and shadow. She carries a knife made from a fish's jawbone.

The lead Mer—he is unscarred, unblinking, his scales etched in runes—steps forward as well. His hands are empty.

The ritual begins.

Mara can feel the words, though no one speaks. The language is current, not sound: pulses of pressure, variations in salinity, heat, and cold layered in meaning. She is not hearing so much as remembering, as if her own body had once known this ritual and forgotten it for a thousand years.

The human woman slices her palm with the blade made from a jawbone. The blood is thick and black, welling up before dripping into the shell's mouth. The Mer does the same, but instead of blood, his wound leaks a clear, blue ichor that fizzes as it hits air.

The shell drinks both.

The rest of the twelve come forward, one by one, cutting and bleeding into the spiral. Each offering is different—some drip, some pour, some barely trickle, but the shell never overflows. It absorbs.

When the last has given, the ring tightens. The twelve form a chain, hand to hand, alternating human and Merfolk. It looks awkward at first, but then Mara sees the magic at work—each grip lines up so the cuts are aligned, so the blood and ichor run together, mixing on the skin before falling to the sand.

The tide comes in slowly and deliberately. It laps at their feet, then their calves, then their waists.

When the water reaches the shell, it reacts.

A light, pale at first, but growing. The shell glows from within, then spills out a thread of energy that wraps around the chain of twelve. Where it touches, the skin fuses, the wounds seal, and a lattice of color spreads across their bodies, spreading in patterns of spiral and net.

The magic is not gentle.

Mara feels the pressure intensify, hard enough to crush bones. She's not in her own body, but it still hurts. The spell is a circuit, the kind that completes only at terrible cost. She feels her teeth crack, her gills close, her lungs empty.

The vision tilts.

The humans and Merfolk begin to sing—not with voice, but with the resonance of their joined bodies. The hum Mara heard in the water before is now a million times louder, a symphony of suffering and purpose. Each note is a fragment of a vow: To live. To endure. To protect the balance.

Mara wants to scream, but the spell will not allow it.

Instead, she is pulled into the spiral. She watches as the magic etches itself into the bones of every participant, inscribing the pattern that will be inherited by all their descendants—human and Mer alike.

The magic is passed. The pact is sealed.

Mara's eyes snap open in the real world, but the vision is not done.

She flails in the water, Notch still limp in her grip, but her limbs move without direction. The spell is running her now, body a passenger in its own skin.

She looks up, and the sky is wrong—split by a rift, white lightning branching into the bone of the clouds. She looks down, and the sea floor is alive with the memory of a thousand years. Every grain of sand, every shell fragment, hums with the same ancient resonance.

Blackwell's ship is just above, its hull blocking out the stars. Harpoons crack the surface, trailing lines that glitter with embedded steel. A net lands, then jerks away as Mara—no, the thing inside Mara—lashes out with a current so dense it fuses the net into a single clump of metal.

The pain is extraordinary.

She barely feels Notch as he's wrenched from her grip. Her hands are claws now, raking through the water, pulling up something profound and angry from the trench below.

The magic is not under control. It is not hers at all.

She remembers the vision—the pact, the spiral shell, the blood.

Her own blood is everywhere now, dissolving into the water as she loses scales, as the net shreds her arms. But the blood is essential. The blood is part of the spell.

She feels the other Merfolk nearby—Coral, Lyla, even the broken ones from the city. Their signatures are all around, a constellation of kin. The magic sees them, claims them, wraps them in its reach.

She opens her mouth, and a scream comes out.

But it is not a scream. It is the chord from the vision, the spell made flesh. It rattles the ships' hulls, boils the surface, turns the water between the boats into a single massive gyre.

Above, Blackwell is screaming, too, but it is nothing compared to Mara.

The magic wants release.

She gives it.

The vision doubles, then splits.

She is back on the ancient shore, but this time the pact is breaking. Humans are older, more complicated; their blood is less willing. The Merfolk are fewer, their lines thin and fractured. The spiral shell is cracked. Instead of joining, the two lines stand apart, hands unclasped, wounds unhealed.

The water is rising, eating the shore. The sky is darker, shot through with storms.

The magic is still there, but it is unbalanced, cycling in tight, destructive loops. It wants to find the other half. It needs it.

Mara feels herself dissolving.

She reaches, desperate, for the thread that joins her to Finn. She does not know if he is alive, if he can hear, but she calls anyway, pushing every scrap of her identity into the scream.

For a second, she thinks she feels him—a warmth, a pressure in her palm, as if he were reaching back.

The vision flickers, then freezes.

Mara is back in her body.

She is deep below the boats, Notch beside her, barely conscious. The water is dark, but she can see every molecule, every current, every fleck of poison. Her hands are bleeding, but her scales have grown back thicker, harder. Her gills are wide open, pulling in everything.

She realizes: The magic is not for her alone. It never was.

She sees the pattern, the spiral. She understands the cost.

The city is in danger, but so is the world above. The only hope is to finish the pact, to heal what broke. To bring the two halves together again.

She must find Finn. She must bring the shell.

And she must survive.

Above, the battle still rages, but the magic has changed the rules.

Every net thrown is tangled, every harpoon warped by impossible currents. The poacher boats are being spun, one by one, into the teeth of the storm. Blackwell's flagship founders, then, are swallowed by a wave as high as the cliffs.

The activist skiffs hold, battered but upright, riding the edge of the whirlpool.

At the center, Mara floats, neither dead nor quite alive, holding the vision's memory in her mind.

She opens her mouth and, for the first time, speaks the words of the ancient language.

The world shudders.

And the vision begins again.

The vision resets, but everything is altered.

Mara floats in a time-lagged lagoon, the world painted with ancient sun and low tide. The air is thick with bird calls and the salt sting of rotting fish, but underneath is a constant undertone: the living current, the aftershock of the pact. All around, the shoreline crawls with humans, dozens this time, and on the far reef, Merfolk ring the drop-off, poised, watching.

The memory is precise, needle-sharp. Mara feels the weight of her own limbs again, but they are not quite hers. She is one of the blue-black Merfolk, standing at the tide line, hands slick with blood. The spiral shell sits between her feet, humming, half-buried in sand and a tangle of eelgrass.

A group of human children approaches, wary, each bearing a piece of driftwood or carved bone. Their leader is a boy; his face painted with the spiral in red ochre. He kneels in the surf, lays the driftwood before the shell, and waits.

From behind, an elder Mer nudges Mara forward. She stoops, takes the wood, and presses it to the mouth of the spiral. The shell vibrates, then releases a thin thread of energy, burning a pattern into the surface of the driftwood—a triple loop, perfect, glowing for a moment before fading into scar.

The boy picks it up and holds it high. Around him, the humans shout, a sound like gulls fighting over a kill.

Mara recognizes the ritual: it is a gift, but also a warning. The spiral is both map and ward, a sigil to mark those who know and those who should never try to understand.

The Merfolk begin the lesson.

They gather at the mouth of the cove, forming a chain, hands locked. On cue, the humans enter the water, their strokes clumsy, desperate. The Merfolk teach by doing: how to read the current, how to ride the surge, how to twist the undertow for speed or safety. The children watch, then mimic, their bodies adapting as their fear turns to hunger.

A tide of learning, literal and brutal. Those who fail are pulled under, spat out onto the rocks, shivering and blue. The ones who survive are marked—on the wrist, on the shoulder, behind the ear—with the spiral, inked in fishbone or rubbed into the skin with crushed shell.

The lessons are not gentle. Every mistake costs blood. But the partnership holds, season after season.

The vision jumps: years, decades, maybe more.

The shoreline changes. New shells, new faces. Humans build houses from the bones of whales, stringing the reefs with woven lines. The Merfolk watch, warier now, fewer in number.

The humans have learned the rudiments of Tideweaving—not the full force, but enough to nudge the currents, enough to cheat death when the storms come. They use it to fish, to travel, to conquer. At first, this is the pact. They protect the Merfolk in return, guard the shallows from other tribes, and build stone markers with the spiral shell chiseled deep.

But the magic is thin, distant. Each new generation forgets more. The rituals become pageant, then rumor, then nothing at all.

In the last flicker of the vision, Mara sees the humans standing on the same shore, but now they are armed with steel, and their eyes are empty. They have tattooed the spiral on their bodies, but do not remember why. The pact is broken. The shell is gone, buried, stolen, or lost to the depths.

The Merfolk are shadows now, retreating into the trench, vanishing from history. The humans laugh and set fire to the tide line.

The vision breaks. Mara's body spasms, tail flaring wide, every scale flashing from jade to silver and back. The cold rushes in, and for a second, she thinks she's drowning, but then her gills snap open, gulping the water in greedy, shuddering lungfuls.

She floats in the black, Notch clutched against her, but the world is wrong, too bright and too fast. Her thoughts fragment, then slam together: the ancient shore, the spiral, the teaching, the loss.

She understands now. The magic is not heritage. It is an obligation; a chain built from memory and muscle and will. It is not meant to be hoarded. It is intended to be shared—if not with the humans, then with someone, anyone, before it dies in the dark.

Above, the water roils. Every pulse is a memory, every current an echo of the pact.

Mara's tail trembles. The colors along her sides burn with new clarity. The pain is everywhere, but it's the pain of birth, not death.

She gasps, hard enough to pop the scars on her lips.

The choice is obvious. She can try to hide this knowledge, keep her people safe for one more desperate generation. Or she can wield it, weaponize it, risk everything on a single hope: that someone—maybe Finn, maybe the next human, maybe some as-yet-unborn freak—will see the pattern, and try to make it whole again.

She stares at the water above, and for the first time, does not feel fear.

Just the weight of the tide, pulling her forward.

When she finally looks at Notch, he is awake, eyes wide with terror and awe.

"Did you see?" he whispers. "Did you see what I saw?"

Mara nods.

His voice is broken, but he continues to speak. "We're not what they think we are. We're not even what we think we are."

"We're a warning," Mara says.

Notch laughs, a wild, bitter sound. "Or a chance."

Mara thinks of the spiral, the blood, the pact.

"We'll see," she says.

And then she rises, dragging Notch with her, ready to face whatever storm is left.

Across the battered curve of the continent, under rain that never quite stops, Finn Gallagher is losing his mind.

He hasn't left the boathouse lab in two days. The interior is a labyrinth of unwashed mugs, Red Bull cans, stacks of weathered notebooks, and the remains of at least one sacrificed pizza. The research equipment takes up every flat surface—seawater samplers, dissected hard drives, and a suite of laptops daisy-chained to a battered generator and taped to every inch of wall: sonar printouts, hand-sketched bathymetry, color photocopies of sixteenth-century maps—Finn's own handwriting runs across every page, sometimes legible, sometimes a fevered scrawl.

He's supposed to be sleeping. Instead, he's hunched over the biggest table, fingers tracing the grain of a parchment so old it sheds dust with every touch.

The document is a captain's log from 1712, the script precise and terrified. Finn's lips move as he reads aloud, each word etched into his brain: "On the third day, the current shifted as if by unseen hands…"

The following line: "We spied blue women among the kelp, their song bending the water. None would believe this, but my men were changed, and the nets came back full for the first time in weeks."

The illustration beside it is crude, but the anatomy is impossible to mistake: the elongated tail, the triple row of gills, the hair streaming like kelp. Finn flips to the next page and the next. Each new log, each scrap of testimony, is more frenzied, more precise. The phenomenon repeats: strange tides, the spiral shell, and always the warning, buried in the footnotes.

He cross-references everything. On a laptop screen, he has a half-translated transcription from a Basque whaler's diary, with the relevant passages highlighted in migraine-yellow. The phrases are similar: "a covenant in the surf," "blood and salt joined," "the mark that wards or calls." Another file is a scan of a Russian folk tale, line-edited by a folklorist who was unfamiliar with the text.

Finn drinks it in, barely blinking.

He's looking for the spiral.

Every witness, every log, every supposed hallucination—it's there. Sometimes carved into a masthead, sometimes tattooed on a sailor's arm. Once, in a Jesuit missionary's diary, it appears as a diagram—a double spiral, one side marked with human faces, the other with "sirens" that resemble Mara's people suspiciously.

Finn's hands start to shake, so he makes a fist and presses it hard against the table.

"Focus," he mutters. "Don't lose it now."

He lines up the papers, matching dates, tides, and places. The pattern is almost too clean: wherever humans and Merfolk meet, the spiral appears, sometimes as a blessing, sometimes as a curse. In every instance, the appearance of the symbol precedes a period of calm, then catastrophe.

He tries to ignore the implication.

Instead, he pulls up the scanned copy of Mara's old note. The first thing she ever gave him—a scrap torn from a kelp wrapper, the spiral drawn in squid ink.

She called it "Memory of the Sea." Said it was both a warning and a guide.

He studies the spiral, overlays it with the captain's log, the folk-tale diagram, the tattoo. The geometry is exact, down to the angle of each curve. There's no way it's random.

Finn flips to the back of the log. There, hidden in the gutter, is a woodcut illustration he must have missed a dozen times. Two groups—one human, one Merfolk—stand at the edge of the tide, joined by a chain of hands, bleeding into a spiral-shaped bowl. The sea behind them is alive with something Finn cannot name, but the implication is clear: the pact is binding, and it is older than the story itself.

His heart hammers. He thinks of Mara, of the way she sometimes stares at him like she's measuring the distance between galaxies, of how her voice always sounds half-drowned in sorrow.

He thinks of the activists, the poachers, the scientists who mocked him.

"It wasn't just legends," Finn whispers, and the words hang in the air, heavy as lead.

He leans back, fingers raking through his hair. For a second, he sits there, breathing in the sour reek of desperation and old coffee.

Then he stands, shoves every crucial page into a waterproof satchel, and slings it over his shoulder.

Outside, the rain is picking up. Lightning shivers over the bay.

Finn looks at the spiral, burned into the back of his retina, and knows what he has to do.

He heads for the docks, never once looking back.

He does not know that, at this exact moment, Mara is rising through the black water, vision of the pact burning in her mind. He does not know that she, too, has seen the future and the past collapse together, and that she is coming for him, ready or not.

But as Finn limps through the night, eyes fixed on the horizon, some part of him senses the current pulling tighter.

The spiral is closing, and this time, he's part of it.

13 Betrayal in the Ranks

The shallows are not safe, but Mara takes the risk. She hovers under the kelp's lacework, breath slowed to nothing, every muscle poised for flight. Above, the world is fractured into wavering slices of blue and brown: Finn's activist camp pressed hard against the tide line, its banners flapping like torn skin. Humans swarm the beach, all energy and friction, throwing up canvas domes and hammering rods into stone, loud as gulls at a carcass.

Mara tracks them in pieces: the red-haired activist is first on her feet, bullhorn slung across her chest like a weapon; two undergrads unfold a solar array, arguing in stage whispers; farther off, a pair of grad students smoke illicit things behind the windbreak, their laughter brittle and afraid. At the center, Finn Gallagher moves like he's everywhere at once, running cables, shouldering coolers, pausing only to check the battered waterproof tablet at his hip. His face looks older since last night, less buoyant, with more lines.

Mara tries to focus on the mission: get the data, then disappear. But her eyes keep drifting to Coral, up on the rock where the sand meets surf. Coral is laughing, for the benefit of the humans. Her gestures are textbook—hands loose, shoulders open, nothing to fear here. But Mara reads the tremor in her fingers, the way she blinks too often, the pulse at the gill line barely suppressed. Her scales are dull, too. Coral is scared.

From the water, Mara can almost taste it.

Next to Coral, Dr. Chen knifes open a water sample with a scalpel and holds it to the light. She squints, whispers something to Coral, who nods and offers up a practiced, "I'll check the pH at the inlets." Her accent is perfect. The smile isn't.

Mara narrows her eyes. That was the cue: test the sample, then rendezvous at the cove mouth. Instead, Coral doubles back, bending to fuss with a loose anchor, her gaze flicking up and down the shore. Mara swears under her breath—if Lyla were here, she'd have spotted the lie already.

Coral rises, stretches, then pads down the sand toward the outer reef, away from the rendezvous point. She glances over her shoulder twice. Mara's tail flicks once, silent as a knife, and she shadows her from below.

It's not subtle, the way Coral moves. She cuts across the old wrack line, boots barely skimming the water, then hurries past a tidepool where a plastic bottle has snared an urchin. Each step is too deliberate, too forced. Mara's suspicion curdles to certainty: this is not about the water samples.

Mara follows, keeping low behind a break of rock. Coral wades out past the kelp, then drops, letting the sea close over her head. For a second, Mara loses her in the glare—then a flicker of silver, a flash of dorsal, and Coral is off, racing for the drop-off.

Mara gives chase. Her copper hair streams behind her, the braid a whip in the current. She calls up a microvortex, riding the slipstream, scales burning as she pushes for speed. The water is thin here, fouled by runoff and the tang of engine oil—every breath stings. But Coral is gaining, shooting deeper, angling toward the bay's far mouth.

There's no sign of fear now, only the sharp, mechanical precision of someone late for a meeting.

Mara clamps down on panic. She cycles through the old training: flatten the body, minimize the wake, let the quarry forget you exist. She's close enough to see Coral's silhouette against the pale mud of the shelf, close enough to read the tension in her shoulders.

At the shelf's edge, a skiff idles. Black, unmarked, too new for a fisher's hands. The engine is off, but Mara hears the hiss of a hydrophone, feels it crawl along her teeth. The man inside is a shadow, but she knows the shape. The posture is military, the face hidden beneath a cap, and the lens glare of cheap night-vision. Captain Marcus Blackwell.

Coral surfaces by the skiff. Mara edges closer, using the column of bubbles from the outboard for cover. She can't make out the words, but the cadence is unmistakable: Coral, pleading and sharp, then Blackwell, flat as a cutting board. He holds up a waterproof phone and taps the screen once. Coral looks away.

"—they're all there. The scientists, the activists, and the mermaid who started it all. Tonight. You have to keep your end—" Coral's voice, higher than usual, pitched by fear.

Blackwell's response is a dead whisper. "You've done well. Now my men can take care of the rest." He thumbs the phone again, then leans in, voice dropped to a register only a hydrophone could love. "You want your city to be safe? Then you stay out of it. Go home. Tell no one. Or I'll hunt you first."

Coral shivers. She starts to say something, but Blackwell's hand clamps over her wrist—brutal, cold, and inhuman in its patience.

Mara recoils. Her stomach turns over; her hands ball into fists. Coral, her own, selling them out for a promise no human could keep.

Coral stares at the horizon, mouth set in a thin line. "You said you'd stop if I gave you the city," she hisses. "You promised."

Blackwell's laugh is barely audible, but it cuts. "I promised I'd try."

Coral lets her arm fall. She doesn't look back as she kicks off the skiff and vanishes into the blue.

Mara lets her go, too stunned to move. She wants to surface and drag Coral back by the hair, wants to scream at her, wants to break every bone in Blackwell's body. Instead, she floats in the half-light, the water pulsing around her.

The old magic feels hollow now.

She waits until the skiff motors away, then curls in on herself, the cold leaking into her core.

Above, the camp is still alive—Finn shouting at the activists, Dr. Chen cataloging samples, Coral returning with a perfect lie on her tongue.

Mara tastes the betrayal, sharp as metal. And for the first time, she wonders if the city was doomed all along.

Mara does not swim back to camp—she detonates through the water, arms slicing, current rippling from her flanks. She pours everything into speed, burns through every trick in the book: dolphin kicks, torpedoes of cold, even the hated surface-pulse that leaves her skin slick with scum. The water is all acid and residue, every swallow a poison she can barely choke down.

It doesn't matter. She has to warn them.

The shallows bite first. As she hits the inlet, the world tilts and the sea goes from salt to septic. It coats her tongue, her gills, and gums up the microfilaments in her fins. Her heart rate spikes. For a second, she's blind, then the current shoves her under the buoy line, and she crashes up near the old jetty, half in the surf, half on the sand.

She's already too late.

Up the beach, the camp is in convulsions. Not the usual scramble of untrained activists but something harder, primal. Finn is on the comm, voice knifing through the fog: "—repeat, this is not a drill, three unknown vessels closing fast, I need all hands—" His hair is wild, his face pinched and grey.

To his left, the red-haired leader is already rallying the younger crew, dragging a camo tarp over the generator and yanking the smaller kids into the dunes. Dr. Chen stands at the edge of the tide, boots sunk in mud, arms loaded with vials and test tubes like bandoliers.

Above them, the sky is knotted with beams of white, floodlights crossing and recrossing as the first of the black skiffs cut the surf. Mara hunches behind a barnacled piling and tries not to vomit.

The skiffs hit land in sequence—three, then two more, then a final monster with a hard-faced man at the helm. Blackwell. He stands straight as a harpoon, every inch of him telegraphing violence, his crew in lockstep behind him.

Nets go first. They are over the sand, catching three activists before they can run. Two others try to bolt for the high grass, but the men in black catch them with weighted lines and drag them back, screaming.

Finn yells into the radio: "Get the footage live! Hit the uplink—do it now!" He shoulders his own camera, aiming it at the invaders, narrating the raid even as the world closes in.

"Three skiffs landing. Unmarked, tactical gear. This is Blackwell's crew. Suppose anyone can see this—" The feed crackles. He ducks as a shot whines past, clipping the flagpole above him. "—They're going for the water next. Mara, if you're out there—"

The signal dies, buried under static.

A man in tactical black grabs Finn by the collar, slams him to the ground, and stomps the camera to shrapnel. Mara winces. She wants to help, wants to call the current and whip the bastards into the rocks, but the water is thick with chemical film. Every time she tries, the power fuses out. Her hands shake.

She tries again. The best she can do is twist a tiny backwash that trips one of the guards. The effect is pathetic.

Finn is hauled to his feet, hands zip-tied behind his back. His eyes scan the beach, desperate, searching for any sign of Mara. She stays hidden, chest heaving, rage a live wire under her skin.

Up the line, Dr. Chen stands her ground. She faces the approaching goon squad with her chin up; the vials still cradled to her chest.

"You have no jurisdiction here," Chen says, voice sharp as glass.

The lead man—short, ugly, probably ex-merc—swings the butt of his rifle into her ribs. She doubles over, but does not drop the samples. He hits her again, and this time, Mara sees something snap. Chen staggers but stays upright, blood in her mouth.

"Move," says the merc.

Chen does, but only after sealing the vials into a hard case and sliding it under her jacket.

Blackwell steps forward, surveying the beach with cold satisfaction. He walks the perimeter, counting his new assets, then signals to the leading boat. Within seconds, the captured crew is lined up at the water's edge, hands tied, faces down.

From her hiding spot, Mara sees the red-haired activist reach for her boot, fish out a tiny comm, and murmur a string of numbers before a guard kicks it out of her hand.

They're all so helpless. So fragile.

Mara's gills flare, scales bristling. Her breath comes in gasps. The water around her starts to spin, but only in a loose spiral—she's too weak for more. Still, the pain sharpens her focus.

She tries again, fighting through the haze, and this time manages to send a tiny surge up the shore. It scatters sand, rips open two net bags, and for a second, the tide shifts enough for the youngest activist to break free. She makes it three steps before a dart tags her thigh, and she drops.

Mara tastes blood, hers and theirs.

On the beach, Blackwell squats next to Finn. He taps the side of Finn's face with a gloved hand. "You're the science boy, right? The one who keeps poking his nose where it's not wanted."

Finn spits at his boots. Blackwell laughs.

"You want to know the secret?" Blackwell's voice is low, meant only for Finn. "There is no secret. Only the strong and the food."

Finn stares, eyes filled with an anger Mara has never seen before.

Blackwell leans in, almost gently. "And your mermaid? Tell her she's next."

He stands, signals his men to load the prisoners.

Dr. Chen is last. She walks on her own, dignity unbroken, though she limps from the hit to her ribs.

Mara watches, helpless. Her hands shake so hard she nearly loses grip on the piling. The magic is a flicker, unreliable, and the world is slipping out of her hands.

The boats load up. The engines roar.

Blackwell turns, scans the waves with those predator's eyes. For a split second, Mara thinks he sees her. He raises a hand in mock salute, then boards.

As the skiffs carve away from shore, Mara slides back into the murk, gills burning, the spiral of rage in her head tighter than ever.

She thinks of the old vision, of the pact, and wonders if the future is just a mirror of the past: the weak, the strong, and the food.

She will not let it end this way.

There is a limit, even to despair.

Mara reaches hers with the slap of Blackwell's boots on the jetty. She's seen enough—her people betrayed, her human allies folded into chains, the future closing like a mouth full of knives. The old pact said to endure, but endurance is a slow, stupid death.

She chooses war.

One instant, she is nothing, a shimmer below the algae line; the next, she launches. Her tail coils, then uncoils with a violence that tears a crater in the mud. She rockets from the water, body slick with oil and cold, and lands dead center on the beach with a sound like a gunshot.

For a second, the world freezes. Every eye turns to her, even the men in black, even Finn, blood streaking his chin.

Mara screams, loud enough to break glass. The air shudders.

She calls the current.

It's not the old magic, neat and clean. This is a brute force, a cannonball in the gut of the sea. The water off the point stands up, a wall three meters high, and slams down onto the beach. The impact scatters men, gear, and nets. Mara is already moving, dragging herself up the sand on raw hands, cutting the bindings on two activists with a snap of her teeth.

"RUN!" she yells, voice raw, human enough to be understood.

The kids don't hesitate—they bolt for the rocks, even as stun rounds spit sand around their feet.

Blackwell's orders are a flurry. "There she is! The red-haired one! Five million to whoever brings her in!" The bounty electrifies the crew. Three men with tranq guns sprint her way; two others swing a reinforced net between them.

Mara ducks the first dart, lets the second graze her shoulder—pain is fuel. She bobs, weaves, and uses a microcurrent to knock the next shot off course. Her hands are numb now, but she grins anyway.

A man tries to tackle her from behind. She whips her tail, clips his knee, and hears the joint go. He screams; she doesn't.

The next wave of poachers comes at her in a wedge, but she's faster. Mara lunges for the net, rips it open with a burst of water pressure. She feels the power fade as the water fouls with blood and chemicals, but she holds the spell long enough to free Finn.

He lands next to her, eyes wide. "Mara—" he manages.

She shoves him toward the breakwater. "Go!"

He hesitates, wants to fight, but Mara pushes him hard enough to leave a bruise. He goes.

She turns, and Blackwell is waiting.

"Thought you'd be bigger," he says, and fires the harpoon.

She dodges, barely. The next shot isn't a harpoon but a tangle line—fine mesh weighted with sinkers. It wraps her left arm, cinches tight. Mara yanks back, but the weights drag her down. The next net catches her tail.

Her gills flutter; her sight narrows to a tunnel. She tries to twist the current, but the water here is dead, every drop laced with poison.

The men close in, clubbing her from all sides. She feels bones give, her vision bursting with color.

Blackwell stands over her, gun to her head. "Hello, monster."

Mara spits in his face.

He grins, then signals to his men. "Bag her."

They wrap her in another net, tighter, then heave her toward the waiting skiff.

She fights. Oh, she fights. But it's not enough. The air is gone;

the water, when it finally comes, is a slurry of microplastics and runoff.

Mara lets herself go limp. Waits for the opening.

She doesn't have to wait long.

The whirlpool is instant, a maw that chews through the tide. It opens right under the skiff, swallowing the crew and the nets and Mara in a single, savage gulp. She's pulled down, down, pressure building in her skull, the world spinning so fast her bones rattle.

Then a hand. Cold as the trench, strong as the tide.

Lyla.

She surfaces next to Mara, eyes wild, hair streaming in perfect plaits. Behind her, a wedge of elite Tideweavers: all muscle, all rage, all blue-black and silver.

"Release my sister," Lyla says, voice deep enough to shake the world, "or face the ocean's wrath."

Blackwell's men flounder, tossed by the vortex, struggling to keep their heads above water. One tries to aim a gun at Lyla; she flicks a finger, and a current snaps the weapon in half.

Lyla pulls Mara free of the net, slicing it with a single movement. The other Tideweavers form a circle around the two, weaving currents so thick that the water boils. They sink, fast, the darkness closing overhead.

Above, the whirlpool widens, devours the smaller boats, and flips the command skiff clean out of the water. Mara catches a glimpse of Blackwell, clinging to the wreck, face twisted in rage and terror.

As they vanish into the trench, Mara looks back one last time.

On the shore, Finn and the other survivors huddle, their faces pale and their eyes wide.

On the deck of the big vessel, floodlights frame Dr. Chen. She's upright, hands zip-tied, but her head is high, eyes scanning the water. For a second, Mara thinks they meet eyes.

Then the ocean closes, and everything is blue.

Lyla and Mara drift, battered but alive, in the deep calm of the drop-off. The other Tideweavers form up around them, a shield wall of living current. In the hush, Mara finally lets herself feel the pain—her torn arm, the burning in her gills, the acid throb in her head.

"You're an idiot," Lyla says. But her voice is tender, and she wraps Mara in a crushing hug.

"I had to try," Mara says.

"You almost died."

"I almost won."

Lyla barks a laugh. "It's not over."

Mara closes her eyes, lets the pain and exhaustion take her.

"No," she says. "It's just getting started."

Above, the night is broken, but the current is already shifting.

14 Shattered Seas

The city is never tranquil, but there are moments—just before the first shift-change, when the younglings are still asleep, when the elder's songs are only whispers, and the currents run slow and thick as honey—when Mara lets herself pretend it could be. She floats just beneath the lattice of pearl and fire-coral, eyes half-lidded, body loose in the updraft, thinking about nothing. Not the war, not her broken arm, not even Finn.

A high-pitched trill rips her from the drift, vibrating straight through her sternum. The old instincts take over before thought can. She kicks off the arch, spinning to face the source. The alarm is everywhere: not sound, exactly, but the kind of wave that makes every scale stand up, a shudder that has been coded into the species since the first cave-Merfolk lost a child to the surface.

The city convulses as one. Every corridor chokes with bodies, each fin and tail and gill responding to the same call. Mara tastes blood in the water, the metallic signature of panic, but she also tastes something else—exhaust, slick and bitter, not from any city engine.

She flashes through the lanes, barely avoiding collisions, as she follows the panic upstream. Around her, the structures vibrate: arches of living coral, hollowed for centuries, flex under the pressure of fleeing bodies. She passes a pack of younglings pressed flat against the ceiling, eyes wild, spines up.

"Get to the caves!" Mara barks, and they scatter, a silver cloud.

The trilling intensifies, then changes. A vibration underneath—slower, heavier, a war pulse. Not warning, but battle.

She rounds the old amphitheater and sees them: overhead, dozens of boats, their undersides black as whale bellies, engines churning the water to silt and shards of oil. Net shadows ripple across the city floor—darts of light, some chemical, some electrical, probe for movement. The first barrage has already dropped—cages, lines, weighted with stones, every square meter mapped and targeted.

She thinks of Coral, and her stomach twists.

The first time they lost the city, it was to a red tide and a cluster of old mines left over from a war no one remembered. The second time, a disease in the kelp caused half the population to starve. The third time, it was humans. Always humans, learning just a little faster every decade.

But this attack is different. This is a culling, surgical, and joyless.

A pulse to her left. She wheels, hand raised—ready to defend, to fight, to die—but it's Lyla, blood already slicking her scales, face all business.

"They're running the pattern," Lyla says, no preamble. "They know every route, every fallback. Like they're inside our heads."

"They are," Mara snaps. "Coral gave them everything. Blackwell has the city's bones in his teeth."

Lyla grimaces. "I'll sweep the outliers. Get the elders and frylings out. You get whoever can still fight."

Mara nods. They don't hug, don't need to. Lyla's gills flare once, a promise, and she's gone, down the main artery toward the old vaults.

Mara scans the field. The main square is a disaster—two nets already settled, bodies thrashing in the mesh. Three divers descend from the lead skiff, suits bristling with unfamiliar weapons. Not the blunt hooks and knives from past years, but rods of something that make Mara's skin ache to see.

She spots Notch, arm splinted, pushing a group of frylings toward a breach in the central spire. He catches her eye, shakes his head—too late, too many.

Mara swims to the edge of the square, ducking under a slab of broken shell. She calls the current just a trickle to edge herself into the kill zone. The moment she moves, one of the divers whirls, aims the rod, and fires. The water between them seethes, an instant cage of needles, but Mara reads the arc and rolls past.

She gathers what's left of her magic, tries to summon an actual current, something big enough to rip the diver away. It almost works—but the water is sluggish, unresponsive. Her hands tingle. There's a burn in the gills she's never felt before, and when she looks up, the diver is unbothered, already lining up another shot.

They've poisoned the water, she thinks, and almost laughs. Of course they did.

The net above shudders as two Merfolk are hauled up, struggling. Mara sees the fear on their faces, sees them lock eyes, and in the last second, wrap tails. She wishes she could look away as the net hits the surface and the engines tear them toward the sky.

A hatch opens above, and a cascade of something pale—crystals? —rains down. Wherever it lands, the coral shrivels, the living structures pucker and twist. Mara knows this isn't just a capture; it's a message.

She darts toward the museum quarter, past three more knots of chaos. Everywhere, the same pattern: nets, darts, chemical agents. Some resist, a few fight back, but most are caught in moments, the tactics perfect.

In the old library, Mara finds two dozen younglings and three elders pressed to the wall, faces blank with terror. She tries to rally, the words coming out in a snarl.

"Listen! We go as a school, tight. I'll break the first net. In the second wave, you dive for the cracks in the floor. If you get separated, keep moving. They're after the big catches—if you make yourself small, you'll live."

An elder glares, voice like sandpaper. "We can't leave the library. It's the last—"

"It's a tomb if you stay," Mara bites. She grabs the nearest fryling by the wrist and shoves her forward. The rest follow, elders, grumbling, but fear wins.

They make it halfway before the first net drops. Mara sees the line and swims at it, flipping up to tangle herself. The netting is charged—an electric jolt spikes her arm, but she grits through, twisting hard, using her own body to open a hole. The frylings stream through, shrieking, a second net dropping behind, but thinner, less charged. A few get caught, but most slip away, diving down through the cracks.

The elders make it too. Mara hangs, winded, in the remnants of the net, then tears herself free and dives after.

Below, the city is worse. The shockwaves of the attack ripple through every tunnel; in places, the water is so fouled it's hard to see. She doubles back to the main square, looking for Lyla.

She finds her at the core, orchestrating a counteroffensive.

Three dozen defenders, most wounded, all determined, arrayed in a spiral behind her. Lyla points, barks orders: break the nets, target the divers, keep the young alive at all costs.

Mara joins, falling into place beside her. "The magic is shot," she pants. "Can barely pull a current."

"They dumped a blocker. Saw it in the current. Fucks with the gills, too." Lyla's mouth is tight. "We've got minutes before they take the next ring."

They share a look: the old, final one. Neither needs to say goodbye.

"Go," says Lyla. "They need you below."

Mara obeys, shooting down into the base of the city, lungs and heart and mind on fire.

She hits the bottom, and the world is different. Here, the magic is almost gone, the water thick as tar, but it's quiet. Mara pauses, lets herself catch up to her own fear, then threads the last of her hope through the narrow passage toward the deep vaults.

She finds Coral there, curled in a ball, alone.

For a second, Mara wants to kill her. She holds the thought, turns it over, then lets it dissolve.

"They lied," Coral sobs, not even lifting her head. "He lied. Said if I gave them the map, he'd leave the city alone."

"You knew what he was," Mara says, no heat in it.

Coral shakes. "I thought I could outsmart them. Protect the hatchlings, at least."

Mara wants to believe her, but there's no time. "Up. Now.

We're moving the last school to the trench."

Coral staggers upright, her tail dragging. "It's my fault. All of it."

Mara grabs her by the shoulder. "Then make it matter."

She pushes Coral ahead, the tunnel closing behind them.

Above, the city is a storm of movement. Mara feels it in every bone: the fight is lost, but the war is not.

She swims hard for the dark.

The deep tunnels are older than the city above—carved by tide, not hand, and haunted by the memory of every collapse. Mara and Coral thread the tightest passages, using the scars of ancient disasters as shelter. Around them, a river of frylings, elders, and wounded defenders flows into the dark. It's not order, but instinct: wherever the light is thinnest, the bloodiest, that's where you go.

A tremor rattles the coral ceiling, sending clouds of stinging dust down onto the evacuees. Mara shields her eyes, then pushes onward, trying to make her body a haven. Behind her, Coral wrangles a tangle of half-grown siblings, her voice shredded but relentless.

They hit a cavern where the current runs in a circle, a dead-end for the hopeless. Mara signals to the crowd: "Keep moving. No stops. Not yet." The survivors ignore her, stacking themselves against the wall, each family pod huddling for its own last stand.

Mara wants to curse, but it's pointless. She grabs Coral by the shoulder. "We need to punch a hole. If they catch us here—"

"I know," Coral says, not meeting her eyes.

Mara finds the two most prominent defenders, both head and shoulders taller than her, with arms like kelp anchors. "With me," she says, and leads them up the chute to the next chamber.

Here, the current is meaner, the water vibrating with the effort of a thousand panicked bodies above. Mara pokes her head through the passage and scans the field. The humans are here, too: three divers at the breach, hands fumbling with what look like plastic grenades—two more, with dart guns trained on the tunnel.

She points at the nearest defender. "Take the right. I'll distract the center. You—wait until you see my signal."

They nod, expressions flat.

Mara stares at the divers, waiting for her own fear to recede. It doesn't, so she goes anyway.

She bursts from cover, snapping her tail in a whip so sharp the lead diver's mask shatters. The next one, startled, fires his dart gun but misses wide. Mara's defender barrels into him, twisting the human in a bear hug, then dragging both down into the tunnel. The third diver panics, drops the grenade, and kicks hard for the surface. Mara grabs the grenade before it can detonate and hurls it up and away.

"Now!" she calls, and the waiting defender detonates the reserve current. The tunnel expands momentarily with the force of the water, flinging Mara and her group through the gauntlet.

The passage is clear for a second.

But the next wave is already here: nets, not dropped but fired, each weighted with a capsule that pops on impact and fills the space with a choking, static-laced foam. The Merfolk defenders slice the first net, but the second lands perfectly, enveloping Mara and three others.

She claws at the mesh, but the foam kills even the faintest spark of magic. Her hands go numb; her tongue thickens. It's only the thought of the frylings below that keeps her moving.

She uses her teeth. Rips a hole just big enough to pull her arm free, then another, then enough for her whole body. The defenders see her trick and mimic it, but not fast enough: one is hit by a dart, his body convulsing, then slack. He floats upward, mouth open, dead eyes turning toward Mara.

She grinds her jaw, then darts for the surface, desperate to find Lyla, anyone.

In the chaos above, the water is neon, lit by bioluminescent blood. Every defender is fighting alone, magic reduced to raw panic, no strategy, no finesse. Mara calls up the last of her Tideweaving, ignoring the pain, and manages to twist the current into a single, lethal whirlpool.

It works. For three seconds, the nearest net is ripped away, and two human divers are smashed together, breaking both their masks. Mara feels the rush, like old times, like victory—but it's too little, too late. The air fills with sound: a new weapon, a frequency tuned to hurt.

It's not just pain; it's betrayal, a resonance that shakes loose every memory of every lost battle. Mara claps her hands to her ears, but it's no use. The water itself is a speaker.

She sees Lyla across the square, holding off a diver with a chunk of broken coral, but bleeding from a new cut on her arm. Mara tries to reach her, but the sound pins her in place. She shivers, tail locked, gills refusing to open.

It is Notch who saves her. He's smaller than she remembers, blood streaking his face, but he barrels into the diver with suicidal joy, head-butting the human off Mara. "Go!" he shouts, voice raw.

Mara kicks for Lyla, dodging another net. All around, defenders are being picked off, each loss tightening the spiral of defeat. She scans for Coral, but only sees a blur of tails, indistinct in the chaos.

The water turns black for a heartbeat—then, with a concussion that nearly stops her heart, the central coral spire explodes. The shockwave rips through the city, collapsing arches and sending debris through every corridor. Mara is slammed sideways, only Lyla's hand on her tail keeping her from being thrown into the open.

"Move!" Lyla shouts, blood streaming from her gills.

They swim for the lower tunnels, dodging shards of living coral and the limp bodies of their own people.

Behind them, the city is a graveyard.

They hit the safe tunnel, where a dozen survivors have already gathered. Lyla crumples, hand pressed to her wound. "We can't hold them," she gasps. "We have to get to the deep caverns. Now."

Mara helps her up. The others look to her, hollow-eyed. "Where's Coral?" someone asks.

Mara doesn't answer. There's no time for that.

She leads them downward, away from the city, into the black.

Behind them, the last song of the Merfolk city is a scream,

then silence.

Finn steadies the binoculars against his brow and pretends his hands aren't shaking. The deck of the little boat is sticky with salt, Red Bull, and someone's blood from the last dockside skirmish, but the only thing that matters is the thin black shadow crawling across the horizon: Blackwell's lead ship.

He has the navigation app open on two different phones. They disagree—one GPS ping keeps sliding; a drift Finn recognizes as deliberate jamming. Blackwell's men are good, but Finn's better. He watches the "ghost" ships dance on the screen, checks the scatter pattern, then snaps the binoculars to his eyes again.

"Anything?" Ava Chen asks, voice tight. She's at the tiller, knees braced against the chop, a GoPro duct-taped to her head.

Finn grunts. "They're bunching up, trying to fake a landing party. But the real show's offshore."

Ava nods, never looking up from the throttle. "We have confirmation on the inside?"

Finn glances at the comms rig, where the grad student, Mona, already sunburned and wired on her own body weight in caffeine, monitors the encrypted feed. "They're prepping a transfer," Mona says, reading from the screen. "ETA on the extraction point is less than an hour. They're using the same route as last time."

Finn swears, then checks his bag: two drysuits, four sets of fins, three ancient GoPros, a satchel of old phones, and a waterproof notepad. The last item makes him smile briefly; Mara would have loved it. He shakes off the memory.

"We go to the buoy field," Finn says. "Blackwell will have snipers on the cliffs, but he's not expecting anyone from below."

Ava frowns, glances at Finn. "You think there's anything left down there?"

Finn looks at her, hard. "There has to be."

Ava doesn't argue. She never does.

He checks his harness and makes sure the old diver's knife is in its proper place. His hands are still shaking, but less. Maybe he's just getting used to it.

The boat slams a wake, and Finn's teeth click. He opens the navigation again and zooms in. The map lights up with the heat trails of the fleet—three fast zodiacs, a support craft, and the transport skiff, separated from the rest by a quarter mile and running dark. Finn taps the blip, double-checks the coordinates.

"That's it," he says, pointing. "The skiff. They're moving the captives now. If we get the footage, we can blow this open."

Mona stares at the readout. "And then what? Blackwell walks?"

"Then everyone knows," Finn says. "The world sees it, and Blackwell doesn't get to hide behind a lie again."

He doesn't add: And maybe Mara sees it too, wherever she is. Perhaps she knows I'm trying.

Ava throttles down, bringing them parallel to the skiff's projected course—the wind shifts, cold and full of rain. Finn shrugs into the drysuit, checks the regulator one last time, then turns to Mona.

"Your job is to stay above water and keep the uplink live. No matter what."

Mona's eyes are enormous. "If I get caught—"

"You won't," Finn says, not entirely sure he believes it. "Blackwell wants the monsters, not us."

Ava is already in the water, a shadow under the hull. Finn follows, feet finding the rungs by touch.

He slips beneath the surface, and everything sharpens. The pain in his lungs, the bite of cold, the low thrum of a thousand engines chewing up the world above. He kicks down, finds Ava's flashlight, and signals.

They move together, practiced. The approach relies on muscle memory—stick to the kelp beds, use the rocks for cover, and never silhouette yourself against open water. Finn's mind flashes back to Mara teaching him, the cadence of her voice, the way she could twist a current with just a flick of her fingers.

He misses her so much he can't even taste it, and that hurts more than the cold.

They reach the buoy field. The skiff is above, silhouetted in the gray light, men in wet suits hauling up the heavy nets. Finn counts bodies: three on deck, one running the winch, two more on perimeter. Probably more inside, but that's a risk he'll have to take.

Ava gestures: go.

Finn swims up the anchor line, then edges under the hull, breath steady, every sense tuned for the impossible.

He hears it first—a low, warbling moan, deep as the trench,

bleeding through the metal of the skiff. Not a human sound. Mara's people.

Finn's heart hammers. He wants to go faster, but forces himself to slow down, to stay alive. He surfaces under the transom, inches from the spinning prop, and latches onto the swim step.

He waits, timing the movement. The crew is busy, distracted by the weight of the net, cursing as the winch jams. Finn eases up, hands barely above the water.

He sees the net come up, dripping. At the bottom, a flash of iridescent scales, a webbed hand, the unmistakable line of a Mer's tail.

Finn locks eyes with the creature. It's a boy, barely more than a fryling, his face pinched in terror.

Finn swears, then makes a decision.

He surges up, grabs the nearest guard by the ankle, and pulls. The man hits the deck hard and screams. The others turn, but Ava is already there, a flash of light in the chaos. She hurls a flare onto the net, blinding the crew, then slashes at the lines holding the fryling.

It works for a second.

The next guard has a gun and fires twice into the water. Finn dives, but feels the shockwave, a punch to the chest.

He claws back up, desperate. Ava is grappling with the winch operator, the deck a tangle of bodies and blood. Finn goes for the net, finds the knife, and cuts, cuts, cuts until the mesh is open.

He grabs the fryling, hauls him free. The boy is gasping, but alive.

Ava is down, a man on her back, hands at her throat. Finn flings the fryling to the water, then barrels into the fight, all teeth and elbows. He gets a fist to the temple, but it barely registers.

He hears Mona's voice, faint on the comms: "The world is watching, Finn. Get the shot."

Finn slams the man's head into the deck, then whips out his phone. He films the net, the boy, the faces of the men, and the blood.

"Smile," he says, voice shaking.

The man spits, then lunges, but Finn dodges, grabs Ava, and together they roll off the deck into the sea.

The bullets follow, but the water is thick and dense, a safety in itself.

Finn finds the fryling, pushes him ahead, then kicks for the shadows. Ava swims beside him, eyes wide, smile even wider.

They make it to the rocks, lungs burning. Finn looks back at the skiff. The crew is screaming as they try to fix the net, but the world is already changing.

He looks at the phone, at the shaky footage. It's enough.

Above, the wind howls. Below, the water is full of new hope.

Finn wipes his mouth, then laughs. He can't stop.

Ava punches his shoulder. "You did it, idiot."

Finn nods, then stares out at the open water.

Somewhere down there, Mara is still alive. He knows it. He can feel it, a thread in his bones.

And as the boat's engine dies in the distance, Finn promises her—out loud, to the sky, to the sea—that he will bring them home.

In the farthest trench, Mara and Lyla lead the last school of survivors into the cold. They don't look back. Not yet.

But they will.

The war is just beginning.

15 Abyssal Shadows

The trench is not a place. It is absence, magnified and pressed into the world with the weight of a planet. Mara follows Lyla and the others until the water is too cold for even memory to float. The younglings press close, moving as a single organism, every tail beating in panic time. When Lyla signals the all-clear, Mara hangs back, lets the survivors melt into the blue-black, and then drifts, alone, down the vertical wall.

The current is dead here. Not dead—starved. The few pockets of energy spiral in on themselves, each barely a shadow of the old rivers that fed the city. Mara curls into herself, tucking her injured arm against her stomach. The gash is ugly, blood ribboning in threads so fine the water itself seems to pulse with her heartbeat. She licks the wound out of habit, but the salt only stings. She tastes metal and defeat.

Below her, the trench falls forever. There is no bottom, only a gradient. She lets herself sink, body loose, hair unwinding in a slow copper flame. At this depth, the world inverts. Every bright thing is hunted; every predator is invisible until it isn't. The only color is the sick blue of desperate light—the kind made by animals too lost to know better.

Mara presses her back to the stone wall. It is cold, but not as cold as what's inside her. She breathes, gills fluttering, each intake a shudder. She wants to cry, but there's no use. The water doesn't care. It never did.

Fragments float up: the city's last song, cut short by the war-pulse; the faces of the frylings, open and round, eyes like moons; the way the nets curled down, graceful as sea-grass, and then snapped shut. She sees Notch's body, limp, and the look on Coral's face when the betrayal bit home. She considers the blue-haired twins, dead before they hit the surface, and the old matriarch's hand, still gripping the library's spiral shell.

Mara shoves it all away. She presses her palms against the rock, skin slick with blood and slime, and reaches.

Tide-Sensing is not like the other magics. It is not something you do; it is something that happens to you. The city elders warned her: never sense on an empty heart. It will fill you with what you lack. Mara opens herself anyway.

At first, nothing. The stone is blank, old as birth, uninterested in her. She pushes deeper, fingers scraping, nails splitting. She feels the static of the poison Blackwell's men left behind—a throb of acid, a low drone in the mineral, already killing the tiny polyps that once lit this canyon.

Deeper still: the ancient signature. The wall is pitted with the bones of her people, a million years of ancestors ground into powder and glued together by pressure and grief. Each fossil is a story, a data point. She feels the echo of old wars, old extinctions. A time when the trench ran with blood so thick the surface turned red for a year—a time when the Merfolk were legion, not refugees.

Mara's mind unspools. She is a child again, learning the first songs from her mother—how to listen to the echo in the shell, how to trace a predator's path from the way the current bends. She is a teenager, breaking her own hand on the city wall to prove she was brave. She is a warrior, teeth bared, arms slicked with poison, dragging an invader down to the mud and feeling the last breath flee his body.

And then she is now: alone, lost, clinging to a rock that will never know her name.

She tries to let go. She no longer wants the burden.

But the wall will not release her. It wants more. It wants everything.

Mara surrenders. She pulls in the dark, lets the trench fill her lungs, lets the pressure crack her ribs. The wall pulses, once, and then a flood of images: a spiral, not drawn but grown, embedded in the stone; a river of light, not water but pure memory, running from the city's heart to this very spot. She sees the old magics—raw, unfiltered. She sees how the currents work, the hidden channels that run beneath the sea's visible surface.

She sees, for a second, the pattern: how the attack on her city was just one move in a war that began when the water first cooled. She sees the humans above, tiny, desperate, building their ships and nets, thinking they are the apex. She sees her own people, splintered by pride, unwilling to evolve.

The wall opens, a fissure of blue light. Mara follows it, deeper still. The water here is not water. It is memory, liquefied, denser than thought.

She drinks it in. The wound on her arm throbs, then goes numb. The salt is a comfort now.

All around her, the bioluminescent creatures have gathered. Some are no larger than a cell; some are so vast their bodies loop back on themselves. They pulse in unison, a heartbeat that is not Mara's but could be. Their light is not pretty. It is honest.

Mara lets the current pull her into the fissure. She closes her eyes.

She expects vision—she is ready for it. But what comes is

sensation, pure and brutal.

She feels every living thing in the trench: the worms that eat sulfur, blind and white, tunnel through the rock. The amphipods, armored and tireless, cleaned the bones of the dead. The slow, stately drift of a jellyfish, ghostly, trailing toxins in a curtain so delicate it's almost a caress.

She feels the predators, too. The fangfish, the nightmare eels, the things too deep to name. She feels their hunger, and the way it is never sated. She feels the moment the net touched down on her city: the ripple as every creature, even the worms, sensed the death above and flinched.

The wall tightens. The pressure is unbearable now. Mara screams, but only inside.

The scream echoes, then returns. It is not her voice anymore.

It is the trench, singing back.

The memory is not a vision—it is a weapon.

Mara sees, in perfect clarity, the first time her people harnessed the current. It was not in defense, not in war, but in rage. The original Merfolk—her ancestors—turned the water itself against the invaders, boiling the shallows until the land walkers fled. The cost was everything. The city burned, but the invaders died screaming.

She sees how humans have learned from this—how they have adapted, grown clever, and begun to poison the water, not just their bodies. She sees how every cycle of violence only made the wall higher between them.

She sees the moment when the pact was made: the spiral shell, the blood, the mixing of the two—the promise, never spoken, to keep the balance.

Mara suddenly understands why the vision keeps coming back. Why were the city elders afraid? The spiral is not a warning. It is a call to action.

She comes back to herself with a jolt. The wall lets her go.

She floats, numb. Her wound is gone, replaced by a thin silver scar. Her scales are duller now, but her eyes burn.

All around her, the trench waits.

Mara blinks once, twice. She knows what must be done.

She has to break the cycle. She has to find the shell. She has to finish the pact, or end it forever.

The current calls her name.

She answers.

She launches up the trench, moving faster than she ever has. The bioluminescent things follow, a cloud of flickering rage and memory. She passes the schools of frylings, sees Lyla tending to the wounded, and sees Coral staring at her own reflection in the stone.

Mara does not stop.

She swims for the surface, for the place where the city died, for the spot where the humans landed their first net. She needs to see. She needs to know.

The water thins, the cold recedes, the light grows harsh and angry. At the surface, the storm is gone, replaced by a sickly calm.

Mara breaches. The air is foul, but she breathes it anyway.

She scans the horizon. The human ships are gone. The city above is in ruins.

But something else is there—a shape, dark and slick, moving against the tide.

A man, on a boat, looking right at her.

Finn.

Mara's heart stops, then starts again.

She dives, letting the current take her to him.

She is ready.

For war, or for peace—she is ready.

The trench is not a place. It is a promise.

And Mara means to keep it.

Above the trench, in air too thin and bright to belong to the world Mara just left, Finn stands at the prow of the activist flagship. "Flagship" is a lie, the kind you tell to make yourself feel tall: the boat is a former research trawler, scarred from three illegal chases, deck warped by fire, and fiberglass patches. The only flag is the blue tarp that covers the broken comm array. Finn wears it like a badge of shame.

He watches the horizon with red eyes. The water is flat, the sky a migraine of white, but Finn knows the pattern: on this coast, nothing stays calm for long.

The crew is down to nine, not counting Mona, who hasn't left the nav bench in sixteen hours. They move like ghosts, unshaven and bruised, the victory high from yesterday's rescue curdling into a hangover. Two of them—both grad students, both named Alex—spend their shifts hunched over the starboard rail, ready to puke or bolt at the first sign of trouble.

Finn's first mate, a fisherwoman with arms like wet rope, breaks the silence. "We can't hold the reef," she says, not even bothering to lower her voice. "Their boats have us boxed. We stay; we drown."

Finn doesn't answer. His hands grip the rail, knuckles paper-white. Under his palm, the old shell—Mara's gift—bites into the flesh. He runs his thumb over the spiral, again and again, feeling the pattern, refusing to forget.

The radio cracks: "This is Mackerel Two, we have three bogies on east vector, repeat, three bogies. Looks like the poacher class. Over."

Finn doesn't flinch. He calls up to the wheelhouse. "Hold course. Confirm all optics are live. If they want us, they're coming through the kelp field."

The mate snorts. "You think that's a plan?"

"It's a plan," Finn says. "It's the only plan we have."

A deckhand brings coffee—thick, burned, and so salty Finn wants to spit. He drinks it anyway.

The crew shuffles around him, pulling tarps, checking old repairs. No one mentions Mara, or the way the water seems empty now. No one says "mermaid," or "ally," or anything that would remind Finn of the night the city fell.

But they all look at the shell, clutched in his fist.

Mona radios in, voice flat. "Confirmed: three enemy vessels. Blackwell's insignia on the lead. ETA twenty minutes. Secondary signature—maybe an escort drone, but it's pinging weird. I think they're jamming our GPS again."

Finn's jaw tightens. He traces the shell's spiral, harder now. "Launch the decoy. Prep countermeasures."

The mate rolls her eyes. "We have countermeasures?"

Finn ignores her. He scans the horizon, sees nothing, but his nerves twitch anyway. He remembers the last conversation with Mara—her eyes, storm-colored, refusing to look at him when she left. He remembers how she said the deep was calling, how she had to go. He remembers hating her for it.

Finn lays the shell down on the tactical map, a salt-stained chart covered in his own frantic handwriting. He marks the probable intercept point, circles it twice, then draws an arrow back to their fallback cove.

The mate leans in, voice low. "They're coming with nets this time. Heavy gear. If you want to get the rest of the crew out, now's—"

Finn cuts her off. "We're not running. Not this time. If

Blackwell gets another haul, there's nothing left to fight for."

She glares, but doesn't argue.

The deckhand comes back, this time with a battered flare gun. He tries to hand it to Finn, but Finn waves him off. "Keep it," he says. "You'll need it more than I will."

The crew finishes prepping the skiff. The other two boats in the fleet—a patched Zodiac and a crabber on its last legs—hold position at the mouth of the cove, ready to close in if Finn gives the signal.

The radio hisses again: "Enemy at five miles. They've got a large net launcher. Looks automated. Over."

Finn breathes in, out. He feels the weight of the world on his shoulders, literal and otherwise. His arms are tired, but his brain won't quit.

He stares at the shell on the map. He wants to throw it overboard and intends to smash it to dust. But he picks it up and slips it into his pocket.

Below deck, the mate corrals the crew for a last briefing. Finn follows, trailing the scent of cold diesel and sweat.

Inside the galley, the map is spread across the table. The crew huddles around, pale faces reflecting the green of the emergency lighting.

Finn clears his throat. "Here's the plan. We force them into the kelp, jam their net, and then turn off the lead boat. Mona's got the uplink—everything goes live to the feed. If we get lucky, they back off. If not…" He lets it hang.

"Maybe we stall long enough for the Coast Guard to care," the mate says, voice dry.

Finn nods. "Maybe."

He doesn't mention the real goal: stall long enough for Mara to come back. For the deep to return her. For anything to change.

The crew grumbles, but agrees. There's no mutiny in them, not yet.

Finn heads back topside. The sun is sinking, bleeding orange into the sea. The enemy ships are now visible on the horizon, black slashes against the flames.

The mate joins him, pulling a cigarette from a pouch. She lights it, offers him one. He shakes his head.

"She's gone, you know," she says, voice low. "The mermaid. She left us."

Finn feels the shell in his pocket. "She'll be back."

The mate squints, shakes her head. "You're the only one who believes that."

Finn watches the enemy ships crawl closer. He watches the mate flick the cigarette butt into the water.

He fingers the shell, tight enough to hurt.

The mate goes below. The deck is his alone.

The sun hits the water, and Finn makes his move. He pulls the shell from his pocket and holds it up to the fading light. For a second, it glows, sharp and perfect, a spiral.

He closes his eyes, feels the old ache.

Then he hurls the shell as far as he can.

It arcs, drops, and vanishes into the ocean with barely a sound.

Finn stands at the bow, knuckles white, eyes full of nothing.

"Come back," he whispers, voice wrecked. "Just come back."

The water answers only with waves.

The enemy ships close in, and the world goes red.

The lab is a cage. Not a metaphor: Dr. Chen sits in a literal box of welded steel, dimensions just wide enough to stretch her legs, just tall enough to stand if she crouches. She counts the bars when the seas get rough—Forty-four, not including the locking panel. At night, the cold seeps into the welds and rises through the floor. Chen does not sleep at night.

She sits, knees up, as the ship rocks through the squall. Above, deckhands shout—Russian, Filipino, American—each voice chopped by the wind and the slap of the waves. The cage sits dead center in the old galley, which Blackwell has converted into a hybrid laboratory, half mad scientist, half taxidermist's den.

On the far wall, past the makeshift fume hood and the jars of preserved sharks, Blackwell holds court with his jar. In it, a tangle of iridescent scales: jade, pearl, something almost red at the edges. The scales float in a suspension fluid, each one perfect and unbroken. Blackwell turns the jar in his hands, watching the light break and refract through it.

Chen watches him watch.

She's hidden three vials under the lining of her coat, tucked between seams meant for pens and scalpels. Every movement risks discovery, but she's learned not to move unless necessary. She's learned a lot, locked in a box.

Blackwell looks up. "Did you know," he says, voice casual as a surgeon prepping a patient, "these scales will regenerate in less than a day? You pluck one off, and the wound closes almost instantly. Like a starfish, but smarter."

Chen doesn't answer. Her eyes track the jar.

He sets the jar down, as carefully as if it were a holy relic. "Imagine the application," he continues. "Human wound healing. Burn units. Soldiers on the front line."

"Imagine the host," Chen replies, words precise and cold. "Sentient. Pain. Dignity."

Blackwell shrugs, an elegant roll of the shoulder. He moves through the galley like he owns every molecule, every ghost of the original captain. The effect would be more impressive if not for the bloodstain on his sleeve.

He unlocks a cabinet and removes a set of glass slides. "You think too small, Dr. Chen. Or maybe too soft."

She wants to spit, but keeps her face neutral. "You could be the first to document an entirely new civilization. Instead, you're butchering them for the scrap value."

Blackwell laughs, genuinely. "And yet you're here, in my lab, instead of at your university, arguing ethics with undergrads."

He slides a microscope across the table, sets a scale on a slide, and motions for the guard to open Chen's cage.

The guard—a kid, maybe twenty, tattoos up both arms—jabs the butt of his gun at the panel. The door groans open. Chen stands slowly, her arms at her sides.

Blackwell waves her over. "You want to see something beautiful?"

She crosses the lab, feigning interest. The scales appear more minor up close, almost like fish scales, but the cellular structure is incorrect. No, not bad—unprecedented. Every cell is a double spiral, with what appears to be microtubules constructed to withstand violence.

Blackwell bends over her shoulder, breath hot on her neck. "They're built for war," he says. "Every part of them is optimized for survival. Even the way they die. Have you seen it?"

"I saw the aftermath," Chen says, voice flat. "Netting, chemical agents, pressure-wave guns. Not much left after that."

Blackwell tsks. "You should see the field tests. When they bleed, the water changes. It's like the sea itself gets angry."

Chen bites her tongue. "Maybe it does."

He circles, hand on the back of her chair. "You want to run tests? I'll let you. But no sabotage, or you'll be back in the box. No more exceptions."

She looks at him, finally, meets his eyes. For a second, she sees the crack in his mask: the curiosity, the hunger to understand, even if only to control.

She plays her hand. "Let me run a full analysis—structure, genome, and chemical. I'll publish your name first. You'll go down in history as the founder, not the butcher."

Blackwell considers. He glances at the guard, then at the jar. "You think I care about legacy, Dr. Chen?"

"I think you care about being right. About being first."

The ship lurches. The guard steadies himself. Chen does not flinch.

Blackwell drums his fingers on the table. For a moment, he looks almost bored. "Fine. You get the lab under guard. No comms. No sabotage." He holds her gaze. "One more warning, and you're cargo."

Chen nods. "Understood."

He pushes her into the chair and slides the jar close. "Start with the scales. Then I'll bring you the blood."

She nods, mouth dry.

He lingers, watching her, then snaps his fingers. The guard locks the cage behind her, but leaves the door open.

Chen bends over the microscope. Her hands shake, but only for a second.

The first slide is a miracle. The scales aren't just armor—they're alive, flexing and rearranging, even in death. She takes notes in her head, knowing he'll confiscate any paper. She counts the layers, catalogs the pigments, and follows the spiral down to its base.

Behind her, Blackwell watches, saying nothing.

She keeps working, faster now. Every slide tells a new story: resilience, adaptation, and the refusal to die.

She remembers the face of the merchild she saw in the net, the way its eyes were blank but not defeated. She remembers what Finn told her, once: the only way to win is to survive longer than your Enemy expects.

She will survive.

She leans back. "You have to see this," she says, her voice calm.

Blackwell comes over. He looks through the eyepiece, his breath hissing.

"I told you," Chen says, letting her pride show. "It's not just biology. It's a strategy."

Blackwell looks at her with a new respect in his gaze. "Maybe you're not as soft as I thought."

She says nothing, lets the moment hang.

The ship shifts course. Above, the shouting grows louder. Chen listens, piecing together the code words: "boarding," "activists," "net launcher ready."

She looks at Blackwell. "What now?"

He smiles. "Now we watch the experiment."

He leaves her in the open cage, microscope and all.

Chen resumes her work, each slide a new weapon, each note a step closer to freedom.

Outside, the sea rages. Inside, the real war has already started.

16 Rising Tide

The trench presses in on Mara until she is barely more than a shadow, a wound in the water. Every motion costs—her battered arm throbs, white pain threading up through her veins with each breath. The cold is so absolute she barely feels it anymore; it has dissolved her, made her something elemental, unrecognizable even to herself. She floats limp against the wall of stone, copper hair a cloud around her ruined face, eyes tracking the slow drift of bioluminescent things with the dead focus of a sleepwalker.

There are no songs this deep, only silence. Not the clean silence of the open water but a drowned quiet, broken here and there by the slow click of distant predation or the groan of a fault line shifting in its sleep. The only color is the sick blue pulse of the creatures that live by eating light. Mara drifts among them, an intruder even here.

She hasn't moved in hours, maybe days. The time has become mush, a slurry of memory and hallucination. Sometimes she remembers the city, the last flash of Lyla's eyes before the current took them apart. Sometimes it is Coral, always Coral, blinking at her in the soft-lit tunnel, the air full of old betrayals. Sometimes it is Finn, lips blue with cold, hands desperate on her waist, voice breaking as he called her name from the wrong side of the water.

Mostly, though, it is the pressure—inside and out—that fills her.

The wound on her arm will not close. The flesh is puckered, white-edged, a spiral of red that matches the marks on her mother's shell. Mara studies it with detachment, as if it were someone else's body. The gills on her right-side flutter unevenly, never quite catching up to the ones on the left. She wonders, not for the first time, if it would be easier to let them stop. If the trench were softer than the pain.

It is not.

A pulse, not memory but real, slices through the gloom. Mara ignores it at first. The trench is full of ghosts; her brain is full of false alarms. But then it happens again—a vibration, sharper, closer, resonant with the signature of living magic.

Lyla.

Mara closes her eyes. "Go away," she says, barely above a thought.

The water shudders. In an instant, Lyla is there, forceful as a torpedo, grabbing Mara's good arm and yanking her out of the crevice where she's wedged herself. The violence is familiar, almost comforting. For a second, Mara thinks she might cry, but the salt won't allow it.

"Enough hiding," Lyla says, the words cutting clean through the water. "You're not dead, so stop acting like it."

Mara resists, but it's a joke. Lyla is stronger—always was. She drags Mara clear of the rock face, out into the shaft of the trench where the light is even thinner.

"You tracked me," Mara says, half accusation, half wonder.

Lyla snorts. "Anyone could. You left a signature a mile wide. Didn't even try to mask your bleeding. The trench is crawling with predators now."

"Let them come," Mara says. She tries to wrench free, but Lyla tightens her grip.

"I'm not here to argue," Lyla says. "I'm here to bring you back."

Mara laughs, or tries. The sound is just bubbles. "There's nothing to go back to. The city is gone. The magic's gone. We lost."

Lyla shakes her once, hard enough to rattle Mara's teeth. "You lost? You think this is about you?"

Mara's tail flicks, but it's a reflex, nothing more. "I failed. I saw it coming and I still—"

Lyla bares her teeth. "I don't care what you saw. I care what you do now. Our people need you. I need you."

Mara lets herself go limp again. "You have the elders. You have the rest."

"The elders are dead," Lyla says, voice flat. "Blackwell's poison got most of them. The rest were caught in the nets. I barely got the hatchlings out before they closed the tunnels." She pauses, then, softer, "There's nothing left but us. The frylings and the broken."

Mara looks at her, tries to read the truth in Lyla's eyes. Finds it, and something else—fear.

"Why me?" Mara asks, not sure she wants to hear the answer.

Lyla is silent for a long time. Then: "Because you're the only one left who remembers how it was supposed to be. Who can call the current without hating it?"

"That's not true," Mara says, but her words have no force.

Lyla pulls her closer, until their foreheads are almost touching. "It is. You think you're special. You saw the spiral because you got the visions? You're not. Every line of our blood remembers it, somewhere. But you—" She bites off the rest, shakes her head.

"What?" Mara says.

Lyla lets her go, pushes off with a violence that is more grief than anger. "You loved them," she spits. "The humans. You tried to make a bridge. I thought you were a fool. Still do, most days. But I see now—it's the only thing left. The war is lost, unless you do something impossible."

Mara blinks. The pain is a little less, for a moment. "They'll never listen," she says. "They only care when we bleed."

"Then bleed for them," Lyla snaps. "Or bleed them out. Either way, choose."

Mara shakes her head. "I can't. I'm not—"

Lyla closes the gap and grabs Mara's face in both hands. "You're not weak. You're scared." She searches Mara's eyes, then, in a softer voice, "So am I."

A current passes between them, old as family, strong as regret.

Mara lets her hands float up and rests them on Lyla's wrists. "You think there's a way out?" she asks.

Lyla looks down, nods once. "There's always a way. But you have to want it."

Mara's gills flutter. The trench is no warmer, but her body feels less heavy, her mind less tangled.

She takes a long, hard breath. The wound throbs, but it's manageable. "Okay," she says.

Lyla's relief is instantaneous, though she covers it with a flick of her tail. "Good. We go now."

She starts to tow Mara upward, but Mara shakes her head. "Wait. The wall—the memory. There's something we need from here."

Lyla stops. "What is it?"

Mara lets go of her arm and floats back to the fissure she had claimed for herself. "The old magic," she says. "I think I can find it. But I'll need your help."

Lyla's eyes narrow, suspicious. "You're not going to try to die again, are you?"

Mara smiles, for the first time in weeks. "Not today."

Lyla sighs. "Fine. Show me."

Mara dives for the crack, Lyla right behind. The trench is still cold, still hungry, but Mara is no longer afraid of being eaten.

She has already survived it and is now ready to feed.

Lyla pulls Mara up through the black, not caring if the climb rips open new wounds. The ledge is nothing but a bump in the endless shaft, just wide enough for two to rest side by side. The abyss stretches below, a mouth so deep the light from above seems like myth.

They rest. Mara sits with her tail coiled, hands loose, shoulders hunched. Lyla is upright, every line of her body announcing: I am not broken, I will never be broken.

It's quiet for a while, just the slow churn of the water and the beat of Mara's uneven gills.

"You were right," Mara says, breaking the silence. "About the humans. They always choose themselves, in the end." She gestures at her arm, the spiral of injury. "I thought I could change that. I thought Finn—" She cuts off, shrugs. "Doesn't matter."

Lyla watches her with a predator's patience. The mask of command is perfect, but something trembles at the corners.

"You were right, too," Lyla says finally, voice lower than Mara remembers. "Not about the humans. About us. Our pride. We let them divide us. You tried to do something new, and I—I punished you for it."

Mara shakes her head. "You protected the city."

Lyla looks away, out into the abyss. "I protected a memory of the city. The real one was gone before the first net dropped." She flexes her hands, the old scars silvering in the blue. "I used to think surviving was enough. But that's just hiding with extra steps."

They sit with that, the silence sharpening until it's hard to breathe.

Then Lyla nods upward, the way she used to point when Mara was a fryling, and the world was simple. "He's still out there, you know. Your Finn. He's got a whole school of humans with him. Activists, liars, fools—but they fight like they want to live. Even after you vanished, he never stopped."

Mara's gills flutter, a reflex she can't hide. "You saw him?"

Lyla smirks, just a hair. "He makes more trouble than any of the frylings. Runs up and down the coast, breaking things, saving what he can." She glances at Mara, and for the first time in a year, her eyes aren't hard. "You picked a good one, even if he is hopeless."

Mara feels something inside her unknot, a muscle she'd forgotten she had.

Lyla leans in and grips Mara by the shoulders. The strength is still there, but now it's a promise, not a threat. "You belong to both worlds now. Stop choosing. Use them."

Mara closes her eyes and lets the words sink in. The current shifts, and for a second, she allows herself to believe it could be true.

They embrace—awkward, fierce, quick. Their tails twine once, then separate. It is enough.

Mara straightens. "What now?"

Lyla bares her teeth, a grin of pure intent. "We get to work."

They start with the simplest tools: fingers, phosphorescence, and the bumpy, ribbed wall of the trench. Mara collects handfuls of bioluminescent algae from the cracks, smearing them across her palms until her skin glows electric blue. Lyla scoffs, but follows suit.

It's like the old lessons, except the stakes are extinction.

Mara sketches the shape of the coastline on the wall—careful, deliberate, correcting every mistake with a swipe of her palm. She marks the city's ruin, then fans out lines for each primary current, mapping the flow as she remembers it. Lyla adds her own notes, overlaying defense grids, choke points, and the hidden tunnels only the oldest Merfolk know.

As they work, Mara feels her hands grow steadier, and her pulse slows. The focus is addictive. Each time she adds a new layer, the image glows a bit brighter, until the map is a living constellation.

"We'll need a relay," Lyla says, tapping a finger on a cluster of glowing dots. "Blackwell's likely to jam anything near the surface. We use the old reef as a blind, send the message through the kelp beds here—"

Mara interrupts, "No. Not the kelp beds. There's a thermal vent, right here." She points to a dark spot off the map's edge. "If we run the current through the vent, it'll amplify the signal. Push it right through the interference."

Lyla's eyes widen. "That's—no one's ever tried that."

Mara grins, showing teeth. "Maybe it's time."

They work in sync, building the plan layer by layer. Every few minutes, Mara pauses to tune the pattern, weaving in side channels or escape vectors. Her hands are a blur, the light from the algae reflecting in her stormy eyes.

The deeper she gets, the more she feels the pressure of the trench—not as a threat, but as an ally. The water here is dense and viscous, with a powerful current. Every gesture carries more weight; every ripple is amplified.

"The trench taught me something," Mara says, voice soft but sure. "The deeper the water, the stronger the connection. It's not just magic—it's memory. Density. Commitment."

Lyla watches, amazed. "You're different."

"I had to be."

Mara draws the final symbol: a spiral, triple-banded, the mark from her visions. The moment the glyph is complete, the whole wall pulses with a blue-green light, brighter than the sum of its parts.

Mara lifts her hand, and the current responds—eager, hungry, ready.

She starts the spell, fingers moving in a new pattern. It's not just Tideweaving anymore; it's something older, more brutal. She braids the energy of the trench with the surface current, knots it with a flourish only she can manage. The effect is immediate: the water shivers, the map flares, and Mara feels the connection spread outward, reaching toward the edge of the world.

Lyla is stunned. "How did you—?"

Mara doesn't answer. She's inside the spell now, driving it harder, letting the old magic course through her bones. The pain is gone; only the work matters.

She finds Finn's signature—buried, faint, but alive—somewhere near the coast. She anchors the message to him, sets the spiral burning, then lets it go.

The current leaps from the wall, a streak of living light, and vanishes into the dark.

Mara slumps, exhausted but exultant.

Lyla helps her up, silent for a long moment. "If the others could see this…"

"They will," Mara says. "If we win."

They look at the map, now etched in pure light.

It's the first time in days that the darkness seems like something they might survive.

Mara floats to the lip of the trench, arms spread, the black below her waiting like a dare. Lyla hangs back, eyes flicking between Mara and the unstable glow of the bioluminescent map.

For a moment, nothing moves but the cold.

Then Mara begins.

She draws the water up with both hands, pulling from the deepest currents, the pressure of a thousand meters stacking in her chest. It hurts, but the pain is now a friend, a guide. She remembers the city's anthem—how it vibrated the walls when sung at full voice—and shapes her own breath to match.

The water answers. It churns around her, a spiral at first, then complex waves that tangle and feedback on themselves. Glyphs appear in the water, loose, messy, then sharper, brighter. She repeats the shell pattern Finn once traced on her wrist, twisting it with new intent. The shape catches, doubling in size, then a hundredfold, until the entire wall is a firework of light and motion.

Every flick of Mara's hands sets another sigil burning: tide arrows, predator warnings, the triple spiral of the old vision. She works fast, frantic, riding the edge of blackout as the energy mounts. The current tugs at her, trying to pull her down, but she leans into it, lets the water braid through her hair and over her skin.

The glyphs glow blue-green, then white. The trench, usually so dead, is alive with a noise that's more vibration than sound.

Mara hears Lyla gasp, the awe and terror in equal measure.

With a final exhale, Mara sweeps her arms upward. The current explodes. The glyphs unspool in a ribbon of pure light, shooting up through the water column, carving a tunnel of color from the trench to the surface.

She rides the wave of exhaustion, almost blacking out, but Lyla catches her, steady as a mooring.

They watch as the signal shoots higher and higher, then disappears.

Mara shivers, but her bones feel new.

Lyla touches her shoulder. "They'll hear it. All of them."

Mara nods, still winded. "Then we get ready."

They settle in the lee of the ledge, watching the last of the glyphs fade from the wall, knowing the message is on its way.

Above, the darkness trembles.

Finn hunches in the stern of the battered skiff, eyes raw, nerves humming with old adrenaline and no sleep. The cove is a crater of stone, the water black and glossy, the only sound the scrape of his boots on the warped deck and the distant chop of a Coast Guard chopper making its pointless rounds.

He spreads the charts on his knees and cross-references positions, but it's just busywork. The activist crew is gone—either scattered or silent. The comms are dead. Blackwell's fleet owns the surface, and Finn is out of ideas.

He stares at the water, at the dull reflection of his own face in the dark. Every plan he tries to imagine dies before it reaches the bow.

He grips the edge of the skiff so hard his fingers go numb.

Then, without warning, the water beneath him flickers.

At first, he thinks it's his brain breaking—hallucination, sunstroke, the final curtain. But the light builds, blue and alien, pushing up from below like a hidden sunrise.

Finn scrambles to his feet. The boat rocks, almost capsizes, but he barely notices.

The glow intensifies. The surface rolls with energy, and then the current forms a pattern—no, a symbol. A spiral, triple-banded, glowing exactly like the shell Mara gave him. The same spiral she used to draw on his palm, back when everything felt possible.

Finn falls to his knees, dizzy.

The water is alive. The spiral opens, lines twisting and looping until they form a string of numbers. He recognizes them instantly: coordinates. A place in the open sea, just outside Blackwell's kill zone—a meeting point.

Then the spiral changes. The lines thicken, pulse, and split into two hands—one human, one unmistakably mer. They join at the center, then blur into a single word, written in the light itself:

TOGETHER.

Finn's breath catches, chest tight.

He laughs, sharp and helpless, then wipes his eyes on the back of his hand.

The spiral flares once more, then vanishes.

Finn doesn't hesitate. He sweeps the maps into a bag, fires up the engine, and points the skiff toward the new coordinates. The air is cold, but he barely feels it.

For the first time in days, maybe weeks, hope burns in him—white-hot and clean.

He guns the throttle, aiming for the rendezvous, already rehearsing what he'll say when he sees Mara again.

Above the water, the sky is empty.

Below, the current races him forward.

The sea is glass, the moon a gash of white on the horizon. Mara floats at the surface, letting the chill numb her, copper hair streaming out behind her like a signal flare. She scans the empty water, alert for danger and hope in equal measure.

Nothing moves at first. Then, far off, a single skiff guns toward her, bow skipping the waves. Mara feels her heart spike, an ancient terror that the boat is an enemy, that Finn is gone, that she is about to die alone.

But then she sees him—Finn, standing at the tiller, face wild, clothes rumpled and soaked with spray. He spots her, and without slowing, kills the engine and vaults into the water.

He surfaces close, arms out, gasping her name: "Mara—"

She is on him before he can finish, hands tangled in his hair, mouth on his cheek, his chin, his mouth. Finn holds her so tight that the water fights to push them apart. Her tail whips around his thighs, pinning him to her.

"I thought I lost you," he whispers into her wet hair, voice fraying at the edge.

Mara pulls back just far enough to look him in the eye. "Never again," she says fiercely.

Finn's laugh is half cry, half disbelief. "You did it. I saw the signal. The whole fucking sea lit up."

Mara smiles. "It worked?"

"Better than worked. The coast is crawling. Blackwell's scrambled every boat he's got, but they're all chasing ghosts."

Mara nods, already planning. "Good. We need the chaos. There are survivors—Merfolk, hatchlings, and fighters. If we move at dawn, we can cut off the net launchers before they reach the city ruins."

Finn wipes the salt from his eyes. "And after?"

"After," Mara says, "we sink their fleet."

Finn blinks. "All of it?"

She grins, the expression so sharp it hurts. "Every last one."

He laughs again, then pulls her close. For a moment, there is no war, only skin and salt and the crazy beating of two hearts in time.

Then reality slaps back. Finn glances over Mara's shoulder, eyes scanning for threats. "How long do we have?"

Mara does a quick mental calculation. "An hour, maybe two. But we'll need a surface relay. Can you get a message to the others?"

Finn nods. "I can. I will."

She kisses him, fast and hard, then releases his neck, tail unwinding.

"I have to go," Mara says. "The others—"

Finn touches her cheek, gently now. "Don't die again. Not if you can help it."

Mara laughs. "I'll try."

She dives, leaving only ripples behind. Finn hauls himself onto the skiff, starts the engine, and heads for the shore, brain already spinning with logistics, codewords, hope.

They will meet again, at the ruin, at dawn.

Mara swims down, fast, retracing the spiral of the message, picking up allies as she goes. Notch is there, battered but smiling; Coral, with a new band of scars but fire in her eyes; even Lyla, arms crossed and waiting, as if she knew Mara would bring the human with her.

They circle, old rivals, new friends, survivors all. Mara gives the plan, voice steady, eyes alight. "We end it tomorrow. No more running."

The others nod. Even the youngest fryling looks ready to fight.

They rest, for a moment, at the edge of the trench, watching the sky for a sign.

Above, Finn races the skiff through the night, leaving a glowing wake behind. At the far cove, Mona and Ava are already waiting, tuning the scanner, prepping the comms. Finn briefs them quickly, voice trembling with joy and fear and something more.

They set up the relay. They check the battery. They wait.

At dawn, the first message arrives—Mara's voice, clear as if she were standing right beside him:

Tomorrow, we end this.

Finn grins, all teeth.

He looks out over the water, to the spot where he last saw her, and whispers:

"We will."

The sea is not quiet, but tonight it holds a promise.

Tomorrow, there will be war.

Tonight, there is only hope.

17 Tempest Rising

Dawn is a bright wound, slicing the ocean open and bleeding gold across the waves. Finn stands on the battered deck of the lead activist boat—technically a retrofitted crabber, though its history is written in duct tape, sun-bleached protest banners, and a hard crust of salt. Around him, the flotilla wakes.

They come in all sizes: rust-eaten dinghies, sailboats with masts mended from salvage, a handful of proper trawlers commandeered by the more moneyed wings of the movement. Finn squints through the fog, counting: forty-two at the muster, but only if you include the two kayaks lashed to an outboard raft, their pilots still asleep in matching life jackets, feet propped on their waterproofed iPhones.

The blockade is a mess, but it's his mess.

He checks the time—05:09, three hours before the media said anything would happen. He likes to be early. Or maybe he no longer sleeps.

Mona mans the radio, her voice coming out in low, caffeinated bursts as she tries to wrangle the smaller craft into an actual perimeter. Finn has tuned her out, mostly, instead focusing on the crackle of the PA: every boat has a bullhorn, and he's got the master key.

He flicks it on. The feedback shrieks, then dies.

"Wake up, heroes," he says, trying not to sound as ragged as he feels. "You got a five-million-dollar armada sitting on your hands, waiting to roll over you. If you're on the blue team, check your GPS and close the gaps."

On the far edge of the circle, a cluster of teenagers—three of them, each with hair so neon-bright it looks toxic in the daylight—raise their fists and yowl, a sound that's almost a howl. Finn grins. The comms are full of static, but the flotilla tightens anyway.

He shifts to a private channel. "Ava, you see them?"

Ava's voice is a midnight rasp. "They're at anchor. No movement on the decks, but I've got at least six bodies in infrared. They're waiting for us to make the first move."

"Copy," Finn says. He hangs up, runs a hand over the deck rail, the wood gone furry with rot and barnacles.

He glances up at the sky. Clouds like bruises, sun just clearing the rim of the world. The perfect day for a bloodbath.

The real battle isn't on the surface.

Mara waits twenty meters below, just outside the kelp forest, her vision adjusted to the half-light that filters down in cold, wet shafts. The ocean here is all edges—sharp with chemical residue, laced with the signatures of a hundred thousand humans who've pissed, bled, and died into it over the last five hundred years. It's a delicate flavor, if you like your adrenaline marinated in existential dread.

Around her, the squad holds formation: eight Merfolk,

handpicked by Lyla and drilled to within an inch of their gills. They move as a single shadow, flickering in the cross-currents, but Mara can pick out every one by the way they hold their tails.

Lyla is to her right, her white hair as still as the grave. The only sign of nerves is the way her jaw flexes on every exhale, grinding teeth against some unspoken fear.

The signal comes as a tremor through the current: two sharp pulses, then a slow draw, the way you call a child home for supper. Mara answers, just a flick of a finger, and the school flows up, hugging the hull of Blackwell's flagship like a rash.

The ship is a monster—bigger than any in the city's memory, all steel and flat black paint and the stink of dead fish. Mara senses the hum of its systems, feels the electric field like static against her bones. She tries to picture the inside, the humans trapped there, running diagnostics and sipping bad coffee, convinced that today is the day they'll finally bag a legend.

She almost pities them.

Lyla shifts, points. The squad splits, each tail slicing for a different quadrant. Mara and Lyla take the port side, slipping under a tangle of old netting that dangles from the waterline like a warning.

They pause in the shadow, reading the vibrations.

Sea-Speaking is not like human talk. It's a pulse, a pressure, a microsecond of intent pressed into the body of the water. Here, in the chop under the poacher's ship, Mara and Lyla build a web of signals, mapping the enemy from bow to stern. Mara picks up the heartbeats: four humans on deck, two more below, and—there—a seventh, pacing near the stern, cold and calm.

Blackwell.

Mara wants to spit. Instead, she signals Lyla: Found him.

Lyla replies: He's mine.

Mara doesn't argue. Lyla's hate is a weapon, and today, they need everyone.

They position themselves directly beneath the flagship's hull, their scales a living mirror for the murky sunlight overhead. Mara flexes her hands, feeling the magic gather, thin and sharp and hungry.

Above, Finn watches as the flagship powers up.

He's been waiting for it: first a low rumble, barely audible over the wind, then the slow-motion ballet of crew emerging on deck. They wear dark uniforms—professional, ex-military, Finn bets—and they move with the cautious confidence of people who know just how many crimes they can get away with.

Ava calls in from the stern. "We've got movement. Deploying the flare in five."

Finn signals Mona, who starts the drone cameras. The sky fills with the buzz of rotors, each one broadcasting live to a thousand news feeds and possibly a million doomscrolling feeds worldwide.

"Go time," Finn mutters.

He grabs the bullhorn and climbs to the prow, boots slipping once on the slick.

He hits the horn: "This is an illegal operation. Stand down. A peaceful flotilla surrounds you. Any aggression will be documented and prosecuted—"

He sees Blackwell step onto the deck, elegant as a shark in a suit.

The captain raises his own megaphone, voice perfectly modulated. "You have no authority here, Mr. Gallagher. You are obstructing a legally sanctioned research mission."

"Bullshit!" Finn yells, the word amplified so loud it peels birds off the water.

The teenagers on the far boat cheer.

Blackwell smiles, a small, private thing. "Please recall that we have permission from the authorities. If you interfere, you will be liable for damages—both material and personal."

Finn's voice is steel. "Try it."

He switches to the closed channel. "Ava, now."

Ava fires the flare. It screams up, a blue-green comet, then pops, raining down a curtain of glittering light.

It's a signal: the net is about to close.

Underwater, Mara sees the flash.

She signals the squad: Go.

In an instant, eight Merfolk slam into the hull of Blackwell's ship, each finding their assigned mark. Mara's fingers flex, and she jams two lengths of bio-cable into the intake of the ballast pump. Lyla attaches an explosive charge—a homemade cocktail of chemical and old magic—directly to the propeller housing.

They peel off, fast as eels, leaving nothing but a smear of blood and adrenaline in their wake.

Above, the poacher ship shudders.

Mara grins, but the victory is hollow—she knows what comes next.

She signals Lyla: Ready for the real show?

Lyla's reply is pure ice: Let's give them a history lesson.

On the surface, Blackwell's crew is scrambling. The flagship lists, ever so slightly, then rights itself. Finn watches as two men in wet suits jump into the sea, knives out, heading for the hull breach.

He cues Mona. "Cut the perimeter. Send the swarm."

Mona's fingers dance. Four drones detach from the nearest skiff, buzzing low and fast, circling the flagship. Each drone carries a camera and a payload: dye for marking, sound for confusion, and a microgrenade, in case things get violent.

Finn watches as the drones force the divers back to the ladder, then pepper the flagship's hull with bursts of iridescent ink. The black paint is now a patchwork of color, every wound lit up for the world to see.

On the PA, Finn shouts, "Every move you make is live! Back

off, and no one gets hurt!"

He hears the teenagers whoop, even over the engines.

For a second, Finn lets himself believe it might work.

But Blackwell is not here to lose.

He lifts the megaphone, aiming it right at Finn. "You've made your point. Now I'll make mine."

The deck guns rotate. Finn hears the whine of motors, sees the targeting arrays flicker. He feels the panic spike in his own chest, the old animal fear.

He thinks of Mara, somewhere in the water below.

He shouts, "Scatter! Break formation! Everyone move!"

But he's a second too slow.

Blackwell gives the signal, and the first net launches.

It's not a net, not precisely. It's a web of polymer and microfilament, laced with weights and sedative pods, designed to capture anything within a hundred-meter radius and drag it to the surface, alive but paralyzed.

The net expands, a monstrous flower. It arcs over Finn's boat, trailing streamers that hiss as they hit the water.

On the deck, Finn watches the sun vanish behind the mesh.

Below, Mara and Lyla see it coming.

Lyla doesn't hesitate. She grabs Mara by the wrist, yanks her hard to the left.

"Now!" Lyla screams, and Mara pulls the current, twists it into a shield around their bodies.

The net slams into the water, wraps around them, but the shield holds—just barely. The pressure is immense, the sedative leaching through the water, but Mara pushes, and the shield explodes outward, shredding the nearest filaments.

She sees Lyla's face—bleeding, but alive.

"Go," Lyla rasps. "Get to the surface. Tell them."

Mara wants to argue, but there's no time. She surges upward, the current propelling her like a bullet.

Finn is fighting to cut the net from the mast when the water next to the boat erupts.

Mara breaches, catapulting up in a spray of foam and blood.

Finn drops the knife.

She lands on the deck, half-fish, half-fury, eyes wild.

Mona screams. Ava stares.

Finn grabs Mara and pulls her behind the wheelhouse.

"They're coming," Mara gasps. "All of them. You need to run."

Finn shakes his head. "We hold. We—"

She cuts him off, voice low and urgent. "You don't understand. This is just the first wave. Blackwell's got more. We have to—"

The PA crackles.

Blackwell's voice, calm as ever: "I see you've met the merchandise, Mr. Gallagher. Shall we negotiate?"

Finn's blood runs cold.

He looks at Mara, then at the flagship, then at the flotilla—half caught in the net, half trying to run, all of them trapped.

He looks at Mara again, sees the fear and the hope fighting in her eyes.

He makes a choice.

He picks up the bullhorn, clicks it on, and screams:

"To anyone who can hear me—sink the flagship."

Then he slams the throttle and aims the crabber straight at Blackwell's ship.

Mara howls, a sound so wild it rattles Finn's bones.

Behind them, the flotilla rallies. Every boat, every soul, every last scrap of hope, surges for the center.

Above, the sky is a wash of color and light.

Below, the ocean prepares to swallow it all.

The war begins at dawn, and neither side is ready for what

comes next.

The lower decks of the flagship are a maze of welded bulkheads and broken promises. Dr. Chen moves through them with the stealth of long practice, the motion of a woman who has measured every guard, every bolt, every blind angle in the space. The two crewmen at her back are defectors—one with a patch over his left eye, the other with a slouch that hides a mind for violence. They say little; they know their jobs.

The hallway reeks of hydraulic fluid and the sickly-sweet stench of bait. Chen's hands are steady, but the heart in her chest is a caged animal. She checks the time, minutes before the following shift change. If she can cripple the capture rig before sunrise, the whole war above will be for nothing.

They reach the engine room. The door is an old Navy hatch, reinforced after the last mutiny. Chen pulls the override—easy, Blackwell never changed the codes—and the defectors file in, quick and silent.

Inside, the noise is total. Banks of control panels blink and hum, everything automated, everything monitored by half a dozen techs in oil-stained coveralls. They're busy, faces hollowed by bad hours and worse pay, all of them staring at the screens that track Mara's people through the water. There is a map of the kill zone, and on it, a hundred ghostly signatures pulse in real time.

Chen feels sick, but pushes it down.

She signals the defectors. They scatter—one to the main breaker, one to the locker with the emergency explosives.

Chen approaches the chief technician, a big woman with buzzed hair and the eyes of a cornered dog.

"Status?" Chen says, voice clipped.

"Ballast is off by point-three, but we've got the schools herded. Commander wants another sweep before we dump the grid."

Chen nods, steps in close, then snaps the woman's larynx with a single jab. The tech drops, gasping, already blue.

The rest of the crew freezes. The one-eyed defector is at the panel, gun leveled. The other swings the crate of explosives onto the deck, a thunk so heavy it silences everything.

"This is a coup," says a voice behind them. Chen turns to see the XO, a former Navy man with an iron rod for a spine.

"Call it what you want," Chen says, moving to the next terminal. Her fingers blur as she yanks wires, flips dip switches, and scrambles the calibration. "This ship is a slaughterhouse. It ends today."

The XO draws his sidearm and aims it at Chen's chest. The defectors aim back.

The standoff hangs, a millimeter from blood.

Above, Blackwell senses the change.

He's standing in the command bubble, watching the skiffs close on his flagship, listening to the chorus of engines and the thud of the net launcher spooling up. The decks shake with every new volley. For a moment, he feels almost alive.

But then the lights flicker. The comms drop too static. The screens that showed Merfolk movement go dark, then flash with a red warning.

He doesn't hesitate. "Deploy the backup grid. Now."

His guard jumps. One slams a fist onto the emergency console. On a panel to his left, the kill switch glows: a last-resort system, wired by a sadist for a moment just like this.

"Launch the tridents," Blackwell says, and his voice is so calm even the guards look up, startled.

Below the waterline, torpedo tubes rotate. The first volley is not meant to kill, just to pin. The tridents are three-pronged, barbed with microtrackers and tipped with a payload of sedative designed to work on bodies twice as dense as human. They cut through the ocean with silent, implacable hunger.

In the engine room, Chen hears the launch. The ship vibrates, a low moan that rattles her teeth.

"NOW!" she shouts, and the defectors unleash hell.

One rips the fire suppression, flooding the room with halon. The other pops the explosives and slams them against the base of the net launcher's control. Chen herself tears the relay from the main board, sending a cascade of sparks through the line.

The XO fires, but the one-eyed man is faster. Two shots, both lethal.

The techs scatter, but the room is already choking with gas.

Chen holds her breath, wraps a rag around her mouth, and sets to work on the backup grid. Blackwell's men have hardwired a second control behind the main panel. It will take minutes she doesn't have.

Her vision is tunneling, her hands shaking now, but she keeps going.

The defectors drag the bodies out of the gas, then return, faces red, eyes leaking.

"You, okay?" one rasps.

"Just get me a clean line to the outside," Chen grates.

The man nods, disappears into the haze.

Chen cuts the last circuit, watches as the lights die, then surge back, this time in manual override.

She laughs—once, bitterly.

But then, on the monitor, she sees the tridents cut through the water.

Her stomach drops.

Underwater, Mara and Lyla have seconds to react.

The tridents are elegant, three-pronged, with tiny jets that correct course mid-flight. The first one misses, but the next arcs, curves, and buries itself in the tail of the Mer to Mara's left.

He screams, the sound a jagged shockwave. Mara feels the current whip, the pain spiking out into the water. The sedative works instantly; the Mer convulses, then goes limp, blood clouding the water.

Mara grabs him, tries to pull the barbs free, but they're engineered to resist even Tideweaving. The microfilament begins to reel him in, dragging him upward.

Lyla sees the next wave coming. She throws herself in front of Mara, tail flicking, arms out. The trident catches Lyla in the forearm, punching through flesh and bone.

Lyla howls, but doesn't stop. She twists, grabs the shaft, and snaps it in half. The sedative blooms in the water, but she fights through, claws the barbs out of her own arm.

They have to retreat. Mara signals the squad, her mind ablaze with panic.

But the tridents are only the beginning.

The reinforced net launches next: a curtain of polymer mesh, laced with capsules of paralytic toxin. Mara sees it coming—so beautiful, almost slow. She calls the current, tries to bend the net, but the water resists; the mesh is designed to negate magic, every knot a node of sonic disruption.

The net hits, and Mara is trapped, along with Lyla and two more.

They fight, but it's all for nothing. The mesh tightens, squeezing the life out of them.

Above, the deck guns fire a third volley: a sound pulse, tuned to the exact frequency that disables Merfolk's gills.

Mara feels her chest seize, her vision flickering.

Lyla's voice, faint and ragged: "Don't let them take you."

On the deck, Finn sees the nets haul up. He sees the bodies inside—Mara, Lyla, two others, thrashing, then still.

His own boat slams into the flagship, metal on metal, the sound a world-ending bell. Finn is thrown over the side, into the water.

He surfaces, gasping. The net is yards away, hauling his friends toward Blackwell's deck.

He screams, but no one hears it over the noise of the war.

In the command bubble, Blackwell watches the net rise, wet and glittering.

He smiles.

"Prepare the extraction bay," he says.

Below decks, the chaos is contained. The halon is vented, the defectors dead or dying. Chen has failed, but she is not done.

She slips out of the engine room, cuts through the dark, heads for the only thing that matters now: the captive tanks, and the hope that something, anything, is left to save.

The last Trident launches, and the sea goes still.

The battle has turned.

Above, Blackwell signals victory. Below, the nets close.

But in the dark, something stirs.

Mara's eyes open, storm-bright. Her hands flex on the mesh, and she whispers the words Lyla once taught her—old, forbidden, last resort.

The current answers.

The war is not over. Not yet.

The world is pain, then whiteout.

Mara wakes in the net. Her body is numb, but every cell screams. The sedative is supposed to paralyze, but it only slows her—the magic in her blood chewing through the poison, metabolizing it into fuel for rage.

Lyla floats beside her, eyes rolled back, lips peeled away from her teeth. The two other Merfolk caught with them are already out, tails limp, gills fluttering uselessly. Above, the hull of the flagship blocks the sun; below, the water churns with the signature of approaching drones.

Mara forces her hands to move, fingers clawing the polymer mesh. She feels the anti-magic nodes vibrate, the mesh humming with the exact frequency to disrupt Tideweaving. Even her thoughts seem to tangle, with every intention doubling back and being weaponized against her.

Lyla's voice, a thread of will: "Ready?"

Mara can't answer, so she pushes her answer into the current, the only way left.

The mesh tightens, hauling them up. The surface is a bright agony, the noise of engines and guns and shouting tearing at her skull. Mara smells human sweat, oil, and blood. She remembers what Lyla said—don't let them take you.

She doesn't plan. She acts.

She reaches for Lyla. They lock hands. For a second, nothing happens.

Then Mara lets the old magic run its course.

The current is a wire, and Mara is the short circuit. The net's disruption frequency is a wall, but Lyla finds the hole, the glitch, the fractional moment when the system resets between pulses. Together, they slip through the gap, then widen it, tearing a path through the mesh and into each other.

Their magic fuses, not in harmony but in pure combustion. It is not beautiful. It is not gentle.

The net shreds, the anti-magic nodes sparking, frying, and then going dead.

The air around them goes silent.

Finn surfaces twenty meters away, spitting seawater, vision

doubled by the slap of his own boat's wake. He wipes his eyes, sees the flagship looming above, nets hanging off both sides, bodies trapped in the filaments.

Then something changes. The net holding Mara and Lyla implodes, collapsing inward, then blowing outward in a shockwave that nearly knocks Finn from the water again. The two Merfolk launch upward, riding a column of current, Lyla's tail leaving a blood comet in the foam.

The cameras catch everything. Finn sees the drones cluster around the scene, every lens hungry for a miracle or disaster. He paddles for the nearest kayak, grabs its rail, and shouts, "Get this to the feed! Get it out now!"

The kid in the kayak fumbles for her phone, jaw slack, eyes huge.

Above, Mara and Lyla hover at the surface, their bodies framed in sunlight, slick with blood and terror.

On the command deck, Blackwell is very still.

He watches the net rupture, the live feed broadcasting to every console on the bridge. His men look to him for orders, but he says nothing for a full ten seconds.

Then, calmly, he says, "Deploy the drones. Full pattern. Target the red one."

His techs hesitate. One says, "Sir, the tridents missed. The nets—"

"Do it," Blackwell says, voice flat. "Use the new program."

The techs comply. From beneath the flagship, a pod of mini-subs launches—small, fast, painted in shark gray. Each drone carries a payload of smart harpoons, programmed to home in on a specific biological signature. They have Mara's.

Blackwell watches as the drones arc around, then dive.

He smiles. "Let's see how magic fares against physics."

Lyla sees the drones first, even before the surface. She signals Mara: Down!

They dive, but the sedative slows Mara, her limbs still leaden. The first drone snaps past, a streak of silver and black, harpoons firing in a tight cluster. Lyla knocks Mara sideways, taking the first shot herself. It glances off her tail, but the next one catches her in the side. The harpoon injects a new toxin, cold and vicious.

Mara screams, both for Lyla and herself.

She reaches the bottom, claws at the rock, and tries to hold on. The drones circle, then close in pairs. Mara wraps her arms around Lyla's body, tries to shield her, but the harpoons stick anyway—needles in her back, her thigh, her tail.

The pain is overwhelming. For a second, Mara loses herself.

Then she hears Lyla, barely a whisper: "Together."

Mara reaches, finds Lyla's hand, and pulls.

The current rushes in, a thousand memories, every lesson, every song. Mara pours herself into Lyla, and Lyla returns it, their magics knotting in a pattern neither of them recognizes but both understand.

It is a new thing, born in agony and desperation.

The water around them warps, the current reversing, folding over itself. The drones are caught in the whirlpool, their sensors blinded, and their harpoons useless. Mara and Lyla ride the vortex, twisting up and up, the pressure building, the pain sharpening into clarity.

At the surface, they break together, screaming.

Finn feels the water change.

He lets go of the kayak, swims for the flagship, and hands grasp the rails on a side ladder. Above, the deck is chaos: the crew is running, alarms are howling, and cameras are everywhere. In the distance, the activist boats swarm, closing the gaps, trapping the flagship in a ring of human desperation.

He pulls himself up and finds his footing on the slippery metal. The deck is a battlefield—bodies, nets, broken tech. Finn ignores it all, searching for Mara.

He sees her, standing on the stern, Lyla at her side, both of them bleeding, both of them alive.

He stumbles toward them, shouting, "Mara!"

She turns, eyes wild, lips torn.

"Finn," she rasps. "They're not stopping."

He grabs her hand. The skin is slick, almost inhuman. "We

have to end this."

She nods, barely able to stand.

He helps her to the edge, where the net rig is being prepped for another launch. The crew is scrambling, confused, and terrified of the red-haired monster that just killed their best tech. Finn sees one of the men reach for a gun, and he steps in front of Mara.

"Don't!" Finn yells. "She's not your enemy!"

The man hesitates, but the gun stays up.

Finn hears a click behind him. Turns.

Blackwell is there, holding a tranquilizer rifle.

"Step aside, Mr. Gallagher," Blackwell says, voice gentle.

Finn doesn't move.

Blackwell sighs. "I warned you."

He fires.

The dart catches Finn in the side. The world tilts.

Mara screams, leaps at Blackwell, claws flashing. He sidesteps, catches her arm, and twists. Mara is strong, but Blackwell is a different breed of predator.

He slams her to the deck and pins her with a knee.

"You could have been famous," he hisses in her ear. "You could have changed the world."

Mara spits blood in his face.

"Maybe I still will," she says.

Blackwell raises the gun, aims for her neck.

Then the deck shifts.

Lyla is not dead. She is very alive and furious.

She climbs the ladder, drags herself up, her body more wound than flesh. She sees Blackwell pinning Mara, sees Finn collapsed, sees the crew cowering.

She calls the current, every last scrap of magic.

The ship tilts, the sea boils, and from the deep comes a wave.

Not a wave—an uprising.

The water rises, lifts the flagship, the deck rolling as if it were a toy. Mara slips free of Blackwell, grabs Finn's arm, and drags him to the rail.

Lyla joins her, together pulling Finn over the side. They fall, hard, into the ocean.

Blackwell stares in horror as his ship lifts, then hangs, half out of the water. The cameras catch everything—his face, the impossible, the undoing.

In the water, Mara and Lyla haul Finn to the surface. He coughs, breathes, then laughs, wild and broken.

"You did it," he says.

Mara looks up at the ship, at the sky, at the cameras.

"We did it," she says.

On every screen, the world watches as the flagship hangs, suspended by a column of water. The activist flotilla circles, cheering. The Merfolk gather below, visible for the first time as a living army.

Above, Blackwell screams orders, but the ship does not respond.

Below, Mara and Lyla hold the current, the magic flowing through them in a double helix, a new pattern, a new world.

The future is written here, in blood and salt and the refusal to die.

Ultimately, the ship sinks. It doesn't capsize—settles back, broken but afloat.

The battle is over.

But the war is just beginning.

Mara and Lyla drag Finn to the shore, where the activists pull them up, wrap them in blankets, capture them with camera flashes, and new, raw hope.

Behind them, the Merfolk vanish, but not all the way.

For the first time, they are seen.

And for the first time, they see themselves.

On the deck of the ruined flagship, Blackwell stares at the sea, at the future that just killed his dream.

He thinks of Mara's last words—maybe I still will—and knows, in his marrow, that she's right.

He sits alone as the world moves on without him.

On the shore, Finn and Mara lean into each other, exhausted, unbroken.

"You still want to change the world?" Finn says, his voice croaking.

Mara laughs. "I want to survive it."

He takes her hand.

"Me too."

They look out at the ocean, at the storm of boats and people and possibility.

For a second, the future looks bright.

Then the sky clouds over, the rain returns, and the work begins.

But this time, they are ready.

This time, it is together.

Blackwell stands at the rail of his shattered flagship, every muscle a wire, every thought honed to a needle. He watches the sea reclaim his empire: drones and nets tangled, the crew huddled in knots, cameras capturing every failure in ultra-high definition. The world watches, and he can taste the shame, coppery and electric.

He tells himself this is just a setback. He's lost more than this before.

He goes below, ignoring the blood trail from his split eyebrow. The corridors reek of ozone and desperation. In the prep room, the dive suit is waiting: custom-built, carbon mesh, with a gel liner that can withstand a white shark's bite. The tank is triple-walled and redundant, and the mask houses a chip that reads brainwaves, amplifies focus, and turns thoughts into microsecond actions.

He pulls it on, locking the suit with fingers that don't shake. The weapon is last: a hybrid between a spear gun and a sound cannon, tuned to disrupt the precise frequency that Merfolk use to work their magic. Blackwell pats the case, almost fondly, then slings it over his back.

He opens the hatch and steps out onto the launch deck.

Nobody stops him. They know better.

The sea is grey and rough, the activist blockade still circling, but Blackwell ignores them. He steps to the edge, sets his mask, and dives.

Mara waits in the cold, feeling the weight of the ocean press her wounds shut. Lyla hangs back; her arm wrapped in kelp to slow the bleeding. The other survivors have scattered, the current thick with their fear and their hope.

She senses him before she sees him.

Blackwell is a line of pure violence in the water, every motion predatory, every thought edged with the hunger to win. Mara watches him drop through the layers, the cold not even slowing him, the suit burning a trail of raw energy through the sea.

She holds her ground. Waits.

He comes to rest twenty meters away, hovering in the blue.

He lifts the weapon, not to aim, but to show it off.

"Nice trick with the ship," Blackwell says, his voice piped through a speaker, obvious, no distortion. "But you know what impresses me more? Evolution."

Mara says nothing. She can feel the pain in her tail, the tear in her gills. But she holds the current, keeps it alive in her chest.

"You could change everything, Mara," Blackwell goes on,

drifting closer. "You and your kind. Imagine what we could learn, working together. Imagine what we could fix."

She bares her teeth. "We did work together, once. You broke it."

Blackwell's eyes narrow, just a hair. "I made you visible. The world knows you exist now. You'll never go back to hiding."

He aims the weapon, steady as death. "You belong in the future, not the past. The future I make, or the one that buries you."

Mara flicks her tail, ready to run, but she knows he's faster, here, now.

She looks behind him, past him, and whispers a word.

The school of jellyfish comes out of the dark, a thousand strong, their bells a wall of shimmering blue and gold. Each one glows with borrowed magic, the light pulsing in rhythm with Mara's heart.

Blackwell pauses, just for a second. Then he fires.

The sound cannon howls, a spike of force so loud Mara can feel it rip the water apart. The jellyfish explode, bioluminescent guts spinning into clouds. Mara dives through the gore, using the flash to blind the sensors on Blackwell's suit. She closes the distance, faster than thought.

He sees her coming. He swings the spear, but she twists, grabs the barrel, and jams it away. The blast tears open a crater in the silt, but misses her by centimeters.

He tries to rip the weapon free, but Mara is stronger. She kicks him in the chest, driving him backward. The carbon mesh cracks, but doesn't fail.

Blackwell headbutts her, hard, the mask splitting her lip. He brings up a blade, small and fast, and slices the side of her face.

Mara ignores the pain. She grabs his arm and bends it the wrong way. The blade falls.

For a moment, they are eye to eye, nothing between them but the current and everything they've lost.

"You could have been a god," Blackwell hisses. "You could have lived forever."

Mara smiles, blood in her teeth. "I don't want forever. I want to live."

She slams her forehead into his, the crack of bone vibrating down the length of his spine—the mask splinters. Mara lets him go, floats back.

Blackwell fires the cannon one more time, point-blank. Mara takes it full in the chest.

But the jellyfish cloud absorbs the blast; the bioluminescence flickers, then burns brighter.

She hangs there, suspended, her eyes storm-bright.

Blackwell empties the magazine, but nothing comes out but bubbles.

His tank is almost empty.

Mara drifts closer, slowly and deliberately.

"You're done," she says.

He tries to lunge, but the weight of the suit pulls him down.

Mara watches as he sinks, the bubbles thinning, the mask leaking. He tries to cut loose, but the suit won't let him. He keeps sinking.

She leaves him there, at the edge of the deep, a monument to what happens when you mistake power for ownership.

Above, on the ruined flagship, Finn watches the drone camera feed.

The world watches with him.

He sees the school of jellyfish, the flashes of Mara and Blackwell locked in battle, and the final blow. He sees Blackwell vanish, alone, into the trench.

A cheer goes up on the deck—small at first, then building. The activists hug, cry, and raise their fists in the air. Some drop to their knees, phones shaking as they stream it all to the world.

Finn smiles, tired and honest.

In the engine room, Dr. Chen makes her last play.

She's bleeding from a cut on her cheek, but she's alive, and the sabotage is ready. She flips the final breaker, shunting every remaining volt into the engine's cooling core.

The lights flicker, then die. The flagship's backup generator groans, then overloads. The entire ship goes black.

On the deck, the crew panics. Some jump overboard, others run for the lifeboats. None of them looks back.

Chen climbs to the surface and meets Finn and Mara on the deck.

"Is it over?" Finn asks, voice hoarse.

Mara looks out at the horizon, where the world's cameras watch the wreck, the water, and the dawn breaking over both.

"Not yet," she says. "But it's a start."

Blackwell's suit hits the bottom. The pressure is intense, but the suit holds up for a while.

He waits, hoping for rescue, for some miracle.

All he hears is the ocean and the faint whisper of Mara's last words.

He wonders what he would have done differently.

He closes his eyes, and the ocean is kind.

Mara finds Lyla on the rocks, bandaging her arm with seaweed. Finn sits beside them, holding Mara's hand, their fingers twined in a way that feels both new and right.

Around them, the shore is alive with activists and scientists, media and locals, every one of them staring at the water, waiting to see what comes next.

Lyla looks at Mara, smiles for the first time in years.

"What now?" Lyla says.

Mara thinks about it.

She thinks about the city, and the frylings, and the chance to build something instead of just surviving.

She thinks about Finn, and Lyla, and Chen, and even Blackwell, somewhere in the dark, learning the last lesson of all.

She smiles.

"Now we live," Mara says.

She slips into the water, Finn behind her, the surface broken and remade by their passage.

For the first time, the ocean feels like home.

The story spreads, out and out, until even the deepest trench can't hide it.

On the horizon, the future waits, sharp as a promise.

But for now, the tide is theirs.

18 Eye of the Hurricane

Mara senses them before she sees them. The pressure in her skull builds, a migraine made from radar, every pulse of the current carrying back the approach of Blackwell's new fleet. Even with her arm shredded and bound with kelp, she can map the perimeter in her head: three vessels, all steel, the lead ship spewing engine oil and discipline, the others holding a net between them like a garrote.

She floats thirty meters below the surface, breath slow, wound hot and angry. Her tail curls around the rocks, braced for recoil. The water is worse than before—hot pockets of chemicals, floating tangles of microplastics that stick to her scales like leeches. She tastes fear in the water, but also hope —the signature of her own survivors gathering in the depths. Somewhere in the dark, Lyla is rallying the hatchlings, prepping for the signal. Above, Finn's drones whine, sharp and eager, their propellers vibrating through the bones of the sea.

Mara closes her eyes, lets the map unfurl:

- The flagship, dead center, prow pointed at the ruins of her old city.

- The net launchers, port and starboard, preloaded with the new polymer, strong, thin, laced with disruptor nodes.

- Beneath, at twenty meters, a string of sensor buoys, each one tuned to her biology, a necklace of traps.

She probes deeper, casting her mind up through the water. Each net has a shadow—a diver waiting to pounce, a sharpshooter with a tranquilizer gun, a drone with a camera eye. Mara can feel the rhythm of the humans on the decks: the nervous fidgeting, the way their hearts spike every time they check a watch.

Her own heart stutters. Then hold.

She signals—not with words, but with a pulse of current. "Now."

She pushes off the rocks and swims straight down, into the cold. The pressure grows, grinding her ribs, flattening her ears. The trench below is a darkness that wants to consume her, but Mara is no longer afraid of darkness.

She tucks her arms, aims herself like a dart, and lets herself fall.

At sixty meters, she twists, opens her gills, and lets the magic come.

Current-Calling is muscle memory by now. She sweeps her hands back, and the water obeys—compressing behind her, stacking up like a spring-loaded fist. The chemical burn on her arm screams, but Mara ignores it. Every ounce of pain is just more fuel.

She rockets up, body a spear, and at the last second, arches into the path of the flagship's hull.

She breaks the surface in a pillar of white water, every scale on her body catching the sun. Her copper hair whips out behind her, a banner of blood and fire. She flies, truly flies, for a heartbeat, before gravity slaps her back to the world.

Above, a drone catches the moment—Finn's, judging by the angle—the lens jitters, then zooms, tracking her flight. Somewhere, Finn is watching, probably cursing, grinning.

Mara lands with a cannonball splash, vanishes.

She is moving before the humans can react. The ships' alarms blare; men scramble to stations, hands grabbing for net lines and triggers. Mara glances up once, sees the deck crew, and bares her teeth.

She wants them to see her.

She wants Blackwell to see her.

She swims parallel to the surface, just under the kill zone, weaving between the sensor buoys. The net drops behind her, too slow, useless. She calls a microcurrent, rides it like a bullet past the first ship.

A diver launches in her wake, trailing a harpoon on a polymer tether. Mara flicks her tail, cuts right, then loops back and wraps the line around a barnacled strut. The diver chokes, stalls, and spins.

On the deck, the crew is shouting, pointing, and shoving one another to peer over the rail. They see her, finally: the flash of copper, the silver-white of her belly, the deep green of her scales. She knows what they think—monster, myth, prize. She dares them to come closer.

Mara surfaces, just once, her head a streak of wet light. She screams—not for help, but for war.

The sound cracks the air.

A bullet follows, trailing a streamer of dye. She lets it miss.

From the flagship, a megaphone blares. The voice is unmistakable: Blackwell, resurrected, amplified, impossible to ignore.

"Nets to starboard! Don't damage the specimen!"

Mara laughs, and it comes out as a chain of bubbles.

She circles, waiting for the second volley. It comes faster this time—two nets, one above, one below, cross-patterned to box her in. She slows, lets the upper net close, then punches through the lower with a roll and a burst of power. The net tears; a chorus of cursing follows.

She tastes the battery acid of new tech in the water. They've upgraded—nodes tuned to her old tricks. Mara grins.

They have no idea what she's become.

She banks left, into the shadow of the support ship. A diver is waiting for her, but this one is smarter: he holds back, weapon at the ready, eyes locked on hers through the mask. Mara pauses, floats just out of range.

He makes the first move, firing a net gun. Mara grabs the net in both hands, flips backward, and yanks him into his own trap. The polymer cinches around his legs; he panics, flails, but Mara is gone before he can process defeat.

Above, the drone watches everything. Mara flashes a hand sign at the camera: a spiral, the old promise.

On the deck of the flagship, Blackwell appears at the rail, white-haired and immaculate in his custom dive suit. He watches her, stone-faced, megaphone dangling at his side. When he finally speaks, it's softer, more dangerous:

"You want to play, then let's play."

He signals to the crew. The net launchers reload. The water around the ships boils with new movement.

Mara edges closer, close enough to see the texture of Blackwell's face, the web of scars under the skin. She knows this is a dare. She also knows she will win.

She calls the current again, but this time, she pulls from the deep, the cold, dense water that slides in from the trench. It's like shoving a fist of glass into the warm surface, and the ships tilt, rocked by the sudden upwelling.

The crew on the deck tumbles. The net launchers falter. Mara uses the chaos, shooting up to the hull and grabbing hold of a ladder. She climbs, just enough to make eye contact.

Blackwell doesn't flinch.

He raises the megaphone, speaks quietly, but the sound cuts through the noise.

"You're not just an animal, are you?"

Mara blinks. It's not a question.

"You're better," Blackwell says.

Mara's fingers flex on the rung. She could launch herself onto the deck, take him now. But she's not here for a kill.

She's here for a lesson.

She lets go, drops backward into the sea, tail snapping in salute.

The humans on the deck lean over, desperate to catch another glimpse. Finn's drone floats above, documenting every second.

Mara circles one more time, making sure every eye is on her. She floats upright, hair fanned, scales burning in the sun.

She is beautiful. She is terrifying.

She is alive.

For a moment, nobody moves. The world pauses.

Then, at a signal from Blackwell, every weapon trains on her at once.

Mara smiles, a flash of teeth and promise.

She dives.

Below, the current calls her name.

She'll meet them in the heart of the kill zone.

She'll show them what magic really means.

But first, she needs to bleed—just enough to make them believe they have a chance.

She can feel Finn's eyes on her, even through the chaos.

She hopes he's ready.

She is.

Mara glides just beneath the surface, body pressed flat against the thermocline, every nerve a tripwire. The ships above form a loose horseshoe, each hull bristling with sensors and men with guns. Mara can feel the static—magnetic, chemical, even the raw heat of the engines, rippling down in bands of distortion.

She slows, lets the world narrow to a pinpoint. She extends her Sea-Speaking, sending out a soft pulse—an invitation, a command. The water answers with a whisper of sonar, the signature of a dozen dolphins sweeping in from the east.

They arrive in minutes, forming up on Mara's flank. Each one flickers with intelligence, their bodies reading the tension in the water, ready for a fight or a party. Mara signals them: Hold formation, then scatter on my mark.

She senses Blackwell's tactical shift before it happens—the crew on the lead ship tensing, the engine revving in a series of short, calculated bursts—the net launcher pivots, aiming a meter ahead of her projected path.

Amateurs, she thinks.

The net fires—a silver cloud, unfurling midwater. But Mara is already turning, and the dolphins break left, pulling the net into a spiral. Mara kicks up, grabs the trailing edge, and flips it with a burst of Current-Calling—the net inverts, doubling back toward the launchers, tangling two divers in the process.

Above, Finn's voice crackles to life. "That was not CGI, people. Repeat: Not. CGI. The net has been reversed. The crew is… they're bailing!"

A cheer rolls through the water—part animal, part human, all adrenaline.

The next wave of attack is smarter: the ships coordinate, laying down a grid of stunners and sonic pingers. Mara feels the sonic hum, tastes the pain as it rattles her teeth. The dolphins chatter, confused and stung, but Mara calls them in tighter, wrapping her own body around the lead animal's flank.

She rides the edge of the sound field, using her scales to absorb and reflect the worst of it. The dolphins adapt, ducking and weaving, their grace making a mockery of the military precision above.

The ships try to close the gap. Mara signals the dolphins, then dives deep and fast. The animals follow, forming a twisting helix behind her.

At thirty meters, Mara slows, lets the dolphins drift ahead, then signals a new wave.

From below, a column of jellyfish ascends—hundreds, maybe thousands, each one aglow with bioluminescent fire. Mara weaves through the mass, fingers trailing through the delicate bells, her magic coaxing them into a living shield.

The jellyfish bloom at the surface, lighting up the water with a wall of blue and green. The ships halt, unwilling to risk the engines or the men against the unknown.

Mara rises with the swarm, her own scales echoing the color, her hair a copper flare in the neon gloom.

Finn's voice again, urgent and awed: "If you're just tuning in, you are witnessing something unprecedented. The water… It's alive. The mermaid—Mara—she's controlling it. She's fighting back."

Mara smiles, baring her teeth for the camera.

The next net comes, but she's ready. She calls a micro-whirlpool, spins it tight, and the net shreds against the vortex. The dolphins leap above the wreckage, chirping triumphantly.

The deck crews go frantic. The flagship begins to pull back, the net launchers stalling as they try to reset. Mara seizes the opening.

She coils, then launches herself up through the wall of jellyfish. For a second, she's framed by living light, the cameras catching every scale, every drop of water streaming from her skin.

The world sees her not as prey but as the thing that ends the hunt.

She lands in the water, disappears, then reappears meters away, dancing through the chaos.

Above, Finn's voice is barely a whisper. "She's free. She's winning."

Mara circles the dolphins once, then twice, in perfect step. The jellyfish wall drifts, blinding the ships and their sensors.

The only eyes that matter now are the ones watching from shore, glued to the feed.

Mara knows it. She glances up, flashes a smile, and for the first time, feels the tide turn inside her.

She is not just surviving.

She is the storm.

She sends a last ripple to the dolphins—Scatter, confuse, regroup at the signal—then dives, vanishing into the blue.

Behind her, the ships scramble, the men shout, and the nets

launch in every direction.

But there's nothing left to catch.

Not today.

The water is empty for a moment. Blackwell's flagship glides forward, the other ships hobbled and drifting. Above, searchlights rake the waves, desperate for Mara, for any sign of the threat they have no tools to name.

Below, Mara gathers herself. Every joint aches; her wounded arm flares. She floats, letting the water pass through her gills, and finds the old center, the memory of the city and family, and the voices that made her.

She thinks of Lyla, of Notch, of the faces lost to nets and poison and pride. She thinks of Finn, glued to the monitor, heart pounding. She thinks of every idiot human who ever imagined a mermaid and decides to give them a new story.

The flagship lumbers overhead. Mara floats up, just meters beneath the hull. She raises both arms, fingers flexing, and calls every drop of power in her blood.

The Tideweaving answers, hungry and wild.

The current bends around her, slow at first, then tighter, denser. She weaves in the memory of every spiral ever etched in coral, every old anthem, every pulse of the city's old heart. The water glows, faint at first, then brightens, a blue-green lantern burning in the night.

The flagship's hull vibrates. Alarms go off above, men

running to and fro, unsure whether the threat is inside or out. Mara ignores them. She tightens her grip on the current, then lets it build, lets it climb.

She rises, inches from the steel, arms stretched wide. The energy is unbearable, every scale on her body burning with it.

Then she releases.

The sea lifts the flagship.

Not all the way—just enough for the hull to break the surface, the whole ship shuddering in a way no machine is meant to survive. For a second, the men on deck hang in the air, weightless. The spotlights swing wildly, pointing in all directions.

Mara hangs below, queen of the undertow.

She rotates her wrists, and the water forms a spiral of dolphins and jellyfish, each layer a different color, each twist a different anthem. The marine life rides the current, circling the flagship in an impossible work of art, a living testament.

On the deck, Blackwell stumbles to the rail, eyes wide. For a moment, he is nothing: not a captain, not a predator, just a man, helpless against the tide.

The glow rises, casting everything in spectral color. Mara lets herself be seen.

Blackwell's hands, which have never known defeat, tremble.

He lowers the gun, lets it fall, and raises his empty hand.

"Stand down," he says, voice barely above a breath. "All vessels—stand down."

Across the water, the smaller ships go silent. The nets retract.

The men on deck drop their weapons, stunned.

In the distance, Finn's voice comes through the drone, choked with emotion. "It's over. She did it. It's over."

On shore, the activists howl. Some drop to their knees. Some weep.

The camera zooms in on Mara, suspended in the glow, her body battered but radiant. Her copper hair burns against the blue; her eyes fixed on the flagship. For a long minute, nobody moves.

Then, slowly, the flagship settles back, the hull kissing the water with a shudder. The spiral breaks apart, dolphins scattering, jellyfish pulsing in wild, frantic joy.

Mara drifts down, away from the surface.

On the deck, Blackwell sags to his knees, mouth open. He is not dead, but the fight has gone out of him.

Above, the drone keeps filming, hungry for every pixel.

Mara surfaces once, just her eyes and the flare of her hair.

Finn catches her in the lens, and for a second, the whole world is only the space between them.

They don't need words.

Mara tips her chin, just a hair. Finn grins, all teeth and salt.

Behind him, the coast is a line of lights and sound and a future that won't be erased.

Mara dives, vanishing into the afterglow.

Finn puts a fist to his heart, the gesture crude but true.

The world sees, and the world remembers.

This is how wars are won.

Below, Mara glides through the wreckage of the battle, her body lit by the last sparks of magic. She finds the dolphins, drifting in a tight circle, waiting for her.

She joins them, swimming in silence, the taste of victory new and unfamiliar.

The water is thick with potential.

Mara breathes it in; lets it settle in her bones.

For the first time, she feels like more than a survivor.

She feels like the future.

On the surface, Blackwell sits alone, his hands open, staring at the horizon.

He will not leave a mark on the world—not the way he hoped.

But somewhere, in the memory of the current, Mara has already erased his name.

There is only the tide, and the stories it carries.

And tonight, the ocean belongs to her.

19 Calm After the Storm

There's a saying among the surface folk: negotiation is war, just wetter. Mara sits at the end of the conference table, hands folded, scales dry and itching where her tail is confined inside the rented wheelchair. The room is all glass and glare, perched above the marina so that the yachts and patrol cutters in the harbor are visible through a smear of seagull shit on the window. Every chair around the table is filled with a human: bureaucrats, scientists, politicians, their names stenciled onto folded cards as if that would keep them from being devoured.

On the opposite side, Finn, in a battered windbreaker and conference-issue name tag, sweats through his shirt. He has not stopped bouncing his knee for the last hour. To Mara's left, a pitcher of water beads sweats onto the legal pad, soaking a sketch Finn made of the city ruins at low tide.

The Minister for Fisheries, a soft-spoken man with a broad smile, is speaking. "I appreciate your… enthusiasm, Miss Ondine. But the economic realities—"

Mara cuts him off with a look. Humans refer to it as the "predator stare." "The economic realities," she says, "are that you will kill the last of us before your grandchildren are born."

A woman in a dark suit, with "Environmental Law" stenciled on her badge, leans forward. "The latest census does not bear that out. You claim three hundred individuals. The scientific

estimate is under one hundred. That is a significant discrepancy."
"We don't trust your census," Mara says.

The Minister sighs. "Be that as it may, the proposal on the table—this 'exclusive zone'—would eliminate fishing rights in three separate bays. That's not tenable. The livelihoods—"

"Your nets killed my cousins," Mara says, voice low.

Finn winces. He tries to intervene, pushes his glasses up the bridge of his nose, but Mara keeps her eyes on the Minister. "Three days ago, your trawler 'Lucky Number' used a drift net in restricted depth. The crew reported dolphins. They lied. They caught my kin and dumped them before you even showed up with your nice blue helicopter."

The woman in the dark suit makes a note. "You have proof?"

Mara nods at Finn. He pulls a thumb drive from his jacket and slides it across the table. "Video from an activist drone," he says. "And, uh, corroborating tissue samples from the stranding site."

He tries to smile, but the room isn't buying it.

The Minister's aide, a young man with a side part and a gold watch, snatches the drive and inserts it into his laptop. The screen flashes: ocean, the drone's jittery altitude, then the blur of bodies in the net, the glint of red hair among the bycatch. Someone retches softly.

Mara keeps her eyes on the Minister. She can smell the panic behind his eyes. Humans don't like losing face.

The Minister clears his throat. "That is… regrettable. But not proof of intent."

Now Mara looks at Finn. He nods, hesitant, then turns to the Minister. "If I may," Finn says, and his voice is steadier than usual, "what Mara is proposing isn't just a conservation corridor. It's a human safety measure. The last incident—" he glances at Mara, "—resulted in fatalities on both sides."

"Industrial sabotage," the aide mutters.

Mara's jaw clenches. She almost says it: You have no idea what I've lost. But instead, she breathes. Finn's hand lands gently on her elbow, a gentle reminder of protocol and patience.

The woman in the dark suit addresses Mara directly. "Would you be amenable to a joint monitoring program? If we establish baseline population numbers—"

"You want to count us," Mara says, "so you can claim we never existed when we're gone."

Another official, older, his voice the brittle edge of a lifetime in committee rooms: "If you want protected status, you must be legible. To policy. To law."

Mara studies the pattern of veins at the old man's temple. She tries to imagine him underwater, eyes bulging, mouth open. She wonders if the Minister has ever swum beyond the hotel pool.

Finn coughs. "Let's talk about the boundaries," he says, redirecting. He unfurls a chart—hand-annotated, splashed with coffee—and points. "This cove is already a no-take zone for spawning rockfish. If we extend the Merfolk exclusion area here, the overlap—"

"We can't set a precedent by ceding the ocean to a mythological species," the aide says, voice gone shrill.

Now Mara moves. She stands, the chair scraping behind her, and every head in the room whips to track her. She is taller than most of them. Her hair burns under the fluorescent lighting, and even on her legs, even in the chair, she radiates something that makes people flinch.

She walks to the end of the table, picks up the Minister's water glass. For a second, the whole room holds its breath, expecting—what? An assassination? A curse? Mara tips the glass, watches the liquid spiral.

"Do you know what this is?" she asks.

"Water," the Minister says, wary.

Mara smiles, but it's a warning. She closes her hand over the rim and flexes her fingers, calling the smallest current, the easiest magic. The water sloshes, then lifts in a perfect column, coiling around her hand like a snake.

Every human in the room recoils. Chairs clatter. The aide knocks over a laptop.

"This is what you fear," Mara says. She lets the column writhe, then spiral into the shape of a shell, the pattern Finn once traced on her palm. "Not that we are monsters. Not that we are too many. But that we will outlast you, even as you poison the ocean."

The woman in the dark suit tries to recover, but her pen hand is shaking. "That display is… unnecessary."

Mara lets the water drop, splattering legal pads and iPhones with salt. "So is genocide."

Finn stands, too. Not as dramatic, but his voice is still compelling. "The proposal stands," he says. "We're not leaving without it."

The old man leans back and watches Mara through heavy-lidded eyes. "Even if we say yes," he murmurs, "what keeps you from sinking our boats? What stops the next war?"

Mara looks at Finn, then back at the old man. "You don't get to ask for mercy and threaten us in the same breath."

Finn says, "The alternative is extinction. For everyone."

A long silence. The Minister looks to his aide, who has closed the laptop and is staring at his own trembling hands. The woman in the suit bites her lip, reviewing her notes. The old man is the first to break, his voice small and resigned. "Draft the treaty."

The Minister hesitates, then nods. "It's a start," he says.

Mara nods once. She sits again, scales prickling, anger boiling off her like steam.

Finn sits, too, relief leaking out of him. He nudges her hand under the table, a secret gesture. She almost smiles.

The treaty is printed, reviewed, and slid down the table to the Minister, who signs it with a ceremonial pen that wobbles in his grip. The woman in the dark suit signs next, then the old man, then Finn.

Mara doesn't sign, but she places her palm on the paper, leaving a wet mark in the shape of the spiral shell.

The Minister eyes it, then stamps the page.

"That's a legally binding wet signature," Finn says, almost giddy.

Mara stands, gathering herself, and faces the room. "We will keep our word," she says, voice ringing.

As she and Finn leave the chamber, the humans watch them go, eyes wide—some with fear, some with something dangerously close to respect.

On the elevator down, Finn leans his head against the glass and watches the harbor slide by.

"You almost exploded back there," he says.

"I almost did," Mara admits.

"Thank you for not," Finn says.

Mara laughs, a low ripple. "We'll see if it's enough."

Below, the water waits. She feels the new current already; a pulse of hope threaded through with doubt.

But it is a start.

If the city is a body, then today it is in surgery. The underbelly of the reef bristles with Merfolk: teams of artisans and hatchlings moving through clouds of silt, wrangling coral fragments and lengths of scavenged steel. The water is milky with work. In the heart of it all, Lyla Pearl floats upright, directing the chaos with staccato flicks of her tail. Where Lyla points, the city listens.

They are remaking the central artery—once a tunnel of pure living coral, now rebuilt with a spine of metal mesh and sleeved with regrowing pink. Three Merfolk brace a girder while a fourth torques it into place. Apply a smooth paste of quick-setting substrate over the seams. The archway is no longer what it was: the old grandeur is gone, replaced by something cruder, yet tougher.

Sunlight filters down through the breakwater above, fracturing into shifting bands that dance over the chaos. The light falls on Lyla's hair, rendering it as white as fever, and turns her scales to a matte blue-black. She circles the site, inspecting, correcting, never pausing.

A youngling with mismatched fins brings a length of net-repellent cable—human salvage, barbed with conductive wires—waiting for approval. Lyla nods, then gestures with a precise spiral of her finger. "Double the ties on the east wall," she says, voice a tuned vibration through the water. "The current pulls hardest there."

The youngling obeys, eyes shining.

Mara glides in from the edge, copper hair streaming like a comet. She pauses at the first new archway, running her hand along the transition from real coral to reinforced mesh. The old part is rough, almost soft, alive with the squirm of polyps. The news is cold and hard, studded with the memory of violence.

She knows why Lyla built it this way. The next attack will not come through kindness.

Mara lets herself drift, watching the workers. They move with the stubborn, beautiful logic of a school, coordinated without ever speaking above a whisper. A pair of young frylings swim circles around her, then dart in close.

"Are you her?" one asks, voice squeaky with emotion.

"Her who?" Mara says, but the smile gives her away.

"The city-saver," the other fryling says, eyes huge. "The humans say you killed a boat with your voice."

Mara shakes her head. "It was a lot of water. And a lot of help."

They don't believe her, but that's fine. Legends are easier to live with than reality.

From above, Lyla barks, "No idle tales!" The frylings scatter, giggling, leaving Mara to float in their wake.

She swims farther in, past the old market square, where the scars of Blackwell's attack are still visible as pockmarks in the coral. Here, the crews are slower, more careful, working to re-etch the glyphs of the city's founders onto slabs of recycled bone. Mara runs her fingers over a half-finished spiral, feeling the weight of history, the grooves worn by thousands of hands before hers.

A young artisan, scales the color of dusk, looks up. "We're using the old stories," she says, pride and worry in equal measure. "Do you think they'll last?"

"If you keep telling them," Mara says, "they will."

The artisan smiles, then returns to her work.

At the far edge of the site, teams are installing the first of the new gates—hybrid barriers that hum with low-grade magic and spark at the slightest touch of electricity. The old wards failed when the water was poisoned. These will not. Lyla stands by the gate, arms crossed, watching as three workers lever it into position.

Mara swims to her, taking the long way around the debris field. The closer she gets, the clearer it is: Lyla has not slept. Her eyes are raw; her hands scuffed from stone and wire.

"Stubborn as ever," Mara says, sidling up.

"Someone has to be," Lyla replies, not taking her eyes off the workers.

For a moment, neither says anything. The water is thick with grit and ghosts.

Mara tries to find the right words. "I thought this would hurt more," she says. "Seeing it like this. Broken, patched. But…"

"But it's ours," Lyla says, finally looking at her. "Every cut. Every bolt."

Mara nods.

Lyla glances at the workers. "They think you're a hero, you know."

"They're wrong."

Lyla smirks, the old competitive glint in her eye. "Maybe. But we need heroes right now."

"Do you?" Mara asks. "Or just survivors?"

Lyla considers, then shrugs. "Same thing, these days."

A billow of sand erupts as the gate locks into place, the workers tumbling in a cloud of debris. Lyla grins, a little too sharply. "Perfect," she says.

Mara lets her fingers trace the curve of the arch, the seam between new and old. "It will hold," she says, more to herself than to Lyla.

"We'll hold," Lyla says, voice soft.

A cluster of younglings floats up, trailing shells and bits of scavenged glass. "Is it true?" one pipes. "Will the humans leave us alone now?"

Mara considers the question, glances at Lyla, then says, "It's true enough."

The younglings seem satisfied, darting away to spread the

news.

Lyla watches them go. "You'll have to teach them, you know. About the old ways. About what it means to be part of the current."

Mara nods, knowing what it means. "I'll start tomorrow."

They float together, sisters in blood and war and rebuilding, surveying what's left.

Mara sees the city as it is: ugly, unfinished, stubbornly alive.

It is enough.

She looks at Lyla, and in the silence, a thousand old arguments dissolve.

They face the new gate, side by side.

For the first time, Mara lets herself believe in the future.

Dr. Chen's new lab is located in the old ferry terminal, which has been reclaimed from rats and rot and retrofitted for the next era of science. She rules it like a queen from her glass-walled throne: at the center, a long counter groaning with vials, mesh sieves, and the latest in 3D-printed pipettes; at the periphery, a ring of tanks brimming with every species of coral and crustacean local to the coast. On the far wall, floor-to-ceiling windows offer a clear view of the protected bay, where the water is so clean it glows.

Today is outreach day, which means chaos. Humans and

Merfolk—none of them quite comfortable in the space—bump elbows and dorsal fins as they work in pairs. The human grad students are obvious: all patched jeans, anxious questions, and hands stained with Sharpie and salt. The Merfolk, in contrast, move with eerie, deliberate calm, fingers trailing over glassware as if mapping it for the first time. Now and then, one will flick their tail and send a wave of brine across the table, to the delighted shrieks of the frylings and the resigned sighs of the interns.

Dr. Chen threads through the melee, pulling up next to a group clustered around a new microscope. "Anyone notice the pH drift in the sample?" she says, voice soft but carrying. A young Merfolk in a borrowed wetsuit blinks huge silver eyes and nods. "Yours?" Chen asks.

The Merfolk flushes blue, then says, "I added algae. For taste."

Chen laughs—a rare, genuine sound. "Next time, clear it with the protocols first."

The human partner, a bespectacled kid with a chronic tremor, raises a hand. "Can we calibrate it? The colorimeter's off."

"Try again. And remember," Chen says, addressing the whole room, "contamination isn't always the enemy. Sometimes it's the hypothesis."

She moves on, checking tanks—the last one houses a pair of tiny anemone colonies, one thriving, the other ghost-pale. Chen taps the glass; the healthy one contracts; the sickly one does nothing.

She calls over a Merfolk with iridescent scars lacing her arms. "What's wrong with this colony?"

The Merfolk peers in, her face unreadable, then points. "The flow is wrong. Not enough food moves past. You feed but don't move the water."

"Exactly." Chen grins, then waves her forward. "Show the others?"

The Merfolk nods, grabs a slender glass rod, and demonstrates: swirling water in the tank with a spiral motion, imitating the natural current. The anemones sway, catching more plankton with every pass.

On the windowsill, a trio of frylings crowd together, faces pressed to the glass. Chen sees what they see: a pod of wild Merfolk in the bay, tails flickering as they patrol the boundary. The frylings chitter in a mix of human and Mer-sign, mimicking the motions.

Chen can't help herself. She steps over and opens the window. "Go on, then," she says. "Ten minutes, but don't chase the squid farm."

The frylings spill out, wriggling into the water with barely controlled chaos.

A few meters down the dock, a figure walks in: Finn Gallagher, hair stuck up in every direction, shirt two sizes too big. He looks lost for a moment, then sees the familiar face at the bench and waves.

Chen hides a smile. "Late as always, Finn."

"Got waylaid," he says, out of breath. "One of the reporters wanted to see the protected zone, and then the—uh, the new crew is here?"

Chen gestures. "Orientation is ongoing. Try not to break anything."

Finn nods, then makes his way to a group running titration

samples. He fits right in, hands-on, already rolling up his sleeves.

Mara arrives next, barely making a sound. She slides into the room from the waterside entrance, her clothes dripping with brine onto the floor. The graduate students freeze, then part to make room, as if someone had just opened a path for royalty.

Mara glances at Chen, then at Finn. Her gaze is softer than Chen remembers.

Chen clears her throat. "Can I have everyone's attention?"

The room quiets, all eyes—human and not—locked on her.

"I want to introduce the latest initiative," Chen says. "It's the first of its kind: a joint human-Merfolk research project, focused on coral restoration and sustainable stewardship of the bay."

A buzz of excitement ripples through the room. The Merfolk exchange glances; the humans lean in.

Chen turns to the nearest tank, where a human and a Mer are working together. "Show them the new camera."

The human pulls out a bright orange unit, sleek and streamlined, with a housing that looks as if it were grown rather than manufactured. The Merfolk partner explains, in clear Mer-sign and halting English, "It works in the deep. It's built from an old shell and plastic. We made it together."

The room applauds.

Chen takes the camera and hands it to the Merfolk. "Want to run the first test?"

The Merfolk nods, then slips the device into a tank and activates it. A live feed appears on the lab's monitor: close-up shots of coral polyps, the subtle movement of tentacles, the swirling motes of plankton.

"See that?" Chen says. "Real-time. No disturbance. No intrusion."

The Merfolk grins, sharp teeth flashing.

Finn watches from the edge, a look of pure pride on his face.

Mara sidles up, whispers, "You're changing them."

"Maybe," Finn says. "Maybe they're changing us."

Mara smiles, a real one.

Across the room, a pair of humans fumble through a set of Merfolk hand signs, trying to ask about a water sample. Their partner, a young Mer with a broken dorsal fin, laughs and answers in perfect English: "You're signing 'clownfish' not 'current.' But it's close."

The humans blush, then try again.

Chen walks the room, checking each station. She sees the subtle shifts: the way the humans are learning to listen, not just observe. The way the Merfolk are picking up lab technique—careful, but never losing their own rhythm. Each is adapting, becoming something new.

She stops by the main tank, where Mara and Finn are watching the feed.

"Do you think it will work?" Mara asks, voice lower than usual.

Chen weighs the question, then says, "We don't have a choice. The old ways nearly killed the reef."

Finn nods. "But we're getting better."

Mara studies him. "You always believed that."

"I did," Finn says. "I do."

Chen feels the weight of the moment, then decides to gamble. "Would you like to take the first team out? Into the field, for the baseline survey?"

Finn looks at Mara, then at Chen. "Us?"

"You," Chen says. "You're the only ones I trust not to screw it up."

Mara straightens, her pride evident. "Then we'll do it."

Chen grins. "Try to bring the cameras back in one piece."

Finn laughs. "No promises."

The lab is noisy again, the tension replaced by a shared purpose.

Chen watches them go—Mara and Finn, side by side, a bridge where before there was only distance.

She looks around her lab, at the teams already prepping for the next experiment.

For the first time in years, Dr. Chen feels optimistic.

At the edge of the dock, the frylings break the surface, waving to the lab.

Mara waves back, her hand a splash of color in the light.

Finn pulls a set of maps from his bag, already plotting the first dive.

The future is bright, and the water holds endless possibilities.

The boardroom is a coffin with windows. Oak panels, ten meters of burnished table, and bottled water lined up like tombstones. At the head, three government appointees in matching gray, each with a stack of legal pads and a digital recorder ticking like a bomb. Down the right wall, the corporate phalanx: five lawyers in suits so dark they eat the light, faces scrubbed to a uniformity of contempt. On the left, the public gallery—two dozen journalists, a couple of marine biologists, a clutch of activists with homemade buttons that say SAVE THE TIDE.

At the witness table, Blackwell sits, smaller than his legend would suggest. He's lost weight since the day of the siege; the suit hangs on his shoulders, and the color in his hair is more salt than pepper now. His hands rest on a battered brief, the knuckles yellow and cracked, and he keeps his eyes on the table until the Chairman calls his name.

"State your full name for the record."

"Marcus William Blackwell," he says, the voice all gravel, none of the old smooth.

The first lawyer—a woman with a carnivore's smile—stands. "Captain Blackwell, how long did Atlantic Harvesting and Research employ you?"

Blackwell doesn't look up. "Fourteen years, seven months."

"And your position at the time of… the incident?"

"I was Chief of Vessel Operations," Blackwell says. "I oversaw all open-water expeditions. Including the ghost fleet."

The Chairman leans forward. "We have your written statement, but we need clarity on your claims regarding environmental violations."

Blackwell opens the brief, pulls out a thick folder, and slides it across the table. "Every log. Every unauthorized chemical dump. Every kill order." His hand hovers for a second, then releases.

The lawyer raises an eyebrow. "These are your own records?"

"Yes, ma'am," Blackwell says. "I kept them myself. I figured someone should."

She flips through the first few pages, then gestures. An assistant collects the folder and passes it to the board.

The second lawyer, an older one, jumps in. "You claim your former employer knowingly ordered the use of unapproved agents in protected waters."

"They did," Blackwell says. "You'll find dates, signatures. And video."

He produces a thumb drive and sets it on the table.

A tech hauls out a projector and wires it to a wall screen. For a second, the room is washed in the blue of the open sea. The first video plays: a cargo vessel in silhouette, men in safety gear dumping barrels overboard. The barrels split open as they hit the water, clouds of phosphorescent chemical curling out.

The lawyer tries to cut in, but the Chairman waves him off. "Let it run."

The following clip is even worse: deckhands in full respirators, rolling cages of captured marine mammals to the edge and pitching them over one by one, with no ceremony. The water churns as the bodies hit.

The third video is just a still: the city, as seen from an ROV—once-living coral now dead, colorless, bleached.

The lawyer looks pale. "Where were these videos taken?"

Blackwell is silent for a second. Then: "Two miles east of the old city. The chemicals sterilized everything in their path. Took the reef with it."

The gallery murmurs. In the front row, Dr. Chen is stone-faced, arms folded. Finn sits beside her; fists balled in his lap.

The lawyer tries to shift the ground. "But you profited from these operations."

"Yes," Blackwell says, "and I'll answer for it. That's why I'm here."

The Chairman looks at him, searching for the old arrogance. There is none left.

Blackwell says, voice cracking, "I saw what we did. I saw what I did. It wasn't just the city. We salted the trench. We took out every last thing that lived there to chase a legend." He shakes his head. "I never saw a war end so fast, or so completely."

The next question is softer. "Why testify now?"

Blackwell looks up, finally, at the board, at the lawyers, at the gallery. "Because I owe them," he says, and for the first time, the room hears the grief. "Because I thought we were the apex. Turns out we were the parasite."

The carnivore lawyer, thrown off, tries to recover. "You claim specific executives ordered these actions?"

Blackwell nods. "I do. And I'll sign the declaration, if you'll have it."

He does, hands shaking as he scrawls his name across the page. The Chairman stamps it, then slides the copy down to the government prosecutor.

The lead lawyer, desperate, objects. "We reserve the right to review—"

The Chairman cuts him off. "You will have that opportunity, counselor. For now, we thank the witness."

Blackwell stands, not sure where to go.

The Chairman says, "One more question, Captain."

He stops, turns.

"If your information is accurate, what would you have us do?"

Blackwell swallows. "Fix what you can. Protect what's left. If there's a way, I'll show you where the worst of it is. Guide your teams. Hell, I'll drive the boat myself."

In the back row, Mara stands, hair a copper halo in the light. For a moment, she and Blackwell lock eyes.

He doesn't expect forgiveness. But he needs her to see he's trying.

Mara nods once. Blackwell breathes.

The Chairman thanks him again, and he leaves the table, moving past the lawyers, past the board, past a future he will never quite fit into.

The gallery erupts, but Blackwell hears only the blood in his ears.

Outside, the sky is storm-gray, the air thick with rain.

He steps into it, lets the water do its work.

They sit on the edge of the world, or what's left of it. Below, the headland drops straight into the bay—a clean plunge, windblown and hard as bone. The evening light slicks the water with gold, turning the surface glassy, and through it Mara can see the city: fractured, but remade, a living thumbprint on the bottom of the sea.

Finn sits next to her, elbows on knees, eyes fixed on the horizon. He's dressed for the weather—old fleece, battered jeans, a scarf that once belonged to his mother. His hands are raw from days spent wrestling with boats, ropes, and bureaucratic paperwork.

The wind whips Mara's hair around her face. She lets it tangle, enables the salt to bite her lips, the memory of blood and war now a faded ache. She flexes her tail, the scales catching the sunset, throwing ripples of color onto Finn's thigh.

He points. "See the new markers?"

She looks: a string of buoys, each flashing a coded sequence—blue for safe passage, red for exclusion, green for nothing but water and luck. The line arcs around the old city and stretches out to the horizon, a boundary both permanent and fragile.

"They wired them with the audio deterrent," Finn says. "Supposed to keep the trawlers away. And anyone else who thinks the sea is for the taking."

Mara grunts, but there's pride in it. "Do you trust it?"

Finn shrugs. "Trust is a luxury. We settle for enforcement."

They lapse into silence. The only sound is the ocean, steady and alive.

Mara props herself on her elbows and dips her tail into the water. The cold shocks her every time, but it's a clean pain. She runs a finger down Finn's wrist, watching the way his pulse jumps.

"You ever think about leaving?" she asks.

"Sometimes," he says. "But the world doesn't get better just because you turn your back on it."

She leans her head against his shoulder. The gesture is awkward—she's heavier than she looks, and Finn nearly tips off the rock—but he steadies them both, laughter rumbling in his chest.

Down in the city, the new coral shines in the low light, a neon-bright hue. Mara can see teams of Merfolk weaving through the arches, carrying bundles of shell and scrap. Lyla is visible at the center, her white hair a signal fire, barking orders and splicing together the broken families.

Above the water, a boat rounds the cove—Dr. Chen's. It moves slowly, carefully, the way ships should in a protected zone. On the aft deck, Chen leans against the rail, binoculars at her eyes, logging every detail. Mara watches her for a while, trying to parse the human need for documentation.

Finn's hand finds Mara's, their fingers tangling in a way that feels old and true. He doesn't say anything, but she knows what he means.

They stay like that for a long time, breathing in the sharp air, watching the last birds' wheel above the rocks. The scars on the city are still evident—whole sections of the old wall are gone, and the market square is now just a memory. But there is new growth, too: patches of hybrid coral, clusters of frylings darting between the shadows.

The water is clear tonight. Mara can see farther than she ever has.

Finn stands, brushing off his pants. "Time to go?"

She nods, then slides off the rock, tail splashing, the shock of cold traveling up her spine.

Finn pulls on his old dive gear, the straps frayed, the wetsuit patched a dozen times. He grins at her, then plunges in, boots first.

They sink together, Mara guiding Finn through the thermocline, her hand on his back. The world grows bluer, quieter, as the chaos above gives way to the slow pulse of the current.

The city comes into focus. From below, it's even more beautiful: the arches rebuilt with metal and hope, the gates humming with soft power, the Merfolk weaving through the streets like they never left.

Lyla greets them at the main gate, arms folded, eyebrow arched. She says nothing, gestures them through.

Inside, the market has been reclaimed. The new stalls are rough but lively, and the air hums with the sound of a dozen languages, human and Mer and everything in between. Mara leads Finn through the crowd, and everywhere they go, eyes follow.

At the center of the square, Mara stops to survey the world she almost lost.

Finn puts his arm around her waist, awkward in the water but unafraid.

"Still think about leaving?" he asks.

Mara shakes her head. "No."

They float there, side by side, watching the city breathe.

Above, the last light fades, but below, the city glows.

It's not perfect, but it is enough.

For tonight, that's all the future they need.

20 Shifting Currents

The city never sleeps now. Even at midnight, the tunnels are alive with blue work lights, the water hissing with the grit of repair. Mara slips through the main artery, following the faint chemical trail that marks the safe path for human lungs. The new design is elegant and brutal, a spine of steel mesh sandwiched between slabs of coral and welded scavenged tile. The old city was a living thing, soft around the edges, its tunnels grown not built, but this—this is a cage that pretends to be a home.

She surfaces in the plaza that was once the heart of the city, now a scaffold forest. Merfolk dart among the pylons, hands rough with work, scales dusted white from pulverized calcium. At the far end, a trio of humans in pressurized suits hang in the current, their limbs jointed and awkward, like marionettes abandoned mid-dance. They are welding a support beam to the hull of the new meeting hall, sparks showering out in little comets before dissolving in the salt.

Lyla is there, white hair slicked to her skull, barking orders in a pidgin of Mer-sign and human handwave. She spots Mara, flicks her tail in a come-here, and Mara glides over, slow, letting the city drift by in its new shape.

"You're late," Lyla says. Her voice is ragged from a day of shouting, every word an accusation.

"I was mapping the east vent," Mara replies. "The juvenile

kelp has tripled since last week."

Lyla grunts, unimpressed. "We need you on load distribution. The cross-tunnel is sagging. Humans say it's safe, but I don't trust their math."

Mara glances at the human trio, busy with their welding. "You trust their torches, though."

"We can't make plasma arcs from shell and kelp," Lyla says dryly. "Not unless you've learned a new trick."

Mara opens her hand, shows the fine web of Tideweaving lines running across her palm. "I can do more than before."

Lyla eyes her, then jerks her chin at the tunnel mouth. "Go show Notch. He's about to drop the ceiling."

The new tunnels are squared off, all right angles and flat planes, built to withstand the kind of pressure that killed the old city. Mara passes through the first checkpoint, where the guard is a Fryingling with bandaged gills and a spear that's more for show than for war. He gives her the slow nod of someone still not used to seeing her alive.

Notch is at the far end, tail wedged between two pipes, arms up to his shoulders in a vat of quick-set substrate. He doesn't see her until she's a meter away.

"Mara," he says, voice muffled by the mask he's wearing. "Just in time."

He gestures at the crumbling ceiling, where a fracture has spread through three meters of load-bearing. "We can't patch from the outside. Lyla says, " You can reinforce from here?"

"Maybe," Mara says, examining the break. The fissure weaves through bone and metal, old and new fighting for dominance.

She closes her eyes and feels the water throughout her body. The current is dense here, packed with the exhale of a hundred workers, the ions from the welders, the slow rot of dying plankton. She threads her hands through the break, following the grain, and lets her will pool in her fingertips.

Tideweaving comes easier now. She can pull a current from nothing, twist it, knot it, and lock it into place. The energy is bright and clean, almost surgical in nature. Mara breathes out, and the crack shudders, closes a fraction. Again, the structure knits, pressure equalized along the seam.

Notch watches, silent. When she's done, he runs his hand over the repair, nods once, then returns to his own work.

Mara floats back, shaking the ache out of her hands.

"Nice," Notch says. "You get stronger every time."

"Not stronger," Mara says. "Just less afraid."

Notch chuckles, dark. "City could use more of that."

She moves on, following the survey markers to the following project site. Along the way, she passes a crew planting juvenile coral onto a grid of recycled rebar. The frylings argue over placement, their voices bright and sharp, but they work in perfect harmony, even as they bicker. Above them, human scientists drift in observation cages, taking notes, adjusting the flow on the nutrient feeders.

Mara remembers when the sight of a human would send the whole city into a frenzy, with alarms blaring and every tunnel on lockdown. Now the humans are everywhere, their suits bright against the gloom, their voices muffled but ever-present.

It makes her skin itch.

She turns into a side passage, seeking a moment of quiet. The old city lingers here: arches carved by hand, walls encrusted with centuries of personal marks, the memorial spirals of families lost to history. Mara brushes her fingers along the wall, finds her own spiral, half-erased by the last attack. She feels the hollow under her ribs, the ache that never leaves.

A shadow flickers behind her. She tenses, then relaxes as a human scientist floats into view, face pressed up against the helmet glass.

It's a young one, a grad student probably, the kind they send down to do grunt work. He spots her and gives a nervous wave.

"Hi," he says, voice tinny through the suit speaker. "Didn't mean to spook you."

"You didn't," Mara lies.

He edges closer, careful, and points at the spiral on the wall. "Is that your family mark?"

"It was," she says.

He fumbles for a tablet, scribbles a note. "We're trying to catalog them. The marks, I mean. For the record. There's a grant for heritage preservation—uh, if you're okay with it."

Mara studies him. His eyes are bright and eager, but there's an edge of fear beneath the excitement. He's seen what her kind can do, even now.

"You can document it," Mara says, "but you have to learn the stories. Not just the marks."

The human blinks. "Would you teach me?"

Mara considers, then nods. "Tomorrow. Bring real food."

He grins, floats off, already planning his next question.

Mara waits until he's gone, then lets herself slip to the tunnel floor, the chill of the stone grounding her.

She sits there, letting the city work around her. Above, the whine of drills, the thump of hammers, the constant drone of life rebuilding itself. It's not the same city she grew up in, but it's alive. That may be enough.

Her hand finds the spiral again, and she traces it, over and over, until the groove is warm from the friction.

She whispers, "I'm still here," just to see if the city remembers her.

The echo comes back, soft but certain.

She rises, heads for the next job.

Outside, the current is already waiting.

The cove is a rumor, a place Mara barely remembers except as a whisper in her mother's warnings: too close to shore, too shallow, infested with sea lice and the drift from old tourist boats. Now it is a laboratory, a proving ground, where the old secrets are supposed to become common knowledge.

She arrives early, skimming just below the skin of the water, her presence unannounced. Already, the humans are there, clustered on the rocky spit at the cove's edge. They have brought everything: bright plastic crates of gear, tents that flap like wounded gulls, laptops in waterproof sheaths. They even have a flag—blue and green, with a spiral in the middle—Finn's idea. Mara can't decide if she finds it ridiculous or touching.

In the shallows, three humans bob in wetsuits, their faces tight behind oversized goggles. They take turns ducking under, then popping up, shouting corrections at each other.

"Too much arm," says one.

"You're supposed to feel the pull, not just flail," says another, splashing him for emphasis.

Dr. Chen is on shore, perched on a boulder with a battered notebook. She's watching everything, jotting notes with an intensity that makes Mara think of predatory birds.

Mara surfaces behind the humans, letting the bubbles announce her. The nearest one—the kid from yesterday's city tour, still sporting a bruise from bumping into a tunnel wall—yelps and almost loses his mask.

Mara laughs, unkind but honest. "If you panic in a cove, the open sea will kill you."

The humans circle up, breathless, eager.

"Show us again?" the kid says, voice damp with hope.

Mara floats on her back, arms wide. "You're thinking too hard. The current is not an enemy, it's a song. Let it carry you. Don't fight."

She flicks her wrist, calls a gentle surge, and lets it roll her backward in a lazy arc. The humans try to imitate, but they're all muscle and no music, their bodies snapping rigid at every shift.

Dr. Chen calls out, "Remember: Mara's technique relies on feedback. You should feel the resistance before you move."

The humans nod, try again.

Mara dives, leaves them to their thrashing, and reemerges by the rocks where Chen is perched.

"Is this how you trained your own?" Chen asks, not looking up from the notes.

Mara shrugs. "Ours start younger. Fewer distractions. Less ego."

Chen snorts. "You underestimate the power of humiliation as a learning tool."

Mara considers, then says, "They have potential. But they're trying to force the sea to listen."

Chen looks up, the corners of her mouth twitching. "You don't think the sea should listen?"

"It's not about force," Mara says. "It's about invitation."

Chen writes that down, underlines it twice.

Back in the water, the kid is struggling. He's managed to ride the current a few body lengths, but his control is shaky, and he wipes out on the next turn, swallowing a lungful of brine. He surfaces, face red, and rips off his mask.

"This is impossible!" he says.

Mara glides over. "It's not. But you're not going to get it in one day."

The kid glares. "You make it look easy."

"It's not easy," Mara says. "Even our frylings take years to master the basic weave. You expect to do it in one morning because you're human?"

The kid opens his mouth, then shuts it, chastened.

Mara softens. "You made progress. Next time, you'll last longer."

The kid grins sheepishly.

Another trainee, a woman with a broad smile and a prosthetic hand, waves Mara over. "Can you show us the sea-talking again?"

Mara hesitates. Sea-Speaking is trickier, more subtle, less about movement and more about intent. But these humans are here to learn, so she nods and gestures for them to follow.

They wade out, water up to their chests, and Mara calls the current with a single finger. She focuses, lets her mind blur at the edges, and sends out a pulse of wanting—not a command, but an invitation.

Within a minute, the water around them shivers. A school of damselfish gathers, flashes of yellow and black swirling around the trainees. The humans gasp and laugh as they try to reach out.

Mara weaves her fingers through the school, guiding their path, and the fish respond, circling tighter. The woman with the prosthetic hand reaches out, and the fish part around her, then settle back, unafraid.

"How do you do that?" the woman asks, awed.

Mara considers. "You don't talk to them. You talk with the water, and the water brings the message."

The woman nods, tries to mimic the motion. The fish scatter, then return, cautious but curious.

On shore, Chen is scribbling furiously.

Mara senses a change in the current, an unease. She looks over her shoulder, sees Finn walking on the beach, eyes on the horizon. He's worried, but trying not to show it.

She waves him in. "Join us."

Finn strips down to swim trunks and wades in, skin already toughened by months of salt. He slides under the surface, holds his breath for almost a minute, then pops up beside Mara.

"Not bad," she says.

"Getting better," he replies, smiling.

She leads the trainees through another round, this time focusing on synchronizing their movements, letting the current set the pace rather than fighting to stay upright. After half an hour, even the slowest human is moving with a kind of grace, if not ease.

They take a break. The kid sits on the rocks, panting. "How did you know we could do this?"

Mara looks at him, then at the others. "You're not so different from us. You have to unlearn everything you were taught about control."

The kid grins. "My parents would hate that."

Mara laughs. "Mine too."

Dr. Chen approaches, shaking out her hand. "You're a natural teacher," she says to Mara.

"Never wanted to be," Mara replies, but she can't hide the flicker of pride.

Chen closes her notebook. "If you ever want a job, I know a university that would kill for you."

Mara snorts. "Maybe after the city is finished."

Finn comes over, wrapping an arm around her shoulders, wet and shivering but happy. "You did well," he says.

"They did better," Mara says, nodding at the humans.

The sun is dropping, painting the cove in gold.

Mara watches the water, sees the ripples left by her students. For the first time, she feels a glimmer of hope that this might work—not just the training, but the entire wild experiment of living together.

She turns to Finn. "Tomorrow, deeper water?"

He nods, grinning. "Race you to the kelp beds."

The trainees groan, but none of them back out.

Mara laughs, and the sound is almost human.

Finn hangs at forty feet, lungs a slow furnace, ears popping in micro-pulses with every meter. He has not worn a dive mask in months—Mara said it was a crutch, and she's right. Now he rides the blur: salt and sting, light searing down through the blue in angled blades. The wetsuit is new—his own design—slick and iridescent, cut to hug every limb and rib, patches of scale-mimic along the forearms and calves. The marketing copy would refer to it as "hydrodynamic." Mara calls it cheating. Finn disagrees;

nothing about this is easy.

Mara hovers above him, upside down, her silhouette wavering against the surface. She is so at home in this element that it makes his human nerves itch. He watches the way she flicks her tail for micro-adjustments, the way her whole body absorbs the current, reads it, and bends with it. She signals: two fingers, then a spiral. Follow.

Finn answers, one finger pointed: Lead on.

They drop together, bodies slicing through the thermocline. At sixty feet, the water goes cold, shocking his chest, making the last bit of air in his lungs shrivel to a hard little knot. Mara never breaks pace; she twists through a stand of kelp, tail painting lazy figure-eights, and Finn has to work to keep up. But he does. He's stronger than he was last year, and the city's workout regimen—swim, then swim more, then swim until your half-dead—has rebuilt him lean and sinewy, with no fat left for comfort.

At the edge of the forest, Mara stops, floats motionless. She holds up a palm—wait.

Finn freezes. She points with her chin, and he sees it: a pod of dolphins, twelve strong, weaving through the dark below.

He feels the tingle of nerves. Last time he tried this, he nearly blacked out, came up retching and shaking for twenty minutes. Mara said it was the side effect of "trying to out-dolphin a dolphin," which is fair.

She signs: Ready? Finn signs back: Yes.

They spiral down, together, closing the distance. The dolphins notice, shift formation, but don't flee. Mara flicks her hands in a new sequence, slow and deliberate. Finn watches, then mimics, adjusting the angle of his wrists, the flare of his fingers. It's not really sign language, not like human ASL, but a grammar built on movement and the shape of intent.

Mara signals: Circle, open, circle.

Finn sweeps his arms, forming a torus in the water. The dolphins slide in, curious. Mara signals again: Echo, then three.

Finn pushes a single note from his throat—not a word, but a shaped burst of air that vibrates his sinuses, a trick Mara taught him. He does it three times, as instructed.

The dolphins answer, their own chatter rolling through the current in clicks and whistles.

Mara beams, her eyes gone vast and wild.

Finn feels the world narrow: it's just him, Mara, and the animals. Nothing above matters. Not the settlement plans, not the politicking, not even his own clumsy humanity. Just the moment.

He wants to say this to Mara, but he's out of time. His chest burns, his arms go leaden. He signals: Up.

Mara nods, and they shoot for the surface. Finn counts the kicks—six, eight, ten. His vision tunnels, but he holds it together, making the air with a gasp that's almost a laugh.

He floats on his back, sky rolling overhead, and Mara surfaces beside him, hair fanned around her face.

She grins. "You almost lost it."

He wipes water from his eyes. "Three minutes, twenty seconds."

She shakes her head, admiring or jealous or both. "Better than last time."

He can still feel the echo of the dolphins, the way their voices resonated through his bones. "Did you hear it? They answered."

"I heard," Mara says. She sounds proud. "You're learning."

He looks at her, all teeth and sun and salt. "I have a good teacher."

They drift, letting the current pull them toward the shore.

Finn's skin is raw from the brine. Not just today—always. It's never really healed since he started training with Mara. The soft skin of his childhood is gone, replaced with something more challenging and less permeable. He likes it. He likes the way his eyes don't sting anymore, the way he can open them for hours underwater and not even blink. He likes the way his body has become a tool, not a burden.

On the rocky lip of the cove, their new settlement is under construction. The architecture is a compromise: above, glass-walled labs and dorms for the human staff, with decks that dip right into the sea; below, the first ever permanent airlock to the Merfolk city, a ring of reinforced titanium and synth-coral that can stand up to a hurricane. The two halves are joined by a wide, sunken stairway—built to allow "maximum cross-species access," as the architects insisted.

He and Mara swim to the dock, where a handful of humans—two researchers, one engineer, and a fryling with a mop—watch them with a mix of awe and terror.

Finn hauls himself onto the dock. His muscles tremble, but only a little. Mara emerges beside him, arms crossed, all confidence.

The engineer, a woman with copper-braided hair, hands Finn a towel. "You made the whole time without a rebreather?"

"Three twenty," Finn says, grinning. "Next time, I'll break four."

The researcher shakes her head. "You're not human."

"Working on it," Finn says.

Mara snorts. "He'll never make the tail."

"Don't need a tail," Finn shoots back. "Just need better lungs."

Mara leans close, whispers, "You have better than that." Then she pulls away, leaving him unsure if it's a compliment or a challenge.

The engineer checks the readout on Finn's suit. "Temperature's steady, no lactic spike. You're adapting fast."

Finn nods, but he's not listening. He's watching the water, the ripples left by the dolphins.

He says, "How's the install going?"

The engineer grimaces. "Slow. The new polymer is too flexible; it shifts under pressure. We're thinking of splicing in some old-school metal bands."

Mara perks up. "Steel or titanium?"

"Stainless," the engineer says. "Too heavy otherwise."

Mara nods. "We can reinforce with kelp cord. My people do it for city gates."

The engineer looks at her, surprised. "Would you help?"

Mara shrugs. "You feed me, I'll teach you."

The engineer laughs, delighted. "Deal."

Finn wraps the towel around his waist, still grinning. "See? Teamwork."

Mara smirks, flicking her wet hair in his face. "I prefer 'mutually assured survival.'"

He laughs, deep and honest.

They walk the dock together, Mara dripping, Finn barely disguised as something human. He loves this—loves the way she never lets him feel sorry for himself, loves the bite in her jokes, the challenge in her every word. He loves the city, even in its half-built state, because it feels like something new, something neither human nor Mer, but both.

They pass a set of glass panels stacked on the dock, ready for installation. Finn stops, runs his hands over the smooth surface.

"Imagine," he says, "when it's finished. Kids from both sides are looking in. No more secrets, no more fighting."

Mara looks at him, skeptical. "You think they'll get along?"

He shrugs. "We did."

She leans against the railing, watching the city below. "It wasn't easy."

He smiles. "The best things never are."

They stand there, side by side, watching the future come into focus. The dolphins are gone, but their song lingers in the water, a memory of what's possible.

Finn feels the burn in his lungs, the ache in his arms, and knows he's alive in a way he never was before.

Tomorrow, they'll dive again. This time, he'll break the four-minute barrier. This time, he'll speak the water's language without Mara's help.

Either way, he's ready.

The tide is theirs now.

The air is full of salt and sawdust. Sunset turns the half-built settlement into a silhouette: glass panels stacked like dominoes, steel supports stretching down into the surf, the skeleton of a stairway spiraling from the bluffs to the tidepools below. Mara stands barefoot in the shallows, skirt hitched, toes digging into the grit as she surveys the chaos.

On the beach, humans and Merfolk work side by side. The humans do most of the heavy lifting—muscle and scaffolding, ropes looped around their waists, shouts of warning and triumph echoing up the cliff. Merfolk handle precision: laying bead after bead of kelp-paste sealant, weaving cross-bracing from cord so thin it cuts your fingers, etching the spiral pattern onto the glass. The two crews are easy to tell apart—humans sunburned and loud, Merfolk slick and sharp and always a little amused—but the lines are already blurring. Mara catches more than one human picking up Mer-sign from a partner, more than one fryling helping a rookie with a stubborn drill.

She spots Finn at the top of the new stairs, clipboard in hand, arguing with the engineer. His hair is a wet pelt, his skin tanned and tight, and he waves the plans so hard Mara thinks they'll take flight.

She calls up, "You're going to lose that if you keep flapping."

Finn shields his eyes and grins down at her. "We need a consensus on the load rating. The human side says we overbuilt. Mer side says humans don't float."

Mara snorts. "Both are true."

He gestures for her to come up, but Mara shakes her head, watching as two humans wrangle a glass panel into place. The water is choppy—wind from the south, and the tide is rising too fast. The panel rocks, nearly tips.

Mara flicks her fingers, subtly, and the water steadies. The panel slides into its bracket perfectly, and the workers let out a shout of approval.

Finn catches her eye. He smiles, a little softer. "Show-off."

Mara shrugs, returns the smile. It's easy these days.

As the sun drops, Lyla arrives, fresh from the city below. She's trailed by a pair of frylings and a human scientist—Dr. Chen, always in the thick of it. Chen carries a tube of rolled-up plans and the battered notebook she guards like a relic. Lyla's arms are full of coiled cable and bundles of shell, all of it dripping seawater onto the sand.

Lyla waves a coil at Mara. "We're ready for the next section. You coming?"

Mara nods. "Let's do it."

They wade out together, Finn and Chen trailing. At the edge of the surf, Mara crouches, grabs the end of the cable, and helps thread it through the underwater guideposts. It's a strange dance—Mara and Lyla diving, Chen marking locations on a tablet, Finn relaying corrections from shore. They finish in half the time the humans predicted.

On the break, the four sit in the wet, eating dry crackers and rationed cheese.

Lyla glances at Finn. "You sure you want the viewing chamber that deep? You'll need special glass, maybe structural reinforcement."

Finn shrugs. Humans love a challenge. Besides, we want the best view."

Chen nods. "We've sourced a blend—old polymer from a decommissioned oil rig, new stuff grown in bioreactors. Strong, light, almost invisible."

Mara eyes the plans. "It won't block the current?"

Chen shakes her head. "Perforated anchor. The water moves through it. No dead zones."

Lyla says, "Good." She glances at Mara, pride hidden behind her usual scowl.

Finn flips the plans and points at a shaded section. "Here's the sticking point. We need a protocol for human visitors, including details on who is permitted to visit, when, and how frequently. The city is worried about crowding, about someone getting lost."

Mara looks at Lyla. "You still think humans are going to swarm us?"

Lyla considers. "Not at first. But the story will spread."

Chen adds, "We can use sign-ups. Rotate the groups, never more than a few at a time."

Mara nods. "And we train them first. No one enters the city without a frying guide."

Finn grins. "That'll keep them in line."

They eat in silence for a while, watching the crews work. The first lanterns are being lit—a human tradition, borrowed and repurposed. Paper globes, each one weighted and set adrift in the shallows, glowing orange and blue as the last of the sun fades.

Lyla is the first to break the silence. "It's working," she says.

Mara looks at her, surprised. "You sound almost happy."

Lyla shrugs. "Better than war."

Chen says, "I heard the city's memorial is almost done. Will you be there for the dedication?"

Mara hesitates. "Maybe."

Finn bumps her shoulder. "You should. They're doing it for you."

Mara laughs, a short huff. "No. They're doing it for all of us."

Finn's hand finds hers under the water, squeezes it.

The night comes on fast. The last glass panel is in place, and the crews are packing up. On the beach, someone starts a fire—driftwood and scavenged pallets, the smoke twisting up in tight spirals. The workers gather around, human and Merfolk alike, eating, talking, sharing the warmth.

Mara and Finn wade out to the edge of the drop-off, the water up to their chests. Behind them, the new stairway gleams in the lantern light, a ribbon of possibility.

Finn looks at her, hair plastered to his forehead, eyes bright. "We're really doing this," he says.

Mara watches the city below, the ghost of the old and the bones of the new. "We are."

He leans in, kisses her—quick and cold and perfect.

She returns it, then splashes him, grinning. "Race you to the deep?"

He laughs. "You'll win. You always do."

Mara shrugs. "Not always."

They dive together, bodies arrowing through the glassy calm. Below, the lights from the settlement scatter across the reef, painting the water in color. Mara feels the current at her back, steady and sure.

She surfaces first, treads water, waits for Finn. He comes up seconds later, laughing, breathless, alive.

On the shore, the lanterns float out, bobbing on the tide.

Mara watches them go, her heart steady.

Above, the world is changed.

Below, the city waits.

And in between—here, in the now—anything is possible.

21 Tides of Tomorrow

Dawn's got knives today, sharp enough to cut the cold off the water and pin Mara's shadow to the wrack. She stands ankle-deep in the lowest tide pool, the sand so fine it stings her scales. Overhead, the new settlement stirs awake—above the beach, the surface buildings cling to the bluffs like barnacles, steel and glass glittering, while below, the sea's own city glows faintly green in the coming light. Her copper hair is a ragged signal flag in the wind, bright even when she knots it back. If the sun sees nothing else today, it'll see her first.

Out past the first kelp tangle, a warband of children combs the flats. Not a pureblood among them. The frylings mix with human kids—some built for land, some barely able to drag themselves out of the water, all of them screaming and splashing as if they own the world. Mara likes this about them. They fight over who can bag the best specimen for the morning's survey, but no one gets to keep what they find. The sea takes everything, sooner or later.

She watches them work: two merboys, tails half-submerged and faces painted with mud, argue over the proper way to snare a limpet. A pair of human sisters, hands already raw from scraping at barnacles, debate whether the pink stuff growing on the rocks counts as "new life" or just "gross." The youngest of the lot—an airbreather with a lisp and an attitude—leads the rest, shouting instructions she barely understands herself. They ignore Mara's presence, which means she's won. She wants them to think this is their world now.

In truth, the kids are better scientists than half the adults up in the research dome. They map by touch, by hunger, by which creatures bite back. Already, they've caught three baby octopus, a rat king of brittle stars, and something with claws that none of the adults will be excited about later.

When the chaos hits a lull, Mara flexes her fingers. She's not supposed to show off the old magic, but rules mean less at low tide. She waits until the children's attention scatters, then calls a slipstream of current—a slow, underwater yawn that spirals along the bottom and corrals every loose shell, pebble, and creature into a gentle vortex at her feet. The swirl is almost silent, but the kids notice; they always do.

"Whoa!" shouts the loudest of them, pointing at the whirling, living catch basin forming in Mara's pool. "Do it again!"

She ignores them at first, letting the effect intensify. The water rises in a neat dome, surface tension giving it a lens-like shimmer. Through the bubble, dozens of tiny creatures—crabs, snails, shrimp—hang in slow motion, confused and beautiful.

The kids crowd closer, disregarding personal space. The youngest merboy floats his chin on the surface and stares up at her, slack-jawed. "Is that real magic?" he asks, voice cracking.

"No such thing," Mara says, deadpan. "It's just water."

He looks skeptical, so she winks. "Water and a little help from the moon."

Above the tideline, footsteps crunch gravel. Finn Gallagher is impossible to miss, even when he tries. He's grown a beard lately—hides his jawline, accentuates the storm in his eyes. He limps a little on bad mornings, but today he's moving quickly, hauling a weatherproof case in one hand and three different pieces of homebrew equipment under the other arm.

"Still showing them the old ways?" Finn calls down, planting himself on a boulder with a theatrical groan. His grin is a challenge, but the lines at the corners of his mouth make it gentle.

Mara flicks her wrist, dispersing the current. The water falls flat, creatures scatter, and a few lucky ones clamber onto rocks, trying to pretend nothing happened. "They're learning faster than you think," she says.

Finn pops the latches on his case, reveals an array of labeled vials and syringes. "If they're anything like you, I should prepare for a minor disaster before breakfast."

"Or a major one," she counters. "Depends on what you're hoping for."

He gestures toward the kids, who are now combing the edge of the pool for survivors. "I'd take chaos over complacency, any day."

Mara squats at the waterline, knees up by her chin. She watches as one of the human girls, the boldest of the two, picks a crab from the swirl and holds it up for inspection. "This one has eggs," the girl says proudly. "Do we keep it?"

"Put her back," Mara says, voice low but firm. "She's more important than you are."

The girl hesitates, then obeys. Mara catches Finn's eye, a silent question. He nods approval.

Finn unspools a length of cord from his kit and wades in, boots sinking in the mud. "All right, crew, gather round. I need a sample from the warm side and the cold side, and I need it before the tide turns." His voice carries, clear even when the wind snaps. The kids obey, form two factions, and immediately fall into competition.

Mara waits until the clamor drowns out the sound of the sea. She drags her hand through the water, fingertips tingling, and checks the temperature. "It's rising faster than yesterday," she says, half to herself.

Finn's already in professor mode, dropping a probe into the pool and tapping at his wrist display. "We're in the sweet spot for algal bloom. If the current stays gentle, we might get a new batch by tomorrow."

Mara grins, baring teeth. "You live for this."

"I do," Finn admits, but his eyes stay on her. "I live for you, too."

She pretends not to hear that, but her gills flare, just for a moment.

The children break into an argument over who gets to dip the next sensor. The Merfolk fryling wins, mostly by threat of tail-slap. Finn hands over the gear, then glances at Mara. "You want to show them the next trick?"

She shrugs. "If they're ready."

Finn calls out, "Listen up! Mara's going to demonstrate something you can't do on land. Watch closely."

The kids line up, dripping and fidgeting, eyes on Mara. She stands, plants her feet in the sand, and stares at the sun. The light is a hammer, even this early, but she takes it all in. She lifts her hands, palms up, and lets the warmth of the pool flow up her arms. The trick isn't really magic, but it looks like it: she tugs a thread of cold from the deeper water offshore, then coils it into the shallows. The temperature plummets. A sheen of vapor forms, the water steaming as if the pool itself is waking up.

The effect ripples, mesmerizing. The kids gasp, then stick

their hands in to feel the difference. One human boy yelps. "It's like ice!"

"Not ice," Mara says. "Just balance."

Finn's impressed, but pretends otherwise. "Think you can teach them to do that?"

She looks at the kids, a doubt crossing her face. "Maybe the ones who sit still for more than a second."

One of the Merfolk frylings raises her hand, uncertain. "How did you move the cold?"

Mara kneels, gestures for the girl to approach. She takes her hand and turns it palm up. "The ocean isn't the same everywhere," she says. "You have to feel the difference. The cold hides under the warm, but it's always moving."

The fryling tries, concentrating so hard her eyes nearly cross. Nothing happens. She frowns, frustrated.

"Try again," Mara says. "Gentle, not hard."

The girl breathes, then does it. A flicker of cool rolls through the pool, barely enough to be felt, but Mara feels it. She nods approval. "That's it."

The other kids crowd in, desperate to try.

By the third attempt, the air is thick with competition. Finn records everything, voice memo running as he narrates for the benefit of future research, or for the pleasure of cataloging the miracle. Mara ignores him and focuses on the students. "Remember," she says, "never use it to hurt."

The men nod, solemn. The human children glance at each other, then at Mara, then at the adults watching from the shore.

Finn calls time. "We've got a lot of samples, but not enough data. Tomorrow, double the cohort."

Mara laughs. "You're going to need more kids."

He grins. "I'll borrow some from the surface school. They can swim, more or less."

A bell rings above, signaling breakfast. The children explode in every direction, some running for the stairs that snake up the bluff, others diving straight for the waterline. Mara and Finn are left alone at the edge of the world, watching the sun finally clear the horizon.

Finn packs his gear, then stands next to her. "You ever get tired of being a legend?"

"Every day," Mara says.

He kisses her cheek, careful not to linger. "Good. That means you're doing it right."

They start up the beach together, sand cold underfoot.

Above them, the settlement sprawls: half built into the bluff, half floating on docks, all stitched together by the same madness that brought them here. The new airlock stairway, engineered by Finn and reinforced by Mara's magic, gleams like a silver snake up the cliff. Glass domes rise from the rocks, green with condensation and the work of a thousand marine biologists. At the seam where land meets water, human and Merfolk banners hang side by side, spiraled together.

It's not perfect, but it works.

Below, the tide pulls at Mara's ankles, as if reminding her what waits beneath. She looks over her shoulder at the sea, at the city they've fought to keep.

She whispers a promise to it, then moves on.

Tomorrow will be another lesson, another day in the water. But for now, the sun is up, the air is sweet, and the future is unwritten.

The children, already forgetting the rules, shout back: "Again! Do it again!"

She smiles a little. Maybe she will.

The world is stubborn, but so is she.

The sand is still cold, but the kids are immune to it. Mara kneels at the high-water mark, draws her finger in a slow spiral, tight at the center, opening wider with each turn. "Again," she says, and the children press in, hands and tails and bare knees splattered with salt and grit.

The spiral is the city's new flag, the mark that every door, hull, and suit sleeve now wears. Finn says it looks like a nautilus. Lyla says it's an old story, something about history folding in on itself, but never breaking. Mara tells the kids it means "keep coming back." No one argues with her version.

She takes the hand of the littlest fryling—a slip of a thing, her scales so thin they're almost transparent—and guides her palm through the pattern, pressing just hard enough to leave a groove. "Now you," she says, and lets go.

The girl's handshakes, but the line comes out cleaner than Mara expects. The other children crowd closer, eager for their turn.

On the tide flat, Finn sets up his gear. The box is new—a

graduation present from the university—and bristles with sensors and vials, a little chemistry lab for anyone brave enough to care about microbe counts before breakfast. He kneels in the shallow, filling one pipette after another, careful not to stir the bottom too much.

"Remember when we couldn't even find healthy kelp within miles of here?" Finn calls, eyes on his sample. "Now look at this."

He holds up a vial. The water inside is almost invisible, but Mara sees the shimmer—millions of plankton, a new galaxy blooming.

She smiles, a private thing. The world ends and begins every morning on this beach.

The children listen with half an ear; their minds are on the sand, the next spiral, the secret war of who can make the biggest or the smallest. The merboy with the chipped tooth draws one so tiny Mara can barely see it, then tries to hide his pride. A human girl, red-haired and wild as a shrimp, digs with both hands, scooping out a spiral crater big enough to trap a hermit crab.

Mara gives a little applause, and the girl bows, then releases the crab and pats it on the shell. "Don't get caught again," she whispers.

It's nearly the lesson's end when the first adult voices drift down from the bluff. Mara glances up, recognizes the silhouettes: Dr. Chen at the lead, flanked by two researchers and a tech dragging a drone on a leash. Chen's hair is slicked back, salt-and-pepper, her stride as quick as the day Mara first met her. She pauses at the edge of the dock, tablet in hand, eyes sweeping the beach like she's trying to inventory every child, every grain of sand.

"Morning," Chen calls. Her voice carries a flat, even tone.

"How's the class?"

"Better than your undergrads," Mara replies.

The tech with the drone groans, but Chen grins. "I believe it."

They make their way down the steps—old quarry stones, still slick from dew—and stop by Finn's station. Chen doesn't waste time. "We need a full read on the outflow before ten. Think you can process samples on the fly?"

Finn nods. "Already started. The tide is shifting north today; you'll get cross-contamination from the kelp beds if you wait."

Chen claps him on the back, almost knocking him over. "Good man."

She turns to Mara. "You'll bring the kids to the dedication?"

"If I can herd them," Mara says. "And if the human ones don't bite."

Chen's smile is a sliver. "I'll bring snacks."

She moves on, already in conversation with the other researchers. Finn flashes Mara a look, half affection, half apology for the interruption.

Mara waves it away, then resumes the lesson. The kids are losing interest in the spirals, distracted by the promise of real food and the rising sun. She lets them break, watches as they scatter—some to the water, others up the path toward the main settlement. The littlest fryling hangs back, her spiral perfect, untouched.

"You want to keep it?" Mara asks.

The girl shrugs, shy.

Mara kneels and lowers her voice. "A spiral only lasts until the next tide," she says. "But every time you make one, it's easier."

The fryling nods, then brushes her fingers over the mark, erasing it with a single pass.

"See?" Mara says. "Now there's room for the next one."

The girl darts away, chasing after the others.

Out beyond the sand, a ripple catches Mara's attention. She stands, shielding her eyes—a familiar silhouette surfaces—the shape unmistakable even after all these years.

Lyla Pearl.

Her hair is more silver than white now, cropped short for efficiency, and her face bears the kind of scars that only come from living past your own legend. She moves with purpose, slicing through the water until she's close enough to the shore that the children notice.

"Lyla!" they shout, racing to the water's edge.

Lyla grins, all teeth. She lets the kids mob her, pulling her in every direction at once, each desperate to show off their spiral, their latest trick, or the weirdest thing they found on the rocks. She endures it with mock patience, rolling her eyes at Mara the whole time.

"Is this what passes for education now?" Lyla calls, voice thick with laughter.

Mara shrugs. "You want to try?"

Lyla feigns horror. "I'd rather face Blackwell again."

The kids don't understand the joke, but they sense the rivalry and double down on it. Soon, there are three spirals in the sand, two made of seaweed, one lined with crab legs.

Lyla examines each, hands on hips. "This one's good," she says, pointing at the smallest. "But you missed a turn."

The merboy with the chipped tooth flushes red, then immediately scrapes a new one, tongue poking out in concentration.

Lyla winks at Mara, who tries not to show her pride.

On the beach, Chen and her crew finish their water sampling and start toward the labs on the bluff. Human and Merfolk researchers cluster at the midpoint, exchanging notes, arguing over tomorrow's forecast, the next batch of eggs, and the optimal temperature for plankton bloom. Mara listens from a distance, content to let others argue over the future. She's already living in it.

Finn walks over, hands in pockets, eyes on Lyla and the children. "She's a natural," he says.

Mara nods. "She's stubborn. That's almost the same."

He stands next to her, shoulder to shoulder. For a while, they watch the surf, the spray, the way the kids run out of energy and then refill themselves just by being near the water.

"You ever think we'd get here?" Finn asks, voice low.

"No," Mara admits. "I thought I'd die before it got this good."

He wraps an arm around her, light as a promise.

A new wave breaks, bringing with it a scatter of silver baitfish. The children shriek and scatter, chasing them up and down the shallows. One human boy, bigger than the rest, wades in too deep and gets toppled by a sudden current. He goes under for a split second, then pops up, laughing and gasping. Mara feels the old urge to dive in after him, but Lyla's already there, steadying the boy, then pushing him back toward shore.

"They're going to be fine," Finn says, as if reading her mind.

"They better be," Mara says. "Or I'll drag them back myself."

He laughs, the sound catching on the wind.

As the children tire, Mara gathers them for a final lesson. She signals with her hand, and they all settle at her feet, shivering and attentive.

"Today, we do something different," she says. "Today, we listen."

She closes her eyes, tilts her head, and hums—not a song, but a vibration, a memory of deep water. The kids try to imitate, but it's too subtle. Instead, she uses her Sea-Speaking, calls out into the bay with a pulse of longing.

The effect is slow, but soon the water answers: first a single ripple, then a pattern, then three shapes breaking the surface.

Dolphins. Sleek, gray, almost ghostly in the morning light.

They arc in tandem, close to shore, then spin and dive, leaving spirals in the foam.

The kids lose their minds, racing into the surf, splashing and shouting. The dolphins circle, curious, then one leaps high and bright, a perfect mimic of the spiral just drawn in the sand.

Mara smiles, letting the sound of their joy fill her.

Finn nudges her. "Show-off," he whispers.

She elbows him, but her cheeks are warm. "Takes one to

know one."

He grins. "I love you."

She says nothing, but she squeezes his hand.

Lyla, still dripping, watches from the rocks. Her eyes meet Mara's, and the old, brittle distance is gone.

For a moment, everyone is quiet: humans and Merfolk, elders and frylings, even the dolphins, all suspended in the hush between waves.

Mara looks at the sand, sees the spiral left behind by the smallest fryling. Already, the tide is pulling it apart, but the center is still there, unbroken.

She traces it once, then steps away, ready for whatever comes next.

22 Echoes of the Deep

Five years to rebuild a world, or just enough of it to fool the eye.

Sunrise splits the horizon, smears the waterline with gold. In the old days, the beach here was bone and oil, the only sound a distant engine and the rattle of gulls picking over plastic. Now it's something closer to alive. The wind still whips hard, but it carries the sweet brine of regrown eelgrass, the sulfur tang of new tidepools. Where once the slope was cut by rusted pilings and broken cement, today it's terraced: stone and glass platforms stepping down to the sand, with each level chiseled for the comfort of a different species. Topside, the buildings run to plain, stubborn rectangles—Finn's idea, keep the lines clean, the function honest. Below, half-submerged domes bulge from the surf like a second, weirder reef: Merfolk architecture, all curves and wild asymmetry, snaking with entrance tunnels so subtle you'd miss them from the air.

The morning is already loud. Children—human, Mer, and every shade between—race up and down the foreshore, shrieking in languages their parents haven't even learned yet. Each time the tide buries the sand in a new wave, the littlest ones dive in, popping up with crabs in their fists or silt on their faces. It's chaos, but it's ordered chaos, like the city below.

Mara stands at the water's edge, watching the sun burn holes in the fog. She's grown taller in the years since the war, but she still holds her shoulders like a fighter—tight, ready for the next hit. Her hair, once a copper tangle, is threaded now with pearls and glass beads, a flag for anyone who's paying attention. Even out of water, the storm-green of her eyes seems to churn. She adjusts the sash at her waist—a leftover from the first Treaty Day, now frayed and faded, but still the only bit of "official" regalia she owns.

Finn stands beside her. He's gone leaner, with the muscle that comes from years of work in salt and sun. There's silver in his beard now, but his eyes haven't lost that drowned-in-possibility look. He wears one of his old university shirts, now patched with a spiral of the city's sigil: a gift from the frylings, who wanted "the soft man" to look more important. On his left wrist, he's strapped a bundle of sensors—a habit he refuses to break, even at a party. His feet are bare, and he's shivering.

"Cold?" Mara asks, nudging him with her tail.

"Just alive," Finn says. "You ever get used to it?"

She snorts. "The cold, or the noise?"

He grins. "Both."

She looks out, counting heads. "It's a good turnout."

He nods. "Lyla said she'd bring the whole crew."

Mara lets that sink in. "I believe her."

A new voice interrupts, sharp as ever. "You should. She runs the city better than the last three elders put together."

Lyla Pearl emerges from the surf, flanked by a dozen Merfolk. Her hair is cropped even shorter than Mara remembers, and streaked with a shock of blue. The scars on her forearms are white and perfect, proof that even time can't erase some stories. She's ditched the old bone jewelry and wears, instead, a cord of silvered kelp that doubles as a blade if you know how to use it.

Lyla wades up, flicks water off her scales, and squints at Finn. "Nice shirt. Lose a bet?"

Finn bows, mock-formal. "Just honoring the city's real power."

Lyla snorts, but her smile is genuine. "We'll see how long that lasts."

The delegation behind her forms a loose half-circle: old faces and new, all of them marked by the hard years but brighter for it. Notch is there, leading a swarm of frylings up the beach. Mara waves, and Notch returns the gesture, careful not to let his charges get too close to the still-wet paint on the new stone markers.

Lyla leans in, voice low. "You look good, Mara. Different."

"I feel different," Mara says, not sure if it's pride or dread in her chest.

Lyla glances at Finn, then back at Mara. "You ready for this?"

Mara nods, but it's a lie. "Are you?"

"Never," Lyla says, then laughs.

Above them, a new sound cuts through the morning: the thump of helicopter blades, fast and low. Everyone on the beach stops; the children point, the adults duck instinctively. The copter banks once, then sets down on the highest terrace, skids biting into the fresh concrete. Mara tenses, but Finn puts a hand on her arm.

"It's okay," he says. "They're with us."

The side door pops open. Dr. Ava Chen steps out, hair slicked back in a severe bun, eyes hidden behind mirror shades. She wears the new uniform: dark, tight, waterproof. Four human scientists follow, each shouldering duffels or dragging crates of equipment. None of them looks comfortable in the sand, but they march anyway.

Chen spots Finn and Mara, then stalks down the stairs toward them, her steps precise and deliberate.

"Morning," Chen says, not waiting for a response. "Is the array set?"

Finn nods, all business. "Local network's up. The sensors are ready, and we have feed from the bottom tunnels."

Chen barks over her shoulder. "Unload the gear. Sort by function. If you drop anything in the tide, you're diving for it."

Her crew scatters, already assembling a field station at the edge of the platform.

Chen turns back to Mara, stripping off the sunglasses. Her face is older, but her smile is still all challenge. "I like the pearls," she says. "Very statesmanlike."

Mara snorts. "You say that like it's a bad thing."

Chen shrugs. "It's just new. You wear it well."

Mara looks at the equipment as the crates are opened with practiced speed. "You brought a lot."

"We always bring a lot," Chen says. "The world doesn't change just because you survived one war."

Mara's smile fades. "Some things change."

Chen softens, just a little. "You're right. They do."

A commotion on the path above: two men in suits, one of whom is pushing a wheelchair. The figure in the chair is all angles, draped in a blanket despite the cold. Mara squints, trying to place him. Finn's hand tightens on her wrist.

"I didn't think he'd come," Finn whispers.

"Who?"

But then she knows.

The chair stops at the top step. The man in the blanket is older, his face nearly caved in by time and gravity, but his eyes are intact: cold, scanning, the eyes of a predator. The hair is whiter than gray, trimmed close to the skull. The suit is expensive, but the hands gripping the armrests are mottled with old burn scars.

Blackwell.

For a moment, nobody moves. The air itself goes tight, waiting for the next disaster.

Then Blackwell lifts a hand, signals the aide to push him forward. He glides down the switchback ramp, moving through the crowd with the kind of arrogance that can't be faked. When he reaches the last terrace, he halts, turns the chair to face the water.

The crowd parts around him, cautious but curious. Even the frylings, trained on horror stories of Blackwell, drift closer.

Mara crosses to him, the sand cool under her bare feet. Finn follows, expression unreadable.

Blackwell's gaze never leaves the sea. "You've rebuilt," he says, voice barely above a whisper.

Mara studies him. The last time she saw this man, he was a monster in every sense of the word. Now, he looks tired.

"We had help," Mara says, not sure if it's forgiveness or just fact.

Blackwell nods, eyes still fixed on the horizon. "It's good work," he says. "Better than we ever managed."

He shifts, and for a moment, Mara sees the old ghost: the man who would've killed a city for a headline, now just another relic at the edge of the world.

Finn leans in, careful. "Why are you here?"

Blackwell answers without looking at him. "It's important to witness history," he says. "Especially when you're not the one writing it anymore."

Mara considers this, then steps back, giving him space. The crowd resumes, the tension melting into a hundred smaller conversations.

Finn shakes his head, quietly amazed. "What next?" he asks Mara.

She surveys the beach. The frylings have begun a new game: rolling a ball of seaweed up the terraces, then chasing it back down to the surf. On the far end, Lyla's team argues over the placement of the ceremonial stones. Near the water, Chen's scientists install a set of transparent domes, already filling them with plankton cultures and coral fragments.

Mara tilts her head, watching the pieces move. "We start," she says. "Like always."

Finn grins. "You're getting sentimental."

"I'll bite you if you say that again," Mara says, but she doesn't mean it.

Together, they wade out, the salt shocking their skin, the future opening up in all directions.

Above the waterline, the city's flag catches the wind: a spiral, endless, stubborn.

Below, the tide calls her name, and Mara answers.

By late afternoon, the party has breached every boundary but the one between air and water. The beach is packed—families clustered on blankets, kids high on salt and sun, researchers in wet gear or formalwear, depending on which tribe claimed them first. The surface food is predictable: bread, cheese, fruit, Finn's attempt at kelp-based beer (a disaster, but no one will say so to his face). The Merfolk tables are stranger: stacks of raw shellfish, shredded sea greens, brined fish that reek and glitter in equal measure. The two crowds mingle awkwardly, but every hour the buffer shrinks, until Mara can no longer tell which voices belong to which world.

At the lip of the terrace, Lyla is holding court. She sits half-submerged in a shallow pool Finn engineered for her comfort ("the throne," he calls it, and she pretends to hate it). Notch and a few other elders flank her, but today she seems to relish the attention from the humans: she's telling war stories, and they're eating it up. Each time she describes a skirmish—especially the ones where Mara bent steel with her hands, or Finn outsmarted a trawler—she points to her accomplices with a roll of the eyes, as if to say, " Can you believe these two? Mara suspects Lyla is making up half the details, but the crowd is too giddy to care.

Finn, meanwhile, orbits the perimeter, checking on every detail. He is happiest in motion, never at the center. Each time Mara sees him, he's ferrying food to a table, helping a child climb a rock, or arguing logistics with Chen's team. When he catches Mara's eye, he winks and mouths, "Surviving?" She gives a so-so gesture, but it's a lie: she's never felt more at home.

Mara sits on the sand, legs folded, tail stretched out in the shallows. The sky is clear now, the sun a hot coin just above the horizon. She listens to the party, letting the noise wrap around her like a blanket. At her feet, three frylings poke at the tiny creatures caught in the surf. Every few minutes, one of them offers Mara a wriggling prize—a sea slug, a crab, a brittle star. She accepts each gift, pretends to examine it with scholarly interest, then releases it back to the water with a secret smile.

Blackwell has kept his distance, up until now. But as the sun dips, Mara sees the old man's wheelchair rolling slowly down the ramp, guided by the same aide as before. The beach around him thins, as if by magnetic repulsion, but Blackwell doesn't seem to notice. He parks at the edge of the lowest terrace and waits, gaze fixed on the surf.

It's Lyla who breaks the spell. She claps her hands once, loud enough to silence a dozen conversations. "Heroes," she announces, "to the waterline!" The word is a joke, but also not: everyone knows who she means.

Mara stands, brushing off sand. Finn materializes at her side, his face sunburned, eyes bright. Chen emerges from the crowd, dragging a stubborn scientist by the elbow, then nods for her team to stay put. Even the frylings get the message; they form up in a wiggling honor guard behind Mara.

The five of them—Mara, Finn, Lyla, Chen, Blackwell—end up arrayed in a loose half-circle at the edge of the tide. The world slows down, as if the party senses something about to happen: the children hush, the researcher angles for a better view.

Nobody has prepared a speech, but Mara feels the expectation gather on her skin. For a second, she's tempted to say nothing at all.

Finn nudges her with his foot. "You get the opening volley," he murmurs. "They'll riot if I go first."

Mara smirks, then looks out at the sea. "Five years ago," she says, letting the sound reach the back of the crowd, "none of you would have come to this beach. You'd have run from the first tail you saw, or tried to net it." She doesn't name the enemy; everyone here knows who it is. "Five years ago, we barely knew how to talk to each other—except when we were fighting."

There's a murmur, not quite laughter.

"I didn't trust any of you," Mara says, looking at the human faces. "Especially the ones who said they wanted to help."

She hears a few gasps, then a quick, nervous laugh.

"But I was wrong," Mara says. "Not because trust is easy. It's not. It's work. Every day, you start over. You get angry, you forgive, you make new mistakes. Sometimes you end up back where you started, and it hurts. But sometimes—" She pauses, scans the kids clustered behind her. "Sometimes you make something new."

Mara steps back and turns to Finn. "Your turn."

Finn scratches his beard, shrugs. "When I was a kid, I wanted to be a marine biologist. Which, surprise, I did. My first research paper got rejected by every major journal, because I said maybe we weren't the smartest thing in the ocean." He glances at the frylings. "Still true."

There's laughter, this time less nervous.

"I spent a lot of years fighting for an ocean that didn't want me," Finn says. "Or so I thought. But it turns out, sometimes you have to lose before you learn how to win." He looks at Mara, then at Lyla. "The city gave me a second chance. I'm not going to waste it."

Lyla snorts, then launches in. "I said the whole thing would fail," she says. "I bet Mara three kelp pies it would fall apart inside of a month. First time a human double-crossed us, or one of ours broke the rules, that'd be it. Back to the old wars." She shrugs. "Lost the bet. I'll make the pies tomorrow."

The humans laugh. The Merfolk join in.

Lyla turns to the crowd. "I still don't trust you all. But that's fine. You don't trust us either. Maybe you never will. But you showed up. You rebuilt the city. You put your frylings in the same schools as ours. You learned the old ways, and you taught us new tricks." She raises her chin. "We're still alive. That's more than I expected."

Chen crosses her arms, then clears her throat. "Science is about evidence. When Finn said he could train me to see what I was missing, I thought, sure. I'll play along. Maybe I can get a paper out of it." She gestures at the party. "I got a community instead."

Her face softens. "I spent years building boundaries. Categories. Everything had a place: human, Mer, other." She meets Mara's gaze. "That was my failure. The ocean doesn't care what you call things. Neither do kids. They want to know what works, and what doesn't." Chen looks at the beach, at the food, at the children playing. "This works. I'm proud to be part of it."

Mara glances at Blackwell, not sure if he'll speak at all.

He surprises her. The voice is ragged, but it carries. "I spent my life building a machine to take the world apart." He turns his head, not quite meeting anyone's eyes. "For years, that was all I wanted. I thought if I controlled it, nothing could touch me. I was wrong."

Silence, but not the cold kind.

Blackwell exhales, the old wolf in him showing through. "You put it back together. With spit, and wire, and hope. And you did it without turning into me." He rolls the chair forward, so the front wheels touch the water. "You don't have to forgive me. I wouldn't, if I were you. But I had to see it with my own eyes."

He stops, then gestures with one trembling hand. "I'm glad I lived to see it."

Nobody speaks for a long time. The sun edges lower, painting the water with a golden sheet.

Mara finally breaks the quiet. "The work isn't done. The city's still small. We're still fighting to keep the currents clean, the poachers out, the corporations from finding new ways to wreck it all." She looks at the delegation behind Lyla. "Some of ours want to go back to the old ways. Hide, or fight, or survive." She turns to the humans on the terrace. "Some of yours would rather forget we ever existed. Pretend this is all a dream, or a myth."

She shakes her head. "But I don't care. Because every time I look at the water, I see frylings." She points at the group of kids now building a fort out of driftwood and shells, a writhing mess of tails and feet and arguments.

"They don't see differences," Mara says. "They only see friends."

Finn wipes at his eyes and laughs. "That's how you build a future. One friendship at a time."

Lyla raises her hands and makes the spiral sign. The crowd picks it up—slow at first, then faster, until every person on the beach, every child, elder, and scientist, is drawing circles in the air.

Chen's team records it. Blackwell sits, watching, a smile barely visible.

The sun touches the horizon, and for a moment, it feels like the world is perfectly balanced: water and land, old and new, loss and hope.

Mara lets herself breathe it in: the cold, the noise, and the messy, beautiful future. She allows herself to believe it's enough.

And when the first stars appear, she's still standing there, at the edge of everything.

As the last light drains from the sky, the air buzzes with expectation. The crowd thickens at the water's edge, frylings at the front, adults stacking behind. Mara paces the boundary, the sand cold under her feet, her nerves sharper than ever. This isn't war, but it feels close—an event that matters, a demonstration the whole world will watch.

The sound system crackles, then resolves into Finn's voice, amplified but still his. "Ceremony starts in ten. Please don't drown, and if you do, sign the waiver first."

Laughter skims the crowd, but Mara's heart knocks inside her ribs. She rolls her shoulders, scanning the assembly. At the far end of the cove, Chen and her team fuss over a cluster of hardware: projectors, drones, and something that resembles a cross between a disco ball and a squid. Lyla's delegation has gathered near the main tunnel, fins flashing with anxious energy. Above, Blackwell and his aide tinker with a set of subwoofers perched on a floating dock, their cables snaking into the deep.

The sky is indigo now, the first stars poking through the smear of twilight. Mara catches Finn's gaze. He gives her a double thumbs-up, then mimes "breathe." She shakes her head, but her smile is genuine.

The crowd shifts, hushes, as Chen's voice comes over the system. "Friends, colleagues, and creatures of the tide: thank you for being here. Tonight, we show the world what cooperation looks like. Or we set the beach on fire. Either way, it's going to be interesting."

The first phase is Current-Calling. Mara moves to the front of the cove, followed by a dozen Merfolk—some her age, some barely older than frylings. She gestures, and they form a ring in the shallows, hands clasped, eyes on her.

Mara draws in the air, the brine, the charge of a hundred anxious hearts. She flexes her hands, fingers wide, then plunges them into the water.

The current answers. It always does.

A spiral forms, tight and invisible at first, then flares into motion: a vortex that yanks silt from the bottom, lifts a dust storm of plankton, and stirs the sand into a rising coil. The spiral rises, two meters, three, shedding silver as it climbs. At the apex, Mara shouts—not in words, but in the bone-deep language of the ocean. The spiral fractures, then branches: a caduceus, a double helix, spinning higher with every breath.

The crowd gasps, then breaks into applause.

Mara signals the next group. Human trainees—half a dozen, led by Finn—wade in. They are ungainly, clumsy, but eager. Finn takes his place opposite Mara, and together they grip the current, pull it across the gap.

For a second, nothing happens. Then the water bows, bends to the human will, and a second spiral forms—slower, softer, but visible. Mara feels the link: the human effort amplifies her own, and the energy builds, a feedback loop humming through her bones. She flicks her tail, signaling more power, and the spirals twine, then merge.

The vortex touches the sky, a ten-meter tower of water, lit from within by starlight and the shimmer of countless plankton. The beach erupts in cheers.

Phase two: Sea-Speaking.

Lyla steps forward, her eyes bright in the near-dark. She hums once, low and resonant, and the water near her glows: a blue-green haze, as if she's bleeding neon into the surf. She gestures, slow and deliberate, and the glow gathers, tightens, then explodes in a burst of bioluminescent fish.

They leap from the water, a living ribbon, then scatter, painting the cove with streaks of light. The frylings howl with delight. Lyla's face is pure joy, unguarded for the first time Mara can remember.

Mara joins her, and together they spin the water, shaping the fish into new forms: a helix, a ring, then a cascade of shooting stars. Each time Lyla changes the pitch of her hum, the fish change color, cycling from blue to gold to ultraviolet.

Above, Chen's team kicks in. Projectors blast colored beams through the spray, fracturing it into a rainbow. Drones drift overhead, dropping tiny packets that burst into new clouds of glittering plankton. The effect is hallucinatory, impossible—like watching the birth of a new planet in slow motion.

Mara loses track of time. She is only current, only motion. The crowd is gone, the fear is gone, the future is now.

Phase three: the symphony.

Blackwell cues the subwoofers. At first, the bass is a suggestion, a pulse at the bottom of the world. But as the vortex rises, the sound grows: a deep, oceanic drone that makes every hair on Mara's body stand up. She recognizes the frequency—an old war song, but twisted, softened, made into something hopeful. The humans on the beach feel it, too. Mara sees their bodies sway, as if the music were a tide and they were just flotsam caught in it.

Mara and Lyla exchange a look, then up the tempo. The spirals intensify, merging into a single column of water that towers above the cove. The bioluminescent fish ride the column, forming rings of light at every meter. Chen's projectors hit the column dead-on, refracting the light into a column of liquid stained glass.

Finn, caught up in the moment, whoops and dives under the surface. He comes up at the center of the vortex, hair plastered to his skull, grinning like a madman.

The finale: every Merfolk, every human trainee, every fryling and adult on the shore, reaches out—literally or in spirit—and the current responds. For the first time, Mara feels the power isn't hers alone. It's a net of intent, of hope, of raw, stubborn will.

The column fractures, then fans out, forming a cathedral of water arches. Inside each, the fish dance, the light shifts, and the sound wraps it all in a single, unified heartbeat.

The crowd is silent. Even the frylings are dumbstruck.

The arches linger, then dissolve. The water falls back to the cove, calm as a sleeping child.

For a moment, all Mara can hear is her own breathing.

Then the world erupts in applause. Not polite, not controlled—just a primal, bone-shaking cheer.

On the shore, Finn catches Mara, hugs her hard enough to bruise. Lyla claps her on the back, laughing so hard she's in tears. Even Chen is grinning, her face wet with spray and something else.

Mara turns, scanning the crowd for Blackwell. She finds him at the edge of the water, wheels sunk in the sand, watching the last of the arches collapse into ripples.

He meets her gaze. Nods, once. For the first time, Mara believes him.

The party resumes, louder than ever. People spill onto the beach, and children imitate the spiral with sticks and hands. The elders of both tribes gather at the center, arguing already about who gets to plan next year's display.

Mara sits on the sand, Finn's arm around her shoulders, Lyla sprawled nearby. She feels the ache of exhaustion, but also the quiet hum of something permanent—a change that can't be unwound.

The tide creeps in, lapping at her feet.

She lets it.

The celebration burns through midnight, then flickers out as quickly as it began. By the time the last fryling is herded home and the beach returns to dark and quiet, Mara and Finn are already gone.

They slide into the water at the far end of the cove, silent as shadows. Mara leads, cutting through the waves with the confidence of a creature born here. Finn follows, slower but surer than he used to be, the awkwardness of his old self replaced by something closer to grace.

They swim side by side, out past the breakwater, beyond the last marker buoy. The lights from the settlement dwindle to a shimmer, then nothing. Here, the ocean is a cathedral of black and silver. The moon throws a ladder across the water, and Mara follows it.

Finn wears a rebreather—Chen's latest upgrade, sleeker than any human gear but still noticeable to Mara's eye. He checks the gauge, then grins at her, a string of bubbles rising to the surface.

They dive.

The reef is three hundred meters from shore, an old patchwork of ruined coral and scaffolded regrowth. Mara remembers when it was a graveyard: skeletons of once-living colonies, the water thick with rot and silt. Now, after years of fighting and cleaning and endless, stubborn hope, it's coming back. Not fast, but steady.

Mara slows, hovering above a clutch of new coral—neon pink, impossible blue, laced with ribbons of kelp. Fish dart between the branches: damselfish, gobies, and a single octopus curled in the hollow of a rock. Mara points it out to Finn, who mimics the animal's arm-wave, then shrugs and does a slow somersault, to show he can.

They settle near the bottom, Mara's tail flicking up a swirl of silt. Finn floats beside her, face mask fogged at the edges, but eyes transparent and open. They watch the reef pulse with life, letting the current rock them back and forth.

Mara closes her eyes, opens her mind to the Tide-Sensing. At first, all she feels is the water's chill, the slow beat of her own heart. But then the reef begins to speak: the chemical signature of growth, the subtle tremor of polyps feeding, the gentle push of a thousand tiny mouths shaping the world around them. It's not language, exactly, but it's communication, and it fills her with a heat that has nothing to do with the sun.

She reaches out and touches Finn's temple. He's learned the trick over the years and lets the connection happen. The sense flows from her to him: he gasps, then laughs, the sound muffled but real.

He mouths, "Show-off."

She grins, then doubles down, pulling in the bigger picture. Beyond the reef, the ocean thrums with possibility. Mara lets Finn see it all: the night migrations of squid, the distant echo of a whale song, the brief, sharp terror as a predator passes in the dark. She holds nothing back.

When she releases him, Finn floats for a moment, stunned.

"Holy shit," he says, the bubbles boiling up from his mask.

Mara laughs, bubbles streaming from her own mouth.

They drift, letting the water carry them. Above, the moon moves west, dragging the stars behind it. Below, the reef grows a little more with every breath.

After a while, Finn rolls onto his back, staring at the surface. "You think it'll last?" he asks, voice soft but audible through the comms.

Mara floats next to him, arms spread. "Nothing lasts. But it's enough that it's here now."

He turns, meets her eyes. "We still have so much work to do."

She thinks about the city, the endless repairs, and the threats from the outside world. "Yes," she says. "But we're not alone anymore.

Finn smiles, and Mara feels the warmth even in the cold water. They float together, hand in hand, letting the silence fill every space.

After a long time, Finn gestures toward the horizon. "Race you?"

Mara shakes her head. "No contest," she says, and for once, lets him have the lead.

They swim into the darkness, two shapes silhouetted against the fractured light.

The ocean is open, infinite, theirs.

www.ingramcontent.com/pod-product-compliance
Lightning Source LLC
LaVergne TN
LVHW010631110826
845149LV00014B/2826

9798999159410